The Midnight Special

1972-1981

Late Night's Original Rock & Roll Show

B.R. Hunter

Designed by Greg Simpson/Ephemera Inc.
Produced by Melcher Media Inc.

VH1 BOOKS | **POCKET BOOKS** | **MELCHER MEDIA**

This book was produced by Melcher Media, Inc.
170 Fifth Avenue, New York, NY 10010
Under the editorial direction of Charles Melcher.

Editors: Gillian Sowell and Genevieve Field
Production Director: Pam Smith
Editorial Assistant: Emily Donaldson
Video Editor: Susan Brownstein

Special thanks to the following:
Aaron Ackermann, Jacqueline Albert, David Ball,
Rob Barnett, Mike Benson, Brian Blatz, Duncan
Bock, Erin Bohensky, Eduardo A. Braniff, Mary
Frances Budig, Lynda Castillo, Frank Chmielewski,
Laura Cohen, Dave Daley, Eddie Dalva, Ruth
Engelhardt, Jeff Gaspin, Smith Galtney, Max
Greenhut, Angie Holcombe, Steve Huang, Josh
Katz, Virginia Lohle and the people at Star File,
Karin Rinderknecht, Jill Newfield, Donna O'Neill,
Ed Paparo, Debra Rohrbacher, Robin Silverman,
Donald Silvey, Paris Speights, Liate Stehlik, Dave
Stern, Kathleen Sweeney, John Sykes, Van Toffler,
Suzy Vaughan, Kara Welsh, Ray Whelan Jr. and the
people at Globe Photos, Annette Rella Wolmark,
and Megan Worman.

Grateful acknowledgment is made to *Record World*
magazine and RCA Victor.

The Midnight Special is distributed
by Paul Brownstein Productions.

An *Original* Publication of
VH1 Books/Pocket Books/Melcher Media

POCKET BOOKS, a division of
Simon & Schuster Inc.
1230 Avenue of the Americas,
New York, NY 10020

ISBN 0-671-01427-7

First VH1 Books/Pocket Books/Melcher Media
trade paperback printing October 1997

10 9 8 7 6 5 4 3 2 1

Cover and interior design by
Greg Simpson/Ephemera Inc.

Printed in the U.S.A.

CONTENTS

FOREWORD

When the immortal Huddie "Leadbelly" Ledbetter first recorded his epic song "The Midnight Special" in the late thirties, he had no way of knowing that rock & roll—a supercharged version of the blues-based music he was playing on twelve-string guitar—would captivate the world fifteen years later. Nor could he have imagined the rapid proliferation of an invention called television. But more than three decades later, forces would conspire to meld rock & roll and television under the banner of a song he brought to the world, with *The Midnight Special*.

Tapped to sing the tune for the show's title sequence, Johnny Rivers would take bold artistic license with Leadbelly's original lyrics, but he retained the tune's hopeful spirit. The song was to become a rallying cry for millions of young people, who were thirsting to see their musical heroes on the newly established "late-night" television format.

The television show, *The Midnight Special,* became a Friday night institution, airing 350 episodes between 1972 and 1981, and spotlighting artists from virtually every genre of popular music. The cross-section of *Midnight Special* episodes profiled here attempts to display that very range and diversity.

Music has always been one of society's mirrors, and the same can be said of *The Midnight Special* because it represented all the quirks, trends, excesses and nuances of our culture in the seventies and early eighties. If our children's children's children were to wonder what life was like at the end of the twentieth century in America, showing them several segments of *The Midnight Special* would be very enlightening indeed.

In researching *The Midnight Special*'s storied past, I came to realize that the show is still a living, breathing entity, even though it went off the air some time ago. It exists in those who were part of making it happen, and that's where its soul resides. This became clear to me during an impromptu reunion of *Midnight Special* staffers in January, 1997, that had been sparked by VH1's interest in re-airing the best of the show. Though many of these people hadn't seen each other for several years, a deep-felt kinship was immediately evident when they got together. "*The Midnight Special* was like a family," more than one person would say.

The impact of *The Midnight Special* was not only felt by the crew and cast, but reached the viewers who experienced the show. This volume is the result of the first effort to chronicle the madness and majesty that made *The Midnight Special* unique. If you were alive during these carefree times, then look back and remember them with fondness. If you were not alive, or weren't old enough to enjoy the fun, then enjoy this book and pine for the days when rock & roll was a way of life instead of a commodity.

Special thanks must be extended to all the wonderful people who gave of themselves to help make this book a reality. Without people like Stan Harris, Susan Richards, Rocco Urbisci, Jacques Andre, Tisha Fein, Ken Ehrlich, Neal Marshall, Debi Genovese, Kari Clark, Paul Brownstein, Paris Speights, Noelle Bogdanovich, Mamush Yamame and of course Burt Sugarman, this book never would have happened. Special recognition is also due to many others, including the people who shared their recollections of *The Midnight Special*: Paul Anka, George Carlin, Dick Clark, Bobby Columby, Harry "KC" Casey, Rick Gershon, Emmylou Harris, John Lee Hooker, Tom Johnston, Lonnie Jordan, Leo Kottke, Steve Miller, Helen Reddy, Todd Rundgren, Barry White, and Verdine White. And a very special thanks to Lou Lamb Smith, Wolfman Jack's widow, also known as Wolfwoman. Additional thanks must be given to designer Greg Simpson, line editor Dave Daley and all the fine folks at VH1, Melcher Media and Pocket Books: Charles Melcher, Dave Stern, Genevieve Field, Gillian Sowell, Erin Bohensky, and Laura Cohen. Thanks to all of you.

This book is fondly dedicated to the memory of my cousin Hank Powers, may his ever lovin' light shine on forever.

B.R. HUNTER

INTRODUCTION

On August 19, 1972, the marriage between late night television and rock & roll was consummated. That's when NBC aired a special 90-minute show—the first *The Midnight Special*—which actually started at 1 A.M. EST. It marked the first time any network had programmed at 1 A.M. or later, and its success was thrilling. The show was hosted by John Denver and besides being a vehicle to present live music, its theme was to encourage young people to get out and vote. It won resounding acclaim, both critically and commercially, and quickly became the basis for something extraordinary—a highly influential weekly series appearing nearly every Friday night for the next decade—and one of the most satisfying experiences of my life.

Before *The Midnight Special*, very few shows dared to combine television and rock & roll, save for short-lived, pioneering 1960s series' such as *Hullabaloo, Shindig* and *Music Scene*. *The Midnight Special* proved once-and-for-all that the irreverent spirit of late-night television, and the power of live pop music, could work well and become very popular. In fact, the show was compelling enough to spawn imitators like *Rock Concert* and *In Concert*. Today there are whole networks devoted to music programming.

But all this success required the hard work and vision of many people, as well as a lot of good fortune and good timing. After working as the executive producer of the 1971–72 Grammy broadcast, and several specials with Dionne Warwick and Jose Feliciano, I wanted to get away from one-time shows and develop a series. The idea for a "get out and vote" program came from Syd Vinnedge, who was working for Grey Advertising at the time. Popular music had proven to be an energizing bond for young people, especially during the tumultuous '60s, so we decided rock & roll would provide the perfect framework to appeal to 18 year olds, who had just been given the right to vote.

The head of NBC's West Coast operations, Herb Schlosser, was wary. He worried that rock & roll artists wouldn't show up on time, might freak on drugs, or do something equally dastardly. With this in mind, we chose a wholesome star with wide appeal to host the first show, John Denver. He didn't look wild enough to scare the network executives, was a great singer, and believed in promoting the importance of voting. I told NBC I wanted to air the show after Johnny Carson on a Friday night, because he always signed off at 1 A.M. with a good rating. The network was still worried. They'd never broadcast at this hour before, didn't know if advertisers would want to sponsor a show that late, and didn't really understand rock music. I believed the whole package was viable, so I told them I would guarantee the show—in other words, front the money for the cost of the show, the air time, plus the potential advertising revenues.

It was a $180,000 risk, and I told Schlosser that if I was going to put up the money for this "experiment," then I was going to have to own the show. At that time the studios and networks owned the shows, but Schlosser fought for it, and finally the network agreed. So with the help of Syd Vinnedge, who had many clients who bought ads, we sold the show out, and I broke even. Based on this success, I told Schlosser I thought we could do it at 1 A.M. every week. Again, he took a big chance, fighting against the norm, to establish a new late-night programming standard. It worked, and soon we had a regular weekly series.

So many staff members deserve recognition and thanks for making *The Midnight Special* so special. Stan Harris was integral in devising the working concept for the show, and masterful at holding up the technical end as both producer and director. He was also easy going, and always able to handle every unexpected crisis with a great deal of diplomacy. Talent coordinator Susan Richards had a fantastic ear for music, and without her, many of the bands never would have appeared. The same goes for Rocco Urbisci, who was a wonderful liaison between the bands and the show. In general, all the staff made bands feel at home, and treated them with a respect that made them want to come back again. Jacques Andre was another skilled behind-the-scenes staffer who helped make it all run smoothly. He had a knack for coordinating many different talented people and still keeping an eye on the budget. Set designer Roy Christopher is credited too infrequently, but he did some great, unique work for *The Midnight Special*. Debi Genovese and Tisha Fein deserve credit for their work, as do my producers Ken Ehrlich, Neal Marshall and Dick Ebersol. Without these people, and many more, there would not have been a *Midnight Special*.

I also want to extend a special thanks to everyone who's ever been a fan of *The Midnight Special*, whether it was during its initial run or today. It's been a pleasure presenting these programs, and I hope you've gotten as much enjoyment out of watching them as I did bringing them to you.

BURT SUGARMAN,
EXECUTIVE PRODUCER

pilot episode

HOST: # John Denver

FEATURING: **Cass Elliot, Argent, Linda Ronstadt, The Everly Brothers, David Clayton-Thomas, War, Helen Reddy, The Isley Brothers, Harry Chapin**

"THE show was revolutionary because all the networks went off the air after <u>Johnny Carson</u>. That was it, and though all the TV and radio stations do it today, in those days no one had thought of programming all night. It was like putting out a magazine, and at the back putting 30 black and white pages, because it was just unsold space. No matter what you're getting for [advertising revenue], you're gonna get an audience, especially on a Friday night when the kids are looking for something. Rock & roll had never been on television before, literally, and NBC was so frightened it hired about 10 Burbank policemen, because they thought if you had rock & roll you were going to have riots.

STAN HARRIS,
PRODUCER/DIRECTOR

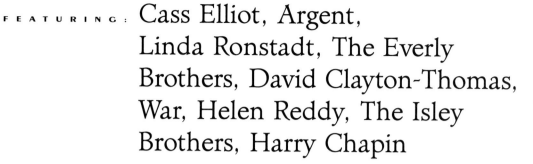

AUGUST 19, 1972

Burt Sugarman's belief in rock & roll and the possibilities of late-night television led him to guarantee NBC the money to produce a pilot episode—thus *The Midnight Special* was born. The pilot episode was aired in August, 1972, garnered excellent ratings, and prompted the network to pick up the show as a weekly offering. Starting regularly six months later, *The Midnight Special* became a 1 A.M. Friday night institution for the next eight years. Though the show opened with host John Denver singing "(Take Me Home) Country Roads," *The Midnight Special's* pilot was an exercise in musical diversity, giving viewers a taste of folk, soul, R&B, rock & roll, and country—and some political activism.

"We're here to try to stress the importance of everybody getting out to vote," said Denver. "It's something a lot of people have been talking about for a long time now, to give 18, 19, and 20 year-olds the chance to participate in local and national elections. And now it seems we have the chance, but there are still about 12 million people who haven't bothered to register."

Later in the program, "Mama" Cass Elliot—whose band, the Mamas & the Papas, broke up in 1968, and briefly reunited in 1971—echoed Denver's sentiments about the importance of casting a vote. "I don't think it's so important who you vote for," she said. "You vote for who you believe in, but the important thing is to vote because it's our way, and the best way."

As the pilot episode rolled on Elliot would teasingly introduce "Leaving on a Jet Plane" as a song "I wrote that I'm letting John sing." In fact, Denver had written the song but never recorded it, giving it instead to Peter, Paul and Mary, who had hit the top spot with it in 1969. Denver sang the song's first verse, and the studio audience was so enthralled they threatened to drown him out with their cheers. Elliot joined him on the song's chorus, and when they faced each other to sing, "Oh babe, I hate to go," the crowd roared their approval. Less than two years later, the flamboyant and talented Cass Elliot choked to death.

Adding a heavier rock element to the pilot was English quartet Argent, which had been formed from the ashes of the Zombies ("Time of the Season") in 1969 by keyboardist Rod

Cass Elliot and John Denver

ARGENT

Harry Chapin

Argent. On their one *Midnight Special* appearance the group played its only charting single, "Hold Your Head Up," a tune that was destined to become deified by classic rock. The group cut a dashing figure. Led by the talented Argent on organ and guitarist Russ Ballard, who wielded a double-necked bass/six-string guitar, Argent proved that they had no problem looking cool while delivering the goods live.

Also appearing was stellar singer Linda Ronstadt, an artist who would subsequently appear more than a dozen times on the show. Ronstadt had recently released a self-titled solo LP, and would climb the charts to pop stardom two years later with "You're No Good."

Yet another type of music represented on this first episode was that of famed vocal duo the Everly Brothers, who had been pop stars since releasing "Bye Bye Love" and "Wake Up Little Suzie" in 1957. The Everlys performed a slow version of their classic "All I Have to Do Is Dream," which spotlighted their pristine vocal harmonies and proved why the song had hit the top of the pop, R&B and country charts in the summer of 1958. Less than a year later, the Everlys would split up as a recording duo for a decade, barely speaking before reuniting in September 1983.

"There are two singers in rock today that stand head and shoulders above everyone else," proclaimed Denver. "That's my friend Harry Nilsson and this man—David Clayton-Thomas." Having recently abandoned Blood, Sweat, and Tears after recording two albums with the group, Clayton-Thomas appeared on the pilot episode backed by the Sanctuary Band. They played two songs, "Nobody Calls Me Prophet" and "Yesterday's Music." The latter tune would actually be recorded by Blood, Sweat, and Tears three years later when Clayton-Thomas rejoined them—and they'd all appear again on *The Midnight Special*.

Rounding out the pilot episode's lineup were War, who would later appear on several spectacular occasions, and Helen Reddy, who would become a regular host of the show. Also included were the Isley Brothers, an R&B group from Cincinnati, Ohio, who had been charting since the late '50s, and folk rock balladeer Harry Chapin, who performed his epic song "Taxi."

1 9 7 3

Humanity saw a year of weary jubilation in 1973 as the Paris Peace Accords ended the Vietnam War. It was also a year of high achievements in the arts, as films like *Last Tango in Paris*, *Mean Streets*, and *The Sting* hit the screens. In the literary world, Kurt Vonnegut Jr.'s *Breakfast of Champions*, *The Honorary Consul* by Graham Greene, and Thomas Pynchon's *Gravity's Rainbow* were published. In music, there was Pink Floyd's *Dark Side of the Moon*, Elton John's *Goodbye Yellow Brick Road*, and Paul McCartney & Wings' *Band on the Run*. On television there was *Kojak*, *The Waltons* and *M*A*S*H*. But at the crossroads of music and television there was one program that would come to define the form: *The Midnight Special*.

Thanks in large part to talent booker extraordinaire Susan Richards, *The Midnight Special*'s inaugural year was one of its most artistically diverse, featuring an array of well-known stars that would set the show's tone for years to come. Richards' love for music, amicable nature and ear for a hit song kept the show well balanced among the contemporary, the cutting edge, and the middle-of-the-road. And while news in the rest of the world was less than cheery—the Watergate Hearings were under way, Vice President Spiro Agnew resigned after pleading no contest to income tax evasion, and the world lost former President Lyndon B. Johnson, painter Pablo Picasso and author J. R. R. Tolkien—*The Midnight Special* became a sanctuary for young people from all walks of life.

episode

HOST: Helen Reddy

FEATURING: Ike and Tina Turner, The Byrds, Curtis Mayfield, Don McLean, George Carlin

"I always enjoyed doing **The Midnight Special**. It was like a big 'be-in,' and it was really comfortable. I remember I did the show during phase two of my career, which was the long hair and the beard. I had gone back to my original roots, which were basically out-of-stepness. You know, being out of step, and swimming against the tide. I think the obligation of an artist is to grow, to be on a journey. You don't know where you're heading, but you have an instinct for taking the turns as they seem to appear."

George Carlin

"Working on **The Midnight Special** was a dream come true for a lot of the staff members. The energy was incredible—from the staff because we were mostly in our twenties and thrilled to be working on the show, and from the studio audience because they had never seen anything like the show before."

Susan Richards,
talent coordinator

It's only appropriate that this new era in television was launched by Helen Reddy, whose then-No. 1 smash, the anthem "I Am Woman," would be the manifesto for feminists fighting for the Equal Rights Amendment. While "I Am Woman" foreshadowed the political and social upheavals of the '70s, this first show also nodded to the musical greats of the '60s, with guest stars Ike and Tina Turner, the Byrds and Curtis Mayfield, and a 1970s' icon, Don McLean, reflecting on the '50s and the death of Buddy Holly with "American Pie."

In a surprise walk-on appearance that welcomed the show to NBC's late night lineup, Johnny Carson's *Tonight Show* sidekick Ed McMahon introduced Reddy, beginning a long relationship between her and *The Midnight Special*. She would be named the show's "permanent guest host" for more than a year starting in mid-1975—the same time a comedian named George Carlin, also a guest on the first *Midnight Special*, would host the first episode of *Saturday Night Live*.

On this episode, several 1960s stars showed they still had great songs and tremendous enthusiasm. Ike and Tina Turner, whose dozen-plus years as a duo yielded numerous pop and R&B hits, started the studio sweating with a spirited cover of Creedence Clearwater Revival's "Proud Mary," a Top-5 hit just two years earlier, before moving into a slow-burning, impassioned duet of Joe Cocker's arrangement of Lennon and McCartney's "With a Little Help from My Friends," an ironic choice considering Tina Turner would later reveal years of physical abuse at Ike's hands.

Curtis Mayfield's silky tenor had already graced an array of hits with the Impressions throughout the '50s and '60s, but he had yet to prove himself as a solo artist when he performed on *The*

Ed McMahon and Helen Reddy

Curtis Mayfield

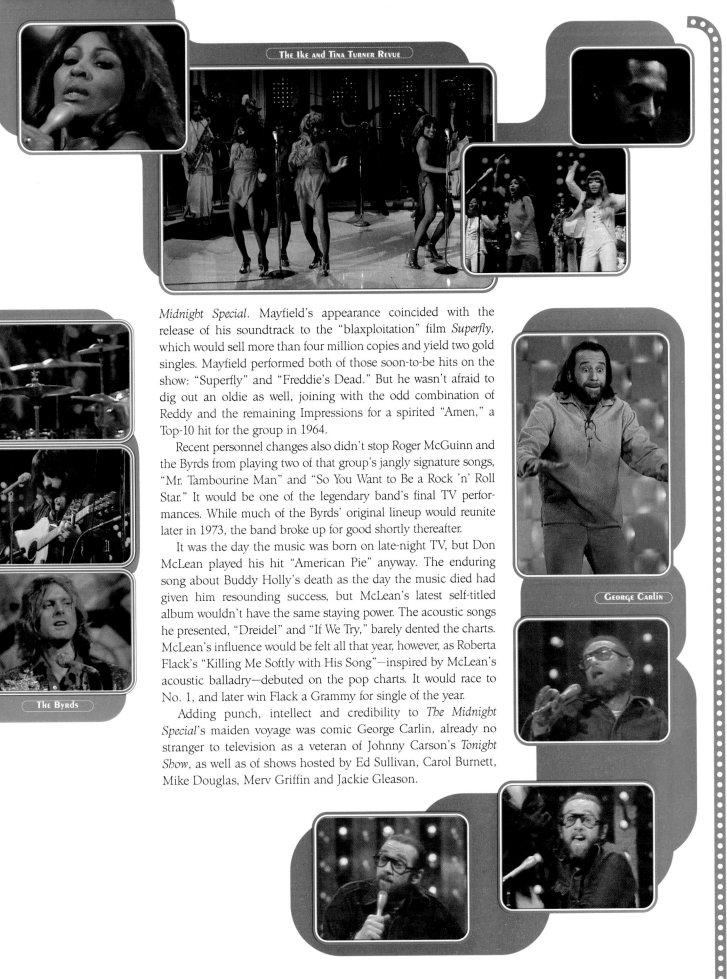

The Ike and Tina Turner Revue

The Byrds

Midnight Special. Mayfield's appearance coincided with the release of his soundtrack to the "blaxploitation" film *Superfly*, which would sell more than four million copies and yield two gold singles. Mayfield performed both of those soon-to-be hits on the show: "Superfly" and "Freddie's Dead." But he wasn't afraid to dig out an oldie as well, joining with the odd combination of Reddy and the remaining Impressions for a spirited "Amen," a Top-10 hit for the group in 1964.

Recent personnel changes also didn't stop Roger McGuinn and the Byrds from playing two of that group's jangly signature songs, "Mr. Tambourine Man" and "So You Want to Be a Rock 'n' Roll Star." It would be one of the legendary band's final TV performances. While much of the Byrds' original lineup would reunite later in 1973, the band broke up for good shortly thereafter.

It was the day the music was born on late-night TV, but Don McLean played his hit "American Pie" anyway. The enduring song about Buddy Holly's death as the day the music died had given him resounding success, but McLean's latest self-titled album wouldn't have the same staying power. The acoustic songs he presented, "Dreidel" and "If We Try," barely dented the charts. McLean's influence would be felt all that year, however, as Roberta Flack's "Killing Me Softly with His Song"—inspired by McLean's acoustic balladry—debuted on the pop charts. It would race to No. 1, and later win Flack a Grammy for single of the year.

Adding punch, intellect and credibility to *The Midnight Special*'s maiden voyage was comic George Carlin, already no stranger to television as a veteran of Johnny Carson's *Tonight Show*, as well as of shows hosted by Ed Sullivan, Carol Burnett, Mike Douglas, Merv Griffin and Jackie Gleason.

George Carlin

2

HOST: **Johnny Rivers**

FEATURING: Wolfman Jack, Steely Dan,
The Spinners, Albert Hammond

"The studio had three stages and the audience sat on the floor. The performers got a lot of energy from the audience, who were essentially attending an amazing concert. The audience was fascinated by the actual taping process too. Often our most enthusiastic audiences were the ones who got to see the bands set up and do their sound checks.

"Taping of an episode could run from 6 to 8 hours. Sometimes we had bands play songs a couple of times each so we could have our pick of shots. If the audience got tired—which they did—Midnight Special, staff members would go out there to get them psyched up. When it was over though, we always had to shoo them out, they didn't want it to end."

Susan Richards,
TALENT COORDINATOR

By 1973, Wolfman Jack's low guttural rasp had been the voice of rock & roll for more than three decades—but always on the radio, enthusing about the latest hits for teenagers everywhere, whether on dates at the drive-in or at home under the blankets with the receiver. Wolfman's trademark excited growl, heard on 1,400 radio stations nationwide, was as recognizable as Richard Nixon's voice. But millions actually laid eyes on the Wolfman for the first time on *The Midnight Special*, where he made his debut TV appearance, only enhancing the dark, spooky, vampire image of rock & roll's most famous DJ.

Festooned in a black cape and fake fangs, the Wolfman proclaimed, "The war is over," and told viewers that *The Midnight Special* would celebrate "good time rock & roll." Truer words have never been spoken. Wolfman Jack became the show's most recognizable figure, as *The Midnight Special*'s permanent announcer, occasional guest host and performer, and regular ambassador in the media. He did a little of everything on this second episode as well, singing an antiracism song called "I Ain't Never Seen a White Man."

Although Wolfman Jack's became the public face of *The Midnight Special*, its voice belonged to someone else: Johnny Rivers, whose soulful cover of Leadbelly's "Midnight Special" became the show's theme. Rivers made several appearances on *The Midnight Special*, including this one, where he performed two songs made famous by others, Carl Perkins' "Blue Suede Shoes" and Huey "Piano" Smith's "Rockin' Pneumonia-Boogie Woogie Flu." Though Rivers loved old songs, he injected them with '70s flair.

Johnny Rivers

Wolfman Jack

Steely Dan rarely performed live, even in their '70s heyday, preferring the perfection of their studio work to the spontaneity and scruffiness of live performance. But just as MTV's *Unplugged* today allows bands like R.E.M. to skip massive concert tours and play one intimate show seen by everyone, *The Midnight Special* offered bands the opportunity to get lots of exposure without actually going on the road. On this night, songwriters Donald Fagen and Walter Becker roughed up their first two big hits from their debut *Can't Buy a Thrill*, "Do It Again" and "Reeling in the Years." Fagen handled lead vocals on the latter, while guitarists Denny Diaz and Jeff "Skunk" Baxter ignited a fiery Telecaster guitar duel that showed off the sound that would become ubiquitous to rock radio for decades.

Where Steely Dan liked to rigidly script their songs, the Spinners preferred to tightly choreograph flashy dance moves and fancy harmonies. Dressed in matching suits, the quintet cut a dashing image, adding soulful stylings to their early hits "Could It Be I'm Falling In Love?" and "I'll Be Around." Indeed they would be—the Spinners would make an additional 15 appearances on *The Midnight Special*.

English singer/songwriter Albert Hammond wouldn't be so lucky. Hammond had a hit with "It Never Rains in Southern California," which he played on the show, but his career hit its own dry spell soon after, despite this *Midnight Special* performance.

Steely Dan

episode 3

AIRED FEBRUARY 16, 1973

HOST: # Mac Davis

FEATURING: **Waylon Jennings, Billy Preston, The Doobie Brothers, Joan Rivers**

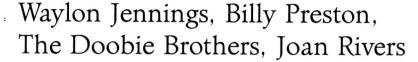

"THE MIDNIGHT SPECIAL WAS ALWAYS live, so you just went out and played. There was a small crowd there, and to be honest we were on the road so much in those days that THE MIDNIGHT SPECIAL seemed like another gig. I never thought too much about the TV end of it, but I knew it was great exposure. I remember we did a couple of songs—I think 'Jesus is Just Alright' and 'Listen to the Music.' Actually, 'Listen to the Music' was written just sitting around playing an acoustic guitar, and it was the only song I ever wrote that I thought would be a hit. I didn't even want to record 'Long Train Runnin',' and it was a much bigger hit."

"I also remember Mac Davis hosted that first MIDNIGHT SPECIAL we did. Mac was a real nice cat."
Tom Johnston, lead singer, The Doobie Brothers

The counterculture arrived late in Nashville, but by 1973, the outlaws had almost taken over Music City. Waylon Jennings, Willie Nelson and Kris Kristofferson were a new breed of country stars, free-spirited, creative visionaries who wanted to make records their way, without interference from their record labels. The "outlaws" were the last great creative boom in country music, before the urban cowboys of the '80s and the faux cowboys of the '90s, and Waylon Jennings not only wrote the songs, he lived the image. In 1973, when he made this first appearance on *The Midnight Special*, performing "You Can Have Her," Jennings was at his creative peak, between his *Good Hearted Woman* and *Ladies Love Outlaws* albums.

The evening's host, Mac Davis, couldn't have been more different from Jennings. Davis was a songwriting machine, not a hardcore honkytonk, and though he would dabble in country, his greatest successes would come from writing "Don't Cry Daddy" and "In the Ghetto" for Elvis Presley, and a decade later, when he would appear in a string of movies with Burt Reynolds. Though Davis played part of "In the Ghetto" acoustically on this show, he opened with the song that established his solo career, "Baby Don't Get Hooked on Me," and he foreshadowed his Hollywood

The Doobie Brothers

future when he played the straight man for a Joan Rivers comedy bit on the show. Later Davis played his "I Believe in Music," popularized the year before by Gallery, and had the audience singing along with the chorus.

While Davis performed songs he wrote that were made famous by others, legendary R&B vocalist Billy Preston—who had played with everyone from the Beatles to Sly & the Family Stone—made the first of his dozen *Midnight Special* performances with a series of cover tunes. Leading a quintet and sporting a two-foot high afro, Preston played acoustic piano on a funkified, organ-drenched rendition of the Beatles' "Blackbird." Later, Preston switched to Hammond organ, doing his best Ray Charles imitation on an abbreviated version of "Georgia on My Mind." Two months later, Preston's biggest hit, "Will It Go Round in Circles," would dominate the charts.

Another band to enjoy huge success soon after its first *Midnight Special* performance was the Doobie Brothers. But despite the national exposure, lead singer and composer Tom Johnston was probably most excited about meeting Wolfman Jack. A self-described "R&B freak," Johnston grew up listening to Wolfman on the radio. The inspiration Johnston gained from listening to years of '50s and '60s music showed in the Doobies' performance of "Jesus Is Just Alright" and "Listen to the Music," which were unequivocally good-time rock & roll, but featured high-octane gospel and an R&B groove thrown in for good measure.

Mac Davis

Joan Rivers

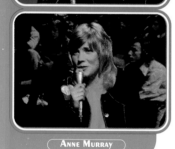

ANNE MURRAY

SONNY TERRY & BROWNIE McGHEE

Backstage at *The Midnight Special* must have felt like the United Nations. Every episode featured a wildly different group of bands speaking a different musical, if not generational, language. The combination of genres gave the show its flavor, but playing one after another, the transition from blues to funk to psychedelic rock could sometimes be as sudden as those kitschy camera angles. Perhaps no combination was stranger than the one on this episode, however, where three artists with different backgrounds—Canadian songstress Anne Murray, country stars the Nitty Gritty Dirt Band and comedian Steve Martin—joined together, and for a bluegrass song no less. Martin, Murray and the Dirt Band played "Shuckin' the Corn" by bluegrass legend Earl Scruggs—with the tuxedo-clad Martin on banjo.

Earlier in the show, performances by Murray and the Nitty Gritty Dirt Band stayed closer to expectations. Murray, a gentle-voiced balladeer, offered easy-listening hits "Snowbird" and "Danny's Song." The NGDB performed a spicy rendition of "Jambalaya," a Crescent City classic that Hank Williams charted with in 1952. Martin befuddled the audience by sticking with the banjo and performing another Earl Scruggs song, an earnest "Sally Goodin"—he stunned the crowd with his quick picking.

There were other great guests waiting in the wings of NBC Studio 4 that night. Don McLean returned for an acoustic performance of "Vincent," which he dedicated to Van Gogh's "Starry Night," using the famous painting as a backdrop for his performance. Also on hand were the Association, a band that was reeling for several reasons: They hadn't had a hit for five years and

Steve Martin

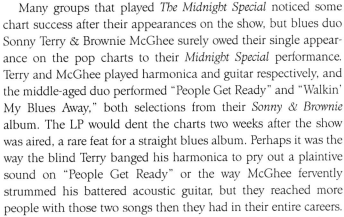

their original bass player, Brian Cole, had recently died of a heroin overdose. Still, the seven-piece outfit ran through a rendition of their 1966 smash "Along Comes Mary," which dovetailed into an impromptu number called "Crazy Songs and Loony Tunes."

Many groups that played *The Midnight Special* noticed some chart success after their appearances on the show, but blues duo Sonny Terry & Brownie McGhee surely owed their single appearance on the pop charts to their *Midnight Special* performance. Terry and McGhee played harmonica and guitar respectively, and the middle-aged duo performed "People Get Ready" and "Walkin' My Blues Away," both selections from their *Sonny & Brownie* album. The LP would dent the charts two weeks after the show was aired, a rare feat for a straight blues album. Perhaps it was the way the blind Terry banged his harmonica to pry out a plaintive sound on "People Get Ready" or the way McGhee fervently strummed his battered acoustic guitar, but they reached more people with those two songs then they had in their entire careers.

Then there were Welsh power-popsters Badfinger, whose Beatlesque pop blend, and association with the Beatles label, Apple, seemed certain to lead to stardom. Their George Harrison/Todd Rundgren–produced album, *Straight Up*, had just been released when they appeared on *The Midnight Special*, playing "No Matter What" and "Suitcase," songs that showed off both Badfinger's earnest harmonics and Beatles/Kinks-like melodic power. Tragedy intervened before fame, however, when guitarist Pete Ham committed suicide two years later, and bassist Tom Evans did the same in 1983.

Don McLean

Badfinger

9

HOST: # Ray Charles

FEATURING: ## Aretha Franklin, Earl Scruggs

"Unquestionably, the hardest part of my job was booking 8 or 10 bands, in advance, week after week. And balance was also important, because we wanted to include enough rock, country, comedy and R&B. A lot of times certain acts wouldn't want to come on the show with certain hosts. Like hard rock bands not wanting to be on with George Burns, for instance. So sometimes that was difficult. But basically, my job was to book the music I thought would become popular and we'd "bank" it. [record several songs that could be used on a later show when the song hit the charts]. We wanted The Midnight Special to have the best groups possible. All in all, it was a wonderful—and very satisfying—job. It was great when the bands would do well on the charts because they'd played the show. It made the artist look good, as well as the show, because we'd had the foresight to book them."

Susan Richards,
talent coordinator

It was an evening for legends. The ninth *Midnight Special* marked the first appearance by Ray Charles, who also welcomed soul sensation Aretha Franklin and bluegrass pioneer Earl Scruggs. Charles opened the show with a riveting rendition of the Beatles' "Eleanor Rigby," while Aretha ripped through "Brand New Me." Then Charles and Franklin wowed the house with an impassioned duet on "Takes Two to Tango," a tune Charles originally cut with Betty Carter in 1961.

Scruggs was part of what's considered to be the greatest bluegrass band of all time, the mid-1940's incarnation of Bill Monroe and Bluegrass Boys with Lester Flatt. Scruggs developed a syncopated three-finger roll on the banjo that allowed him to play clusters of notes with amazing speed and clarity, inspiring the Stanley Brothers as well as a generation of Grand Ole Opry stars. His unique style gave the impression he was playing even faster than he was; his prancing banjo and soaring voice making bluegrass seem more high-energy than ever. But Scruggs' appearance on *The Midnight Special* came at a time when he was feeling stifled by bluegrass, and tired of playing the same songs he had for years.

So he started sitting in with Bob Dylan, Joan Baez and the Byrds, and reaching out to a younger audience. On *The Midnight Special* with the Earl Scruggs Revue, which featured sons Randy, Gary and Steve, Scruggs turned toward country-rock, complete with drums and long hair that alienated bluegrass fans the same way Dylan angered the folk community by playing electric guitar at the Newport Folk Festival less than a decade earlier. A new audience listened: right after his *Midnight Special* performance, Earl Scruggs hit the pop album charts for the first time in years.

Ray Charles and the Raylettes

Earl Scruggs

Aretha Franklin and Ray Charles

10

HOST: # The Bee Gees

FEATURING: ## Gladys Knight & the Pips, Jerry Lee Lewis, Johnny Nash

"The first time I hired the Bee Gees I thought it was Benny Goodman, because I had never heard of the Bee Gees and Goodman was also known as BG. But they were terrific, and they played the show a lot after that."
Stan Harris,
producer/director

"When the Bee Gees hosted Episode 10 they were the first band to do it. Before that only solo artists had hosted. I remember everyone was very curious as to how it would work and how the television audience would react, but they ended up doing very well. Personally, I thought they'd do fine because I knew they were witty and cute and talented. I had a close personal relationship with them, especially with Barry, and this was a big reason they kept coming back to do the show."
Susan Richards,
talent coordinator

Manchester, England, would acquire a new buzz years later, when the working-class, industrial town would help spawn post-punk in the early '80s, with Joy Division, The Smiths and Factory Records, the British rave craze in the late '80s with Stone Roses and Happy Mondays, and later, Britpop and Oasis. But at the time Episode 10 was aired, a very different Manchester band was storming America—the Bee Gees. The brothers Gibb made their *Midnight Special* debut the same night as another family band, Gladys Knight & the Pips. And joining the lineup of '70s pop and '60s soul was one of the '50s architects of rock and roll, Jerry Lee Lewis.

Lewis would be back three weeks later, hosting an oldies show, but on this episode he showed the same vigor and boogie-woogie that turned "Whole Lotta Shakin' Goin' On" and "Great Balls of Fire" into Top-5 smashes back in 1957. Also appearing for the first time was American singer and guitarist Johnny Nash, who had a hit with the soft stylings of "I Can See Clearly Now," as well as a cover of Bob Marley's "Stir It Up."

One of the episode's lightest moments came when Robin Gibb introduced Nash, who was to play Marley's soon-to-be reggae classic. "There's a new sound around today," said Gibb, "called Redge-Jay." After an uncomfortable pause, his brother Maurice tried to correct him. "Ray-gay, ray-gay" he prompted, in hushed tones, as both brothers smiled impishly.

Later the Bee Gees joined Jerry Lee Lewis for a medley of rock & roll classics including "Money," "Good Golly Miss Molly," "Long Tall Sally," "Jenny Jenny," "Tutti-Frutti" and "Whole Lotta Shakin' Goin' On," the high-pitched harmonies of the Bee Gees blending with Jerry Lee's fiery pounding.

Johnny Nash

Jerry Lee Lewis

The Bee Gees

episode

AIRED
JULY 20, 1973

25

HOST: Joan Baez

FEATURING: Wilson Pickett, Bloodstone,
Black Oak Arkansas,
The Pointer Sisters

"THERE WAS A GUY NAMED JIM DANDY, WHOSE ACT ... WELL ... HE WORE TIGHT PANTS AND HE'D BE ON THE STAGE, AND ALL THE GIRLS WOULD COME AND GRAB HIM AT THE CROTCH AND HE WOULD GET AN ERECTION. EVERYBODY KNEW IT WOULD HAPPEN AND YOU COULD SEE IT. HE WAS PRETTY WELL ENDOWED FOR A YOUNG GUY. ANYHOW, ON THAT FRIDAY AFTERNOON [THE DAY THE SHOW WAS TO AIR], THIS GUY FROM DETROIT CALLS ME WHO WAS INVOLVED WITH THE [ADVERTISING] AGENCY. HE SAYS "YOU'VE GOT TO CUT THIS [PART OF THE SHOW] OUT." NOW IT'S ABOUT TWO HOURS BEFORE THE SHOW CAN BE SEEN IN NEW YORK. I SAID "HOW CAN WE DO THAT?" SO I CALLED BURT SUGARMAN AND TOLD HIM WHAT THEY WANTED AND HE AGREED WITH ME THAT THERE WAS NO WAY OF CUTTING IT OUT. SO I SAID TO THIS AGENCY MAN, 'I DON'T KNOW WHAT YOU'RE TALKING ABOUT. I WAS LOOKING AT HIS FACE, I DON'T KNOW WHAT YOU WERE WATCHING.' THAT'S HOW WE LOST CHEVROLET AS A SPONSOR."

STAN HARRIS
PRODUCER/DIRECTOR

Episode 25 was significant because it was Joan Baez' first appearance on the show. One of the most beloved folk singers and political activists of a generation, Baez had been instrumental in helping Bob Dylan's career in the early sixties, and would be welcomed to *The Midnight Special* with open arms by a large and enthusiastic studio audience, as well as millions of home viewers. Baez opened the show with a stirring interpretation of "The Night They Drove Old Dixie Down." She sang several other numbers on the show, including a duet with her sister (and fellow songwriter) Mimi Farina on "Best of Friends."

Additional spice was added to the show with the performance of legendary soul singer Wilson Pickett. Pickett—whose *Mr. Magic Man* album had just hit the charts—chose to perform two songs from his 1970 live album *Wilson Pickett in Philadelphia*, including the Top-20 "Don't Let the Green Grass Fool You." That song had become his first gold single in 1971, and Pickett ran through it with the fervor and grace that only he could offer.

Causing a furor with the *Midnight Special* advertisers, fiesty southern rock sextet Black Oak Arkansas made their first showing on the program, playing some of their high-octane music and wowing the audience. Black Oak Arkansas would release *High on the Hog* in late 1973, the album's title taking on a humorously ironic sheen in light of their encounter with Chevrolet. On this night, the outfit played such energetic selections as "Fever in My Mind," "Dance to the Music Tonight" and "Hot and Nasty," none of which had yet been recorded when the show was aired during the hot month of July, 1973.

JOAN BAEZ

WILSON PICKETT

BLACK OAK ARKANSAS

Plenty of new sponsors jumped at the chance to be part of *The Midnight Special* by the time Billy Preston returned to the show six weeks later, riding his chart-topper "Will It Go Round in Circles," backed by a full horn section. Steely Dan was back as well—but without singer David Palmer, who had been replaced by two female backup singers, so a reprise of "Reeling in the Years" had a glossier feel. Guitarist Skunk Baxter's skidding, wah-wah sound later shone on two other songs, "Show Biz Kids" and "My Old School," both of which were new to most listeners, but would become classic rock staples.

Performing on Episode 31 was renowned bluesman Bo Diddley, who showed up playing his trademark rectangular electric guitar on his theme song, named of course, "Bo Diddley." Also making his first appearance on *The Midnight Special* was drummer Buddy Miles, who had previously played with legendary blues-rockers the Electric Flag, as well as in Jimi Hendrix's Band of Gypsies. Miles still had stars and stripes on his drum kit when he appeared, leading his power trio through an exceptional version of his signature song, "Dem Changes." Miles also dueted with Preston on a soulful, horn-driven version of George Harrison's "My Sweet Lord." Miles and Preston traded passionate vocals on the tune, inspiring the audience to get up off the floor and sing, dance and clap, demanding an encore. Miles and Preston obliged the crowd, reprising the song's "Hallelujah" chorus until long after the credits rolled.

Bo Diddley

Billy Preston, Buddy Miles

episode

AIRED
SEPTEMBER 28, 1973

35

HOST: **Seals & Crofts**

FEATURING: T. Rex, Arlo Guthrie, Uriah Heep, Paul Butterfield, Ramblin' Jack Elliot, Leo Kottke

Seals & Crofts

Paul Butterfield

T. R

Arlo Guthrie

While *The Midnight Special* always featured an eclectic mix of legends and popular sensations, it steered clear of the cutting edge and the pre-punk underground already developing in reaction against bloated art-rock, dull guitar bands, and '70s soft-rock balladry. Then came T. Rex, whose glittery glam-rock and swaggering style had the British music weeklies buzzing and would inspire descendants on both sides of the Atlantic.

In typical *Midnight Special* style, the introduction of singer Marc Bolan and T. Rex to America would be made by none other than easy-listening maestro Dash Crofts who, bowing to the hype, quipped "This guy has made as many headlines in England as Watergate has here." T. Rex opened with the gritty and glammy "Hot Love." Later in the show they dove into "Bang a Gong (Get It On)."

And "get it on" they did. Bolan swung and staggered, parodying every known rock & roll move even while indulging in them, dropping to his knees for a blazing guitar solo and trading wild wails with his backup singers, while a dry ice machine billowed smoke. Bolan, still on his knees, assaulted his six-string with a tambourine, which he soon threw into the crowd, demanding, "Come on—get it on, America!" It was the kind of exciting showmanship that kept late-night viewers pinned to the screen. Unfortunately, T. Rex would soon implode, and Bolan died in a car crash four years later at age 29, his promise unfulfilled, his legacy unforgettable.

How to follow that? Why not with something completely different—folk troubadour Arlo Guthrie getting it on with his piano, playing "Bling Blang." In addition to the "Alice's Restaurant" man and Marc Bolan, the show also featured cartoonish hard rockers Uriah Heep and blues legend Paul Butterfield. At the center of it all were hosts and '70s sentimentalists Seals & Crofts, playing "Diamond Girl" and "We May Never Pass This Way (Again)," which had overwhelmed the airwaves all year.

Two important guitar players, Ramblin' Jack Elliot and Leo Kottke, wrapped up the evening. Elliot had become part of the growing folk movement in the early '60s, influencing Bob Dylan and others. On his sole *Midnight Special* performance, Elliot piloted his six-string acoustic Guild guitar through a tune called "Talkin' Fishin' Blues." His matter-of-fact picking was neatly complemented by the dazzling showmanship of the young Kottke, who would go on to play the show four more times in the next year.

36

HOST: # Gladys Knight & the Pips

FEATURING: ## Focus, B.B. King, Earth, Wind & Fire

Earth, Wind & Fire

Focus

Before the music charts fragmented into a different list for every taste, and radio play lists became as singular and specialized as a phlebotomist, the Top-40 had room for lots of different styles—as did *The Midnight Special*. And when Gladys Knight & the Pips hosted, it didn't matter how different the bands were, there was always a party going on in NBC's Studio 4. Knight and her band (Edward Patten, William Guest and older brother Merald "Bubba" Knight), exuded a contagious aura of fun. Their joking and laughing set the stage for a relaxed vibe, which swelled as the evening's song list grew. Knight & the Pips opened the show with an exhortation to "watch your mouth," the crisp "Daddy Could Swear, I Declare," which had hit the Top-20 a few months earlier.

Then they yielded to Dutch art-rockers Focus, who had fans leaping out of their seats in excitement over a breakneck-tempoed version of their smash "Hocus Pocus." Indeed, the speed with which the quartet negotiated "Hocus Pocus" was breathtaking and a testament to the band's skill and tight playing. If Jan Akkerman's guitar pyrotechnics weren't enough to bring a crowd to life, there was always Thijs Van Leer's organ and flute playing, as well as his manic array of multiple octave yodels, yelps, whistles and screams.

Today the logo identifying "stereo" broadcasts is as normal to television shows as commercial interruptions. But *The Midnight Special* was the only show of its time to broadcast in stereo via FM simulcast in many cities, which meant homes equipped with the proper receiver could enjoy sound as alive as that heard by the studio audience. They couldn't join right in at home, though, as one woman in the audience did during bluesman B.B. King's set, seconding that emotion when King belted, "I've been downhearted, baby" in the midst of his classic "How Blue Can You Get?" In the spirit of the blues, King barely cracked a smile, even though he too was back on the Top-40 charts at the time.

Los Angeles-based R&B outfit Earth, Wind & Fire—named for the three elements of lead singer Maurice White's astrological sign—were still more than a year away from their biggest hit, the celebratory "Shining Star." But for the rapt *Midnight Special* audience, the soulsters crooned, "Evil," a song from their first gold record, *Head to the Sky*, and "Power," from 1972's *Last Days and Time*.

Gladys Knight & the Pips

B.B. King

AIRED
OCTOBER 19, 1973

FEATURING: New York Dolls, Bachman-Turner Overdrive, Mott the Hoople

"PAPA DEE NEVER MISSED A GIG. I THINK AT THAT TIME SOMETHING HAPPENED WITH HIS FATHER OR HIS MOTHER. THEY DIDN'T PASS AWAY OR ANYTHING, BUT I THINK ONE OF THEM WAS ILL, AND HE HAD TO GO TO DELAWARE.

"BUT The Midnight Special WAS ONE OF MY FAVORITE SHOWS TO PERFORM ON BECAUSE THEY WERE VERY CREATIVE, AND THEY ALLOWED US THE FREEDOM TO PLAY THE ROOT OF THE SONG, AND ITS DURATION. WE WOULD ADD AND CREATE DIFFERENT STUFF FROM WHAT IT SOUNDED LIKE ON RECORD, BECAUSE THAT'S HOW WE CREATED IT ORIGINALLY. I LOVED THAT. THEY WERE LIKE THE FIRST MTV, EXCEPT THEY WERE LIVE."

LONNIE JORDAN,
WAR KEYBOARDIST

The underground and the mainstream came together on this October evening, even if no one would recognize that for several years. But the two new bands that debuted together nationally, the New York Dolls and Bachman-Turner Overdrive would—in distinctly different ways— have a profound impact on bands and radio for years to come. A year later, BTO would begin a decade-long rock radio reign with "Takin' Care of Business" and "You Ain't Seen Nothin' Yet." And the New York Dolls would influence the entire New York CBGB art-punk scene, including the Talking Heads and Blondie.

The androgynous Dolls—akin to Detroit's MC5—would go on to define the New York "glitter" rock sound and attitude, credited by *Spin* for helping "not only sire New York's heady '70s under-ground (the Ramones, for instance...)" but also teaching "English punks (the Damned, the Sex Pistols) how to spit, swagger and roar." Their music—trashy, stylish, drug-addled, romantic, urban gutter-punk—had been described by one critic as "the Rolling Stones circa 1964," and for their only *Midnight Special* appear-ance, they tore through versions of "Trash" and "Personality Crisis." The latter song would become not only the Dolls' signa-ture song, but an anthem for the burgeoning New York scene. Toward the end of the song one enraptured fan was briefly caught by the *Midnight Special* cameras. Slightly effeminate in dress and manner, the young man was grooving right in front of the stage, trying his best to sing along. Both he and the Dolls offered living-room viewers a glimpse of the kind of scene usually reserved for the "in" crowd at clubs like Max's Kansas City in New York.

Glitzy Brits Mott the Hoople—another glam-rock outfit who called Hereford, England home—had similar roots, not to men-tion an album produced by the godfather of glitter, David Bowie. The band, led by Ian Hunter, hit the States right after working with Bowie on their essential album *All the Young Dudes*. Bowie himself penned the hit title track, which became a mantra for

WAR

New York Dolls

Bachman-Turner Overdrive

Mott the Hoople

young gay men, and appearances by groups like Mott the Hoople and the New York Dolls on national TV were certainly integral to further cementing a relationship between lifestyles: androgyny and glitter rock.

Hosting the show was a decidedly non-glitter and non-androgynous band, War. They opened the show with a particularly spirited version of their highest-charting hit, "Cisco Kid." The Long Beach, California, outfit was missing one of its pivotal players, percussionist Papa Dee Allen, who had traveled home for a family emergency. But even without the group's elder statesman, War was a force of nature, a shuffling blues-rock band spearheaded by the bright baritone saxophone of Charles Miller and Lee Oskar's piercing harmonica. The absolute high point of the show (and one of *The Midnight Special*'s most wonderful performances ever) was War's haunting, scratchy, gospel-tinged funk classic "Gypsy Man." The band was given the opportunity to stretch out and develop the tune as they would in a "real" concert setting, so they allowed the song to unfold slowly and gracefully. Driven by the majestically impassioned lead vocals of bass player B.B. Dickerson and the backing vocals of keyboardist Lonnie Jordan and guitarist Howard Scott, Miller mapped out a smoky solo on tenor sax, while Scott played a terse "chicka chicka" rhythm. As the song wound down, harmonica and sax traced the melodic chorus in tandem, their instruments weaving a web of glorious tension.

"Gypsy Man" would take on a sad significance for War almost fifteen years to the day later, when founding member and percussionist Papa Dee Allen would expire on stage from a brain aneurysm as the band was playing the song.

e p i s o d e

AIRED
NOVEMBER 16, 1973
TAPED AT THE CLUB
MARQUEE, LONDON
ON OCTOBER 20, 1973

42

HOST: # David Bowie

FEATURING: ## Dooshenka, Marianne Faithfull, The Troggs, Carmen

"DURING THE REHEARSAL, A MEMBER of THE BRITISH CREW ASKED ME WHAT I THOUGHT of DOOSHENKA. 'LONG LEGS AND SEXY,' I REPLIED, TO WHICH THE GRIP LAUGHED AND WALKED AWAY. THROUGHOUT THE DAY SEVERAL OF THE BRITISH CREW APPROACHED ME AND ONE SAID 'I BET YOU'D LIKE TO ROCK WITH THAT LONG-LEGGED BEAUTY, AY?' I COULDN'T FIGURE OUT WHY THE CREW TOOK THIS PERSONAL INTEREST IN WHAT I THOUGHT OF DOOSHENKA. . . . I FIGURED IT OUT WHEN SHE CAME IN TO THE MEN'S ROOM AND TOOK A P**S ALONGSIDE ME. WHEN I EMERGED, THEY WERE WAITING FOR ME AND ONE SAID, 'BET YOU'VE NEVER SEEN A GIRL IN AMERICA TAKE A P**S LIKE THAT BEFORE!'"

Rocco Urbisci,
co-producer

Early '70s rock had no more fascinating or inspirational character than David Bowie. Of the era's best records, if Bowie didn't make it himself (*Hunky Dory, Low* and *Ziggy Stardust*), he probably produced it (Mott the Hoople, Lou Reed's *Transformer*). So it only made sense for the *Midnight Special*'s first road trip to be to England, for a show assembled by David Bowie. The surreal, multimedia package he dubbed the "1980 Floor Show" was a concept based on George Orwell's book *1984*, which Bowie wanted to turn into a rock opera. Bowie even had a troupe of incredibly limber dancers spell "1980 Floor Show" with their bodies

The costumes Bowie designed for the show were spectacular, proof that he was the vanguard of the glitter movement. One outfit consisted of a plastic red corset, decorated with two huge black feathers that spanned the distance from his waist to beyond his ears. Another outfit was stitched from a fishnet-like material, and with it Bowie wore a black jockstrap slung low enough to reveal a tuft of pubic hair.

It was a fertile period for Bowie, who released five albums during a nineteen-month span over 1973–74, and the songs he played on *The Midnight Special* would almost all become standards: A ragged-but-right version of "Space Oddity," intercut with footage of launching rockets and spaceships, and "Jean Genie" and "Time," from *Aladdin Sane*.

But Bowie's theatrics weren't the only ones in town. He had chosen the beautiful Dooshenka to announce the show. Blessed with a perfect face, platinum blonde hair, and a mysterious Hungarian accent, Dooshenka glamorously introduced Bowie and the other acts—Marianne Faithfull, the Troggs and the obscure Spanish classical quartet Carmen.

David Bowie

Dooshenka

Mick Ronson

Besides the elements that were part of the show, there were also strange things going on during the actual taping. Marianne Faithfull was scheduled to do a version of her hit Rolling Stones cover "As Tears Go By." But the combination of lengthy lyrics and much pre-show partying caused her problems. She decided to lip-synch the song—a concept that ran counter to the whole *Midnight Special* live performance ethic—but she received permission from the producers anyway. By showtime the backstage festivities had taken their toll; her recall of the lyrics was barely adequate to cover up the lip-synching. Often her recorded voice could be heard confidently belting verses her lips hadn't even reached. Worse still, and unbeknownst to the television audience, was that the producers actually placed sandbags on Faithfull's feet in an attempt to keep her from toppling over. Bowie seemed both amused and embarrassed later, when they dueted on Sonny & Cher's "I Got You Babe."

In her autobiography Faithfull remembers the "1980 Floor Show" as a pleasant experience, recalling, "I did 'I Got You Babe' in a nun's costume. The nun's habit was David's idea. What I loved was doing my version of the Nöel Coward song 'Twentieth Century Blues.'" The song made a lasting impression on her; more than 20 years later, Faithfull would release an album of the same name.

The network censors had a memorable night as well. One incident involved the gold lamé hands that eventually ended up draped around Bowie's fishnet-clad chest. It seems the censors thought Bowie's original idea—to have the hands covering his groin—was a bit too risqué. Later, censors objected to Bowie using the word "wanking," which at least impressed the show's staff, surprised that the buttoned-down censors even knew what "wanking" meant.

Also riding on Bowie's flashing coattails that night were the Troggs. It had been five years since the Troggs' last hit, so they wheeled out their hugely successful smash "Wild Thing," and proved themselves to be one of the smoothest—and straightest—acts of the evening.

"When we went to London to do the show with Bowie, he wanted us to use this friend of his, Dooshenka, who was one of the most beautiful women I'd ever seen. So Mick Jagger decides he's going to play a trick on me, and he fixes me up on a date with her. Mick was a friend of David's, you know. When Rocco told me she was he, I felt like the guy in that picture The Crying Game. Those were very strange days, but they were a lot of fun."

Stan Harris,
producer/director

1974

Perhaps it's only fitting that a musician named Sly (Sly Stone) hosted *The Midnight Special* on the evening that a disgraced President Richard M. Nixon resigned his office rather than face certain impeachment for his Watergate-related crimes. Nixon's successor, Gerald R. Ford, then pardoned Nixon, sparing him and the country the ordeal of a president on trial. But many of the president's closest advisers—"all the President's men," as *Washington Post* reporters Bob Woodward and Carl Bernstein dubbed them in their book— did face prison time.

In the arts, Hollywood would lose one of its pioneers, Samuel Goldwyn, while the music world would lose arguably its greatest jazz composer, Duke Ellington.

Roman Polanski's *Chinatown* and Francis Ford Coppola's *The Godfather, Part II* invaded movie theaters, while Frank Robinson became baseball's first black manager and Hank Aaron shattered Babe Ruth's career home run record.

And *The Midnight Special* rolled right along. The show's share of the coveted Nielsen rating grew steadily in its first 15 months, averaging 4.5 million viewers per episode by May 1974. In late May a special tribute to the show ran in *Record World* magazine, profiling the "behind the scenes" personnel, citing the show's achievements and calling it a "success story." The 1974 season ended with a bang, as *The Midnight Special* celebrated its 100th show with Charley Pride captured live at the Tulsa State Fair with friends Ronnie Milsap and Doug Kershaw.

episode

52

HOST: Steve Miller

FEATURING: Brownsville Station, Genesis, Tim Buckley

"WHEN you look at <u>The Midnight Special</u> today, you can see that every band in the world was coming through there on a regular basis. It's one of the definitive documents of what was really going on in music then. But I just wanted to be a musician, not a celebrity, not a pop star. I always considered myself a musician, and once I got in there, man, I wasn't gonna let go.

"I had done lots of European television shows where we played whole concerts and all this stuff, but I think <u>The Midnight Special</u> was the second time that I had performed on American network TV. I think for the show I had on no shirt, a vest, hair to my shoulders and silver platform shoes. It's always funny to look back and see what you were doing 25 years ago. At that point we'd already been playing for seven or eight years, and been on the road forever, so we were no strangers to gigging. I have always really enjoyed playing live. That's my expertise, and as long as I'm alive I'm sure I'll be playing."

STEVE MILLER

The Midnight Special's sophomore season introduced a segment that would become a staple of the show—Wolfman Jack honoring singles that sold a million copies. Some of the bands would last for years, like the first recipients—Loggins & Messina, who had hit it big with "Your Momma Don't Dance." Others would be nostalgia trips, like the New York quartet Stories, who performed their only hit, "Brother Louie," a No. 1 smash about the politics of interracial relationships. As part of the million-sellers segment of Episode 52, Wolfman Jack gave a gold album award to host Steve Miller for "The Joker" (which would eventually go platinum).

Miller, resplendent in a loud red flowered shirt and metallic bell-bottom trousers, then threw a musical curveball by opening the show with a rendition of "The Joker" that had a markedly different vocal melody from the familiar recorded version. The crowd was riveted. Miller's haunting slide guitar and languid vocals piloted the song, while his deft quartet—Dickie Thompson (organ), James "Curly" Cooke (acoustic guitar), Jack King (drums) and Gerald Johnson (bass)—vamped behind him with characteristic aplomb.

Later performing a new composition called "Fly Like an Eagle," Miller wowed the crowd again, drawing a considerable

Tim Buckley

Steve Miller

Brownsville Station

Peter Gabriel

ovation from the audience for a song that wouldn't be released for another three years. It was a fascinating performance: "Fly Like an Eagle" debuted on this landmark *Midnight Special* as a funky, spacey tune, appreciably less pop-oriented than it would later become on record. Even its lyrics would be honed later. Miller also displayed his deep blues roots—he was taught blues guitar at age nine by legendary bluesman T-Bone Walker—sharing guitar solos and vocals with renowned Chicago blues harmonica player (and former Muddy Waters sideman) James Cotton on a version of the great Jimmy Reed's "Big Boss Man."

Respected singer/songwriter Tim Buckley also stepped up to display the talent that had made him a critical favorite since his 1967 self-titled debut. Playing a twelve-string, electric guitar, Buckley fronted a four piece consisting of bass, drums, guitar and keyboards on two songs, the passionate "Do You Ever Think of Me" and the driving, soulful blues of "Honey Man." Less than two years later Buckley would succumb to a drug overdose. Along with Nick Drake and Scott Walker, Buckley remains one of the most revered psych-folk avatars ever.

"I've known this group of crazy wackos for quite a while," said Miller, introducing Brownsville Station, the short-lived trio from Ann Arbor, Michigan, whose huge hit "Smokin' in the Boys Room" burned up the charts in January 1973, peaking at No. 3. They liked elaborate costumes—guitar man Michael Lutz wore a white fringed suit with rhinestones and knee-high boots, singer Cub Koda sported a striped referee's shirt and matching wristbands—but not as much as the next band.

"They're into theater rock," was how Miller introduced the Peter Gabriel–led Genesis, whose new <u>Selling England by the Pound</u> had just introduced them to the international stage. Miller's intro was a classic example of understatement, because at that time Genesis was <u>really</u> into theater rock. So much, in fact, that the long-haired Gabriel would appear wearing sparkling makeup, green eyeshadow, a bright multicolored cape, white gloves, and bat wings on his head. Also appearing in Genesis was another soon-to-be-megastar, a young bearded drummer named Phil Collins.

Genesis

61

AIRED: MARCH 29, 1974

HOST: # The Guess Who

FEATURING: Wishbone Ash, Sha Na Na, David Essex, Leo Kottke

The Guess Who

"Of the television I'd done up to that point, <u>The Midnight Special</u> was great. It was an impressive show because on other shows I had spent plenty of hours in the studios waiting for something to happen. On <u>The Midnight Special</u> they were ready. It was beautifully done. I don't know how they accomplished that, both from a technical standpoint and from the perspective of getting so many bands to play live. And it <u>was</u> live. It was also unusual because they weren't into putting music into categories. You gotta hand it to them. Back then there was a distinct idea of the "counterculture," and I remember thinking how odd it was that any of us who thought we were part of that were allowed access to the power. We were invited in, and pretty much allowed to do whatever we wanted to do. So <u>The Midnight Special</u> had a real hopeful feeling to it. It felt very new, exciting and loose."
LEO KOTTKE

Canada's The Guess Who had hit the charts four years earlier with "American Woman," but they were still a hot commodity when they hosted *The Midnight Special* in early 1974. Lead singer Burton Cummings was one of the most respected front men in rock, and he and his band tore through a gutsy version of that anthemic tune before turning the stage over to progressive British hard rockers Wishbone Ash and '50s rock & roll troubadours Sha Na Na. The latter performed a medley of Bill Haley's beloved "Rock Around the Clock" and Dion and the Belmonts' "Teenager in Love." Sha Na Na's greaser haircuts, synchronized dance moves and dead-on harmonies brought back everything about the '50s except President Eisenhower.

The London-born David Essex, making his third *Midnight Special* appearance (he played on a boat sailing up the Thames on Episode 43 and also guested on the episode hosted by Ike and Tina Turner), showcased three songs from his *Rock On* album. His set included the title track, which sold a million copies and became a Top 5 smash in the first months of 1974.

Youthful guitar virtuoso Leo Kottke, who was quickly gaining a reputation as one of the foremost instrumental stylists in the world, performed only one track, "Bean Time," that night, but his ability to simultaneously play both the song's bass and melody lines wowed the crowd.

David Essex

Leo Kottke

Sha Na Na

HELEN REDDY

Helen Reddy hosted the first *Midnight Special* ever, and she would go on to host the show more than anyone else. For almost two years, she served as the show's "permanent guest host," responsible for keeping things moving smoothly, doing the voice-overs for tributes to other artists, and also performing her own songs. Reddy's presence on the show kept it squarely in the middle of the road, and though some of the harder-rocking acts might have been dissuaded from appearing when Reddy was hosting, her familiarity to audiences and wholesome image helped keep the show's ratings high.

"I'M NOT SURE WHY I WAS CHOSEN TO HOST SO OFTEN, BUT I THINK I WAS ONE OF THE FEW POP MUSICIANS—WITH MY THEATRICAL BACKGROUND—WHO COULD ACTUALLY STAND UP AND READ A LINE. HOSTING WAS HECTIC, BUT <u>THE MIDNIGHT SPECIAL</u> WAS A LOT OF FUN. IT WAS VERY GOOD EXPOSURE FOR ME, PLUS I WAS HAPPY TO BE A PART OF GIVING EXPOSURE TO A LOT OF BANDS.

"I REMEMBER I HOSTED THE FIRST SHOW [AIRED 2/2/73]. MY SON WAS BORN ON THE 12TH OF DECEMBER, SO HE WAS IN THE DRESSING ROOM AND I'D FEED HIM BETWEEN TAKES. BUT I'M A THIRD-GENERATION PERFORMER, AND I DON'T REMEMBER THE FIRST TIME I WALKED OUT ON STAGE. SO THERE WAS NEVER ANY FEAR FOR ME, IT WAS JUST SOMETHING I DID. I HAD A VERY HECTIC SCHEDULE AT THE TIME, BECAUSE I NOT ONLY HAD AN INFANT, BUT I HAD A TOURING SCHEDULE, SO A LOT OF THE BANDS THAT WERE ON THE SHOW I NEVER EVEN SAW OR GOT TO MEET. I WOULD COME IN, AND I WAS PRETTY MUCH IN THE SAME WARDROBE FOR THE ENTIRE SHOW, SO THEY WOULD JUST TAPE ALL

MY INTROS ONE AFTER THE OTHER. I WOULD TURN TO ONE CAMERA AND SAY 'PLEASE WELCOME SO AND SO,' AND THEN TURN TO ANOTHER CAMERA AND SAY, 'HERE'S A GREAT BAND, BLAH, BLAH, BLAH,' THEN SAY MY GOOD EVENINGS AND GOOD NIGHTS, AND I'D BE OUT OF THERE. I WOULD ALSO TAPE MY SONGS. I USUALLY GOT TO DO A SONG OR TWO, WHICH BECAME DIFFICULT, BECAUSE WHEN YOU'VE GOT TO COME UP WITH DIFFERENT MATERIAL EVERY WEEK, YOU REALLY START DIGGING FOR SONGS. BUT IT ALSO GAVE ME A CHANCE TO DO SOME STUFF THAT I HADN'T DONE ON ALBUMS.

"I REMEMBER I HAD ONLY ONE PROBLEM WITH BURT [SUGARMAN]. I COMPLAINED THAT I WAS ALWAYS IN FRONT OF THIS SAME SET, WAS JUST SICK TO DEATH OF IT, AND COULD WE PLEASE HAVE SOMETHING DIFFERENT? SO WHEN I CAME IN THE NEXT WEEK, I WAS IN FRONT OF A BLACK VELVET CLOTH. THAT WAS MY NEW SET. IN THE ENTIRE TIME I HOSTED THE SHOW THAT WAS MY ONLY COMPLAINT, AND I THOUGHT HE HANDLED IT WITH A GREAT DEAL OF HUMOR."
Helen Reddy

episode

AIRED:
AUGUST 2, 1974
TAPED AT THE TEXAS
MOTOR SPEEDWAY,
COLLEGE PARK, TEXAS
ON JULY 4, 1974

79

HOST: # Leon Russell

FEATURING: **Willie Nelson, Waylon Jennings, Doug Kershaw, Rick Nelson**

"WHAT I REMEMBER MOST ABOUT College Station is how hot it was. That summer day on July 4th, the humidity made it feel like it was over 100 degrees. All of us, the crew and the staff, walked around in shorts and the crowd were about 100 percent barechested, including several girls. This was an unruly crowd, drunk, hot. We kept them cool by watering them down with firehoses. Those were the days.

"We had made a deal with Shelter Records to televise Willie Nelson and friends at the Forth of July picnic. Part of the deal was that we would have to use Shelter's audio and video truck. Both equipment and crew were below sub-par.

"Waylon Jennings had just completed his six- or seven-song set, all the way through. After he was finished, Jacques Andre [associate producer] came to me and said, 'Rocco you've got to go talk to Waylon and tell him he has to go do his songs again. The audio track is unusable.' So I made this dead man walking trip to Willie Nelson's trailer where the musicians hung out. I knocked on the door—and I don't know if you remember who David Allan Coe was, but he was a country singer who claimed to have killed someone [Actually, Coe claimed to have killed someone while he was already in prison serving time for

By now, Willie Nelson's famed Fourth of July picnics have become as much of an Independence Day tradition as fireworks, but *The Midnight Special* was there in the beginning when it joined him for the second such party. Because the taping was at a mobile location, the crew was compelled to use equipment and staff from an outside source, and production of this episode turned into something of an adventure.

Famous but always cooperative "outlaws" Waylon and Willie, as well as singers Doug Kershaw and Rick Nelson, sailed through the glitches and what the camera operators captured—in what was actually take two of the proceedings!—was host Leon Russell kicking off the set with a rousing version of "Jambalaya." Nelson and Kershaw were in his backing group, and they traded solos on acoustic guitar and fiddle respectively before Waylon stepped to the microphone to sing one of the celebratory song's verses. Rick Nelson then took the stage, performing "Someone to Love," then his famed "Garden Party," a song that went to No. 6 in 1972. After Rick Nelson's bow, Kershaw moved into the front-man role. He performed "Louisiana Man," much to the delight of the crowd. One woman was so thrilled with the selection that she disrobed from the waist up and sat on her friend's shoulders, shouting approval at Kershaw, who, looking pleased, continued undaunted.

Leon Russell

Doug Kershaw

Willie Nelson

Waylon Jennings

Rick Nelson

another crime. It later came to light that he was lying about the murder.] He opens the door—Coe, dressed in black is whittling on some wood with this huge hunting knife. I said, 'I've got to come in and talk to Waylon.' So I walked into the trailer and sitting there at the end of the trailer drinkin' and smokin' were Willie Nelson and Waylon Jennings. I walked in and said [clears throat]

'Mr. Jennings?'

'Yeah?'

'It seems we had a technical problem . . .'

"Then David Allan Coe says, 'Boy, you're standing in my light.' It was the only time I felt cold all day.

"Then Waylon said, 'What you want? What's that got to do with me?' Thank God for Willie who said 'Waylon, this gives you a chance to go out there and do your set right.' Everyone laughed except David Coe who kept on whittling.

"And Waylon says, not amused, 'Boy, get the f**k outta my face.'

'Yes, sir, but the director says if you don't do the songs again it won't be on the show.'

"I excused myself, and I ran out of the trailer. I waited what seemed to be an eternity and then the trailer door opened. Out stepped Waylon Jennings and as he walked past me he says, 'You've got a lot of balls, boy. I'll give you that.'

'Yes, sir.'

'We gonna have f**kin' audio this time? And pictures?'

'Yes, sir.'

"So he came out and just before he did the concert again, he tapped the mike and said 'Is this thing on?' And the crowd went crazy."

Rocco Urbisci,
co-producer

AIRED:
AUGUST 9, 1974

80

HOST: # Sly & the Family Stone

FEATURING: ## Roger McGuinn, Elvin Bishop, Little Feat

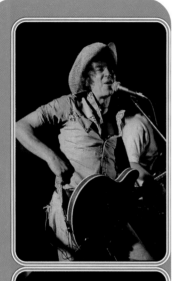

Elvin Bishop

Just as President Nixon exited the White House, Sly Stone was at the end of a long run as one of the nation's top soul singers. When Sly & the Family Stone hosted the show on August 9, they had just released *Small Talk*, an album that would be the group's last gold record. Sly and Company ran through a litany of old hits on the show—"Thank You (Falettinme Be Mice Elf Agin)," "Time for Livin'," "Family Affair," "Dance to the Music," "I Want to Take You Higher," "Stand" and "If You Want Me to Stay"—underscoring the combo's status as bona fide superstars. But unfortunately it was not to be long lived. Though the hits soon dried up for Sly Stone, he will always be regarded as one of the pioneering soul singers and composers of our time.

Nixon and Stone weren't the only icons in free-fall. Roger McGuinn, the founder of the Byrds, was promoting his second solo album, *Peace on You*, which was not well received. Another expatriate from a famous band was also on hand for *The Midnight Special*'s 80th episode—Elvin Bishop, the lead guitarist with the Butterfield Blues Band until 1968, now pushing a solo album of his own. Less than two years later, Bishop would become a regular on *The Midnight Special* and also on the charts with "Fooled Around and Fell in Love."

Perhaps the most engaging aspect of Episode 80 was the appearance of Little Feat, a country/gospel/rock/boogie/funk/R&B outfit from Los Angeles that was about to hit the charts with *Feats Don't Fail Me Now*, their fourth album. On this show they would perform two songs from the release, the deeply funky "Tripe Face Boogie" and "Willin'," a truck driver's beautiful lament. Little Feat would go on to co-host *The Midnight Special* with Emmylou Harris in 1977, but in 1974 the group was just on the cusp of major acclaim.

Sly & the Family Stone

81

HOST: # Little Richard

FEATURING: Golden Earring, Kool & the Gang, Aerosmith, Eddie Kendricks

ittle Richard was no stranger to the charts, but he was a *Midnight Special* rookie when the original mover and shaker of rock made his debut with a rousing version of the show's theme song. Golden Earring followed Little Richard with their epic "Radar Love," followed by suave funkmasters Kool & the Gang, who were still years away from their crossover success with "Celebration," but Top-40 veterans nevertheless with "Jungle Boogie" and "Hollywood Swinging." Inexplicably, the group played neither of these songs, opting instead for "Funky Stuff," from 1973's album *Wild and Peaceful*.

Wild but never peaceful were Aerosmith, who paused from a hectic touring schedule to debut on *The Midnight Special* with a smoldering "The Train Kept A Rollin," recorded for *Get Your Wings* in 1973. Later in the show they played their signature tune "Dream On," which would go down in the annals of rock history as one of the decade's defining anthems.

Also making a showing on *The Midnight Special* that August night was ex-Temptation Eddie Kendricks, who had piloted the legendary soul group as its lead singer from 1960 to 1971. Kendricks, who had enjoyed monstrous pop and R&B chart success with "Boogie Down" over the previous year, performed "Keep On Truckin' (Part 1)," much to the delight of the attendees.

Aerosmith

Little Richard

Kool & the Gang

episode
AIRED:
AUGUST 30, 1974

83

HOST: # B. B. King

FEATURING: John Lee Hooker, Bobby "Blue" Bland, Big Mama Thornton, Papa John Creach, Joe Williams, Zulu, Paul Butterfield's Better Days, Jimmy Whitherspoon

"I REMEMBER THEY MADE THREE OR FOUR ATTEMPTS TO GET ME ON **THE MIDNIGHT SPECIAL**. IT WAS A GREAT SHOW, AND IT WAS THE THING BACK THEN. SO THEY FINALLY CAUGHT UP WITH ME AND I WENT ON. IT WAS THE FIRST TIME I'D EVER DONE A BIG NATIONAL SHOW LIKE THAT, AND I FELT NERVOUS, BECAUSE IT'S RUNNIN' THROUGH YOUR MIND THAT PEOPLE ARE LOOKING AT YOU ALL OVER THE WORLD. BUT ONCE IT GOT GOING I WAS FINE.

"PAPA JOHN CREACH WAS ON THAT SHOW. YOU DON'T SEE MANY PEOPLE WHO CAN PLAY BLUES ON VIOLIN, BUT HE AND SUGARCANE HARRIS REALLY COULD. THAT WAS MY KIND OF BLUES. I LEARNED TO PLAY THE GUITAR WHEN I WAS A KID FROM MY STEPFATHER. HE TAUGHT ME TO PLAY THE WAY HE PLAYED YEARS AGO. I FIRST RECORDED IN 1948, AND I MET B.B. KING IN ATLANTA, GEORGIA AROUND 1951. HE WAS A GREAT GUITAR PLAYER. HE STEPPED ON IT, AND HE DID IT RIGHT. HE'S A NICE MAN—SUCH A GENTLEMAN. HE'S GOT NO BIG EGO AT ALL, HE'S JUST A DOWN-TO-EARTH GUY. WE USED TO HANG OUT, DRINK, PARTY TOGETHER.

Theme shows had been part of *The Midnight Special* practically since its inception. Episode 13 was the first "theme" show, consisting of "oldies and solid-gold moments." Though regular shows would always champion a diversity of styles, these theme shows displayed *The Midnight Special*'s imagination and resources. Whether it was country, heavy metal, jazz fusion, disco or oldies, each theme show would take on a cohesive life of its own. Other theme programs included million sellers, anniversary shows, Christmas shows, the "British invasion," all-international acts, all comedy, and Southern rock.

But of all the theme shows *The Midnight Special* would put together, this was its most fully realized. Assembling some of the greatest living blues artists of the previous fifty years, the show gave B.B. King an opportunity to teach America about the blues, using some experts in the form as examples. As of this writing most of the artists are dead, but for several of them, *The Midnight Special* was the widest exposure they would ever enjoy.

On this episode, B.B. King would say "The blues is really everything to me. Most of the friends I have, I made them through music. And it's been able to keep me and the family eating for years. A lot of [kids] don't even know a lot of the blues giants today, and I think it's a sad, sad thing. I think this is a part of our culture, and they should be taught to respect them. You've given us a chance tonight to show that the blues can be presented as well as any other type of music, and you can see that we have a rainbow of people here tonight. One thing young people don't realize is that a lot of their idols have listened to the many [blues] greats. Bessie Smith was the Aretha Franklin of her day."

With that, Wolfman Jack introduced a film clip of Smith singing in 1929.

Particular highlights of the show included John Lee Hooker's rendition of the "Boogie with the Hook," Bobby "Blue" Bland's organ- and horn-infused version of "Goin' Down Slow," and Big Mama Thornton's impassioned reading of "Ball and Chain"—which was enough to give many a watcher the chills. The riveting combination of King, Hooker and Papa John Creach jammed on an unrehearsed rendition of a King brainchild, aptly called "Gettin' It Together."

Joe Williams

Papa John Creach

John Lee Hooker, B.B. King and Papa John Creach

"A whole bunch of people were influenced by me. European people, Z.Z. Top, the Stones, Van Morrison. He loves John Lee Hooker. He plays a bunch of my stuff, and he's on a lot of my records.

"Big Mama Thornton was a great lady, and a great singer, too. She didn't get her justice like she should have, but she was so good. I worked with Big Mama around '51, '52, '53, something like that. She used to sing "You ain't nothin' but a hound dog, hangin' 'round the door," and Elvis got that from her. I knew Elvis real well, and he was a nice guy, too.

"I knew Big Joe Williams real well. He was a great singer. I was on the same bill with him, and did the same shows, but he never sang in my band. Bobby "Blue" Bland, too. Boy, he was a great singer. I worked with him a lot.

"I've had a great life, and I'm fortunate to have always played music. It's amazing when you can do something you love deep down in your heart."

John Lee Hooker

episode 84

AIRED:
SEPTEMBER 6, 1974
TAPED AT ATLANTA
FULTON COUNTY
STADIUM ON
AUGUST 5, 1974

HOST: **Marvin Gaye**

BURT SUGARMAN, EXECUTIVE PRODUCER: "MARVIN DIDN'T ALWAYS LIKE TO COOPERATE. ONE TIME WE WERE SUPPOSED TO REHEARSE, AND HE WAS TWO HOURS LATE. SO I WENT TO HIS FATHER'S HOUSE TO GET HIM, AND HE WAS SLEEPING. SO I WOKE HIM UP AND SAID 'MARVIN, YOU WERE SUPPOSED TO REHEARSE TWO HOURS AGO.' HE SAID, 'FRANK SINATRA DOES IT HIS WAY, AND SO DO I.'"

JACQUES ANDRE, ASSOCIATE PRODUCER: "THE MARVIN GAYE SHOW WAS SUPPOSED TO BE DONE IN WASHINGTON, D.C., AT THE CAP ARENA, BUT WHEN WE GOT TO WASHINGTON, BURT CALLS STAN AND ME TOGETHER AND SAYS, 'THE GUY WANTS AN EXTRA $20,000 TO SHOOT AT THE CAP ARENA, SO WE'RE NOT DOING THE SHOW.' WE'D ALREADY BROUGHT CAMERAMEN FROM CALIFORNIA AND A TRUCK FROM NASHVILLE, BUT HE SAID, 'FIND SOMEPLACE ELSE TO DO THE SHOW.'"

STAN HARRIS, PRODUCER/DIRECTOR: "GAYE HAD A CONCERT SCHEDULED IN ATLANTA A COUPLE OF DAYS LATER, SO WE MOVED THE WHOLE CREW TO ATLANTA."

The most ambitious *Midnight Special* show ever produced, this episode featured an entire concert by one of the greatest soul singers of all time, Marvin Gaye. The concert footage was cut with footage of various prerecorded interviews, including several sadly prophetic talks with Gaye's father, who would kill his son a decade later after a family argument. By 1974, Gaye was already a certifiable superstar, having released the sensitive, sensual and socially conscious albums *Let's Get It On* and *What's Going On.*

Gaye liked to do things his own way, but there were more than a few problems surrounding the production of the Atlanta show, and they couldn't all be attributed to Gaye's attitude.

Despite all of the behind-the-scenes maneuvering, the show itself was an unqualified success. Gaye's ensemble included four male backing vocalists as well as string and horn players, all of whom reacted to Gaye's every passionate gesticulation with the precision of a small combo. Everything except Gaye's voice, slightly ragged due to a recent illness, sounded seamless. Highlights included Gaye's rendition of his 1972 smash "Trouble Man," the title song from a movie starring Robert Hooks. Opening the show with this number, Gaye—bedecked in foothigh platform shoes and a red skullcap—sat down in the middle of the song at an acoustic piano, pounding out a few bluesy riffs before picking his microphone back up and finishing the tune.

Throughout the evening, Gaye reacted to the throng with charisma and sensuality. During his version of the Holland-Dozier-Holland classic "How Sweet It Is to Be Loved by You," Gaye beseeched the attendees to love one another and to "turn to the person next door and give them a great big kiss." During "Distant Lover," the singer dropped to one knee to sing, "Come back home, girl" with a passion that drew shrieks from the women and raw shouts of approval from the men. Likewise, his

MARVIN GAYE

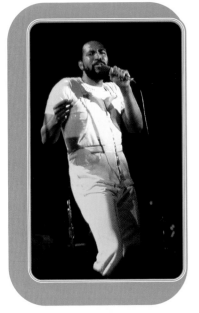

evocative reading of "Come Get to This" set the crowd swooning. But it was the moments with the elder Gayes that spoke volumes about the legendary man behind so many painfully lovely songs.

MRS. ALBERTA GAYE [Addressing her son]: "I enjoyed your show. I really don't see you that much because I'm lookin' at the people, but I thought the concert was beautiful. I get my joy when the people scream and they love you."

MARVIN GAYE: "Music is my love. It's all I know. But if I didn't have musical talent I'd probably be a doctor because I like to make people feel better."

MRS. ALBERTA GAYE: "I don't know what I would have done without your father. He was very strict, and he kept you from getting into all different kinds of trouble."

MARVIN GAYE [somewhat unconvincingly]: "I know I'm better for it."

MARVIN GAYE SR. [Addressing his son]: "I'm gonna give to you now, before these cameras and before these people—I think you're wonderful, myself. As long as I know you have a humble mind, and as long as you know the Lord upstairs; and you can call on him, and respect the people. I think you are a really wonderful person and I'm gonna give that to you as my son, and I'm proud of you."

Marvin Jr. looked at the ground, perhaps embarrassed that his father needed a public forum to finally praise him. Marvin Sr. offered his hand, which his son gladly accepted, throwing his arms around his dad's neck and kissing him on the cheek. As the screen faded to black, the camera lingered on the face of an uncomfortable Marvin Sr.

ANDRE: "WE MOVED IT TO ATLANTA FULTON COUNTY STADIUM. WE HAD A CAMERA TRUCK, BUT ON THE WAY THE TAPE TRUCK WAS IN AN ACCIDENT. SO WE HAD CAMERAS, BUT WE DIDN'T HAVE ANY TAPE. AND WE HAD NO WAY OF FINDING TAPE IN ATLANTA. SO WE DISCOVERED THAT THE UNIVERSITY OF ATLANTA HAD TAPE MACHINES, BUT THEY WERE NOT ALLOWED TO USE THEM FOR COMMERCIAL PROGRAMMING. THE MAYOR OF ATLANTA, ANDREW YOUNG, TRIED TO HELP US GO IN THERE AND DO EVERYTHING, BUT HE COULDN'T GET THE TAPE FROM THE UNIVERSITY EITHER. SO JIMMY CARTER, WHO AT THAT TIME WAS THE GOVERNOR OF GEORGIA, GOT US THE TAPES."

HARRIS: "SEVERAL YEARS LATER I DID A SHOW WHEN CARTER WAS PRESIDENT, AT THE FORD THEATRE, AND THERE WAS A BIG RECEPTION AFTERWARD WHERE EVERYONE WAS BEING INTRODUCED TO HIM. EVEN BEFORE I WAS INTRODUCED HE SAID 'STAN HARRIS, HOW ARE YOU?' I WAS QUITE IMPRESSED, BECAUSE I'D ONLY MET HIM FOR A FEW MINUTES. HE DIDN'T EVEN KNOW GLEN CAMPBELL!"

Marvin Gaye and Mrs. Alberta Gaye

Marvin Gaye Sr. and Marvin Gaye

episode 87

AIRED:
SEPTEMBER 27, 1974

HOST: # Randy Newman

FEATURING: Maria Muldaur, Dr. John, Flo & Eddie, Ry Cooder

Randy Newman

Ry Cooder

Randy Newman might have been the 1970s' best-known unknown songwriter, simply on the strength of his "I'm a Pepper, You're a Pepper" jingle for Dr. Pepper, a commercial theme that then funded his iconoclastic career. But Newman wrote plenty of hits for other people as well that no one knew he was behind, including the song with which he opened this *Midnight Special*, "Mama Told Me Not to Come," a No. 1 for Three Dog Night. After a knowing "Betcha didn't know I wrote that one" wink, Newman, on piano, performed the earnest "Simon Smith and the Amazing Dancing Bear," the mournful "I Think It's Going to Rain Today" (covered by Judy Collins in 1966), and the hilarious "Political Science." Newman introduced the latter as a song "for all you good fascists. It's about bombing the hell out of everybody."

Newman's first guest was Maria Muldaur, riding high on the popularity of her self-titled debut and her hit "Midnight at the Oasis," and who was on the verge of releasing her second effort, Waitress in the Donut Shop. Her first song was a track from that album, the jazzy, Dixieland-ish "Sweetheart." Later in the show Muldaur would sing "Squeeze Me," another song from Waitress, which was followed by a heart-wrenching take on the Billie Holiday staple "Lover Man." On this tune, Muldaur was backed by a tasteful group consisting of acoustic bass, piano, drums, electric guitar, two trumpets, two saxophones, and a trombone.

Next up were several performers who were not afraid to use props to augment their music. First came Dr. John, the well-known New Orleans pianist. Known to his friends as Mac Rebennack, the good Doctor purveyed a mixture of funk, R&B and glitter, infused with a healthy dollop of good old-fashioned Crescent City voodoo. Dr. John hit *The Midnight Special* wearing full makeup and a multicolored headdress, looking more like a character actor than a highly touted musician. His band resem-

Dr. John

bled a group of traveling gypsies, from the organ player with a luminescent eye patch to the guitarist, sporting full African garb. The combo performed two songs from Dr. John's recently released *Desitively Bonnaroo*, including the rollicking title track and the swampy "Let's Make a Better World."

Mark Volman and Howard Kaylan (a.k.a. Flo & Eddie), had formed the Turtles in 1963, but had subsequently broken up the band, briefly joined Frank Zappa's Mothers of Invention, then released two albums as a duo. Apparently Zappa's sense of the absurd had rubbed off on the pair: Flo flew down from the ceiling in a cloud of dry ice while Eddie got busy making noise. Both he and Eddie were clad in full face paint and capes, announcing, "Most rock concerts end with a big send-up, so if you're waiting for that you can leave now." After this sensational introduction, Volman and Kaylan changed into their "normal" clothes and sang a beautiful version of the Turtles' 1967 chart-topper "Happy Together."

One of the finest moments that evening was the solitary song that guitar hero Ry Cooder performed. Cooder's one-and-only performance on the show was "Ditty Wah Ditty," played solo on acoustic guitar. The track, originally written by Arthur Blake, had been recorded by Cooder on his defining solo effort, *Paradise and Lunch*, released earlier in 1974. On the album version of "Ditty Wah Ditty," Cooder had welcomed legendary "stride" pianist Earl "Fatha" Hines to perform a duet, effectively linking the past, the present and the future of music. Cooder's tasteful, hyper-skilled playing on *The Midnight Special* gave the masses yet another brief glimpse of musical genius at work.

Flo & Eddie

94 HOST: Barry White

FEATURING: Eric Burdon

"The Midnight Special was one of the greatest music television shows that was ever done. It allowed the artists to do their music exactly the way they wanted to do it. I remember how excited and happy I was when they told me that The Midnight Special wanted me to host an episode of the show. I think it was my first experience on network TV. I remember feeling very nervous about everything, because I had so many things to worry about. Normally, if you are an artist, that's all you've got to worry about. But I had me and the Love Unlimited, and all of us had hits, so we were under a pressure grind to play all the hits that we had right then. The Midnight Special was a great promotional tool, though, because it exposed everybody who was somebody at the time."

Barry White

While White's performance was fantastic, his forte in the early '70s was studio work:

"The force that drives me is not money, it's not publicity, it's not even hit records. It's music. When I go into the studio, the whole world ceases, everything stops, and I'm in a suspended world of my own. That's what

lights . . . camera . . . enter the ultra-charismatic singer / songwriter / keyboardist / producer / arranger / conductor Barry White, his 40-piece Love Unlimited Orchestra, and ex-Animal and War front man Eric Burdon. Burdon was more of a legend than a star at that juncture, having had numerous hits, starting with the biggest, "House of the Rising Sun," in 1964. A decade later, Burdon performed "It's My Life," an Animals hit from 1965, a version of The Who's "The Real Me," and the apropos 1967 Animals' song "When I Was Young," for an appreciative *Midnight Special* audience.

White, on the other hand, was a star on the rise that year, having recently hit No. 1 with his soulful, sensual classic "Can't Get Enough of Your Love, Babe." He had also hit the charts less than two weeks before the airing of the show with "You're the First, the Last, My Everything," a song which would quickly vault to No. 2 after his appearance. White had also piloted the Love Unlimited Orchestra to the top of the charts on the instrumental "Love's Theme," with which the ensemble kicked off the show— White wielding the conductor's baton.

BARRY WHITE AND THE LOVE UNLIMITED ORCHESTRA

Barry White and the Love Unlimited Orchestra

Eric Burdon

drives me, to get that feeling. And what comes out of that feeling? Many, many things. Drumbeats, bass notes, horn lines, string riffs, melodies, lyrics, all kinds of things come out of that suspension of time. I remember 'Can't Get Enough of Your Love, Babe' was the only song [at that point] for which I had written the bass line. We were in the studio recording it, and all the people had their parts. So I went back into the control room to hear the song, but I felt there was something missing. Everybody was telling me 'You're wrong. This is a smash like it is, blah blah blah.' And I said 'Yeah, I know you're right, it is a good song, but I'm not sure it's the song it could be if that bass line was changed.' So I went back into the studio, called all my guys back into that room—and I had the greatest f**kin' musicians in the world—and I changed one thing: the bass line. When they started playing the song with that new bass line, one of them just hollered out in the middle of a take, 'This is a damn smash!'

"'You're the First, the Last, My Everything' was brought to me by a guy named Peter Radcliffe. He'd been shopping the song for 22 years. The original title was 'You're the First, the Last, My In Between.' So I said to him, 'You're not gonna believe this song when you hear it again.' I changed it around and it became a very large hit; number two, I think."

Barry White

1 9 7 5

Two separate women—Lynette "Squeaky" Fromme and Sara Jane Moore—tried to assassinate President Ford within a matter of weeks in 1975—and he wouldn't pardon either one. This was also the year that Teamster boss Jimmy Hoffa disappeared, and the year Sony introduced the possibility of watching a movie at home with its Betamax technology. Robert Altman's *Nashville* was in the theaters, and Jack Nicholson would give an Oscar-winning performance in *One Flew Over the Cuckoo's Nest*. *Starsky and Hutch* was popular on the tube, while Dylan's *Blood on the Tracks*, Patti Smith's *Horses* and Bruce Springsteen's *Born to Run* were popular on turntables. 1975 was also the year Arthur Ashe became the first black men's singles champ at Wimbledon.

1975 was a pivotal year for *The Midnight Special*, too. It had already proved itself to be diverse, cutting edge, and middle-of-the-road—all at once—but could it be resilient to the impending radical changes in music and the music industry? Helen Reddy began her 35-episode stint as "permanent guest host" in 1975. During a period of almost two years, commencing on July 18, 1975 (Episode 129), Reddy became as recognizable a personality as the show had ever known. Her moderate appeal kept the show anchored by song craft and soft rock & roll, though the frothing waters of disco were threatening to turn the music world on its ear. This was also the year when *The Midnight Special* debuted its "salutes" feature, a phenomenon that would pay tribute to more than 50 artists. The first salute would occur on Episode 128, with comedian Flip Wilson doing a tribute to—who else?—Helen Reddy.

episode 103

HOST: **Electric Light Orchestra**

FEATURING: Linda Ronstadt, Rufus featuring Chaka Khan, The Ohio Players

Linda Ronstadt

In a May 1974 issue of *Record World* magazine, E.L.O. drummer Bev Bevan said, "I think [*The Midnight Special* has] probably done us more good than any other thing I can think of in America. I'm sure it must have helped us sell many thousands of records."

With this statement, Bevan neatly packaged the appeal of *The Midnight Special* to artists and record companies. In fact, he and his band would host *The Midnight Special* for the first time on January 17, 1975, and soon thereafter E.L.O. would enjoy their biggest American hit at the time, the Top-10 "Can't Get It Out of My Head." And just to prove they had rock & roll in their hearts, as well as virtuosity in their playing, the septet rolled out a vibrant cover of Jerry Lee Lewis' "Great Balls of Fire," with wild-haired guitarist and group leader Jeff Lynne handling the vocals. The group would later match itself with a rendition of another early rock & roll classic, "Roll Over Beethoven."

Perhaps the most engaging E.L.O. performance of the night, however, was their version of the bluegrass standard "Orange

Electric Light Orchestra

Blossom Special," later popularized by Johnny Cash. The song showcased violinist Mike Kaminski, whose keening playing lent a dark undercurrent to the tune's upbeat, racing melodies.

Linda Ronstadt and her band celebrated their hit album *Heart Like a Wheel* by wearing miniature hearts on their stage outfits. They played three of the biggest hits from that double-platinum LP: the anthemic "When Will I Be Loved," the beautifully scathing "You're No Good" and the steel-pedal-laden Lowell George composition, "Willin'."

Making their fourth appearance were Chicago soulsters Rufus, featuring Chaka Khan, who graced the room with several songs, including Reddy's "I Am Woman" and the Beatles' "We Can Work It Out." They also played the funky "You Got the Love" from their breakthrough 1974 album *Rags to Rufus* and "Pack'd My Bags," a song from their *Rufusized* album, which had hit the pop charts less than two weeks prior and would burst into the Top 10 after their appearance on *The Midnight Special*.

Rounding out Episode 103 were The Ohio Players, a quintessential 1970s funk band, who riveted the audience with their hit "Jive Turkey."

Rufus Featuring Chaka Khan

HOST:

The Marshall Tucker Band

FEATURING: Olivia Newton-John,
The Charlie Daniels Band,
Poco

Olivia Newton-John would ultimately appear almost two dozen times on *The Midnight Special*, but on this early performance, she was the relative newcomer in a field of established heavyweights. Known more for her mellifluous songs and crystalline voice than for her raucous country spirit, Newton-John was not expected to hold a candle to her fiddle-playing, Southern-fried boogie company. Then she opened her mouth, for heart-melting performances of "Let Me Be There" and Bob Dylan's "If Not for You," and it was apparent that her spirit was singular and her intentions were pure.

The Marshall Tucker Band's only appearance on *The Midnight Special* lit up the house, as the great band was making the most memorable music of its career. Named after a piano tuner who owned their rehearsal space, the South Carolina rock/pop/country sextet had formed in 1971, releasing their eponymous debut two years later. Shortly after hosting *The Midnight Special*, the group would have its first charting single, "This Ol' Cowboy." Opening the show with this number, flutist Jerry Eubanks teamed up with special guest fiddler Charlie Daniels, as the two players formed the song's main riff with serrated, simultaneous lines, and lead guitarist Toy Caldwell sang its melancholy, matter-of-fact refrain.

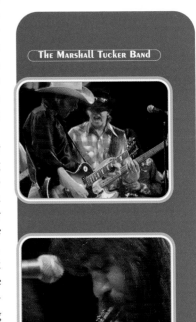

The Marshall Tucker Band

The Charlie Daniels Band

Later Charlie Daniels and his band did a set of their own, including their distinctive ode to Southern rock, "The South's Gonna Do It," which paid homage to Elvin Bishop, ZZ Top, Barefoot Jerry, and the show's host.

Poco, a group that had weathered many personnel changes since its formation in 1968, here consisted of founder Rusty Young (dobro, banjo, pedal steel guitar), future Eagle Timothy B. Schmit (bass), George Grantham (percussion) and Paul Cotton (acoustic guitar). Sitting on the *Midnight Special* stage, which had been transformed for this show to resemble the interior of an old saloon—replete with woodstove pipe, casks and the like—the country-rockers ran through "Whatever Happened to Your Smile," with Schmit on vocals. They then played a tune from 1973's *Crazy Eyes* called "Sagebrush Serenade," on which Cotton sang lead. *The Midnight Special* audience loved Poco's electric, "High and Dry," which they had recorded on their 1974 *Cantamos* (Spanish for "We Sing") LP. During this song Young would show off his horseshoe-shaped pinky ring, which flashed his band's distinctive logo across the screen.

Poco

HOST: Clive Davis

FEATURING: Blood, Sweat, and Tears, Barry Manilow, Martha Reeves, Melissa Manchester, Loggins & Messina, Gil Scott-Heron

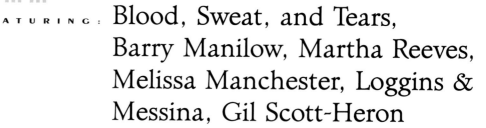

"**The Midnight Special** wanted to have Ringo, and Ringo was being hounded by Nilsson, who was hanging out and drinking with John Lennon and him all the time. Nilsson wouldn't let them out of his sight. So the show told Clive, 'Hey, we can get Ringo.' And Ringo probably said, 'If you get me you have to take my friend Harry, because we travel together.' And Clive said 'Okay, why not?' But I actually don't remember much about the show, other than the fact that we were just trying, to be musically efficient."

Bobby Columby,
Blood, Sweat, and Tears

This was the first *Midnight Special* to be hosted by a behind-the-scenes player instead of an artist. The evening celebrated both the genius of Clive Davis, the founder of Arista Records, and the artistry of his acts, which included Janis Joplin, Blood, Sweat, and Tears, Loggins & Messina, and Barry Manilow. Davis was instantly recognizable to people within the music industry, yet the public knew only his artists—a dilemma for the producers, as *The Midnight Special* was always hosted by a household name. The solution? Prime the audience with a photo montage of the record mogul with an array of stars before sending him on-stage. This presentation was made by an artist who was also relatively unknown, but well respected in the musical community, Harry Nilsson. Nilsson himself had been introduced by a man known to virtually everyone: Ringo Starr. Starr knew his purpose, joking, "Nobody knows who you are, so I've come to introduce you."

But Clive Davis' artists needed no introductions, for they wrote the songs the whole world sang. Barry Manilow appeared wearing a glittering, baby-blue silk shirt with a huge white collar and studded with blue rhinestones. Sitting alone at his white piano, Manilow ran through his first hit, "Mandy."

From Mandy to Janis—the show aired footage of the late, great Joplin performing an amazing version of "Try (Just a Little Bit

Clive Davis

Ringo Starr and Harry Nilsson

Harder)," complete with horns, from a late '60s show called "Music Scene" that had been owned, produced and directed by *The Midnight Special*'s own Stan Harris and where several *Midnight Special* crew members had also worked. Then Blood, Sweat, and Tears—reunited with singer David Clayton-Thomas—played "You've Made Me So Very Happy" for Davis, crediting him for their being a band in the first place. It was a fitting tribute to Davis, but also a sentimental favorite for the show, since Clayton-Thomas had also appeared on the first *Midnight Special*.

Some of Davis' biggest hitmakers, like Martha Reeves, Melissa Manchester and Loggins & Messina, also honored him and played. But perhaps the evening's most inspiring performance was by Gil Scott-Heron, who was a pioneer of a style of music that would later be dubbed "rap," though he would never sell many records himself. Davis introduced Scott-Heron's socially conscious jazz, funk and African hybrid by saying, "Every free-thinking adult should have an open mind to what Gil Scott-Heron is saying." With that, Scott-Heron launched into a song called "The Bottle," a track that melded urgent social commentary with groove-heavy, percussion-dominated backing music.

Barry Manilow

Martha Reeves

Gil Scott-Heron

116

HOST: # Earth, Wind & Fire

FEATURING: LaBelle, Leo Sayer

"WE'D JUST PUT OUT 'SHINING STAR' WHEN WE HOSTED <u>THE MIDNIGHT SPECIAL</u>. THOSE SHOWS WERE GREAT BECAUSE YOU ACTUALLY PLAYED LIVE IN FRONT OF AN AUDIENCE. IN THOSE DAYS, IF YOU LIP-SYNCHED, YOU DIDN'T GET THE SAME LEVEL OF RESPECT BECAUSE PEOPLE WEREN'T SURE IF YOU REALLY COULD PLAY. SO THAT WAS THE BEAUTY OF THE SHOW. BACK THEN MUSIC WAS ON NETWORK TELEVISION, SO PEOPLE REALLY CHECKED IT OUT. IT WASN'T LIKE TODAY, WHERE YOU HAVE MTV OR BET. TODAY YOU HAVE DIFFERENT CHANNELS FOR DIFFERENT KINDS OF MINDS. BUT IN THOSE DAYS WE'D BE ON THE SAME SHOW WITH LINDA RONSTADT AND THE EAGLES. IT WAS MIXED TOGETHER. IT WASN'T LIKE YOU WERE SEPARATE FROM ANOTHER GENRE OF MUSIC. IT WAS JUST MUSIC. MUSIC SHOWS TODAY ARE MORE SHOW BUSINESS-Y, AND SOCIAL COMMENTARY DOESN'T SELL [LIKE] IT USED TO. AT THAT TIME MUSIC WAS COMBINED WITH A LEVEL OF CONSCIOUSNESS AND SOCIAL COMMENTARY. IF YOU WERE GOING TO BE A MUSICIAN YOU HAD TO MAKE A CERTAIN AMOUNT OF COMMITMENT. NOWADAYS EVERYONE KNOWS IT'S ABOUT MONEY. IT WAS ABOUT MONEY THEN, TOO, BUT THERE WAS A COMMITMENT THAT TOOK THE MUSIC TO ANOTHER LEVEL.

"ANOTHER THING THAT WAS GREAT ABOUT <u>THE MIDNIGHT SPECIAL</u> AUDIENCES WAS THAT THEY REALLY LOVED THE ARTIST. NOW YOU HAVE AUDIENCES THAT ARE MORE

B ands liked to come back to *The Midnight Special* for many different reasons, whether for the people, the exposure, or for some, simply the chance to play live on television. Other shows asked groups to lip-synch, which was always a dicey prospect before a live audience. For Earth, Wind & Fire, in the midst of a string of eight hit records when they hosted this *Midnight Special,* playing live was the incentive—and indeed, they had a fiery stage show. On this episode they opened with their No. 1 hit "Shining Star," then quickly burst into "Mighty Mighty," which, in true rock & roll fashion, ended abruptly with a huge flash and a puff of smoke. Earth, Wind & Fire welcomed LaBelle who, dressed in shiny, silvery space-age outfits, played their propulsive, sexually charged smash "Lady Marmalade," which taught many Americans the only French they would ever learn—*Voulez-vous coucher avec moi?* or "Do you want to go to bed with me?"

EARTH, WIND & FIRE

Earth, Wind and Fire

LaBelle

117

HOST: Rod Stewart & the Faces

FEATURING: Keith Richards

critics. You might be on-stage and have half the audience taking notes saying 'I don't know if I like this.' Because we're living in an information society, everybody's got an opinion. Back then people just flowed with you. They're more cynical today. As an entertainer today, you know the public knows you stay at great hotels and you ride in limousines, so on some level there's a little animosity toward what you do, because they know if you make it, you might leave them behind. There might be a disparity between your economics and your status versus theirs. In the <u>Midnight Special</u> days there was less of a divide between performer and audience.

"We were one of the first black crossover bands, and <u>The Midnight Special</u> let Middle America into our vibe. We were building momentum at that point, but <u>The Midnight Special</u> really helped us a lot, and the people were always really nice to us, and treated us right. In those days, any high-level exposure was great. That was sort of like the birth of music as we know it today because that was the first time America had really opened up to all types of music. In a lot of ways we really had a lot more racial harmony then we have now. Music cuts through all the s**t."

Verdine White,
Earth, Wind & Fire

pisode 117 marked the first occasion that superstar Rod Stewart visited the show. Backed by the famed Faces— pianist Ian McLagen, drummer Kenney Jones (who would join The Who in 1978), guitarist Ron Wood (who would join the Rolling Stones in 1976), and bassist Tetsu Yamauchi—the performance included live footage that was taped by *The Midnight Special*. Wearing a brilliant, shiny yellow jumpsuit with a red sash and a polka-dotted kerchief, Stewart looked every part the rock & roll prince. The group opened the show with a version of the Bobby Womack/Valentinos tune "It's All Over Now," and followed with a medley of Sam Cooke tunes, "Bring It On Home to Me" and "You Send Me." Later in the show Rolling Stone Keith Richards would join the fray, dueling with Wood and firing off some dark, propulsive licks on Chuck Berry's "Sweet Little Rock and Roller." Richards also augmented their rendition of Cooke's rock staple "Twistin' the Night Away." Less than nine months later, the Faces would permanently disband.

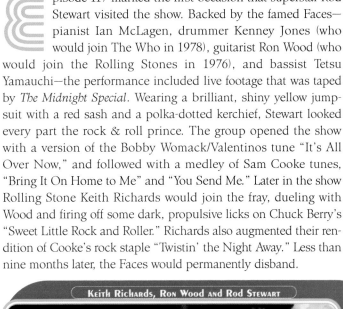

Keith Richards, Ron Wood and Rod Stewart

episode
AIRED:
MAY 9, 1975
TAPED AT
THE UNIVERSITY
OF CHICAGO ON
MARCH 12, 1975

119

HOST: Wolfman Jack

FEATURING: The Ohio Players, Roxy Music, Graham Central Station, The Strawbs, Larry Gatlin

Wolfman Jack

Perhaps no '70s band had more impact than Roxy Music, whose suave, sophisticated art-rock blurred the boundaries between rock, pop and punk, and inspired bands of the '80s new wave and new romantic movements, as well as the '90s martini-swilling cocktail nation. Debonair crooner Bryan Ferry created the decade's most romantic music: charming, elegant, refined, but funky and danceable. 1975 found the band at its creative peak; though Brian Eno had departed, their mid-1970s records *Stranded, Country Life*, and *Siren* were their best. For their only *Midnight Special* appearance, Roxy Music dug deep into *Country Life* for "Out of the Blue," "The Thrill of It All," and "A Really Good Time," operatic tales of love lost and found in clubland.

The University of Chicago college crowd saw mostly funk during the rest of the evening. The Ohio Players opened the show with "I Want to Be Free," from their explosive No. 1 *Fire* album. They would play a total of eight times on *The Midnight Special*. After Roxy Music, Graham Central Station played. The funk-oriented group was led by bassist Larry Graham, who had held up the bottom end of Sly & the Family Stone's music from 1966 to

The Strawbs

Roxy Music

1972. In May 1975, Graham was about to release his *Ain't No 'Bout-A-Doubt It* LP, which would climb to No. 22 and become the highest charting record of Graham's solo career. The sextet performed, among other songs, the propulsive "Feel the Need," a track from the 1974 *Release Yourself* album. This appearance on *The Midnight Special* would also be the only one ever for Graham Central Station.

Another rare treat was a performance by the British progressive/Celtic/folk group the Strawbs (they made two showings in all). Originally known as the Strawberry Hill Boys, the group was formed in 1967. By May 1975 they had released *Ghosts*, an album from which they chose two songs for *The Midnight Special* audience, "Lemon Pie" and "The Life Auction Medley."

Country singer Larry Gatlin would later lead the famed Gatlin Brothers, but when he debuted on *The Midnight Special*, he was known as the writer of some of Tom Jones', Elvis Presley's, Glen Campbell's and Kris Kristofferson's best '60s material. Gatlin did hit with "Delta Dirt" in 1974, but that was to be his only solo appearance on the singles chart.

Graham Central Station

In 1976, the United States' bicentennial year, Democrat Jimmy Carter was elected the 39th President, defeating Gerald Ford. That year the Supreme Court would also make two landmark decisions. It ruled capital punishment was not unconstitutional, and it overturned a Missouri law requiring women to get their husband's approval prior to having an abortion. An earthquake in Guatemala killed upwards of 20,000 people, while the supersonic *Concorde* shortened flying time between America and Europe to a few hours. *All the President's Men* was made into a film in 1976, starring Robert Redford and Dustin Hoffman as the plucky reporters bringing down a president, while Sylvester Stallone portrayed a heroic Philadelphian prizefighter in *Rocky*. On television, *The Muppet Show* was a hit, while the Eagles released *Hotel California* and The Band filmed their farewell concert at San Francisco's Winterland. The 1976 Summer Olympics, held in Montreal, were boycotted by 32 African and Asian countries. The U.S.S.R. took home 47 gold medals, while 14-year-old Romanian gymnast Nadia Comaneci scored seven perfect 10s and win three golds.

1976 was also full of highlights and disappointments for *The Midnight Special*. The year began with Episode 151, a repeat of a Paul Anka–hosted show from 1974, on which he welcomed guests like James Brown, the Ohio Players and the Guess Who. This show set the tone for the year, as *The Midnight Special* started relying more heavily on repeated episodes and a large revolving cast of recurring guests. But these trends certainly didn't mean the show was running out of ideas. A great deal of preparation still went into each new episode, and the diverse booking (now handled by Debi Genovese) was still attracting big stars as well as younger, unknown artists on their way up. One major-league star who barely slipped through *The Midnight Special's* web was Bob Dylan, who agreed to be taped for the show, but later rejected the tapes—in one account because he thought the show looked too "slick." Captured during his famed 1976 "Rolling Thunder Revue," the Bob Dylan show would become known as "The Lost Episode."

THE LOST EPISODE

NEVER AIRED
TAPED APRIL 22, 1976
STARLIGHT BALLROOM
BELLEVUE BILTMORE
HOTEL, CLEARWATER,
FLORIDA

HOST: # Bob Dylan

FEATURING: ## Rolling Thunder Revue
Including: Joan Baez,
Roger McGuinn

"Of all the <u>Midnight Special</u> shows I did—and that was over 200 episodes—the two I was proudest of were the Marvin Gaye show in Atlanta and the Dylan show in Florida. It was a great disappointment that the Dylan show never aired, because the lighting was beautiful, the composition was wonderful and the music was absolutely sensational. It was Dylan at his best. It had a nice feeling because it was simple. It presented the music simply, and it wasn't pretentious at all."

Jaques Andre,
ASSOCIATE PRODUCER

Bob Dylan and Phil Ochs

Had it actually aired, "the lost episode" of *The Midnight Special* would have been a huge coup for the show. But some things are too good to be true, especially when dealing with an artist like Bob Dylan. The concept was to catch Dylan in the midst of the second leg of his ground-breaking "Rolling Thunder Revue," a tour that featured a large entourage of Dylan's closest musical friends. Dylan was enjoying his most fertile creative period in years, having just released "Blood on the Tracks" and "Desire"—which would prove to be his best work of the '70s—in the preceding 15 months.

The initial idea was to rent a studio in which to film the show. As it turned out, Dylan and company were using the Starlight Ballroom of the Clearwater Biltmore Hotel to rehearse, so the show was taped there. The Ballroom was like a long tunnel, with a 20-foot-high, entirely black ceiling, and scaffolding was brought in to serve as seats for the audience.

Dylan opened the show on solo acoustic guitar with "Mr. Tambourine Man," "The Times They Are A-Changin'," "It's Alright Ma (I'm Only Bleeding)," "Girl From the North Country," "Don't Think Twice It's Alright" and two takes of Blonde on Blonde's "Visions of Johanna." Later in the evening he performed a raucous rendition of "Like a Rolling Stone," a graceful reading of "One More Cup of Coffee," the tender "Oh Sister," the steel-pedal-driven "Tonight I'll Be Staying Here with You," and indulged co-producer Rocco Urbisci's request for

Bob Dylan's Rolling Thunder Revue

"Most Likely You'll Go Your Way and I'll Go Mine." Dylan also dueted with Joan Baez on "I Pity the Poor Immigrant," then turned the stage over to Baez, who performed "Dancing in the Street," "Swing Low, Sweet Chariot" and her classic "Diamonds and Rust." Other highlights included Baez, Dylan and ex-Byrd Roger McGuinn's teaming on "Knockin' on Heaven's Door."

Why would Dylan later ask that such a stirring performance never air? In *Behind the Shades*, Clinton Heylin's biography of Dylan, Heylin quotes band member Howie Wyeth, who claimed that Dylan got into a fight with a *Midnight Special* staff member. Others have speculated that Dylan didn't like all the close-up shots of himself. Either way, it was a difficult time for Dylan, still reeling from the suicide of close friend and left-wing folkie Phil Ochs just two weeks earlier. Ochs had desperately wanted to be a part of the Revue, and Dylan took his death badly. The anger and regret that energized Dylan's performance that evening may have ultimately tainted the evening for him, but the lost episode will go down in history as one of the great shows never seen.

In September 1976, the jettisoned *Midnight Special* show was replaced with a one-hour Dylan performance from a show in Fort Collins, Colorado. It garnered low ratings and disparaging reviews. Dylan also released an album called *Hard Rain* from the same performance (it included tracks from a Fort Worth, Texas show too), which dropped quickly out of sight.

Bob Dylan's Rolling Thunder Revue

e p i s o d e

AIRED:
OCTOBER 22, 1976

170a

HOST: Paul Anka

FEATURING: Elton John, Joan Baez, Chubby Checker, Jim Croce, Peter Frampton, Herman's Hermits, Frankie Valli & the Four Seasons

"I was on TV starting back in the '50s. I was on Ed Sullivan 20 or 30 times; Perry Como, Dinah Shore, Dean Martin, Hullabaloo, which I hosted many times, The Tonight Show, Coke Time, Hollywood Palace, Jackie Gleason, American Bandstand. There was really a sense of urgency with television back in those days, especially on Ed Sullivan. The orchestra was 50 yards away, maybe in another room, you were hearing them through a speaker, and you could never hear yourself as loudly as you wanted to. There was also a feeling of nervousness there because it was live. If you blew it, you blew it. I think, in terms of the 'vibe,' American Bandstand was probably the closest to The Midnight Special because you sang your record and you had a good loud sound. It was relaxed and you were really among friends. Except, of course, The Midnight Special was live.

"Prior to The Midnight Special, when pop music was in its infancy, you were kind of looked down upon by television. You were hot, you had the hit record, but [they'd say] you know, 'We also have the ballerinas on the show.'

This show was a "greatest hits" montage of taped and live performances. By popular demand, it would be re-aired four times over the remainder of *The Midnight Special*'s reign on late-night television. Elton John made his first-ever appearance on the program, performing two songs that would become favorites—"Bennie and the Jets" and "Your Song." On the same day, he hit the American pop charts—this time with an LP called *Here and There*, which included live performances from 1974, recorded in New York and London. The album would prove to be a bit of a commercial disappointment for John, as it only went to No. 4. That almost seemed a failure for the prolific pianist/singer/songwriter, who in a five-year stint between 1971 and 1976 released eleven Top-10 albums, including seven that went to No. 1! John would become a frequent attraction on the show—just weeks later, he would smash his way to the top of the charts for four weeks with Kiki Dee on the peppy "Don't Go Breakin' My Heart."

Following John was an eclectic selection of artists and songs. Joan Baez returned with a version of Bob Dylan's "Simple Twist of Fate," also ironic, following "The Lost Episode." Then Anka—a longtime regular of television music and variety shows—dug out his 1959 chestnut, "Put Your Head on My Shoulder."

Paul Anka

Chuck Berry

Elton John

Frankie Valli

FRAMPTON

Peter Frampton

Jim Croce

Herman's Hermits

No one had really embraced pop music as they did in the time of <u>The Midnight Special</u> or in the late '60s. So you knew you weren't in totally friendly waters, as you were on <u>The Midnight Special</u>. <u>The Midnight Special</u> was really the epitome of 'It's us, we love you, we know what this music's about, and let's go.'

"The atmosphere of the show itself was always exciting, too. Everybody was very professional and the audience was really wild. On most of the other shows the audience was staid and not that enthusiastic. But <u>The Midnight Special</u> had all of the ingredients of a 'happening.'

"TV usually is not indigenous to the kind of atmosphere of live performance, and doing <u>The Midnight Special</u> was like you were doing a live concert and someone was filming it. They were right up close, as opposed to 'Let's be careful, let's separate the crowd from the performers, etc.'

"Television is television. You don't have everything going for you in a sense, because you're dealing with a lack of space, you're adhering to technicalities, and definitely there's the time factor. When I'm performing live there are cases I like to ad-lib and take my time. There are parameters, and I don't know that you can 'get off' as readily as you would with live performance. You're reaching a lot of people, but you have to stay within the restrictions and parameters. <u>The Midnight Special</u> was the closest to a live performance feeling that you could get on TV."

Paul Anka

Episode

AIRED:
AUGUST 6, 1976

181

HOST: # James Brown

FEATURING: Elton John / Kiki Dee, Alice Cooper salute, Peter Frampton, Seals & Crofts, Rhythm Heritage, J. D. Souther

Elton John and Kiki Dee

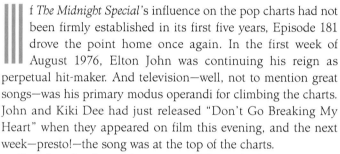

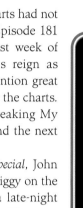

Alice Cooper

If *The Midnight Special*'s influence on the pop charts had not been firmly established in its first five years, Episode 181 drove the point home once again. In the first week of August 1976, Elton John was continuing his reign as perpetual hit-maker. And television—well, not to mention great songs—was his primary modus operandi for climbing the charts. John and Kiki Dee had just released "Don't Go Breaking My Heart" when they appeared on film this evening, and the next week—presto!—the song was at the top of the charts.

One day after his performance on *The Midnight Special,* John appeared on *The Muppet Show* and dueted with Miss Piggy on the same song. John's one-two combo gave America a late-night Friday, prime-time Saturday jolt of the infectious tune. The song was so infectious, in fact, that it became John's first No. 1 single on the pop charts in Britain, and stayed there for six weeks. He stayed at New York's Madison Square Garden almost as long, starting a series of shows on August 10 that grossed more than $1.2 million in ticket receipts, and shattered the Rolling Stones' mark for most sold-out shows at the famed arena.

The Midnight Special's salute to Alice Cooper may have come as a surprise to the many Americans who had written him off as a miscreant due to his highly theatrical, gory stage show. But Cooper was a star in his own right who had recently hit No. 12 with his ballad "I Never Cry." The salute included footage of Cooper in concert as well as a set of interviews with the performer, which revealed him to be a soft-spoken, even thoughtful man, fresh from raising $200,000 for charity on his previous tour a far cry from the on-stage demon he portrayed.

1976 was also a big year for Peter Frampton, and his performance of "Baby, I Love Your Way" pushed the single into the Top 15 the week after the show aired. But Frampton's real success was *Frampton Comes Alive!*, the double live album he had recorded at Winterland in San Francisco and released in January. The album would bounce in and out of the top position on the charts, including one three-week stint at the top directly after

James Brown

Frampton's late-summer *Midnight Special* appearance. *Frampton Comes Alive!* would ultimately become the best-selling live album of all time.

Frampton warmed up the mike for the godfather of soul himself, James Brown. On this, his fifth visit, Brown belted his classic "Sex Machine," and later the new "Get Up Offa That Thing," the title track to an album he had released earlier that year. Later in the evening, the indefatigable Brown sang the title track from his signature *It's a Man's Man's Man's World*, an LP he had recorded in 1966. Showing up also for the fifth time were Seals & Crofts, who had become old friends of *The Midnight Special*. They would perform their Top-10 "Get Closer" from the gold 1976 album of the same name, and later "Goodbye Old Buddies" from the same work. *Get Closer* would become the duo's last Top-40 entry, and they would only tape one more *Midnight Special* before fading into the annals of the 1970s.

Other performers included Rhythm Heritage, a precise Los Angeles studio group assembled by producers Michael Omartian and Steve Barri. The group had captured the country's attention in early 1976 when they hit No. 1 with "Theme From S.W.A.T.," the ABC series starring Steve Forrest. The group's sound was crisp and concise, which made it perfect for soundtrack work. On this show they would perform "Baretta's Theme (Keep Your Eye on the Sparrow)," a tune that had just exited the charts after peaking at No. 20.

Rounding out the lineup was country/rock singer/songwriter J.D. Souther, who had previously formed Longbranch Pennywhistle with future Eagle Glenn Frey and had been a principal member of the Souther, Hillman, Furay Band in 1974 and 1975. In the latter project, Souther's mates included ex-Byrd Chris Hillman and ex-Buffalo Springfield and Poco member Richie Furay. On this evening Souther sang three songs from his recently released *Black Rose* album, including the title track, "Silver Blue," and "Banging My Head Against the Moon." It was to be Souther's only appearance on *The Midnight Special*, though he would hit the Top 10 three years later with "You're Only Lonely."

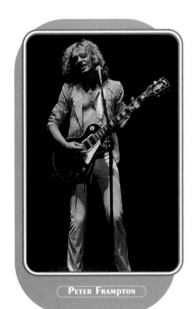

Peter Frampton

J.D. Souther

197

HOST: **Diana Ross**

FEATURING: **Jermaine Jackson, Tata Vega, Commodores, Franklyn Ajaye**

JERMAINE JACKSON

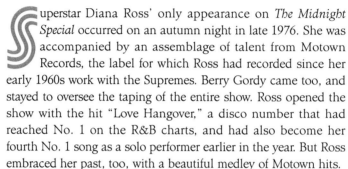

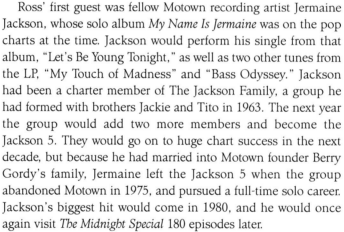

Diana Ross

Commodores

uperstar Diana Ross' only appearance on *The Midnight Special* occurred on an autumn night in late 1976. She was accompanied by an assemblage of talent from Motown Records, the label for which Ross had recorded since her early 1960s work with the Supremes. Berry Gordy came too, and stayed to oversee the taping of the entire show. Ross opened the show with the hit "Love Hangover," a disco number that had reached No. 1 on the R&B charts, and had also become her fourth No. 1 song as a solo performer earlier in the year. But Ross embraced her past, too, with a beautiful medley of Motown hits.

Ross' first guest was fellow Motown recording artist Jermaine Jackson, whose solo album *My Name Is Jermaine* was on the pop charts at the time. Jackson would perform his single from that album, "Let's Be Young Tonight," as well as two other tunes from the LP, "My Touch of Madness" and "Bass Odyssey." Jackson had been a charter member of The Jackson Family, a group he had formed with brothers Jackie and Tito in 1963. The next year the group would add two more members and become the Jackson 5. They would go on to huge chart success in the next decade, but because he had married into Motown founder Berry Gordy's family, Jermaine left the Jackson 5 when the group abandoned Motown in 1975, and pursued a full-time solo career. Jackson's biggest hit would come in 1980, and he would once again visit *The Midnight Special* 180 episodes later.

Another Motown artist to appear on the show was Tata Vega, a contemporary gospel vocalist from Queens, New York. Vega debuted songs from her *Full Speed Ahead* album, including the title track, "Been on My Own (Too Long in the Wilderness)" and "Never Had a Dream Come True." Also joining the fray were the Commodores, a popular R&B group that had been formed in Alabama in 1970. Led by vocalist/saxophonist Lionel Richie, the group was making its second *Midnight Special* showing, and was boasting a Top-15 hit album in *Hot on the Tracks*, from which they would perform "Come Inside," "Fancy Dancer" (which would crack the Top 40), and the Richie ballad "Just to Be Close to You." Richie would start recording as a solo artist in 1981, and would leave the Commodores for good the next year, becoming a huge star in his own right.

SPECIAL SALUTES

This popular segment of the show was originally the brainchild of associate producer Rocco Urbisci. In mid-1975 *The Midnight Special* hired Tisha Fein to coordinate the newly established feature. A semi-regular vehicle to give recognition to hot bands and to favorites of *The Midnight Special*, the salutes segment began on Episode 128. On this show Flip Wilson would pay tribute to HelenReddy, an artist who had hosted Episode 1, and who would begin her nearly two-year, 35-episode stint as "permanent guest host" the very next week. In all, *The Midnight Special* would salute more than 50 artists, usually calling upon the show's host to orchestrate the salute. Sometimes the saluted artist would make a personal appearance, or they'd be represented by promotional clips, footage of them performing live, or a retrospective video overview of their career.

TISHA FEIN, SPECIAL SALUTES COORDINATOR: "I started doing salutes on *The Midnight Special* because I had done special salutes for radio. I had gotten people like Van Morrison and Brian Wilson in his sandbox. So the folks at *The Midnight Special* heard that I was interviewing all these people and they interviewed me [for the job]. We all hit it off, and it was basically love at first sight. So I started writing Wolfman Jack's dialogue, then I ended up booking a lot of the show. It was 24 hours a day, and it was a hell of a life for a young California girl. The salutes ranged from Elton John to Olivia Newton-John, and from Eric Clapton to Patti Page. We covered the gamut. We got Frank Zappa, who thought it was sleazy, but we let him say that, so it stayed in. And we had Alice Cooper, who talked about his character in the third person. We got Chuck Berry, who showed how he played gospel on the piano when he was a kid, and then when his mom wasn't listening he'd throw in a boogie woogie beat. I got everybody—all my heroes, and those who became my heroes. It was the best gig anyone could have had. It was very immediate, very intense and very exciting."

Chuck Berry

Wolfman Jack

Van Morrison

Brian Wilson

TOM JONES

Glen Campbell

Welshman Tom Jones performed on *The Midnight Special* three times before he was asked to host the show at the end of 1976. Jones had enjoyed his first chart success in 1965, but by December 1976 he had gone nearly six years without a hit. What to do? Host *The Midnight Special*, of course. As with so many others, the show helped bring Jones back into the public eye, and sure enough, within two weeks of his performance, "Say You'll Stay Until Tomorrow" peaked at No. 15 on the pop charts, and topped the country list. On this program Jones would perform no fewer than 10 songs, and hint at the same techniques he would use to get attention in the '80s and '90s as well—performing quirky, unexpected covers of popular hits with verve and sass. On this show, he covered The Amazing Rhythm Aces' 1975 hit "Third Rate Romance" and the Beatles' "Get Back." In later years, he'd try Prince's "Kiss" and EMF's "Unbelievable."

Jones welcomed Glen Campbell to the program, himself no stranger to *The Midnight Special* either, as a veteran of eight other shows. Campbell avoided his biggest hits, "Rhinestone Cowboy" and "Southern Nights," for a nostalgic look back at his brief, and little-known, spell with the Beach Boys. He ran through a medley of hits—including "Good Vibrations," "Help Me Rhonda," "Little Surfer Girl" and "Surfin' U.S.A."—which Campbell played with the band when he toured with them in 1964 and 1965, playing bass and singing Brian Wilson's parts. "That'll raise your voice an octave or two," he quipped, remembering those years.

But a moment that was both one of the most sublime and ridiculous in *Midnight Special* history came when Jones and Sly & the Family Stone teamed up to perform a version of Sly's "Everyday People." Jones and Stone engaged in an abundance of silliness before getting down to business, but eventually channeled that energy into the song. The most marked difference

TOM JONES

between the two men was their voices. Jones relied heavily on brawn to hit the notes, while Stone's voice was soulful, yet not the least bit grainy. The pair's incompatibility was immediately evident, as Jones, straining to reach for the high notes in the song's chorus, all but drowned out Stone. To make matters worse, after every chorus, when the camera would cut to the Family Stone, and specifically the women singers, Jones could be heard unloading an arsenal of grunts and groans. All the performers seemed to enjoy singing "Everyday People," even if it wasn't exactly the song Sly had recorded in 1969.

Jones' duet with country singer Lynn Anderson on "Don't Go Breakin' My Heart" was almost as strange a pairing as his duet with Stone. The duo's lackluster rendition of the peppy Elton John/Kiki Dee original almost lapsed into self-parody. Anderson would later perform "Stand by Your Man," a song she had recorded in 1969, less than a year after Tammy Wynette had brought the song to No. 1 on the country charts and into the Top 20 on the pop charts.

It was a year filled with extremes. On the positive end, there were films like *Star Wars* and *Annie Hall*. The Sex Pistols led the punk vanguard, and Elvis Costello recorded *My Aim Is True*. Alex Haley's *Roots* made an impact on the small screen in a landmark television adaptation, and the re-usable U.S. space shuttle *Enterprise* made its first peopled flight. In the sociopolitical realm, President Carter granted pardons to almost all Vietnam-era American draft evaders.

But as in any year, there was plenty of bad, too. Carter warned that the energy crisis could induce a "national catastrophe," and called on Americans to make "profound" changes in their energy consumption. Deaths in 1977 included political activist Steven Biko and American actress Joan Crawford. It was also the year that the first cases of AIDS were discovered in New York City. But one of the most profound events that occurred in 1977 was the passing of the king. On August 16, Elvis Presley, one of the most triumphant, tragic figures of our time, died at age 42.

Perhaps it's only fitting that 1977 marked the death of rock's principal architect, because disco was entering the popular music scene. The success of a film called *Saturday Night Fever* and its soundtrack album would shape the path of popular music for the next several years and the direction of *The Midnight Special* for the remainder of its existence. The album sold 30 million copies worldwide, effectively turning the music world on its ear and influencing even stalwart rock & rollers to try their hand at wooing the dance crowd. Of course the 1977 *Midnight Special* episodes placed paramount importance on music, and in accordance with the rising popularity of disco, the show would begin to welcome more disco artists. In the process, the show became a fascinating portrait of America in the late '70s, celebrating the mechanized excesses of disco, the lasting appeal of roots music, the enduring popularity of comedy and the everyperson allure of TV sitcoms. With shows hosted by Aretha Franklin, Loretta Lynn, KC & the Sunshine Band, George Carlin and Gabe Kaplan (television's "Mr. Kotter"), *The Midnight Special* distilled everything contemporary (mixed with glimpses of the past) into the episodes of 1977.

KC & the Sunshine Band

FEATURING: ABBA, Heart, Gordon Lightfoot, Jose Feliciano, Andy Kaufman

"THE first time we played **The Midnight Special**, I think it was in the middle of 1975. I remember being nervous as hell because it was our first American network TV appearance. Of course we went on to do the show many times. I think it was a great show because it was the only show at the time that had the proper facilities and equipment to allow the proper reproduction of music and sound. And everyone was really professional. They'd always give you a good soundcheck, and didn't just shuffle you off as another band. Later on when I hosted, they'd ask me 'What bands do you want on your show,' and I'd make a couple of suggestions for bands that were hot at the time. I think I pitched ABBA and the Bay City Rollers, because they were certainly both hot then."

HARRY (KC) CASEY

This diverse show featured up-and-coming hard rockers, a caustic cutting-edge comedian, an easy-listening troubadour, and the kings and queens of disco, but what this show really did was cement the status of KC & the Sunshine Band as regulars. With their catchy, R&B–flecked disco sound and strong visual appeal, the group's television magnetism would contribute directly to their five No. 1 smashes between 1975 and 1980. It would also garner them many appearances on *The Midnight Special*. Opening the show with the horn-spiked invitation to boogie "(Shake, Shake, Shake) Shake Your Booty," Harry (KC) Casey and company gave the audience a taste of their party-starting dance grooves. Later in the evening they performed the racy "Get Down Tonight" and the extra-funky "That's the Way (I Like It)." Their resounding success, though attributable to a number of factors (primarily the inclusion of the group's "Boogie Shoes" on the wildly successful *Saturday Night Fever* soundtrack) was due in large part to the indefatigable spirit of *The Midnight Special*.

Swedish pop group ABBA performed "Dancing Queen" on this episode and, within a month, the song topped the charts. It would go on to be the groups biggest seller and their first gold single in the United States.

Another band that had been heating up in the previous 11 months was Heart, the women rockers from Seattle who were making their foray into the world of *The Midnight Special*. The

HEART

Gordon Lightfoot

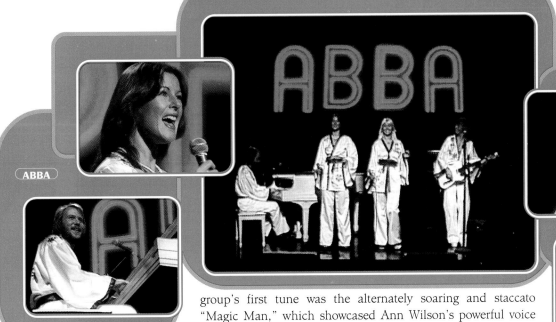

ABBA

group's first tune was the alternately soaring and staccato "Magic Man," which showcased Ann Wilson's powerful voice and roared into the Top 10 that October. That hit, along with the platinum success of their debut album *Dreamboat Annie* (on this show they played the album's title track as well as their first Top-40 hit, "Crazy on You"), would propel Heart to success after their first appearance on the program. The band would go on to sell 20 million records, and make six more appearances on *The Midnight Special*.

Also showing off his songwriting talents was Canadian balladeer Gordon Lightfoot, who sang "Wreck of the Edmund Fitzgerald," a song based on the tragic wreck of a vessel loaded with iron ore in Lake Superior two years earlier in which 29 crew members died. The song was as topical as it was absorbing. Later in the program, Lightfoot sang "Race Among the Ruins," the second single from his platinum *Summertime Dream* album.

Also of note on this program was the first appearance by comedian Andy Kaufman, who would become a regular on the show in the coming years. Kaufman, who died of lung cancer in the mid-1980s, also became a regular on *Taxi*, *Late Night with David Letterman* and *Saturday Night Live*—where he once barely won a phone-in poll that asked whether he should be allowed back on the show.

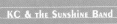

KC & the Sunshine Band

episode 214

AIRED:
APRIL 22, 1977

HOST: George Benson

FEATURING: Van Morrison, Etta James, Dr. John, Carlos Santana, Tom Scott

Dr. John and Etta James

This show epitomized everything that was great about *The Midnight Special*: spontaneity, virtuosity, soul, and an unpretentious love for great music. It was also a milestone for the program because it was the first showing by two legends: Van Morrison and Etta James. The show also boasted one of the finest aggregations of talent the program had ever seen. But the story goes that Morrison's appearance on the show was either thanks to—or in spite of—a little help from the Grateful Dead's Jerry Garcia and Bob Weir.

It was a tribute to *The Midnight Special*'s good reputation to have Van Morrison on the show, and before an expectant audience, host George Benson announced, "Over the 20-year history of rock music, only a small group of writer/performers have left a permanent stamp on the contemporary scene. Now as the history of rock is being written by various experts, my next guest is being universally recognized as one of those personalities. Please welcome, making a very rare television appearance, Van Morrison."

Morrison performed three tunes from his 1977 LP *A Period of Transition*. Co-produced by Dr. John, the album was Morrison's first release in three years, and was celebrated as a comeback for the heralded songwriter. Everyone in attendance was glad he had returned to the public eye,

Benson would introduce R&B pioneer Etta James with even

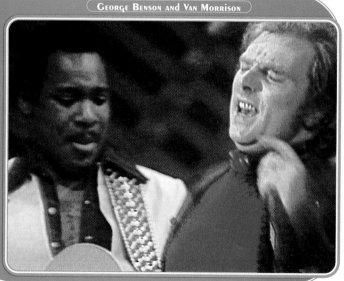

George Benson and Van Morrison

"WE THOUGHT WE HAD A CHANCE TO GET THE GRATEFUL DEAD AND VAN MORRISON ON THE SHOW, SO STAN [HARRIS] AND I FLEW TO MILL VALLEY TO MEET WITH JERRY GARCIA AND BOB WEIR. I WASN'T CONVINCED THE DEAD WERE GONNA DO <u>THE MIDNIGHT SPECIAL</u>, BUT HEY, I WAS GONNA GO TO MILL VALLEY AND MEET JERRY AND BOB AND THEN VAN MORRISON. WE TOOK THE 'COPTER OVER AND A CAR PICKED US UP AND TOOK US TO GARCIA'S HOUSE. SO HERE I AM SITTING WITH JERRY AND BOB, AND DOING MY BEST PITCH ABOUT GETTING THEM ON THE SHOW. BOB AND JERRY SHOWED US A TON OF CONCERT FOOTAGE THAT THEY HAD FILMED OF THEMSELVES. WE EXPLAINED THAT SUGARMAN AND THE NETWORK WOULDN'T ACCEPT CONCERT FOOTAGE AND WANTED THEM TO DO THE SHOW LIVE.

"FINALLY JERRY SAYS, 'TELEVISION? LET ME EXPLAIN SOMETHING TO YOU. THE REASON WE'RE THE GRATEFUL DEAD AND WE HAVE LONGEVITY IS BECAUSE WE DON'T DO TV AND PEOPLE COME AND SEE US IN CONCERT. BUT YOU'RE A COOL KID AND I LIKE THIS GUY, SO WHY DON'T WE SMOKE A DOOB.'

"SO THEY BRING OUT A DOOB, AND I TAKE A HIT, AND I PASS IT TO STAN. IT'S THE KIND OF DOPE THAT MAKES YOU LAUGH. ALSO, YOUR HEARING DIMINISHES WHEN YOU GET HIGH, SO STAN GOES DEAF [HARRIS HAS HAD A WELL-DOCUMENTED AND OFTEN-JOKED-ABOUT HEARING

George Benson and Van Morrison

problem since he was in his early twenties]. So I say, 'Thank you very much, we have to go meet with Van Morrison, now.'

"The deal was that the Grateful Dead driver would take us down to Morrison's house. And by the way, the Grateful Dead driver had serious dreads and was in some kind of 1951 Buick with hot pink dice hanging from the mirror. We get to Morrison's house and it was like a Frank Lloyd Wright kind of house. We walk in and it has no furniture in it. Zero furniture, except for two chairs, and at the end of the wall is an old 1950s swing which really creaks. Stan and I are sitting there laughing— and if you ask me what about, I don't remember. Finally a girl comes in and says, 'Mr. Morrison will meet with you.' So in comes the first guy, wearing Farmer Johns, beard down to here, looking like a bad Woodstock character. Three or four more guys come in, and finally in comes this red-headed guy on crutches. Stan and I laugh, and then suddenly realize, this is Van Morrison.

"'You guys want to come over here?' he said.

"Now I'm gonna tell you the exact conversation,:

"'Hi Van, my name is Rocco Urbisci, I'm with The Midnight

more deference, calling her "a legendary performer and a strong influence on us all." James would perform the explosive, organ and electric guitar-spiked "Tell Mama," then sang a duet with Dr. John on a song of reconciliation called "I'd Rather Go Blind." Other highlights included two Benson/Santana duets on the Benson instrumentals "Breezin'" and "Valdez in the Country." Santana was not wholly familiar with the songs, but his technical acuity, combined with Benson's "trial-by-fire" tutelage on the tunes' complex themes, would help the pair get through with a near-seamless precision.

The whole ensemble would get together for versions of Morrison's classic "Moondance" and Sam Cooke's "Bring It On Home to Me." On the former song Santana would take a blazing solo, then turn the spotlight to Benson, who would scat-sing the notes he was playing. The next solo was taken by Dr. John, who would yield to saxophone phenom Tom Scott, who blew a blazing, upper-register solo before giving way to James, who took the song to the next level with her entrancing scat singing.

Carlos Santana and George Benson

Van Morrison

Special and we're really glad you're going to be on the show.'

"Then Stan said, 'We're with The Midnight Special.'

"So I can feel my eyes are welling up red, and I suddenly realized that Stan is now stone deaf.

"Then Van said, 'How many songs do you want me to do on the show?'

"I said, 'We'd like you to do about four.'

"Then Stan said, 'We'd like you to do about four songs.'

"Then Van turned to Stan and said, 'I suppose you would like one of my songs to be "Moondance"?'

"To which Stan replied, 'I would really love it if one of those songs was "Moondance."'

"Finally, I said, 'We've gotta stop. I'm f**ked up, he's f**ked up,' and I explained what happened back at the Dead camp with Jerry and Bob.

"Van laughed and said, 'I'll tell you what, when you get un–f**ked up and you get back to L.A., give me a call.'

"Then Van turned to Stan and said, 'I hope you're not the audio man.'

"And Stan turned to me and said, 'What did he say?'"

Rocco Urbisci, co-producer

WOLFMAN JACK

"Old Wolfman Jack. He sure could talk."
John Lee Hooker

"I was a true fan of Wolfman Jack. His background was a story unto itself, and he was one of the most colorful presenters of rock & roll in the whole entertainment business."
Dick Clark, CREATOR, American Bandstand

"I don't think Wolfman Jack got enough credit for his importance on The Midnight Special. Bob was a wonderful guy, and meant a lot to the show. I remember the first time I went to see him. He had these wolfman teeth on. And he had this cape, and he said [Urbisci puts on his best gravelly Wolfman voice] "Come on in, kid, what's goin' on? You want me to do this TV show?"

"I said, 'we're looking for an on-camera announcer and I think you'd be great, but you've gotta meet the producers. When they ask you if those are your real teeth, tell them yes. Whatever you do, do not take the teeth out. Tell them you went to the orthodontist, and you had them chiseled and pointed, and you believe you're the wolfman.'

"He said he would, and he wore the damn cape. So he shows up to meet Burt [Sugarman] and Stan [Harris], and says, 'Yeah, I'm

The musical offerings of *The Midnight Special* were always diverse, wide-ranging and unpredictable. But at the center of it all was one constant—Wolfman Jack, the raspy, impassioned, and only slightly mad rock & roll animal. The Wolfman provided more than passion, though; he was a link to the beginning of rock & roll, one of rock's leading ambassadors, and one of its most easily recognized personalities.

The Midnight Special only cemented his fame. First came the all-important name change—from Bob Smith to Wolfman Jack, all the better and more mysterious to captivate listeners who for years would only know his voice, not his face. Wolfman held sway over his audiences from XERF-AM, a station located across the border from Del Rio, Texas, whose 250,000-watt transmitter reached most of North America. Word of mouth soon spread about his uncompromising style, and the great music he was spinning, and by 1965, Wolfman had moved to another border station, XERB-AM, which was located near Tijuana. He quickly attracted a new group of fans from Southern California, all the way into regions of Alaska and Canada.

One of the youngsters influenced by his radio voice was burgeoning filmmaker George Lucas, who would use Wolfman in his 1973 film about coming of age in the early '60s, *American Graffiti*. It was that film, combined with his regular gig on *The Midnight Special* that unveiled his face—as well as his voice—to the public. The film would earn four Academy Award nominations, and Wolfman Jack was on his way from cult figure to media legend.

Wolfman would influence many bands, including ZZ Top, who recorded "Heard it on the X," a tribute to his DJ career. Canadian rockers The Guess Who also had a 1974 Top-10 hit with "Clap for the Wolfman," featuring bits of dialogue from the man himself.

After *The Midnight Special*, Smith would host a show called *Rock and Roll Palace* on The Nashville Network (TNN), and in 1984 Wolfman Jack became even more animated than usual, when his cartoon series *Wolf Rock TV* joined ABC's Saturday morning line-up. All the while, Wolfman credited his voice for his success. "It's kept meat and potatoes on the table for years for Wolfman and Wolfwoman," he would say of his Camel

Wolfman Jack.' And I remember Burt saying 'So what's with those teeth?'

"'I went to the orthodontist, man, and I had these teeth made. Cost me $10,000,' he said."
Rocco Urbisci, co-producer

"The idea was to have one identifiable person do the announcing, and Rocco was really into what I did on radio. So I go to interview with Stan Harris, wearing these

weird teeth, and wearing some really weird clothes, looking very vampirish. Well, I meet with Stan and he doesn't get fazed easily. That's why he's such a good director, because he's so laid back, and knows how to handle everybody. He asks me all sorts of questions, and I'm conducting the whole thing with these teeth on, which look very real.

"After about 15 minutes, he asks me if they are my own teeth.

And my manager jumps up and says, 'Please, Stan, don't talk to Wolfman about his teeth. He's very self-conscious about them.' So this really freaks Stan out. He goes back to Rocco after the interview and says, 'Okay, we'll use him, but he's really weird.'

"At the first show, I go up to the booth to say hello, and while we're talking I took out the teeth and laid them on the counter. [Stan] just looked at them, and I've never seen anybody laugh so hard."
Wolfman Jack, Record World magazine article, 1974

"Wolf enjoyed doing the shows, and he loved that they were live. That was his biggest inspiration. He really enjoyed working with the different acts, too. In June 1973, we moved to New York for one year, and he commuted back and forth and paid his own way, which cost him more than he was making on the show. But he believed in the show, and that's why he did that."
Lou Smith, Wolfman Jack's widow

"I think so much of The Midnight Special, it damn near costs me money to do the show. I pay my own plane fare each week from New York, and for the money I get paid to do the show, we just about break even. I do it for the love of the show. I'm part of a very creative thing

here, and my trip is to try to expose new talent."

Wolfman Jack, <u>Record World</u> magazine article, 1974

"Wolfman was a prize. We had more laughs. Whenever we did a 'Best of' or compilation show, he'd be the host. One time, I wrote him an opening line: 'Hello to all you hip cats, you cool cats, and my lawyer, Stanley Katz.' He was all over it. Stanley Katz riffs everyhwere. And it became a thing between us. 'I got me the biggest lawyer in Hollywood that nobody ever heard of, Stanley Katz.' Then that infectious laugh, 'eee, eee, eee.' We used to put people on. 'This is my lawyer, Stanley Katz. Tell 'em all the gigs you got goin' for me, man.' We'd make up something ridiculous. We got a lot of mileage out of Stanley.

"Ten years later I get a call from a guy in Chicago. He's doin' a blues show with Buddy Guy, Albert King, some real tasty players. He wants Wolfman to host it. And he says to me, 'I was told you know his lawyer, Stanley Katz.' In an insane moment I say, 'Yeah.' I give him Stanley's number . . . my fax machine. A few minutes later the fax rings and I answer, 'Stanley Katz.' It's the guy from Chicago. He goes into his rap. And I say, 'This is my private line. How'd you get this number?' He says, 'Neal Marshall gave it to me.' I say, 'That

cigarette-perpetuated sound. "A couple of shots whiskey helps it. I've got that raspy sound.

Wolfman Jack died of a massive heart attack on July 1, 1995, but not before writing an autobiography called *Have Mercy*, named after his signature phrase. His widow Lou Smith recalls, "He came up the stairs. When he got to the landing, four steps from the top, he said 'One more time' in a happy voice with a big grin—that was all he said. He reached the top of the stairs, put out both arms as if making an entrance to a big room, I walked three steps toward him, and he fell forward on me and knocked me unconsious. When I came to I was underneath him. His heart had exploded, like dropping an egg on the floor, he never knew what hit him. That's how the doctor explained it to me.

"From the first meeting Wolfman and I knew we were soulmates in this lifetime and would continue to be in the spiritual world."

assh**e. I'll kill him. Now I gotta change it.' Then I called Wolfman, left him a message. 'This is your lawyer, Stanley Katz. You won't believe this, I got you a deal for a real gig.' He called me back and said, 'I already got the gig, man. Just wanted to see how far you'd take it. Eee, eee, eee, eee.'"

Neal Marshall, producer

"We already knew Wolfman [when we first appeared on <u>The Midnight Special</u>]. We'd done some radio shows with him and he was quite a wild man. Actually he wasn't that much of a wild man, he just seemed like it. That was the idea. That's what made him what he was—his portrayal of being a crazy guy. But he was actually

a really nice guy. I remember hearing him on the radio when I was a kid in the early sixties. He was famous. He played a lot of stuff I liked—all the good R&B."

Tom Johnston, Doobie Brothers

"<u>American Graffiti</u> came out in the latter part of June 1973. That was a big beginning as far as the public eye was concerned. Prior to that he was underground. Nobody knew what he looked like. I think radio was really in his soul, because he always felt he had a deep communication with the people. He said at times when he was on the radio he felt that he was really touching someone. Since he died, I have received letters from fans that are now in their fifties or sixties, people who say this and that happened or 'he saved my life because I was driving and falling asleep and Wolf said, 'Wake the hell up' to me on the radio.' I'm real happy that he did have a good impact on people's lives, and he'd be very glad to hear it. He just liked people."

Lou Smith, Wolfman Jack's widow

221

HOSTS: Emmylou Harris and Little Feat

FEATURING: Bonnie Raitt, Neil Young, Weather Report

"I REMEMBER I did "QUEEN of the Silver Dollar" with LITTLE FEAT, and THAT was THE best version of THAT SONG we ever did. IT was definitely the New Orleans funk version. The Midnight Special pretty much mirrored music that was happening at the time—good and bad and mediocre and cutting edge. I have some recollections of that show, because I was there, but I don't know whether I actually watched it at the time because I was always on the road, and I didn't watch much TV anyway. It was really like another gig. But just being on the show with all those people was great. I had been a huge Jessie Winchester fan when I was a folk singer, and my then-husband Brian Ahearn had produced one of his records. I'd been a fan of Bonnie's since I saw her at the Philadelphia folk festival and she played and sang so beautifully. I saw Joni Mitchell and Bonnie Raitt at the same festival, when I was still struggling in the clubs. That would've been around 1971, and they were so good I wanted to say, 'Okay, I quit.'

"When I think about the show now, there was a real Washington, D.C., connection because I was living and working in that area and I remember being in the studio with Lowell and Little Feat north of D.C., when they were doing Feats Don't Fail Me Now. And of course Bonnie had been on the

ith the passing of Elvis Presley, Marc Bolan, and Lynyrd Skynyrd's Ronnie Van Zant, 1977 would be a year of rock-star deaths. While this show seemed like a family reunion, with old friends and tourmates Little Feat, Bonnie Raitt and Emmylou Harris, it too would soon be touched by tragedy.

With the Southern blues-funk band Little Feat as her backing band for her first appearance on The Midnight Special, Harris opened with the melodic "Queen of the Silver Dollar," before moving on to material from her three mid-1970s country-rock masterpieces, Elite Hotel, Luxury Liner and Quarter Moon in a Ten Cent Town.

Harris would then defer to her able backups, who performed their signature tune "Dixie Chicken," as she and Bonnie Raitt lent their vocal support to the seductively funky chorus. The refrain would be followed by the song's drunken central guitar riff, which was created by the metallic scrape of Lowell George's slide on the strings of his blonde Stratocaster. At this performance, George seemed inspired, as each bent note he coaxed out of his guitar sounded like an aural manifestation of the pain in his soul. George had founded the band in 1969, but by 1977 his behavior was becoming increasingly erratic, and he was contributing few songs to the group's repertoire. He would die of a drug-related heart attack in an Arlington, Virginia hotel room fewer than two years later, leaving behind a fine body of work but even more unfulfilled potential.

Emmylou Harris

Bonnie Raitt

Little Feat

Also dovetailing nicely with the show's "keep it in the family" theme was Neil Young, whose *American Stars 'n' Bars* album—featuring unreleased studio tracks from the previous three years and backing vocals by Emmylou Harris—would be released the following month. Young contributed concert footage of "Like a Hurricane," a song from the forthcoming album that he wrote while sick with a high fever. Though it never hit the pop charts, "Like a Hurricane" would become one of Young's most recognizable songs thanks to several cover versions and years of radio play.

Making their first—and only—appearance on the show was Weather Report, one of the foremost electric jazz ensembles of the '70s and '80s. They played the fat, visceral "Birdland"—then all over the radio—at a faster tempo than they had recorded it, underscoring their virtuosity on the tune's hairpin twists and turns. Saxophonist Wayne Shorter would contribute punchy, majestic horn bursts to the tune, while Jaco Pastorius, always economical in his hand movements on the bass, would add his falsetto scat-singing to frame the song's catchy main theme. Pastorius would later suffer from alcoholism and heroin addiction, and would die in 1987 from massive head wounds he sustained in a brawl outside a bar.

Coincidentally, this show would be re-aired as Episode 388 14 months to the day after the death of Lowell George.

road with them, and that was when I actually spent time with her. There was a real organic connection between us all. Lowell became such a dear friend and champion of mine, and was such a wonderful soul. He seemed very vibrant and full of life. I was really surprised that he died so suddenly.

"But I wasn't that familiar with Weather Report, and my only connection with them really was a strange one. When I first went on the road with Gram [Parsons] we played a little club in Boulder, Colorado. We were scheduled to play several shows, and we were unprepared because Gram's idea of rehearsal was that you'd just sit and play song after song after song that had nothing to do with the show. So we never got beginnings, endings and middles of the songs. And then we got up to play our first show, and I'd never done anything like it, so I said 'Well, I guess Gram knows what he's doing, and at some point it'll fall together.' But of course it didn't. It was just a train wreck on every song. So we were about to get fired, and the club got closed down for a noise infraction because Weather Report had played before us and were so loud. So I was sort of grateful to Weather Report for not making us look bad. In those days off we did some real rehearsals and got it together and became a good little band."

Emmylou Harris

Weather Report

AIRED:
OCTOBER 7, 1977

HOST: **Kenny Rogers**

FEATURING: Debby Boone, B.J. Thomas, Carly Simon, Supertramp, Andy Gibb, Bob Marley & the Wailers

Kenny Rogers and Debby Boone

The death of Elvis Presley ended one rock era but, but the first U.S. tours by The Clash and Elvis Costello started another, and at *The Midnight Special*, a new era began when Stan Harris passed the producer's duties on to Ken Ehrlich. But as if immune to British punk and the American New Wave, *The Midnight Special* continued to spotlight the decidedly mainstream. Enter the affable Kenny Rogers, the diametrical opposite to the independent-minded outlaw spirit of Waylon Jennings and Willie Nelson. Roger's polished, suburban and slick voice would bring country through a commercial revival.

Rogers opened the show looking back at his own past, with his first hit, the First Edition's "Just Dropped In (To See What Condition My Condition Was In)," and then dueted with Debby Boone on the Eagles' "Desperado," appropriate because Rogers helped discover Don Henley when he played in an L.A. band called Shiloh in the late '60s. Rogers then modestly introduced one of his own songs: "I don't know that I seriously consider myself a songwriter, but just recently I've written a song I'm particularly excited about." The song, "Sweet Music Man," would be recorded by Tammy Wynette, Anne Murray and Dolly Parton.

Also on the show was B.J. Thomas, the Texas-bred singer who first hit the charts with Hank Williams' "I'm So Lonesome I Could Cry," and then achieved even greater success with the Bacharach/Hal David–penned "Raindrops Keep Fallin' on My Head," from the Paul Newman/Robert Redford film *Butch Cassidy and the Sundance Kid*. Making his first *Midnight Special* appearance since 1975's "(Hey Won't You Play) Another Somebody Done Somebody Wrong Song," Thomas proved that he could make an impact with material other than light pop fare, delivering a swinging, horn-driven version of "Play Something Sweet (Brickyard Blues)" as well as a version of his current chart entry, "Don't Worry Baby." Though he never recorded it, Thomas' version of "Brickyard Blues"—written by famed New Orleans musician

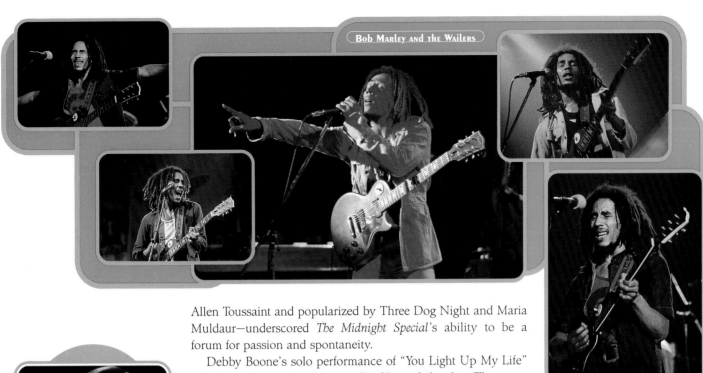

Bob Marley and the Wailers

Debby Boone

Debby Boone

Allen Toussaint and popularized by Three Dog Night and Maria Muldaur—underscored *The Midnight Special*'s ability to be a forum for passion and spontaneity.

Debby Boone's solo performance of "You Light Up My Life" added another tie-in with popular films of the day. The song, also the title track to the Didi Conn movie of the same name, would go on to sell a million copies, top the charts for an astounding 10 weeks, and win the Academy Award for best original song. Yet another tie-in with film on this episode was a clip from *The Spy Who Loved Me*, with its marquee song "Nobody Does It Better"—a song written by Marvin Hamlisch and Carole Bayer Sager, and sung by Carly Simon. Other highlights of the show included the first appearance by Supertramp (albeit an outside clip), performing "Give a Little Bit," and Andy Gibb's sanitized funk/pop tune "(Love Is) Thicker Than Water."

The biggest disappointment of the show was the taped appearance of Bob Marley & the Wailers, whose music was described by Rogers to be "as political as it is entertaining." Not that Marley's renditions of "Jammin'" and "Get Up, Stand Up," which melted into "Exodus," weren't spellbinding; they just lacked the immediacy of a live *Midnight Special* appearance. One of the most explosive performers in the world, the reggae superstar was slated to be on the program live, but according to Rogers (as he introduced a tape of Marley and his group captured in concert in London), Marley had sustained a foot injury that would preclude his live performance. In fact, the press had been told Marley had been injured playing soccer, but the full story was much more troubling. Though he had originally torn the nail off his big toe playing soccer, it never healed properly, and became so infected that his doctor ordered it amputated. But Marley's strict Rastafarian faith wouldn't allow amputation, so Marley instead had a skin graft on the toe. Three and a half years after this show aired, Marley was dead of the cancer that started in that same big toe.

The world would lose former senator and Vice President Hubert H. Humphrey, Pope Paul VI, his successor Pope John Paul I and American illustrator and painter Norman Rockwell in 1978. Who drummer Keith Moon also died this year. Herman Wouk's *War and Rememberance* and Mario Puzo's *Fools Die* were hot novels, and the world's first "test tube" baby was born in England. *Grease*, starring John Travolta, and *Animal House*, starring John Belushi, were in movie theaters, and Springsteen's *Darkness on the Edge of Town*, Van Halen's first album and Meatloaf's *Bat out of Hell* were in record stores. It was also the year that "Son of Sam" killer David Berkowitz received a sentence of life imprisonment, and People's Temple cult leader Jim Jones orchestrated the murder-suicide of 917 people in Guyana.

This was also a wild year for *The Midnight Special*. The show's content veered unpredictably from week to week, with Aretha Franklin hosting one week and Shaun Cassidy at the helm the next. Yvonne Elliman and Allman Brothers guitarist Dickie Betts hosted on consecutive weeks, as did Crystal Gayle, Elvin Bishop and Mac Davis. Todd Rundgren hosted a show that would be one of the year's finest, and Patti Smith was interviewed as well. Because there were many types of music fighting for the soul of the show, 1978 was one of *The Midnight Special*'s most interesting years. Most of the performances were still live. Artists and record companies were warming to the idea of videos, but they hadn't achieved the foothold they would later enjoy. Of course bass-heavy dance music was becoming more and more entrenched in the national psyche, and *The Midnight Special* would continue to be buffeted by disco's big waves. 1978 marked the first appearance by choreographer Jeff Kutash, who would later lead his dance troupes through many performance numbers to the latest dance hits. But *The Midnight Special* still had rock & roll in its heart, as evidenced by the Ted Nugent heavy-metal show which, in typical *Midnight Special* fashion, would be followed by a theme disco show featuring, among others, Chic and Rick James.

episode

AIRED:
JANUARY 27, 1978

253

HOST: Aretha Franklin

FEATURING: Four Tops

Four Tops

Aretha Franklin and Four Tops

As the Sex Pistols played their last show in nearby San Francisco, *The Midnight Special* still struggled with redefining the show for "the disco years," as new producer Neal Marshall called them, as he took over from Ken Ehrlich. His first episode featured the inimitable Aretha Franklin, who performed songs from her *Sweet Passion* and *Almighty Fire* albums. She would also duet with the legendary Four Tops on a version of Stevie Wonder's "Isn't She Lovely." And like any superstar of Franklin's caliber, she also did things her own way despite Marshall's admonitions.

NEAL MARSHALL, PRODUCER: "I got the full range of emotions—from exhilaration to trepidation and back again—during my first week on the show. The host was Aretha Franklin, one of my all-time favorites. What a way to start. I got a call from her agent, who said she's rehearsing in North Hollywood and would like to go over the introductions so she wouldn't have to read them from cue cards.

"I get to this rehearsal hall, and there she is, the greatest R&B / gospel singer of our time working out with this sensational band, and I'm stittin' there and sayin' to myself, 'Now I know why I left law school.' This is too good. After the rehearsal we go through the intros, which she gets in a heartbeat. Then she says, 'I wanna show you something. I had a special costume made just for *The Midnight Special*.'

ARETHA FRANKLIN

"Her assistants wheel in a rack of clothes, and there it is. How do I describe this? Remember when Neil Armstrong and Buzz Aldrin landed on the moon? They were wearing this outfit . . . a big, silvery, shiny moon suit. My heart dropped into my shoes. I tried to explain why I thought this wasn't a good idea: Lighting problems. Lack of production time. I did it badly. She had her heart set on wearing it.

"On the day of the show, let's just say that Aretha was not my best friend. Debi [Genovese] had booked the Four Tops to sing with Aretha. Aretha loved them and vice versa. During rehearsal Aretha decided she wanted to sing harmony with the Tops. It wasn't working, and I was dying. How am I gonna say anything about music to Aretha Franklin? No way. I went up to the control room, hoping that it would sound better on the small speakers. No way. So, I say to Tommy [director Tom Trbovich], 'What are we gonna do about this?' And he says, 'Sounds like a producer's problem to me.' I take a deep breath and figure, What the hell. Going down the stairs, it crosses my mind that my first show could be my last.

"I walk onto the stage. Aretha and the Tops are taking a short break. And I say, 'Aretha, may I talk to you for a moment?' She says, 'Sure.' I say, 'Maybe off to the side would be good.' She says, 'These are my friends. Anything you have to tell me, you can say in front of them.' The moment of truth had arrived. Just as I'm ready to spit it out, Levi Stubbs, the lead singer for the Tops, chimes in, 'While we're all here, I wanna suggest that Aretha should lead on this song because she's the greatest singer in the world. We're her guests on the show, and she's trying to be gracious, but nobody can sing this song like she can.' God, I wanted to kiss him. Aretha looks at the other Tops, who agree with Levi, and she says, 'Okay.' Then, she turns to me with a sly smile and says, 'What is it that we need to talk about?' And I said, 'I just wanted to let you know that now that I've seen it on camera, I love that space dress.'"

266 Journey

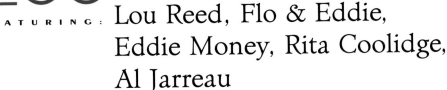

FEATURING: Lou Reed, Flo & Eddie, Eddie Money, Rita Coolidge, Al Jarreau

JOURNEY

It has been repeatedly noted that while only several thousand people bought the first Velvet Underground album, everyone who did went out and started a band of their own. In fact besides the Beatles, Lou Reed and the Velvets have arguably inspired more groups than any other outfit. Whether it be Sonic Youth, REM, Stereolab or Galaxie 500, the Velvet Underground's influence on contemporary music has been profound.

Reed agreed to host the show, but backed out when network censors refused to let him perform "Walk on the Wild Side," deeming a line that reffered to oral sex too indecent even for late-night television. But Reed did agree to be interviewed for the show, and sunglasses on and cigarettes blazing, talked with friends Flo & Eddie about everything from the censoring of his song to his public image.

Often referring to his professional persona as "he" and to himself as "me," Reed's words came fast and furious: "I have various tangent manifestations of the same character, and [reviewers often discuss] the dark depths of my psyche and dig out the tawdry, bitter, angst and germ that exists in some kind of Kierkegaard-ian, existential, metaphysical hassle. That'll put you through a Pollyanna trip backward."

Reed's decision to boycott gave Journey a lucky break, and the band's first major exposure since adding new singer Steve Perry.

With Perry on board and producer Roy Thomas Baker at the helm, Journey had just released *Infinity*, an album that would prove to be the band's U.S. breakthrough, with the single

Wolfman Jack and Eddie Money

JOURNEY

Flo & Eddie and Lou Reed

Eddie Money

"Wheel in the Sky." Journey opened the show with that hit, Perry sporting a crisp, all-white suit and the band—bassist Ross Valory, guitarist Neil Schon, keyboardist Greg Rollie and drummer Aynsley Dunbar—churned out the song with the punch and precision of an outfit confident of commercial success.

Another fledgling artist poised on the brink of major success visiting the Friday night institution for the first time was Eddie Money. The son of a New York City policeman, Money attended the NYPD police academy, but quit the force in 1977 and moved to Berkeley, California, where he was spotted by legendary music impresario Bill Graham. Graham became his manager and helped him get a record deal with Columbia and release his debut, with soon-to-be hits "Baby Hold On," "Two Tickets to Paradise" and "Don't Worry," each of which he performed on *The Midnight Special*.

Also on this episode, an outside clip of Linda Ronstadt, who performed her covers of the Temptations' "The Way You Do the Things You Do" and "Words," both songs from 1977's million-selling *Anytime . . . Anywhere*. Another highlight was soul-jazz vocalist Al Jarreau's silky stylings on the smooth, vibes-driven "Better than Anything." The Latin-flavored tune brought down the house.

episode

AIRED:
JUNE 2, 1978

271

HOST: **Crystal Gayle**

FEATURING: Tom Petty & the Heartbreakers, The Band, Wolfman Jack with Robbie Robertson, Eddie Rabbitt, Chuck Mangione

Eddie Rabbitt

Eddie Rabbitt

Country songstress Crystal Gayle hosted this episode, but Southern rock was the real story—from the recently departed The Band, to the then-unknown Tom Petty & the Heartbreakers. "The show we have for you this morning has something musical for everyone," said Gayle, introducing the show after playing her hit, "Don't It Make My Brown Eyes Blue." "A touch of jazz feeling with Chuck Mangione, country flavor with Eddie Rabbitt, and then there's my first guest. Two things keep him happy—chasing women and playing rock & roll. And if he's as good with the ladies as he is with his music he's a very happy man. Here's Tom Petty & the Heartbreakers!"

With that, Petty and his band kicked into a rousing "American Girl," with Mike Campbell's guitar ringing brightly, Benmont Tench's organ punctuating the melody, and Petty shaking his head wildly, spitting out the chorus. It would be a timely debut on the show for Petty and company, who would really explode two years later with *Damn the Torpedoes*. Later in the show, they added enthusiastic performances of "I Need to Know" and "Listen to Her Heart."

Wolfman Jack provided the next introduction, rasping:

"One of the premier rock groups to stand the rock of ages is simply called The Band. Their music has been a driving force through the '60s and into the '70s. On Thanksgiving Day, 1976, The Band created an event of historical significance—their farewell concert at San Francisco's Winterland."

With that, the countrified voice of Band drummer Levon Helm singing "Up on Cripple Creek" rang forth, as a clip from *The Last Waltz*—the feature film that chronicled The Band's farewell show—was aired.

"Sitting with me is Mr. Robbie Robertson," continued Wolfman. "He's the producer of *The Last Waltz*. As you know, Robbie was the lead guitar player for The Band. He was also instrumental in writing and doing sound and production."

"The Band," Robertson explained, "after doing 16 years on the road, had come to the conclusion that it was no longer a

Tom Petty & the Heartbreakers

progressive or an aggressive move for us. So to experiment in music and the media and the things we really wanted to do, we decided to take a pass on the road and do a final concert and have some of our dear old friends [Neil Young, Van Morrison, Muddy Waters, Joni Mitchell, Bob Dylan, et al.] join us. It became a true collaboration between film and music."

In explaining how The Band had originally hooked up with Dylan, Robertson said, "It's very vague. I don't know why [Dylan] got in touch with us. We got a message in 1965 to come and visit [him] and talk. We did, we played a little bit of music and the next thing you know we were touring around the world together. There was an aspect of music that he was extraordinary at, and our background in rock & roll and Southern music, that combination was a lot of fun."

The final clip from the film that was shown was that of Dylan singing "Baby Let Me Follow You Down" with Robertson's serrated guitar tone slicing at the rest of The Band's earthy, deep-rooted pulse.

"The Band is like a train," said Robertson to *The Midnight Special* audience. "And it's time to pull it into the station while it's still shining."

After a commercial break, Gayle would introduce her next guest. "Chuck Mangione is the master of fusion music. He combines great melodies and hot rhythms to form an exciting musical experience. His latest album, *Feels So Good*, has just gone platinum, so here's Chuck Mangione, who will make you feel so good."

With that, master trumpeter and keyboardist Mangione, backed by tenor sax, bass, guitar and drums, stepped into his most well-known song, the funky instrumental title track. When guitarist Grant Grissman took the song's first solo, Mangione sat down and complemented him beautifully on a Fender Rhodes, adding the keyboard's dynamic rhythmic accents to the song and displaying his multi-instrumental dexterity. Later in the show Mangione would take to the Rhodes again, playing terse, choppy riffs over the whirling, churning chord progression of "Hide and Seek," before picking up the trumpet to solo.

Crystal Gayle

Chuck Mangione

Todd Rundgren & Utopia

FEATURING: Warren Zevon, Exile, Carlene Carter, Meatloaf

"Hosting <u>The Midnight Special</u> was fun. It wasn't the first network TV program that I did, but I did get more attention and consideration from <u>The Midnight Special</u> than for any other show. After all, I didn't host that many shows. It really evolved through several phases, but it was really a hip show. The great thing was that the show often had the most incongruous meeting of new artists and old artists. Rock was relatively less enfranchised [in the early days of <u>The Midnight Special</u>], and it was part of the evolution of music in general. Rock music went from being really rare on TV, like in the sixties with the <u>Smothers Brothers</u>, occasionally <u>Ed Sullivan</u>, and <u>Shindig</u> and <u>Hullabaloo</u>. When they all went off the air there were only little ghettos for pop music, because most of the music was still our parents' music, and that accompanied everything. Then as time went on, rock music became more and more ubiquitous. It's to the point now that you don't have rock TV shows because the music is everyplace. It's in the commercials. It's in the movies. It's so ubiquitous now that it's almost pointless to have a weekly pop music show where half a dozen artists would all play.

multi-instrumentalist/producer Todd Rundgren wore as many hats as anyone in music during the '70s and '80s, performing his own theatrical rock (with Utopia), writing crisp, piano-driven pop albums, producing countless records by everyone from Meatloaf to the Psychedelic Furs, and playing with Bruce Springsteen's E Street Band. In his fifth appearance on the show, but first as host, Rundgren showed off his range of styles, while also introducing Warren Zevon to a national audience.

Dressed in clothes as dramatic as his songs—a metallic red shirt with a photo of Marilyn Monroe across his chest and sparkling silver trousers—Rundgren and Utopia opened the show with "Real Man," with the crowd pressed against the stage, cheering wildly. Then Rundgren retreated to the piano for "Sometimes I Don't Know How to Feel," before switching to the drums (and also singing) on the funky "You Cried Wolf." Finally, he strapped on a guitar for "Love in Action," where a quick-cut editing technique emphasized the song's staccato chorus.

Zevon, though he also played piano and was trained classically, couldn't have been more stylistically different from Rundgren. He wasn't trying to fashion perfect piano pop, but rather sang about twisted, oddball characters in ugly situations, making cutting comments on media and society on the way. For the show, Zevon provided outside clips that he had produced

Carlene Carter

Meatloaf

Todd Rundgren & Utopia

Todd Rundgren & Utopia

himself. These were the early days of music video production, and it was evident that Zevon was lip-synching on "Werewolves of London," perhaps because Fleetwood Mac's rhythm section (drummer Mick Fleetwood and bassist John McVie) played on the record, and Zevon couldn't find a live band to match that for the video. Zevon cannot be faulted for lack of enthusiasm, however. In the second clip, "Nighttime in the Switching Yard," from his outstanding *Excitable Boy* album, Zevon took the lip-synching charade so seriously that at one point he spun around, staggered, and knocked over the microphone stand.

Other highlights included Exile, who did a sensual version of their only pop hit, the slinky, deceptively funky "Kiss You All Over." Also making the scene was country legend Carlene Carter, daughter of country singers June Carter and Carl Smith, who performed two songs, including "I Once Knew Love," solo on the piano. But who would have guessed that the performer still going strong two decades later would be Meatloaf? Rundgren introduced an outside clip of the follow-up single, "Paradise by the Dashboard Light"—which had debuted on the charts less than two weeks earlier and would crack the top 40—with these words: "I produced his album, and now it's selling briskly." Briskly was an understatement; the album would go on to sell 12 million copies (and counting).

"MOST ARTISTS CAN'T EVEN PLAY LIVE ANYMORE, AND THEY GET TURNED OVER SO QUICKLY NOWADAYS THAT MOST OF THEM WOULD BE COMPELLED TO LIP-SYNCH IF THEY WENT ON. IN THOSE DAYS YOU WERE A LAME POP ARTIST IF YOU HAD TO LIP-SYNCH YOUR MATERIAL. AS I RECALL, <u>The Midnight Special</u> HAD NO ABSOLUTE POLICY ABOUT IT. IF AN ARTIST INSISTED ON LIP-SYNCHING THEIR THING THEY COULD DO THAT, BUT WE ALWAYS PLAYED LIVE. IT WAS A GOOD PERFORMING ENVIRONMENT BECAUSE THEY REALIZED SOME OF THE BANDS WERE GOING TO COME IN THERE AND GET LOUD. USUALLY IN THOSE DAYS, WHENEVER YOU DID A TV SHOW THEY WOULDN'T PUT UP WITH ANY TYPE OF VOLUME BECAUSE THEY SAID 'THE DIRECTOR'S GOTTA TALK TO THE CAMERAMAN WITH EARPHONES, AND THEY CAN'T HEAR, AND YOU'RE TOO DAMN LOUD.' THEY WOULD ENCOURAGE PEOPLE TO LIP-SYNCH, JUST FOR GENERAL EASE. THEY USUALLY DIDN'T INVEST A LOT OF TIME, BUT WITH <u>The Midnight Special</u> YOU HAD A DRESS REHEARSAL, AND THEY ALLOWED YOU TO DO THE NUMBER SEVERAL TIMES. THEY'D USUALLY DO TWO OR THREE TAKES JUST SO THEY WOULD HAVE SOME EXTRA ANGLES TO SHOOT FROM. IT WAS DEFINITELY A WINDOW INTO AN EVOLVING MUSIC BUSINESS."

Todd Rundgren

Warren Zevon

Disco may have been the rage, but rock & roll never went away, even during the late '70s, as this episode proved. Featuring an array of heavy rockers and power popsters—most of whom are still recording and touring today—it would become one of the most explosive *Midnight Special* episode ever.

Appropriately enough, Ted Nugent, perhaps the most excessive and cartoonish rocker of the '70s, hosted the show. Known as the "Motor City Madman," Nugent tapped the pulse of the burgeoning heavy-metal market by juxtaposing his highly quotable, conservative political viewpoints (pro-guns, anti-drugs) with images of cars, sex and violence in his music. All the attention helped Nugent score five straight platinum albums, including *Weekend Warriors*, which hit the charts just two weeks prior to the show. "We got a record comin' out, and it's all about you out there," said Nugent, introducing the new song "Need You Bad." The rest of his set spanned his career, including a furious rendition of his signature tune, "Cat Scratch Fever," as a wild-eyed throng mobbed the rim of the stage.

Making their first and only *Midnight Special* performance on this show were Chicago power popsters Cheap Trick. On their smash hit "Surrender," guitarist Rick Nielsen showcased an arsenal of kicks, spins, and rock & roll maneuvers while frantically picking his trademark checkerboard guitar. Robin Zander, singing lead vocals and clothed in a sharp all-white suit, contrasted sharply with the figure cut by hardworking drummer Bun E. Carlos, who had clearly mastered the art of puffing on a cigarette while drumming maniacally. The studio audience was enthralled with the quartet. At the song's conclusion, Nielsen threw his guitar into the crowd, who tore after it like a World Series foul ball hit into the stands, or Elvis' scarf on the "Aloha Hawaii" specials.

Also making their debut on the show were Australian heavy-metal mavens AC/DC, whose fourth album *If You Want Blood You've Got It* would hit the pop charts just weeks after their showing. Fresh off a tour opening for Aerosmith, AC/DC would be introduced to *The Midnight Special* audience by that group's lead singer, Steven Tyler. It would be another nine months

Ted Nugent

Cheap Trick

AC/DC

before AC/DC would hit pay dirt with *Highway to Hell*, but their spark as a live outfit was clear on this night. Their one selection, "Sin City," was led by guitarist Angus Young, who parlayed his bundles of nervous energy into solid, blues-based playing and a high-wire stage act. The wiry ax-man's take on Chuck Berry's "Duck Walk" maneuver was credible, but when he threw himself onto the stage while desperately picking out a piercing series of one-note runs it was clear that Young was the axis on which the band rotated. Singer Bon Scott, clad in a sleeveless denim jacket that exposed his many tattoos, wailed out his lines like a man who'd been stabbed, and rocked nearly as hard as his guitarist did. Scott died in February 1980 after an all-night drinking binge, and wouldn't see his band dominate the '80s hard-rock scene with albums *Back in Black*, *Dirty Deeds Done Dirt Cheap* and *For Those About to Rock We Salute You*.

Heartland popsters REO Speedwagon, who hosted an earlier show, also made an appearance, via an outside clip of "Say You Love Me or Say Goodnight," recorded in Kansas City. In a rare and odd oversight, guitarist Kevin Cronin mis-introduced the clip as "Roll with the Changes," another song from their *You Can Tune a Piano but You Can't Tuna Fish* album.

Thin Lizzy's contribution was also prerecorded, a version of "Cowboy Song" captured live at London's Rainbow Club.

As for Aerosmith, Tyler and Nugent introduced the group's contribution—a clip from the Robert Stigwood film *Sgt. Pepper's Lonely Heart's Club Band*, in which Tyler and Aerosmith guitarist Joe Perry (cast as villains) sang the Lennon/McCartney gem "Come Together." It was a fine way to end a blazing show. In some ways this show would signal the end of an era on *The Midnight Special*. The next episode would be a theme disco show, hosted by Wolfman Jack, on which the Jeff Kutash Dancers would make their debut. The raucous Episode 296 would be an apropos swan song for the show, as the next episodes emphasized its shift toward dance music and away from live rock & roll.

"THERE WERE A COUPLE OF WORDS HE HAD TO LEAVE OUT, AND HE DID. THE PROBLEM I REMEMBER HAVING WAS WITH THE SOUND LEVEL. IT WAS TOO LOUD, SO THEY MADE HIM TURN HIS EQUIPMENT DOWN AT SOME POINT. THERE WAS SOMETHING ABOUT THE UNION, BECAUSE THEY WANTED HIM TO TURN IT DOWN. TED WASN'T THRILLED. BUT IN GENERAL, THE SHOW WAS SO MUCH FUN, AND WE HAD A BALL WHEN WE WERE WORKING TOGETHER. WHEN I THINK BACK ON ALL THE SHOWS I'VE DONE OR ALL THE PEOPLE I'VE WORKED WITH, I STILL HAVE THE WARMEST REGARDS FOR THE PEOPLE ON <u>THE MIDNIGHT SPECIAL</u>. IT WAS A GROWING-UP STAGE FOR ALL OF US, AS WELL AS FOR TELEVISION."
DEBI GENOVESE, TALENT COORDINATOR

1979

In 1979, the economy, energy crisis, and the hostage-taking in Iran presaged the eventual defeat of President Carter. Iranian militants forced the Shah of Iran into exile, and the American-friendly leader was replaced by the Ayatollah Khomeini, who took nearly 100 U.S. Embassy staff hostages— and didn't release them until 30 minutes after President Reagan took office in 1981. Arthur Fiedler, the conductor of the Boston Pops Orchestra, died, as did Sex Pistol bassist Sid Vicious and heralded jazz composer Charles Mingus. Karen Silkwood posthumously won $10.5 million in damages for negligent exposure to nuclear contamination, and Three Mile Island narrowly averted a full-scale nuclear meltdown. *Apocalypse Now* and *Kramer vs. Kramer* were doing brisk business in the theaters, while Pink Floyd's *The Wall* and Tom Petty's *Damn the Torpedoes* were burying themselves deeply in music enthusiasts' consciousness.

1979 also still found dance music en vogue, but a musical style called "new wave" was also rearing its head. And like any cultural mirror, *The Midnight Special* reflected those trends right back onto its audience. Shows hosted by The Cars and Blondie were interspersed with those hosted by Bob Welch, Peaches & Herb and the Captain and Tennille. Furthermore, 1979 was the year the show introduced a new feature, the audience dance segment, and it was the first time the audience became as much a focus as the performers themselves. Jeff Kutash's dancers were also playing a larger role, sometimes performing several times during a show. Even Wolfman Jack assumed a new look, often shown in a raised booth, complete with blinking lights, that resembled a DJ's stand. Poised above the frothing studio audience, Wolfman would stand, announcing the next song, outside clip, or—less and less frequently—the next live act.

FEATURING: Sarah Dash, Peaches & Herb, Audience dance segment, Queen

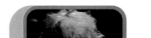

"I remember getting tickets and going down to see Blondie on The Midnight Special with some friends. In those days they would book the shows in the most eclectic way possible to generate the widest possible audience. You'd have your token new wave act with your bearded, aging, mainstream rock act mixed with an R&B act, and they'd also be somewhat reflective of what was happening on the charts at the time. In this case Blondie came to town, and we were really excited. I remember they had the studio set up so that there were two stages simultaneously at opposite ends of the studio. We got there early to get to the front of the stage, and I remember looking over the equipment and trying to figure out which stage would be Blondie's. We knew their setup; what the drum kit looked like; there was a keyboard, and their equipment tended to look a little bit different from that of, say, REO Speedwagon or somebody like that. Blondie had a cheesy little Farfisa keyboard setup, and their equipment looked a little less world-weary than that of other bands.

"I recall Debbie Harry was wearing that skin-tight pink patent leather dress that she wore on the second Blondie

The Midnight Special was a long way from CBGB's, the punk and new-wave mecca of New York's East Village where Blondie, Television and the Talking Heads got their start. Blondie was the first of the CBGB bands to take a more deliberate commercial approach, crossing over to mass appeal with the dance-flavored "Heart of Glass." Meanwhile, *The Midnight Special* had taken on the feel of an *American Bandstand* knockoff. With more emphasis on dancing than on the live presentation of music, Blondie appeared and mimed its way through the difficult-to-reproduce-live "Heart of Glass." As if not even trying to fool the TV audience, the whole last verse of the song consisted of footage of a couple gyrating wildly on the dance floor.

Commercialization—appealing to the widest audience possible—was keeping *The Midnight Special* afloat. Even though she herself had fallen victim to lip-synching, one such form of that commercialization, Deborah Harry underscored the fact that the show had turned to disco to provide its primary musical undercurrent with her opening remarks:

"Welcome to *The Midnight Special*," she said. "It's really a pleasure to host this show. Usually our band plays an ancient form of music that is still heard and seen in some places today. It's called rock & roll." [some applause.] "But now, everybody is dancing to a heavy bass-line beat." With this she introduced her first guest, disco's Sarah Dash. As if to fly in the face of the show's late 1970s norm, however, Blondie later played an

Peaches & Herb

Queen

Blondie

record. And of course all the young boys in the audience, myself included, were drooling on our leather jackets. In those days Debbie was quite a feminine image to behold, and that made it all the more interesting. For one reason or another, after their set I was able to sneak backstage when one of the security goons was unaware. I was sort of young and thin at the time, and was kind of punky, and it would have been possible for them to mistake me for one of the band members. I was coiffed in a modern fashion, and had I been caught in a photograph with the band I wouldn't have looked terribly dissimilar. So I went back there and introduced myself as a fan. Debbie could see that I wasn't a stalker, I was just a typical goofball; a coy, drooling, record-collecting goofball. We spoke for about five minutes. I asked them about their tour plans and their recording plans, because that was my modus operandi at the time, my standard slate of questions. So I had Debbie and Chris Stein autograph the inside of my leather jacket before security discovered me and showed me the way to the door. I remember Debbie stuck up for me and told the security guys to hang on and to let me have a moment before they tossed me out onto the cold sidewalk. I remember she said 'He's okay. We'll be through in a minute,' and she kindly continued to have a conversation with me for a moment. She was great."
Rick Gershon,
audience member

inspired live version of "One Way or Another," and the rocking power pop of their "Sunday Girl" was equally riveting, diluted only by the extended shots of people dancing.

Sarah Dash appeared in a low-cut red dress with a substantial slit up the leg. Originally a member of the R&B/soul group LeBelle, Dash's self-titled album would hit the charts a day after the show, perhaps aided by purchases by the audience members that joined her on stage, dancing like mad, to her hit "Sinner Man."

Harry also introduced her next guest with subtle disdain. "You are about to enjoy the second coming of this group," she said. "The first time around in the '60s they did the good old-fashioned rhythm and blues thing. Now they're back with a great new sound. Shake your groove thing, Peaches & Herb!" With that, the soul duo from Washington, D.C., wearing matching shiny silver outfits and accompanied by several dancers, performed their sensation, "Shake Your Groove Thing," much to the delight of those who had tuned in for some bona fide disco dancing. Later in the show, Peaches & Herb played their sentimental ballad "Reunited," which would later become their biggest hit.

Another disco-oriented aspect of the show was the newly added "audience dance segment." On this episode the Bee Gees' quintessential disco smashes, "Stayin' Alive" and "Night Fever," were introduced by Wolfman Jack, who presided over the dance floor like a disenchanted ship's captain determined to go down with his vessel.

Audience Dance Segment

episode

AIRED:

JANUARY 26, 1979

305

The Village People

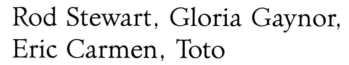

FEATURING: Rod Stewart, Gloria Gaynor, Eric Carmen, Toto

Gloria Gaynor

Toto

pening this show with its breakthrough hit "Y.M.C.A." was campy disco group the Village People, whose onstage costumes were more identifiable than their given names. Formed in 1977 by French producer Jacques Morali after seeing costumed men in gay discos in New York, the group would become a huge hit in both the straight and gay communities, let alone sports stadiums. But their success did not preclude their being censored. On this performance of "Y.M.C.A.," lead singer Victor Willis was compelled to sanitize the song, changing the words from "You can make out with all the boys" to "You can hang out with all the boys." No matter. *The Midnight Special*'s wildly dancing crowd didn't know the difference—nor did they care—as they were just there to dance. Later the group would play "Macho Man," during which the camera cut to several shots of the audience doing push-ups, while the band members themselves would flex, pump their fists, and undulate their hips to jibe with the song's theme.

Next up was *Midnight Special* regular Rod Stewart, whom the Village People were excited to introduce. David Hodo, the construction worker, fingered his microphone absentmindedly while Randy Jones, the cowboy, drew his gun. But it was Willis, the policeman, who introduced Stewart like this: "This latest hit asks the question you should ask yourself every morning when you look into the mirror: 'Da Ya Think I'm Sexy?'" With that, Stewart's ultimately self-absorbed video clip was shown. It portrayed a spiky-haired Stewart watching a film of himself on stage singing "Da Ya Think I'm Sexy" while he seduces a woman in his bedroom.

And the disco kept coming. Gloria Gaynor followed with her No. 1 disco smash "I Will Survive," with her backing musicians offstage. It would be Gaynor's second of four appearances on *The Midnight Special*, and she would go on to host the show in June 1979.

Also on the show was Eric Carmen, who had led the pop group the Raspberries from 1970 to 1974, and was appearing on the show as a solo act for the sixth time. He sang his recent hit "Change of Heart," followed by "Baby I Need Your Lovin'," the Holland-Dozier-Holland classic that Johnny Rivers had taken to No. 3 in 1967.

The Village People

Rod Stewart

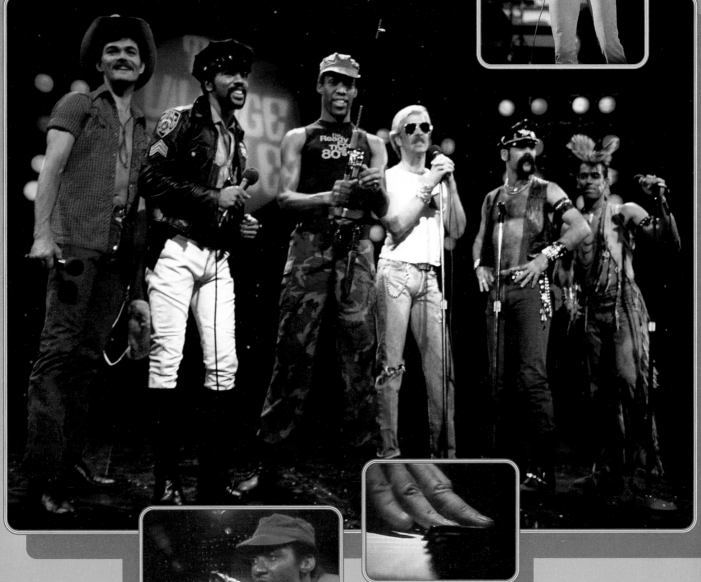

episode

AIRED:

FEBRUARY 16, 1979

308

HOST:

Alice Cooper

FEATURING: Olivia Newton-John, Instant Funk, Chic, Tanya Tucker, The Cars

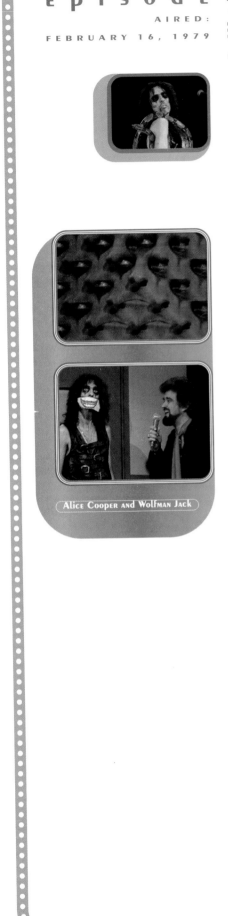

Alice Cooper and Wolfman Jack

Alice Cooper

Before Marilyn Manson, before Tipper Gore and William Bennett launched their demagogic attacks on rock music, there was Alice Cooper, '70s rock's resident master of theatrical—and occasionally demonic—histrionics. Cooper hosted *The Midnight Special* on the heels of his autobiographical *From the Inside*, an album based on his months in a psychiatric hospital being treated for alcoholism. But in typical Cooper fashion, even his own demons were used as fodder for cartoonish excess. Wolfman Jack opened the show lying in bed in a mental ward, introducing Cooper as "The master of madhouse rock," as Cooper, dressed head-to-toe in leather, played his new album's title track joined by dancing, lifesize liquor bottles. As each new bottle joined the merriment, the band played a corresponding song: a Scottish reel for a kilt-clad, Celtic-dancing whiskey bottle; "Dixieland" for Southern Comfort; and of course "Tequila" for that Mexican beverage.

Cooper didn't just introduce the evening's guests, he gesticulated like a vampire through a door marked "Alice's Madhouse," which revealed the next act. Who would have thought that the guest behind the door would be the sugar-sweet girl-next-door Olivia Newton-John, performing "A Little More Love."

Following that came Philadelphia's Instant Funk, who lip-synched their way through their only hit, "I Got My Mind Made Up (You Can Get It Girl)," which hit the charts the day after the show aired.

The Cars

Tanya Tucker

Olivia Newton-John

The "madhouse" was used throughout the show, and even for comic effect more blatant than the incongruity of Olivia Newton-John's presence. Cooper and Wolfman Jack quickly slammed the door shut when a smiling image of Richard Nixon appeared and garnered boos and hisses from the partisan audience. The audience preferred watching Cooper feign biting the head off a boa constrictor while he played "Billion Dollar Babies," which they greeted with appreciative hollers.

In addition to the Cooper's macabre act, Chic performed "Le Freak," and country singer Tanya Tucker covered Buddy Holly's "Not Fade Away." But there was hope. The Cars brought one of the first blasts of new wave and skinny ties to *The Midnight Special*, driving through a ragged, energetic "My Best Friend's Girl" from the group's well-produced album.

It was just what we needed—then it was back to Cooper. Returning to the show's theme, the episode's last number was Cooper's apropos rendition of "Inmates (We're All Crazy)," also from his *From the Inside* album. The evening definitely ranks as one of the most bizarre *Midnight Special* episodes ever.

318

HOST: The Beach Boys

FEATURING: Blondie, Tavares, Bad Company, McGuinn, Clark & Hillman

The Beach Boys

How times change. By 1979, even the Beach Boys had to go disco. Hosting *The Midnight Special* for the first time, the California sun-and-funsters finally found their way back on the charts with a disco remix of their '60s song "Here Comes the Night," which bore just a slim resemblance to the original. On this evening they'd perform the updated arrangement to a *Midnight Special* audience that had come to expect dance music, as well two other songs from their latest album, called *L.A.*, short for Light Album. Then they dug out the time machine for expert versions of "Good Vibrations" and "Surfin' U.S.A."

But the tides were high for a musical sea-change, which Blondie would help provide, as new wave supplanted disco. The new popularity of new wave was evident from the recycled footage from Blondie's previous appearance on *The Midnight Special* just five months earlier, as "Heart of Glass," "One Way or Another" and "Hanging on the Telephone" had only grown in stature.

Of course, disco wasn't dead yet, and neither was guitar rock. Still riding the momentum from their appearance on the *Saturday Night Fever* soundtrack, R&B sibling quintet Tavares ran through "Strait from Your Heart" and "Never Had a Love Like This Before." They would also do the requisite performance of their big hit "More Than a Woman," their Bee Gees-penned song from that best-selling soundtrack. Then Bad Company sent along concert footage of some of their biggest hits: "Feel Like Makin' Love," "Can't Get Enough" and "Rock and Roll Fantasy."

The Beach Boys weren't the only old-timers on this show altering their sound in an effort to reach new fans. *Midnight Special* old friend Roger McGuinn returned, joined by two other founding members of the Byrds, Gene Clark and Chris Hillman. The trio had just released a reunion album of sorts, simply titled *McGuinn, Clark & Hillman*, which achieved modest success. Their approach was decidedly different though. The three songs they played from the new album—the single "Don't You Write Her Off," "Backstage Pass" and "Surrender to Me"— were catchy, but lyrically more lightweight, and leaned on keyboards much more than the Byrds ever did.

The Beach Boys

Tavares

Nick Gilder

Steve Martin

FEATURING: Steve Martin, Nick Gilder, Yvonne Elliman, A Taste of Honey, Donna Summer, Teddy Pendergrass, Kenny Rogers

Wolfman Jack

This show featured a mélange of footage from previous episodes. Hosted by Wolfman Jack, who would introduce the bands as if they were playing live, the show was a winner even though regular viewers might have felt cheated by the "greatest hits." The show's first "guest" was comedian Steve Martin, who jammed on banjo with the Dirt Band's John McEuen. Taken from Episode 290, the pair would play the bluegrass number "Pitkin County Turn Around," which would later show up on Martin's album *The Steve Martin Brothers*, a 1981 album divided between comedy and Martin's surprisingly fine banjo skills.

The audience probably had to be reminded who some of the musicians were, since pop music is by nature ephemeral, and pop fame can be fleeting. There was Nick Gilder's one-hit wonder "Hot Child in the City," originally aired during the hot summer in 1978; and Yvonne Elliman's "If I Can't Have You," a tune taken from the popular *Saturday Night Fever* soundtrack. Written by the Bee Gees, it would be Elliman's biggest hit. Lastly, A Taste of Honey proved how poorly the Grammy award for Best New Artist predicts a lasting career. "Boogie Oogie Oogie," performed here, would be their biggest hit, and their career faded as the disco era ended.

Then there were the bigger stars. Also chronicled on this show were performances by Donna Summer, who played her gold, Top-10 hit from 1977, "I Feel Love;" Teddy Pendergrass, who chipped in with his biggest pop hit, "Close the Door;" and Kenny Rogers, who performed his "Love or Something Like It," the single that preceded "The Gambler." In all, this show did not have the seamless feeling that customarily accompanied a pre-booked show. However, the song selection was strong, the artists diverse, and their performances solid.

A Taste of Honey

1980

In the dawn of a new decade, President Carter ended diplomatic relations with Iran and announced economic sanctions as a result of the hostage situation. Norman Mailer's *The Executioner's Song* and Tom Wolfe's *The Right Stuff* were popular books of the year. The arts lost French author and philosopher Jean-Paul Sartre, American author Henry Miller, comedian Jimmy Durante, movie director Sir Alfred Hitchcock, and John Lennon of the Beatles.

Meanwhile, the wreck of the *Titantic* was found, and Mount St. Helens erupted, killing 36 people. *Dallas* fever gripped the nation, as the "Who shot J.R.?" episode of the evening soap garnered the largest rating ever for a regular TV program up to then, drawing 88.6 million viewers. Ronald Reagan won the presidency in a landslide victory over Jimmy Carter, becoming the United States' 40th president, and films like *Coal Miner's Daughter*, *The Empire Strikes Back* and *Raging Bull* enchanted moviegoers. The Winter Olympics were held in Lake Placid, New York, and the American hockey team beat the feared Russians, capturing the gold medal for the first time since 1960. 1980 was also a year that found the Police's *Zenyatta Mondatta*, the Pretenders' eponymous debut, and the J. Geils Band's *Love Stinks* all over the radio.

In *Midnight Special* land, the "Outrage" talk and comedy segments became regular attractions in 1980. Though they debuted in late 1979, these segments would be an early harbinger of the show's new direction, which was heading more and more toward a variety show format. There were still live musical performances, but repeated shows, reliance on outside clips and reused segments from past shows were becoming common. There were still dancers of all kinds to gyrate their hips to songs like "Funkytown" and "Call Me," and by Episode 369 *The Midnight Special* even introduced a Top-10 countdown. The countdown featured the Steve Merritt Dancers, who did mini-skits and undulated to the rhythms of the hottest hits in the nation. Forced to come up with new twists to compensate for the growing dearth of live talent, *The Midnight Special* was beginning to lose the element that made it unique, becoming a combination of a Hollywood talk show, Casey Kasem's *America's Top 40* and Dick Clark's *American Bandstand.*

episode 355

AIRED:
JANUARY 11, 1980

HOST: **Dr. Hook**

FEATURING: Prince, Cliff Richard,
Outrage comedy segment

"The bomb scare, that's my favorite story. On the other side of NBC Studio 4 was a special dressing room, because when Flip Wilson had his show produced in the studio, he wanted his own dressing room far away from everybody else, so they made him one. It was a very nice suite and we used it as our office. Anyhow, Rocco [Urbisci] was working in there. In the meantime, I got a call in the control room, and they said 'We want you to get everybody out of there in five minutes, there could be a bomb.'

"So Rocco was in this room, and he couldn't hear anything because it was all soundproofed. I said to the audience, 'I've just gotten a call from the Burbank police department, and they said the electric company has got to turn off the lights for five minutes, and they don't want anyone in the studio when the lights are off.' So everybody left and they put chains on the doors, because that was the only way to lock [them]. So there were about four bands and [several hundred] kids that had to leave the studio. And Rocco comes out, and he can't believe it. There was nobody there."

STAN HARRIS,
producer/director

Cliff Richard

Timely bookings were always a hallmark of *The Midnight Special*, and this episode welcomed Prince, an artist who would become one of the most successful and prolific superstars of the 1980s. When this show was aired, Prince was in the midst of supporting funkster Rick James on a U.S. tour. Meanwhile, the-artist-still-known-as-Prince-at-that-time had recently hit the pop chart with his second album for Warner Bros. Thanks in part to his performance on the show, the self-titled album would become his first of many platinum efforts. "I Wanna Be Your Lover," which he performed on this evening, would go gold. Though he was described as "The strangest act I ever put on the show" by one *Midnight Special* staffer, one thing was irrefutable about Prince: his musical talent. He would play all the instruments on (and self-produce) his first five albums, including the triple platinum *1999*, actually released in 1982.

Cliff Richard's appearance on the show helped him achieve a Top-10 hit with "We Don't Talk Anymore," a tune that would become one of his five Top-40 hits in America in 1979–80. Though he'd been making records since the late '50s, it was by far the most consistent success Richard would ever enjoy in the United States. Referred to as "Britain's answer to Elvis Presley," Richard was the most successful pop star in British history, charting a staggering number of songs in his homeland. As of this writing, Richard boasts more than 105 entries into the U.K. Top-40 in his fabled career.

Dr. Hook hosted the show, and while the band had more than 30 hit albums in Australia, they were enjoying American success with the smooth ballad "When You're in Love with a Beautiful Woman." Though they performed one of their biggest hits ever on this show, Dr. Hook were still best known around *The Midnight Special* for a near-smash that thankfully never happened.

Dr. Hook

JOY GRDNIC

SANDRA BERNHARD

RUFUS SHAW JR.

PAT McCORMICK

Outrage Comedy Segment

"So the studio is completely empty. Now you have to understand that five minutes prior to that there were 230 people there. The first thing I think is, 'I've F**kin' died. My penance is I'm going to spend my life in this empty studio.' And I hear this chain—like Jacob Marley's chain—being pulled, and I'm freaking out. 'Where'd the audience go? Where'd the show go?' I'm thinking. And I see this security guard, and his face is in the little window in the door. And I run up and I bang on the door and go, 'What the F**k is going on? Where's the show?' 'Bomb scare, bomb scare!' he says.

"And I think, 'Get me the F**k outta here.' So we go outside to the parking lot.

"There were five bands that night. One of them was Dr. Hook. The bomb scare went on for over an hour, so a couple of members of the Hook band started to do some acoustic sets and basically had a sing-along with the crowd. That would never happen today. Finally we get the official notice. They can't find the bomb, but they're going to dismiss the show. No taping today."

Rocco Urbisci,
co-producer

episode 358

AIRED: FEBRUARY 1, 1980

HOST: **The Captain and Tennille**

FEATURING: **Crystal Gayle, The Commodores, Dolly Parton, The Village People, Olivia Newton-John, Willie Nelson, Andy Kaufman**

The Captain and Tennille

By this time, *The Midnight Special* had a lot of footage in its vaults, and was able to draw on it when a show's lineup needed augmentation. This episode was such an affair, featuring an array of soft rock/pop (The Captain and Tennille, Crystal Gayle, Dolly Parton), country (Willie Nelson), disco (The Village People), R&B (The Commodores) and comedy (Outrage comedians, Andy Kaufman). Hosted by *Midnight Special* pros Daryl "The Captain" Dragon and his wife Toni Tennille, (veterans of more than 20 previous appearances) who were enjoying what would be their final No. 1 hit, the show ran smoothly—despite its decidedly middle-of-the-road and not entirely up-to-date leanings.

After opening the show themselves with their chart-topping "Do That to Me One More Time," The Captain and Tennille's first three guests proceeded to do just that—dust off songs previously played on *The Midnight Special*: Crystal Gayle's 1977 hit "Don't It Make My Brown Eyes Blue," the Commodores' 1979 smash "Still," and Dolly Parton's late-1977 single "Here You Come Again." Then came the Village People's first hit, "Macho Man" and Olivia Newton-John's 1975 chart-topper "Have You Never Been Mellow" followed by Willie Nelson's "Blue Eyes Crying in the Rain," a song Nelson recorded in 1975, but written by Fred Rose in 1945. Though this show looked smooth, there was some discontent behind the scenes, as producer Neal Marshall remembers.

NEAL MARSHALL, PRODUCER: "For me, *The Midnight Special* was a delicious musical smorgasbord. I worked with some great rock & roll bands, R&B artists, country music acts. The salutes and mini-documentary pieces we aired were also a treat. Robbie Robertson talked with Wolfman about the making of *The Last Waltz*, and I got a chance to spend some time with Martin Scorsese. There was a down side—disco. It drove me crazy. Yes, there were some really good acts—Donna Summer and Chic come

Willie Nelson

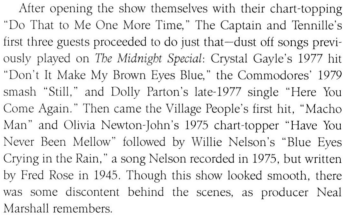

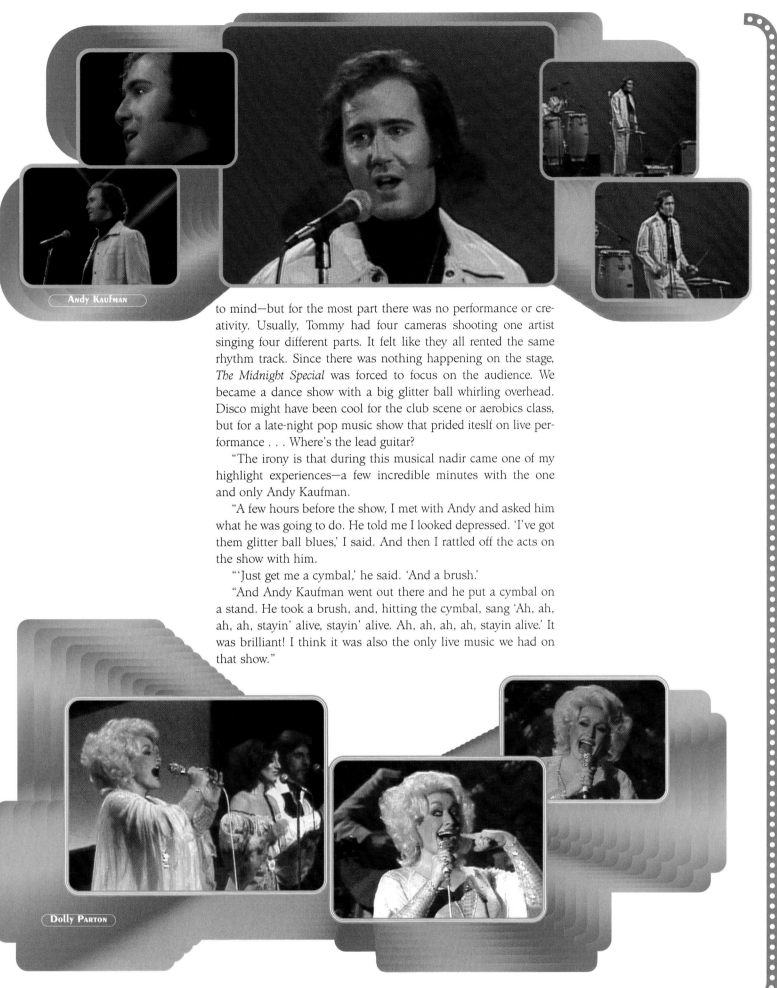

Andy Kaufman

to mind—but for the most part there was no performance or creativity. Usually, Tommy had four cameras shooting one artist singing four different parts. It felt like they all rented the same rhythm track. Since there was nothing happening on the stage, *The Midnight Special* was forced to focus on the audience. We became a dance show with a big glitter ball whirling overhead. Disco might have been cool for the club scene or aerobics class, but for a late-night pop music show that prided iteslf on live performance . . . Where's the lead guitar?

"The irony is that during this musical nadir came one of my highlight experiences—a few incredible minutes with the one and only Andy Kaufman.

"A few hours before the show, I met with Andy and asked him what he was going to do. He told me I looked depressed. 'I've got them glitter ball blues,' I said. And then I rattled off the acts on the show with him.

"'Just get me a cymbal,' he said. 'And a brush.'

"And Andy Kaufman went out there and he put a cymbal on a stand. He took a brush, and, hitting the cymbal, sang 'Ah, ah, ah, ah, stayin' alive, stayin' alive. Ah, ah, ah, ah, stayin alive.' It was brilliant! I think it was also the only live music we had on that show."

Dolly Parton

episode 369

AIRED: APRIL 18, 1980

HOSTS: # Sissy Spacek and Levon Helm

FEATURING: **Beverly D'Angelo, Phyllis Boyens, Queen, Rupert Holmes, The Spinners, Anne Murray**

BEVERLY D'ANGELO

BEVERLY D'ANGELO and Sissy Spacek

Actors generally shouldn't sing. But this episode of *The Midnight Special* may have been the exception to that rule. The show was a celebration of *Coal Miner's Daughter*, the film based on the rags-to-riches life of country superstar Loretta Lynn. Sissy Spacek's portrayal of Lynn would win her an Oscar for best actress—a long way from her debut in Andy Warhol's graphic *Trash*—but on this show, Spacek seemed to want a Grammy as well.

Spacek and costars Beverly D'Angelo and Levon Helm (the former Band drummer) did all their own singing in the movie, and 16 of those outside clips made the bulk of this show. Helm, of course, was no stranger to performing. The real surprise was the sensitive, tender voice of D'Angelo, whose stirring turn as Patsy Cline induced shivers, and Spacek's gritty, heartfelt and passionate versions of Lynn's greatest hits. D'Angelo didn't shy away from Cline's most memorable tearjerker: the mysterious, weeping "Crazy." She belted out the bouncy "Walkin' After Midnight." and the heartbreaking "Sweet Dreams," recorded by Cline just before she died in a 1963 plane crash. Music fans responded as well: the *Coal Miner's Daughter* soundtrack stayed on the charts for five months.

Before the *Billboard* charts splintered into separate listings for dozens of different music styles, the early 1980s was probably the last time when rockers like Queen and Pink Floyd could share space in the Top-5 with the Captain and Tennille, Kenny Rogers and the Spinners. The segment of the show that included a look at the charts—which became more pronounced on *The Midnight Special* as music shows like Casey Kasem's *America's Top 40* and *Solid Gold* proliferated on TV—became one of the most diverse sections of the show. Indeed, Queen's "Crazy Little Thing Called Love" and The Spinners' "Working My Way Back to You" cover were featured this week—some updated soul and operatic rock.

But something *The Midnight Special* had on all these Johnny-come-lately shows was its extensive video library of '70s performances, so the "Golden Moment" nostalgia clip reared its head on this show flashing back to 1973 for Anne Murray's "Snowbird."

Levon Helm, Sissy Spacek, Phyllis Boyens and Beverly D'Angelo

Richard Tee

HOST: # Chevy Chase

FEATURING: **The Rolling Stones, Benny Mardones, Irene Cara, Richard Tee, Johnny Nash, Richard Belzer, Steve Merritt Dancers**

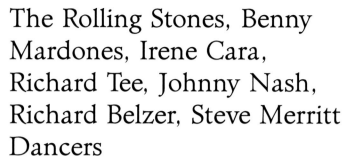

Just a few weeks away from the election of Ronald Reagan, the host of *The Midnight Special* was Chevy Chase, the comedian perhaps best known for his devastating portrayal of the previous GOP president, Gerald Ford, as a bumbling klutz. But Chase, like D'Angelo (with whom he would soon star in the *Vacation* films), aspired to a musical career of sorts, and released an album this year, not long after leaving *Saturday Night Live* after four wildly successful seasons.

Chase performed three campy covers—Randy Newman's caustic, controversial "Short People," Bob Marley's reggae standard "I Shot the Sheriff," and "Sixteen Tons," a late '40s country lament written by Merle Travis, but taken to No. 1 by Tennessee Ernie Ford. Chase's voice, to put it nicely, was somewhat limited.

Chase welcomed the Rolling Stones—or at least the Rolling Stones' new video for "Emotional Rescue." But Benny Mardones did appear in person. Who? Benny Mardones— whose *Never Run Never Hide* LP was on the charts, riding the hit "Into the Night," which would climb to No. 11 in 1980, then reappear in the Top-20 nine years later, perhaps making "Into the Night" the only song to hit both *The Midnight Special* and the MTV Top 20 Video Countdown. Mardones would also play "Hometown Girls," a tune from the same album, on this show.

Adding spice to the *Midnight Special* proceedings on this evening was the multitalented singer and actress Irene Cara, whose starring role in the movie *Fame*, and a hit soundtrack single of the same name, gave the 21-year-old time in the spotlight. Cara would be to early 1980s soundtracks what Kenny Loggins would be to the middle of the decade, charting not only with "Fame," but with the even more infectious "Flashdance (What a Feeling)" a few years later, though her movie career petered out after cameo roles in *D.C. Cab* and *Killing 'Em Softly*.

Rounding out *The Midnight Special* lineup was Johnny Nash, whose performance of "I Can See Clearly Now" from 1973 was shown as a "Golden Moment" from the good old days. Richard Belzer, then a fledgling nightclub stand-up comic, added his routine. And the Steve Merritt Dancers saluted several popular songs with their tightly choreographed dance routines, including Eddie Rabbitt's "Drivin' My Life Away," Paul Simon's "Late in the Evening," and Diana Ross' "Upside Down."

Chevy Chase

Chevy Chase and Wolfman Jack

Steve Merritt Dancers

e p i s o d e

398

HOST: # Stephanie Mills

FEATURING: The Pointer Sisters,
Leo Sayer, Pete Townshend,
707, John Cougar

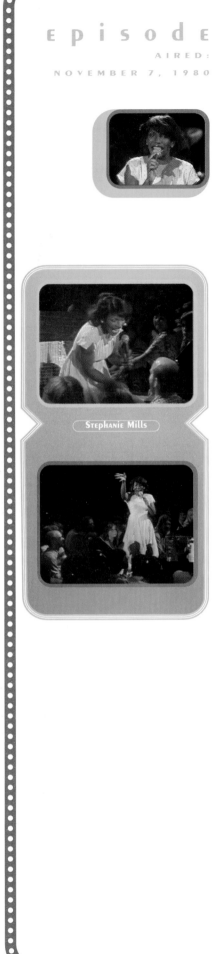

Stephanie Mills

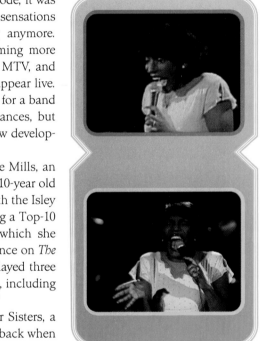

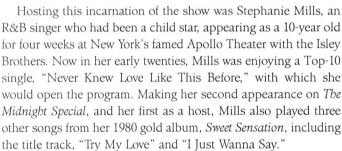

A s *The Midnight Special* neared its 400th episode, it was still attracting established stars and newer sensations alike, albeit seldom in a "live" setting anymore. Videos, once a luxury, were slowly becoming more common for bands to make, even before the birth of MTV, and bands were happy to show off their clip, rather than appear live. *The Midnight Special* made chart success a prerequisite for a band to appear, which resulted in some superstar performances, but also in the show revealing its age by missing some new developments in music.

Hosting this incarnation of the show was Stephanie Mills, an R&B singer who had been a child star, appearing as a 10-year old for four weeks at New York's famed Apollo Theater with the Isley Brothers. Now in her early twenties, Mills was enjoying a Top-10 single, "Never Knew Love Like This Before," with which she would open the program. Making her second appearance on *The Midnight Special*, and her first as a host, Mills also played three other songs from her 1980 gold album, *Sweet Sensation*, including the title track, "Try My Love" and "I Just Wanna Say."

Mills' first guest on the show would be the Pointer Sisters, a soul group that had been formed in Oakland in 1971, back when Mills was still a precocious youngster. Originally consisting of sisters Ruth, Anita and Bonnie Pointer, the trio was bolstered by youngest sister June in the early 1970s, and the group would go on to sing background vocals for many rock acts, before making their own music with a danceable, high-energy disco flair. The Pointer Sisters were represented on this show by clips of them singing "He's So Shy," a tune from their *Special Things* LP that had debuted on the charts in July, and would remain there for six months, peaking at No. 3.

Also on hand for this show was *Midnight Special* veteran Leo Sayer, the English songwriter who would make more than a

Pete Townshend

Leo Sayer

The Pointer Sisters

John Cougar

dozen appearances on the show all told. Having had back-to-back No. 1 smashes in the States in the mid-1970s ("You Make Me Feel Like Dancing" and "When I Need You"), Sayer was trying to repeat his prior successes on the strength of his album, *Living in a Fantasy*, and its single, the Sonny Curtis/Jerry Allison (of "I Fought the Law" and "Peggy Sue" fame) penned "More than I Can Say," which Sayer invested with heartfelt romanticism and a desperate, needy edge.

Also appearing on this show would be two certified songwriting superstars—one who had had major success in the previous 15 years, and one who would have major success over the next 15. As leader of the legendary English band The Who, Pete Townshend had written some of the best-known and most popular songs of the rock era. Here, in his second *Midnight Special* appearance, he was promoting *Empty Glass*, his most successful solo album. Containing songs like "Rough Boys" and "A Little is Enough" (both of which Townshend performed via outside clips on this show), the album also contained "Let My Love Open the Door," a song that would become his most well-known solo song.

Johnny Cougar. John Cougar. John Cougar Mellencamp. John Mellencamp. The names changed, but the music has remained consistently good. For two decades, Mellencamp has made stirring roots music deserving of the name; music that is tied to a place and a tradition. Mellencamp's songs, filled with images of the Midwest, of rebellion and youthful anxiety, of dislocation and relocation, became as much a part of Americana as the farmhouses and pink houses, hot dog stands and youthful last stands that he sang about so passionately. On this *Midnight Special*, one of his first television appearances, Cougar played two rootsy stomps from his *Nothin' Matters and What If It Did* album, both of which became two of his first hit singles—"This Time" and "Ain't Even Done with the Night."

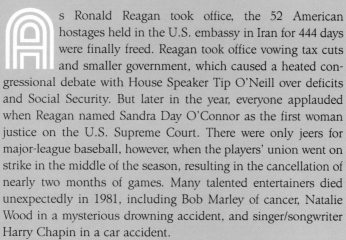

1 9 8 1

As Ronald Reagan took office, the 52 American hostages held in the U.S. embassy in Iran for 444 days were finally freed. Reagan took office vowing tax cuts and smaller government, which caused a heated congressional debate with House Speaker Tip O'Neill over deficits and Social Security. But later in the year, everyone applauded when Reagan named Sandra Day O'Connor as the first woman justice on the U.S. Supreme Court. There were only jeers for major-league baseball, however, when the players' union went on strike in the middle of the season, resulting in the cancellation of nearly two months of games. Many talented entertainers died unexpectedly in 1981, including Bob Marley of cancer, Natalie Wood in a mysterious drowning accident, and singer/songwriter Harry Chapin in a car accident.

1981 would also find *The Midnight Special*'s final episodes being produced, and many of them were hosted not by musicians, but by television and film stars. Larry Hagman, who played television's evil J.R. Ewing on the nighttime soap opera *Dallas*, hosted Episode 408, welcoming guests like Marie Osmond and George Burns. Other 1981 hosts included movie star Lily Tomlin, Lynda Carter (television's "Wonder Woman"), former baseball catcher Bob Uecker, and *Taxi* star Marilu Henner. 1981 was the year that *The Midnight Special* finally became a variety show, as performers found easier ways to get their music heard—namely a new network called MTV, which first aired on August 1, 1981. MTV would become the most influential force in rock & roll in the years to come, placing new importance on conveying image and music through video. This shift to interest in videos on the part of both performers and the viewing public would untimately cause the demise of *The Midnight Special*, which had been one of the most resilient, diverse and interesting music shows ever.

Lily Tomlin and Hall & Oates

Martha Davis and Robert Hilburn

Who had the most big hits of the '80s? Madonna? Michael Jackson? Prince? Wrong. It was Hall & Oates. "Daryl Hall and John Oates had their first hit single in 1976," said host Lily Tomlin in her introduction. "And they've had at least one a year since then. And while they've written most of their own material through the years, their current release is a new version of the old Righteous Brothers hit 'You've Lost That Lovin' Feeling!'"

Though several other artists had covered the song previously (Dionne Warwick, Roberta Flack, Donny Hathaway), Hall & Oates' version proved the most popular, nearly cracking the Top-10. But it wouldn't be the last people would hear of their album, *Voices*. On this evening, the most successful vocal duo ever played two other songs from the album that would become hits, "How Does It Feel to Be Back" and "Kiss on My List."

Later Tomlin welcomed the Police, a young trio about whom she would say: "A year ago, on a shoestring budget the Police embarked on a worldwide tour that included stops in the subcontinent of India and the Middle East. Now they're back in America with their biggest hit yet." Indeed, the Police were in the midst of a 33-date American tour, but there was no sign of them live on the show. Instead, the group's Top-10 single, "De Do Do Do, De Da Da Da," was represented by an outside clip of the

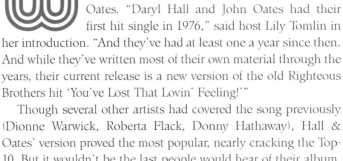

Lily Tomlin

group playing their instruments and singing outside in the snowy environs of a ski resort.

Next up was rock critic Robert Hilburn of the *Los Angeles Times*, one of the most respected daily rock critics, who enthused about the Motels: "[They're] one of the most exciting bands in the country, mix[ing] the energy of new wave with the musicianship of mainstream rock & roll. It's the same pattern that the Cars, the Police and the Pretenders have used to great success in recent years, and this could be one of the biggest bands in the country in the next few months."

Well, maybe not. But the Motels did at least have two hits that still get played during '80s nostalgia fests, "Suddenly Last Summer" and "Only the Lonely." On this show, Davis piloted her group through the jagged, synth-driven pop of "Envy," from their album *Careful*. It was clear that the Motels were no strangers to playing live, as Davis responded when Hilburn asked whether she took naturally to singing. "I was always very shy," she said, "But when I got on stage, all of a sudden, I didn't know what had inhibited me. I still remember the first time I played. It was on Halloween night in San Francisco. There was one guy who was stark naked and painted blue right in front of me. I was like, 'I'm not sure about this gig.'" Of course, Davis would have no such worries on *The Midnight Special*.

episode

AIRED:
FEBRUARY 6, 1981

44

HOST: Lynda Carter

FEATURING: Charles Grodin profile, Gail Davies, Devo, Robert Hilburn interview with Devo, T.G. Sheppard

Lynda Carter

osted by the lovely Lynda Carter, previously known as television's "Wonder Woman," this version of *The Midnight Special* featured more talk and less rock than virtually any other episode. Carter, having recorded an album of songs called *Portrait* after *Wonder Woman* was canceled in 1979, was also pursuing work as a Vegas nightclub act. Violating that cardinal rule about actors not singing, Carter offered several numbers on this show, including "Last Song" and "Tumble Down Love."

Actor Charles Grodin, who played the doctor in 1968's *Rosemary's Baby*, was profiled by Albert Brooks on this show. Grodin would go on to star in 1978's *Heaven Can Wait* and win an Emmy for writing *The Paul Simon Special*. He was promoting two 1981 films, *The Great Muppet Caper* and *The Incredible Shrinking Woman*, and would go on to author three books, including one called It *Would Be So Nice If You Weren't Here*, and to host a popular and provocative talk show.

From a musical perspective, the focal point of the show was Devo, new-wave stars from Akron, Ohio, including college professors who formed the group on a dare. Their name was based on the tongue-in-cheek theory that human beings were in a state of genetic and cultural "devolution," but perhaps their success proved otherwise. "Whip It" provided one of new wave's sharpest images—the band dressed in yellow radiation suits and using upside-down flowerpots for hats—not to mention a defining sound, futuristic, robotic beats, a bubbling bass line, and punchy keyboards. Their influence would extend into the '90s, as alternative bands like Nirvana and Soundgarden started covering Devo tunes.

The other musical guest on this episode was country singer and Tennessee native T.G. Sheppard, who would soon hit the pop album charts for the first time with his *I Love 'Em All* album. In 1984 Sheppard would score a minor hit with "Make My Day," a duet with Clint Eastwood inspired by Eastwood's movie *Sudden Impact*.

Albert Brooks

Charles Grodin

Devo

T.G. Sheppard

episode

AIRED:
FEBRUARY 20, 1981

413

HOST: Marilu Henner

FEATURING: Michael O'Donoghue,
Peter Ustinov, Firefall,
Sir Douglas Quintet

The Midnight Special's focus continued to drift away from music during these last months, toward more of a variety-show format featuring sitcom stars and other actors. Marilu Henner epitomized this new approach when she hosted this episode, surrounded by more actors than bands. Known to the world as the only female taxi driver on the Emmy-winning "Taxi," Marilu Henner would introduce herself to the *Midnight Special* audience by saying, "Before we really get rolling, I just want you to know that it's a dollar for the first mile and ten cents for each block after that. And trunks and guitar cases are extra in my cab." But there weren't many guitar cases anywhere near the set this evening. The episode itself would prove to be a big show-business "love-in," as Henner talked affectionately about her "Taxi" co-stars—Judd Hirsch, Tony Danza, Danny DeVito—and they all raved about her.

Henner then raved about guest Michael O'Donoghue, describing him as "America's poet laureate of bad taste," who, "as head writer of the original *Saturday Night Live,* gleefully, and with malice aforethought, forced sex, violence, and vulgarity into millions of American homes."

PETER USTINOV

His bald head and demure look masking a reeling, twisted mind, O'Donoghue started offensive and stayed that way. "My sentiments are summed up best by a little love poem I'm working on now. It's entitled, 'Jesus May Love You, But I Think You're Garbage Wrapped In Skin,'" he said. Later Mr. Mike would give the television audience a guided tour of his cabinet of curious collectibles, including a statuette of a saluting Nazi woman and Christ on the cross in a bottle.

MARILU HENNER

In an altogether different vein, this show also featured an interview with award-winning actor Peter Ustinov, who won Oscars for best supporting actor in 1960 and 1964 for his roles in *Spartacus* and *Topkapi*, respectively. "The theater and movies are to me an intellectual and emotive sport," he said. "I think you need the same reactions as you do playing a match of some sort. At the end of a long or wearing performance you are covered in cold perspiration, even if it's a winter's night. It's exactly the same mental and physical effort and discipline as a sport."

With little live music save for the subpar Colorado band Firefall, the highlight of the show was Doug Sahm's Sir Douglas Quintet. Though Sahm had formed the outfit in 1964, their commercial success never matched their critical acclaim. They recorded infrequently, and with an ever rotating lineup. But Sahm managed to coerce original members Johnny Perez and Augie Meyers to rejoin in the early '80s, added his son, Shawn, on guitar, and released *Border Wave*—an album that arguably wouldn't have dented the pop chart if not for *The Midnight Special*. On this show they would play their biggest hits, 1969's hippie anthem "Mendocino," and "She's About a Mover" from 1965, as well as a cover of the Kinks tune "Who'll Be the Next in Line."

Firefall

episode 418

HOST: **Skip Stephenson and Byron Allen**

FEATURING: **Robert Urich, Cathy Moriarty, Creedence Clearwater Revival, Waylon Jennings, Yarbrough & Peoples**

Byron Allen

O n this day the music died, there also wasn't much music. Ironically, the show that helped revolutionize the relationship between television and rock & roll, popularizing dozens of bands in the process, went out with a bunch of sitcom stars, and few musicians. The last hosts of *The Midnight Special* wouldn't be Wolfman Jack or some other appropriate rock & roll icon, but comedians Skip Stephenson and Byron Allen, two of the hosts of TV's *Real People*.

Moreover, the featured stars weren't up-and-coming new wavers, or '70s favorites returning for a fond farewell, but actors Robert Urich and Cathy Moriarty. Urich, the star of *Soap*, *S.W.A.T.* and later *Spenser: For Hire*, was in his final days on *Vega$* at the time, and his acting abilities were praised by noted observers like Bart Braverman and Howard Cosell. The Bronx-born Moriarty, who starred opposite Robert DeNiro in *Raging Bull*, went on to a successful but low-key career as a character actress in films like *Neighbors*, *Kindergarten Cop* and *Soapdish*.

At least there was some music. Robert Hilburn interviewed country superstar Waylon Jennings, who made his eighth *Midnight Special* appearance. But while Jennings was on the charts again with *Leather and Lace*, an album recorded with his wife, Jessi Colter, he too was having more success with TV and film. His theme to TV's *Dukes of Hazzard* would be one of his last hits, and Jennings also appeared in *Urban Cowboy*.

An outside clip of a rare live appearance from John Fogerty made the evening memorable. Creedence Clearwater Revival had essentially broken up a decade earlier, reuniting only to play guitarist Tom Fogerty's 1980 wedding, but the band

Skip Stephenson

Cathy Moriarty

wanted to promote a live concert album, originally called *Live at Royal Albert Hall*. It was later renamed *The Concert* when Fantasy Records discovered that the wrong tape had been used, and that the album actually chronicled a 1970 performance from Oakland not London. The video footage aired on this episode corresponded with the album's content, as the group cruised through several of its classics, including "Proud Mary," "Green River" and the song that got it all started, "The Midnight Special." Creedence leader John Fogerty would keep a low profile for years, finally re-emerging in 1985 with a wildly successful solo album, *Centerfield*. Creedence Clearwater Revival was inducted into the Rock and Roll Hall of Fame in 1993.

Dallas soul duo Yarbrough & Peoples, who had been "discovered" by members of the Gap Band, would be the final live act on the last original *Midnight Special*. They would play two songs from their 1980 gold album, *The Two of Us:* "Easy Tonight" and ironically enough, their Top-20 hit "Don't Stop the Music." But the music did stop. Though old episodes of *The Midnight Special* would be rerun for the next several weeks, and the pilot episode appropriately reaired on May 1 as the series officially closed, the music stopped, after more than 400 episodes and almost nine highlight-filled years.

Waylon Jennings

Yarbrough & Peoples

Robert Urich

SONG INDEX

The Midnight Special was remarkable in many ways, but perhaps its most impressive statistic was its longevity. Literally, the show welcomed thousands of guests, who performed thousands more songs. Until now a proper accounting of every episode has not been available, but this song index exhaustively recounts every appearance in the show's nearly nine-year life span. From amazing—and sometimes incongruous—duos (Ray Charles and Sarah Vaughn; Dionne Warwick and Johnny Mathis; Tom Jones and Chuck Berry) to intriguing and amusing cover tunes (Jose Feliciano doing "Purple Haze;" The Pointer Sisters interpreting "Wang Dang Doodle"), The Midnight Special brought us magical moments.

In this list you'll see names you know: members of rock's elite as well as a bevy of familiar artists hailing from the land of R&B, folk, blues, jazz, bluegrass, country, soul, or a combination of any of these styles. You'll recognize many of the songs, and maybe they'll bring back memories of driving in a car on a warm summer day with the windows down singing at the top of your lungs. On the other side of the coin, you'll undoubtedly see a number of songs and artists you don't recall. But reach back into your memory because in their day, these performers were big. The names in this index, recognizable or not, are significant because they were all part of The Midnight Special, a show that celebrated and embodied the 1970s and one of the most vibrant periods in music history.

1972

Pilot, Episode 140, 171, 280, 423
HOST: JOHN DENVER
John Denver, "(Take Me Home) Country Roads," "Goodbye Again"
John Denver/Cass Elliot, "Leaving on a Jet Plane"
Linda Ronstadt, "Long Long Time," "The Fast One"
Argent, "Hold Your Head Up," "Tragedy"
The Isley Brothers, "Pop That Thang"
War, "Slippin' into Darkness"
Helen Reddy, "I Don't Know How to Love Him"
The Everly Brothers, "All I Have to Do Is Dream," "The Stories We Could Tell"
David Clayton-Thomas, "Yesterday's Music," "Nobody Calls Me Prophet"
Harry Chapin, "Taxi"

1973

Episode 1
HOST: HELEN REDDY
Helen Reddy, "I Am Woman"
Ike and Tina Turner, "I Can't Turn You Loose"
Curtis Mayfield, "Superfly"
Don McLean, "Dreidel"
Rare Earth, "We're Gonna Have a Good Time"
Helen Reddy, "Peaceful"
Kenny Rankin, "Comin' Down"
The Byrds, "Mr. Tambourine Man," "So You Want to Be a Rock 'n' Roll Star"
The Impressions, "Preacher Man"
Helen Reddy/Curtis Mayfield/The Impressions, "Amen"
Ike and Tina Turner, "With a Little Help from My Friends"
Don McLean, "If We Try"
Rare Earth, "I Just Want to Celebrate"
Helen Reddy, "Come On John"
George Carlin, comedy spot

Episode 2
HOST: JOHNNY RIVERS
Johnny Rivers, "Blue Suede Shoes"
Steely Dan, "Do It Again"
Paul Williams, "Out in the Country"
The Spinners, "Could It Be I'm Falling in Love"
From the movie *Deliverance*, "Dueling Banjos" (outside clip)
Merrilee Rush, "Start Again"
Albert Hammond, "It Never Rains in Southern California"
Wolfman Jack, "I Ain't Never Seen a White Man"
Johnny Rivers, "Rockin' Pneumonia-Boogie Woogie Flu"
Paul Williams, "I Won't Last a Day without You"
The Spinners, "I'll Be Around"
Albert Hammond, "If You Gotta Break Another Heart"
Merrilee Rush, "Comfort and Please You"
Steely Dan, "Reeling in the Years"
Johnny Rivers, "Got My Mojo Workin'"
The Ace Trucking Company, comedy spot

Episode 3
HOST: MAC DAVIS
Mac Davis, "Baby Don't Get Hooked on Me"
Billy Preston, "Blackbird"
The Doobie Brothers, "Jesus Is Just Alright"
Billy Paul, "Me and Mrs. Jones"
From the movie *Deliverance*, "Dueling Banjos" (outside clip)
Waylon Jennings, "You Can Have Her"
Joan Rivers, comedy spot
Billy Preston, "Georgia on My Mind," "That's the Way God Planned It"
Mac Davis, "I Believe in Music"
Billy Paul, "Brown Baby"
Mac Davis, "Dream Me Home"
The Doobie Brothers, "Listen to the Music"
Mac Davis, "Home," "Half and Half (Song for Sara)"

Episode 4
HOST: HARRY CHAPIN
Harry Chapin, "Sunday Morning Sunshine"
Blood, Sweat and Tears, "Rosemary"
Curtis Mayfield, "Freddie's Dead"
Kerrie Biddell, "Spirit in the Dark"
The Hollies, "Magic Woman Touch"
Timmy Thomas, "Why Can't We Live Together"
Harry Chapin, "Sniper"
The Hollies, "He Ain't Heavy, He's My Brother"
Curtis Mayfield, "Superfly"
Blood, Sweat and Tears, "Hip Pickles," "Snow Queen"
Harry Chapin, "Taxi"
The Committee, comedy spot

Episode 5
HOST: ANNE MURRAY
Anne Murray, "Snowbird"
Nitty Gritty Dirt Band, "Jambalaya"
Steve Martin, comedy spot
Don McLean, "Vincent"
The Association, "Along Comes Mary," "Crazy Songs and Loony Tunes"
Badfinger, "No Matter What"
Sam Neely, "Loving You Just Crossed My Mind"
Sonny Terry and Brownie McGhee, "People Get Ready"
Don McLean, "Dreidel"
Anne Murray/Steve Martin/Nitty Gritty Dirt Band, "Shuckin' the Corn"
Anne Murray, "Danny's Song"
Don McLean, "If We Try"
The Association, "Names, Tags, Numbers and Labels"
Badfinger, "Suitcase"
Sonny Terry and Brownie McGhee, "Walkin' My Blues Away"
Sam Neely, "Rosalie"
Anne Murray, "I Know"

Episode 6
HOST: PAUL WILLIAMS
Paul Williams, "Old Fashioned Love Song"
Sha Na Na, "Hound Dog," "Yakety Yak"
Seals & Crofts, "Hummingbird"
Edward Bear, "Last Song"
Loretta Lynn, "One's on the Way"
Ravi Shankar, "Tilak Shyam"
Paul Williams, "Drift Away"
Sha Na Na, "I Wonder Why"
Loretta Lynn, "Coal Miner's Daughter"
Seals & Crofts, "Summer Breeze"
Edward Bear, "Close Your Eyes"
Lakshmi Shankar, "Nata Nagara"
Paul Williams, "That's Enough for Me"

Episode 7
HOST: PAUL ANKA
Paul Anka, "Girl"
Bobby Darin, "If I Were a Carpenter," "Dream Lover," "Splish Splash," "Roll Over Beethoven"
Paul Anka, "Diana," "Puppy Love," "Lonely Boy," "You Are My Destiny," "My Home Town," "Goodnight My Love," "(All of a Sudden) My Heart Sings"
The Coasters, "Poison Ivy," "Charlie Brown," "Yakety Yak"
Tammy Wynette, "Kids Say the Darnedest Things"
The Edwin Hawkins Singers, "Oh Happy Day"
The Doobie Brothers, "Natural Thing"
George Jones, "What My Women Can't Do"
The Doobie Brothers, "Listen to the Music"
George Jones/Tammy Wynette, "Let's All Go Down to the River"
The Edwin Hawkins Singers, "New World"
Paul Anka, "Jubilation"
The Ace Trucking Company, comedy spot

Episode 8
HOST: LOU RAWLS
Lou Rawls, "A Natural Man"
The O'Jays, "Backstabbers"
From the movie *Deliverance*, "Dueling Banjos" (outside clip)
The Grass Roots, "Midnight Confession"
Honey Cone, "Want Ads"
Lou Rawls, "Memory Lane," "It Was a Very Good Year," "Old Folks"
Brewer & Shipley, "One Toke Over the Line"
The O'Jays, "Love Train"
George Burns, "Mr. Bojangles"
George Burns/Honey Cone, "You Made Me Love You"
The Grass Roots, "Love Is What You Make It"
From the movie *Deliverance*, "I'm My Own Grandpa" (outside clip)
Lou Rawls, "Dead End Street"
The Committee, comedy spot

Episode 9
HOST: RAY CHARLES
Ray Charles, "Eleanor Rigby"
Aretha Franklin, "A Brand New Me"
Ray Charles, "Georgia on My Mind"
Ray Charles/Aretha Franklin, "Takes Two to Tango"
The Earl Scruggs Revue, "T For Texas"
Raelets, "Shake"
Ray Charles, "I Can Make It Through the Days (But Oh Those Lonely Nights)"
The Earl Scruggs Revue, "Everybody Want to Go to Heaven"
Ray Charles, "What'd I Say"
Freemen and Murray, comedy spot

Episode 10, 328, 422
HOST: THE BEE GEES
The Bee Gees, "To Love Somebody"
Jerry Lee Lewis, "Whole Lotta Shakin' Goin' On"
Gladys Knight & the Pips, "Neither One of Us"
Frank Welker, comedy spot
Johnny Nash, "Stir It Up"
The Bee Gees, "Lonely Days"
Jim Weatherly, "You Are a Song"
The Bee Gees/Jerry Lee Lewis, medley: "Money," "Good Golly Miss Molly," "Long Tall Sally," "Jenny Jenny," "Tutti Fruitti," "Whole Lotta Shakin' Goin' On"
Skeeter Davis, "One Tin Soldier"
The Bee Gees, "I Saw a New Morning"

Gladys Knight & the Pips, "I Heard It Through the Grapevine"
The Bee Gees, medley: "New York Mining Disaster 1941," "I Started a Joke," "Massachusetts," "How Can You Mend a Broken Heart"
Johnny Nash, "I Can See Clearly Now"
Skeeter Davis, "End of the World"

Episode 11
HOST: BILL COSBY
Bill Cosby, "Ursulena (With Your Washing Machina)"
Ray Charles, "Early in the Morning"
Billy Preston, "Will It Go Round in Circles"
David Brenner, comedy spot
Steely Dan, "Reelin' in the Years"
Taj Mahal, "Sounder," "Cheraw"
Fanny, "All Mine"
Waylon Jennings, "Lovin' Her Was Easier," "Good Time," "Charlie's Got the Blues," "Only Daddy," "That'll Walk the Line"
Bill Cosby, "I've Got to Be Strong"
Billy Preston, "Outa-Space"
Taj Mahal, "Texas Woman Blues"
Fanny, "Last Night I Had a Dream"
Bill Cosby, "I Lost My Baby At the Dance Last Night"

Episode 12
HOST: DOC SEVERINSEN
Doc Severinsen, "I Just Want to Celebrate Celebrate"
Dobie Gray, "Drift Away"
Vicki Lawrence, "The Nights the Lights Went Out in Georgia"
Jerry Butler, "Western Union Man," "Only the Strong Survive"
Country Joe McDonald, "Couleene Anne"
Hoyt Axton, "Jambalaya"
Doc Severinsen/Henry Mancini, "Brothers Go to Mothers"
Not Cut of Friends, "Indian Warrior"
Jerry Butler, "Ain't Understanding Mellow"
Doc Severinsen, "Last Tango in Paris," "Does Anybody Know What Time It Is," "Introduction," "Twenty-Five or Six to Four," "Beginnings"
Country Joe McDonald, "Hold On It's Coming"
Hoyt Axton, "Less Than the Song"
Dobie Gray, "In Crowd"

Episode 13, 293
HOST: JERRY LEE LEWIS
Jerry Lee Lewis, "Great Balls of Fire," "High School Confidential," "Drinking Wine Spo Dee O'Dee," "Cold Cold Heart"
Chubby Checker, "The Twist," "Huckle Buck"
Lloyd Price, "Stagger Lee," "Where Were You on My Wedding Day"
Del Shannon, "Runaway," "Keep Searchin'"
Little Anthony, "I'm Alright," "Tears on My Pillow"
The Shirelles, "Soldier Boy," "Tonight's the Night"
Freddie Cannon, "Tallahassee Lassie," "Way Down Yonder in New Orleans"
Jerry Lee Lewis/Linda Gail Lewis, "Roll Over Beethoven"
The Penguins, "Earth Angel"
The Ronettes, "Be My Baby," "Walkin' in the Rain"
Del Vikings, "Come Go with Me"
Bobby Day, "Rockin' Robin"

Episode 14
Host: Johnny Nash

Johnny Nash, "Stir It Up"
Gladys Knight & the Pips, "If I Were Your Woman"
The Raspberries, "I Wanna Be with You"
Chi Coltrane, "Thunder and Lightning"
Kenny Rankin, "You Are the Sunshine of My Life"
Johnny Nash, "Groovy Feeling"
Tom T. Hall, "The Year That Clayton Delaney Died"
Gladys Knight & the Pips, "Neither One of Us"
Johnny Nash, "I Can See Clearly Now"
The Raspberries, "Let's Pretend"
Kenny Rankin, "In the Name of Love"
Chi Coltrane, "You Were My Friend"
Tom T. Hall, "Old Dogs, Children and Watermelon"
Johnny Nash, "Merry-Go-Round"
Freemen and Murray, comedy spot
Andrew Johnson, comedy spot

Episode 15
Host: Burns and Schreiber

The Hollies, "Long Cool Woman in a Black Dress"
The O'Jays, "Love Train"
Mark Almond, "What Am I Living For"
The Crusaders, "Put It Where You Want It"
The Incredible String Band, "Black Jack Davy"
Ronnie Dyson, "One Man Band"
Mark Almond, "Just Another Road Song"
The Incredible String Band, "Old Buccaneer"
The Crusaders, "Don't Let It Get You Down"
Mark Almond, "The City"
Kenny Colman, "Last Tango in Paris"
Burns and Schreiber, comedy spot
Steve Martin, comedy spot

Episode 16
Host: Chubby Checker

Chubby Checker, "Let's Twist Again"
Danny & the Juniors, "At the Hop"
Little Anthony & the Imperials, "Going Out of My Head"
The Skyliners, "This I Swear"
Lloyd Price, "Personality"
The Shirelles, "Baby It's You"
Jimmy Clayton, "Just a Dream"
Chubby Checker, "Pony Time"
Ben E. King, "Spanish Harlem"
Danny & the Juniors, "Rock and Roll Is Here to Stay"
The Ronettes, "Baby I Love You," "Do I Love You"
Lloyd Price/The Skyliners, "I'm Gonna Get Married"
Chubby Checker, "Limbo Rock"
Little Anthony & the Imperials, "Two Kinds of People in the World"
The Shirelles, "Will You Still Love Me Tomorrow"
The Skyliners, "Since I Don't Have You"
Ben E. King, "Stand by Me"
Chubby Checker, "Slow Twistin'"

Episode 17
Host: Gladys Knight & the Pips

Gladys Knight & the Pips, "Friendship Train"
Dr. John, "Right Place, Wrong Time"
The Staple Singers, "We the People"
John Stewart, "Road Away"
Gladys Knight & the Pips, "Daddy Could Swear I Declare"
Skylark, "Wildflower"
Gladys Knight & the Pips, "I Don't Want to Do Wrong"
Dr. John, "Such a Night"
The Staple Singers, "Respect Yourself"

John Stewart, "Chilly Winds"
Skylark, "Woodstock"
Gladys Knight & the Pips, "Neither One of Us"
Robert Klein, comedy spot

Episode 18
Host: Paul Williams

Paul Williams, "My Love and I"
Slade, "Gudbuy T'Jane"
The Stylistics, "Betcha By Golly, Wow"
Argent, "God Gave Rock and Roll to You"
The Statler Brothers, "Flowers on the Wall"
Gunhill Road, "Back When My Half Was Short"
Paul Williams, "Let Me Be the One"
Stylistics, "Break Up to Make Up"
Sydney Jordan, "Sunday Morning Sunrise"
Argent, "Hold Your Head Up"
The Statler Brothers, "The Class of '57"
Slade, "Cum On Feel the Noize"
Gunhill Road, "Mr. Keyboard"
Paul Williams, "We've Only Just Begun," "Rainy Days and Mondays"
The Stylistics, "I'm Stone in Love with You"
Argent, "It's Only Money Part 2"
Paul Williams, "I Never Had It So Good"

Episode 19
Host: Curtis Mayfield

Curtis Mayfield, "Superfly"
Canned Heat, "Let's Work Together"
The Spinners, "One of a Kind Love Affair"
Jose Feliciano, "Simple Song"
Tufano-Giammarese, "Music Everywhere"
Ravi Shankar, "Ahir Bhairav"
Canned Heat, "Harley Davidson Blues"
Jose Feliciano, "Compartments," "Light My Fire"
The Spinners, "I'll Be Around," "Could It Be I'm Falling in Love"
Curtis Mayfield, "If I Were Only a Child Again"
Leroy Hutson, "Love Oh Love"
Tufano-Giammarese, "I'm a Loser"
Curtis Mayfield, "Back to the World"
Lakshmi Shankar, "A Bhajan"
Canned Heat, "Woodstock Boogie"

Episode 20
Host: Jim Croce

Jim Croce, "Operator"
Little Anthony & the Imperials, "Dance to the Music"
Savoy Brown, "Tell Mama"
Bobby Womack, "It's All Over Now"
Shawn Phillips, "Anello (Where Are You)"
Barbara Fairchild, "Teddy Bear"
Jim Croce, "Roller Derby Queen"
Wishbone Ash, "Jailbait"
Bobby Womack, "Nobody Wants You When You're Down and Out"
Savoy Brown, "Coming Down Your Way"
Shawn Phillips, "America"
Jim Croce, "You Don't Mess with Jim," "Speedball Tucker," "Bad Bad Leroy Brown"
Little Anthony & the Imperials, "La La La at the End"
Jim Croce, "Careful Man"

Episode 21
Host: The Bee Gees

The Bee Gees, "I Gotta Get a Message to You"
Wilson Pickett, "In the Midnight Hour"
Steve Miller Band, "Living in the U.S.A."
John Kay, "I'm Movin' On"
Jimmie Spheeris, "The Original Tap Dancing Kid"
The Bee Gees, "Alexander's Rag Time Band"
The Bee Gees/Wilson Pickett, "Hey Jude"
Maxine Weldon, "Johnny One Time"
John Kay, "Moonshine (Friend of Mine)"
The Bee Gees, "Run to Me"
Wilson Pickett, "Mr. Magic Man"
The Bee Gees, "Morning of My Life," "Holiday," "Let There Be Love," "My World"
Steve Miller Band, "Shu Ba Da Du Ma Ma Ma Ma"
Jimmie Spheeris, "Beautiful News"
The Bee Gees, "Wouldn't I Be Someone"
The Muledeer and Moondoog Medicine Show

Episode 22
Host: Paul Williams

Paul Williams, "Someday Man"
Electric Light Orchestra, "Roll Over Beethoven"
Kris Kristofferson, "Loving Her Was Easier"
Commander Cody and His Lost Planet Airmen, "Smoke, Smoke, Smoke (That Cigarette)"
Rita Coolidge, "I'll Be Your Baby"
King Harvest, "Dancing in the Moonlight"
Paul Williams, "That's What Friends Are For"
Kris Kristofferson/Rita Coolidge, "I Never Had It So Good"
Commander Coy and His Lost Planet Airmen, "Jailhouse Rock"
Brewer & Shipley, "Black Sky"
Kris Kristofferson, "Out of Mind, Out of Sight"
Electric Light Orchestra, "Kuiama"
Rita Coolidge, "My Crew"
King Harvest, "A Little Bit Like Magic"
Brewer & Shipley, "Yankee Lady"
Paul Williams/Kris Kristofferson/Rita Coolidge, "Me and Bobby McGee"
Paul Williams, "Look What I Found"

Episode 23
Host: Jose Feliciano

Jose Feliciano, "California Dreamin'"
Johnny Winter, "Jumpin' Jack Flash"
The Staple Signers, "Oh La De Da"
Savoy Brown, "Shot in the Head"
Tower of Power, "So Very Hard to Go"
Stories, "Brother Louie"
Jose Feliciano, "Compartments"
Johnny Winter, "Johnny B. Goode"
The Staple Singers, "Be What You Are"
Tower of Power, "What Is Hip?"
Jose Feliciano, "Papa Was a Rolling Stone"
Johnny Winter, "Rock and Roll"
Savoy Brown, "Jack the Toad"
Stories, "Top of the City"

Episode 24
Host: Smokey Robinson

Smokey Robinson, "Want to Know My Mind"
Rare Earth, "Hey Big Brother"
The Stylistics, "You'll Never Get to Heaven"
Bonnie Bramlett, "Good Vibrations"
Martin and Finley, "It's Another Sunder"
Rare Earth, "Big John Is My Name"
Smokey Robinson, "Sweet Harmony"
The Miracles, "What Is Heart Good For"
Bonnie Bramlett, "Celebrate Life"

The Miracles, "Tears of a Clown"
The Stylistics, "You Are Everything"
Rare Earth, "Hum Along and Dance"
The Miracles, "Don't Let It End (Till You Let It Begin)"
Smokey Robinson, "You Are the Sunshine of My Life"

Episode 25
Host: Joan Baez

Joan Baez, "The Night They Drove Old Dixie Down"
Wilson Pickett, "Don't Let the Green Grass Fool You"
Black Oak Arkansas, "Fever in My Mind"
Bloodstone, "Natural High"
Steve Goodman, "Somebody's Else's Troubles"
Black Oak Arkansas, "Dance to the Music Tonight"
The Pointer Sisters, "Cloudburst"
Joan Baez, "Joe Hill"
Mimi Farina, "In the Quiet Morning"
Wilson Pickett, "International Playboy"
The Pointer Sisters, "Naked Foot"
Joan Baez/Mimi Farina, "Best of Friends"
Black Oak Arkansas, "Hot and Nasty"
Joan Baez, "Love Song to a Stranger," "Prison Trilogy"
Bloodstone, "Never Let You Go"
Steve Goodman, "Would You Like to Learn to Dance"
Joan Baez, "Rider Pass By"

Episode 26
Host: Dionne Warwick

Dionne Warwick, "I Say a Little Prayer"
Kenny Rogers and The First Edition, "Coming Through the Rye"
Johnny Mathis, "Killing Me Softly with Her Song"
Dionne Warwick/Johnny Mathis, "My Love"
Malo, "Momotombo"
Kenny Rogers and The First Edition, "Something's Burning"
Leo Kottke, "Vaseline Machine Gun #2"
Johnny Mathis, "To the Ends of the Earth"
Bud Brisbois, "Miss Ma-Tazz"
Kenny Rogers and The First Edition, "Lena Lookey"
Malo, "Hala"
Bud Brisbois, "Baby Hand Your Love on Me""
Alan Bursky, comedy spot
Dionne Warwick, medley of Burt Bachrach hits

Episode 27
Host: Al Green

Al Green, "Let's Stay Together"
Foghat, "She's Gone"
Bobby Womack, "Nobody Wants You When You're Down and Out"
Livingston Taylor, "Good Friends"
The Stylistics, "Point of No Return"
Al Green, "Tired of Being Alone"
Ramblin' Jack Elliott, "San Francisco Bay Blues"
The Stylistics, "I'm Stone in Love with You"
Foghat, "I Just Want to Make Love to You"
Bobby Womack, "Harry Hippie"
Al Green, "Call Me"
Livingston Taylor, "Over the Rainbow"
The Stylistics, "Stop, Look and Listen"
Al Green, "How Can You Mend a Broken Heart," "Here I Am"

Episode 28
HOST: THE BEE GEES

The Bee Gees, "New York Mining Disaster 1941"
Herman's Hermits, "I'm Henry the VIII I Am"
Gerry and the Pacemakers, "How Do You Do," "I Like It"
Wayne Fontana and the Mindbenders, "Game of Love"
The Hollies, "Long Cool Woman in a Black Dress"
The Searchers, "Needles and Pins"
Billy J. Kramer and the Dakotas, "Little Children"
Gerry and the Pacemakers, "Ferry Cross the Mersey"
Herman's Hermits, "Mrs. Brown, You've Got a Lovely Daughter"
Wayne Fontana and the Mindbenders, "A Groovy Kind of Love"
The Hollies, "He Ain't Heavy, He's My Brother"
The Bee Gees, "Turn of the Century"
The Searchers, "Sweets for My Sweet"
Herman's Hermits, "There's a Kind of Hush"
Gerry and the Pacemakers, "Don't Let the Sun Catch You Crying"
The Bee Gees, "I Can't See Nobody"
The Searchers, "Love Potion #9"

Episode 29
HOST: RICHARD PRYOR

Electric Light Orchestra, "Roll Over Beethoven"
Doug Kershaw, "Fisherman's Luck"
Joe Walsh, "Tend My Garden"
Albert King, "Don't Burn Down the Bridge"
Melissa Manchester, "If It Feels Good"
Joe Hicks, "Train of Thought"
Melissa Manchester, "Easy"
Doug Kershaw, "Diggy Diggy Lo"
Joe Walsh, "Rocky Mountain Way"
Albert King, "I'll Play the Blues For You"
Doug Kershaw, "Louisiana Man"

Episode 30
HOSTS: LORETTA LYNN and MARTY ROBBINS

Loretta Lynn/Marty Robbins, "The Midnight Special"
Loretta Lynn, "One's on the Way"
Marty Robbins, "Don't Worry 'Bout Me"
George Jones/Tammy Wynette, "We're Gonna Hold On"
Tanya Tucker, "Blood Red and Goin' Down"
The Earl Scruggs Revue, "Caroline Boogie"
Tom T. Hall, "Spokane Motel Blues"
Loretta Lynn/Marty Robbins, "Singin' the Blues"
Tammy Wynette, "Stand by Your Man"
Charlie Rich, "Behind Closed Doors"
Marty Robbins, "A White Sport Coat," "Devil Woman," "El Paso"
Don Gibson, "Oh Lonesome Me"
George Jones, "The Race Is One"
Loretta Lynn, "Love Is the Foundation"
Conway Twitty, "You've Never Been So Far"
Loretta Lynn/Conway Twitty, "Louisiana Woman, Mississippi Man"
Johnny Paycheck, "She's All I Got"
Johnny Rodriguez, "Bosier City Backyard Blues"
Tanya Tucker, "Delta Dawn"

Episode 31
HOST: BILLY PRESTON

Billy Preston, "Will It Go Round in Circles"
Steely Dan, "Reeling in the Years"
Bo Diddley, "Bo Diddley"
Maureen McGovern, "The Morning After"
Buddy Miles, "Them Changes"
Billy Preston/Buddy Miles, "My Sweet Lord"
Ned Doheny, "I Can Dream"
Gladstone, "Natural Inclination"
Billy Preston, "All Spaced Out"
Steely Dan, "Show Biz Kids"
Bo Diddley, "Bo Diddley-Itis"
Billy Preston, "Music's My Life"
Buddy Miles, "Thinking of You"
Steely Dan, "My Old School"
Billy Preston, "That's the Way God Planned It"

Episode 32
HOST: MAC DAVIS

Mac Davis, "Something's Burning"
The Edgar Winter Group, "Keep Playing That Rock and Roll"
Harold Melvin & the Blue Notes, "The Love I Lost"
Mark Almond, "Neighborhood Man"
Chuck Berry, "Roll Over Beethoven"
The Edgar Winter Group, "Frankenstein"
Mac Davis, "I'll Paint You a Song"
Chuck Berry, "Bio," "Carol"
Ravi Shankar, "Sindhi Bhairavi"
Mac Davis, "Naughty Girl"
The Edgar Winter Group, "Rock 'n' Roll Boogie Woogie Blues," "Hangin' Around"
Mac Davis, "Lonesomest Lonesome"
Mark Almond, "Get Yourself Together"
Mac Davis, "I Believe in Music"

Episode 33
HOST: CURTIS MAYFIELD

Sly & the Family Stone, "Everybody Is a Star"
Helen Reddy, "Delta Dawn"
Curtis Mayfield, "Future Shock"
Jim Croce, "I've Got a Name," "Bad Bad Leroy Brown"
War, "Gypsy Man"
Gladys Knight & the Pips, "Where Peaceful Waters Flow"
Wilson Pickett, "Get Me Back on Time Engine 9"
The Bee Gees, "Lonely Days"
Curtis Mayfield, "Back to the World"
Wilson Pickett, "Don't Knock My Love"
Natural Four, "Can This Be Real"
The Bee Gees, "Run to Me"
Curtis Mayfield, "Right On for the Darkness"

Episode 34
HOST: WILSON PICKETT

Wilson Pickett, "Land of 1000 Dances"
Canned Heat, "Dust My Broom"
The Chi-Lites, "Stoned Out of My Mind"
Brian Auger's Oblivion Express, "Whenever You're Ready"
Curtis Mayfield, "Freddie's Dead"
B.W. Stevenson, "My Maria"
Wilson Pickett, "Funky Broadway"
Brenda Patterson, "Dance with Me Henry"
Spooky Tooth, "Cotton Growing Man"
Canned Heat, "Lookin' for My Rainbow"
Wilson Pickett, "Never My Love"
Brian Auger's Oblivion Express, "Listen Here"
B.W. Stevenson, "Don't Go to Mexico"
The Chi-Lites, "Oh Girl"
Wilson Pickett, "In the Midnight Hour"

Episode 35
HOST: SEALS & CROFTS

Seals & Crofts, "Diamond Girl"
T. Rex, "Hot Love"
Arlo Guthrie, "Gypsy Davy"
Uriah Heep, "Stealin'"
Paul Butterfield's Better Days, "New Walkin' Blues"
Seals & Crofts, "Dust On My Saddle"
T. Rex, "Bang a Gong (Get It On)"
Arlo Guthrie, "Bling Blang"
Ramblin' Jack Elliot, "Talkin' Fishing Blues"
Uriah Heep, "Sweet Freedom"
Seals & Crofts, "We May Never Pass This Way Again"
Leo Kottke, "Bean Time"
Paul Butterfield's Better Days, "Broke My Baby's Heart"
Seals & Crofts, "Ruby Jean and Billie Lee," "Pop Goes the Weasel"

Episode 36
HOST: GLADYS KNIGHT & THE PIPS

Gladys Knight & the Pips, "Daddy Could Swear I Declare"
Focus, "Hocus Pocus"
Stories, "Mammy Blue"
B.B. King, "To Know You Is to Love You"
Gladys Knight & the Pips, "Heavy Makes You Happy"
Focus, "Sylvia"
Chris Smither, "Mail Order Mystics"
Earth, Wind & Fire, "Evil"
Gladys Knight/B.B. King, "The Thrill Is Gone"
B.B. King, "How Blue Can You Get"
Stories, "Broken Love"
Gladys Knight & the Pips, "Midnight Train to Georgia"
Focus, "House of the King"
Earth, Wind & Fire, "Power"
Wolfman Jack/Monda, "Ling Ting Tong"
Focus, "Focus III"

Episode 37
HOST: THE BEE GEES

The Bee Gees, "Massachusetts"
Chuck Berry, "Maybellene"
Lee Michaels, "Do You Know What I Mean"
King Crimson, "Lark's Tongues in Aspic Part 2"
The Bee Gees/Chuck Berry, "Reelin' and Rockin'," "Johnny B. Goode"
The Bee Gees, "Lay It on Me"
Monty Python's Flying Circus (outside clip)
Apple and Appleberry, "Landlord"
The Bee Gees, "Alive"
Lee Michaels, "Barefootin'"
Chuck Berry, "Sweet Little Sixteen"
The Bee Gees, "Bye Bye Blackbird"
King Crimson, "Easy Money"
Barbara Mason, "Yes I'm Ready"
Lee Michaels, "Same Old Song"
The Bee Gees, "Alone Again"

Episode 38
HOST: WAR

War, "Cisco Kid"
New York Dolls, "Trash"
Mott the Hoople, "All the Way from Memphis"
Danny O'Keefe, "Good Time Charlie's Got the Blues"
Climax Blues Band, "Shake Your Love"
War, "Me and Baby Brother"
Bachman-Turner Overdrive, "Hold Back the Water"
Mott the Hoople, "Rose"
War, "The World Is a Ghetto"
Climax Blues Band, "Constant"
Danny O'Keefe, "Angel Spread Your Wings"
Bachman-Turner Overdrive, "Gimme Your Money Please"
New York Dolls, "Personality Crisis"
Piper, "Bungle Rye"
War, "City Country City"

Episode 39
HOST: SLY & THE FAMILY STONE

Sly & the Family Stone, "Stand"
Mark Almond, "Get Yourself Together"
Melissa Manchester, "Oh Heaven How You've Changed Me"
Frankie Valli & the Four Seasons, medley of hits
Sly & the Family Stone, "Higher"
Freddy Weller, "The Perfect Stranger"
Mark Almond, "The City"
Sly & the Family Stone, "Thank You (Falettinme Be Mice Elf Agin)"
Atlee Yeager, "I Wanna Be Alone with You"
Frankie Valli & the Four Seasons, "Let's Hang On"
Freddy Weller, "The Roadmaster"
Little Sister, "I'm the One You're the One"
Frankie Valli & the Four Seasons, "The Scalawag Song"
Sly & the Family Stone, "If You Want Me to Stay," "Dance to the Music"

Episode 40
HOST: CHUCK BERRY

Chuck Berry, "Tulane"
The Edgar Winter Group, "Free Ride"
Johnny Taylor, "Who's Making Love"
Fleetwood Mac, "Miles Away"
Shawn Phillips, "Technotronic Lad"
Edgar Winter, "Dying to Live"
Chuck Berry, "Bio"
Muddy Waters, "Can't Get No Grindin'"
The Edgar Winter Group/Rick Derringer, "Rock and Roll Hootchie Koo"
Chuck Berry, "School Days," "Johnny B. Goode," "Got It and Gone"
Shawn Phillips, "Spaceman"
Muddy Waters, "Got My Mojo Working"
Fleetwood Mac, "Believe Me"
Johnny Taylor, "I Believe in You"
Chuck Berry, "Rock and Roll Music"

Episode 41
HOST: JERRY LEE LEWIS

Jerry Lee Lewis, "Breathless"
Ike and Tina Turner, "River Deep Mountain High"
Flash, "Dead Ahead"
B.B. King, "Hummingbird"
Ballin' Jack, "This Song"
Jerry Lee Lewis, "Hold On I'm Coming"
Ike and Tina Turner, "Nutbush City Limits"
Jerry Lee Lewis, "Chantilly Lace"
B.B. King, "Why I Sing the Blues"
Dalton & Dubarri, "Any Other Man But Me"
Flash, "Psychosync"
Jerry Lee Lewis/Linda Gail Lewis, "Jackson"
Jerry Lee Lewis, "Lonely Weekends," "Silver Threads Among the Gold"
Dalton & Dubarri, "Take a Change"
Jerry Lee Lewis, "Whole Lotta Shakin' Goin' On"

Episode 42, 82, 169, 231
HOST: DAVID BOWIE

David Bowie, medley: "Sorrow," "1984," "You Didn't Hear It from Me," "1984" David Bowie, "Sorrow"
Carmen, "Bulerias"
David Bowie, "Everything's Alright," "Space Oddity," "I Can't Explain"
Marianne Faithfull, "As Tears Go By"
David Bowie, "Time"
The Troggs, "Wild Thing"
Carmen, "Bullfight"
David Bowie, "Jean Genie"

Marianne Faithfull, "20th Century Blues"
The Troggs, "I Can't Control Myself," "Strange Movies"
David Bowie/Marianne Faithfull, "I Got You Babe"
David Bowie, "1984"

Episode 43
Host: Peter Noone

Gilbert O'Sullivan, "Ooh Baby," "Get Down"
The Bee Gees, "Bad Bad Dreams," "Don't Wanna Be the One"
Peter Noone/Herman's Hermits, "No Milk Today," "There's a Kind of Hush"
Electric Light Orchestra, "Showdown," "Ma-Ma-Ma Belle"
Gilbert O'Sullivan, "Who Knows Perhaps Maybe"
Peter Noone, "Last Blues Song"
David Essex, "Rock On"
Manfred Mann's Earth Band, "Joy Bringer"
Robin Trower, "Lady Love," "Man of the World"
David Essex, "Lamplight"
Manfred Mann's Earth Band, "In the Beginning"
Peter Noone, "Getting Over You," "Oh You Pretty Thing"

Episode 44
Host: Procol Harum

Procol Harum, "Conquistador"
Humble Pie, "Oh La De Da"
Alvin Lee/Mylon Lefevre, "Rockin' Till the Sun Goes Down"
Procol Harum, "Whiter Shade of Pale," "Grand Hotel"
Humble Pie, "I Don't Need No Doctor"
Alvin Lee/Mylon Lefevre, "Carry My Load"
Procol Harum, "Fires Which Burn Brightly," "Drunk Again"
Humble Pie, "30 Days in the Hole"
Steeleye Span, "Cam Ye O-er Frae France"
Alvin Lee/Mylon Lefevre, "The World Is Changing"
Procol Harum, "T.V. Caesar," "Rule Brittania"

Episode 45
Host: The Four Tops

The Four Tops, "Can't Help Myself"
Dr. Hook & the Medicine Show, "The Cover of Rolling Stone"
Mott the Hoople, "Drivin' Sister"
John Mayall, "California Campground"
Todd Rundgren, "Black Maria"
The Four Tops, "Love Music," "Reach Out I'll Be There," "Standing in the Shadows of Love," "Love Music"
Dr. Hook & the Medicine Show, "Life Ain't Easy"
Shawn Phillips, "Baby's Breakthrough"
Todd Rundgren, "Hello It's Me"
John Mayall, "Room to Move"
Mott the Hoople, "Hymn for the Dudes"
The Four Tops, "Sweet Understanding Love"
Dr. Hook & the Medicine Show, "Insane Asylum"
The Four Tops, "Keeper of the Castle," "One Woman Man"

Episode 46, 72
Host: Loggins & Messina

Loggins & Messina, "My Music," "Danny's Song," "Your Mama Don't Dance," "You Need a Man/Coming to You," "Sailin' the Wind"
Billy Preston, "Space Race," "How Long Has the Train Been Gone," "I'm So Tired"
The Guess Who, "Albert Flasher," "Undun," "Straighten Out," "Star Baby," "Glamour Boy"
Leo Kottke, "Vaseline Machine Gun #2"
Martin Mull, comedy spot

Episode 47
Host: Jose Feliciano

Jose Feliciano, "Purple Haze"
Sha Na Na, "Get a Job," "Sh-Boom"
Linda Ronstadt, "You're No Good"
Clarence Carter, "I'm the Midnight Special"
Roger McGuinn, "Mr. Spaceman"
Jose Feliciano, "I Like What You Give"
Sha Na Na, "Tossin' and Turnin'"
Freshflavor with Richie Havens, "Prometheus Bound"
Linda Ronstadt, "Love Has No Pride"
Jose Feliciano, "I Want to Learn a Love Song"
Roger McGuinn, "Sweet Mary"
Clarence Carter, "Slip Away"
Jose Feliciano, "Susie-Q," "The Midnight Special"

Episode 48
Host: Marty Robbins

Marty Robbins, "Gotta Travel On"
Tanya Tucker, "Jamestown Ferry"
Johnny Rodriguez, "Pass Me By"
Doug Kershaw, "Mama's Got the Know How"
Marty Robbins, "20th Century Drifter"
Barbara Mandrell, "Show Me"
Bobby Bare, "Detroit City"
Marty Robbins, "(Take Me Home) Country Roads"
Tanya Tucker, "What's Your Mama's Name"
Charlie Rich, "Break-Up (medley)"
Doug Kershaw, "Cajun Joe (Bully of the Bayou)"
Barbara Mandrell, "The Midnight Oil"
Barbi Benton, "Top of the World"
Charlie Rich, "Behind Closed Doors"
Marty Robbins, "Beyond the Reef"
Marty Robbins/Barbi Benton, "Help Me Make It Through the Night"
Johnny Rodriguez, "Bosier City Backyard Blues"
Bobby Bare, "The Mermaid"
Marty Robbins, "Cool Water," "Tumbling Tumbleweeds," "El Paso"
Marty Robbins, "My Woman My Woman My Wife"

Episode 49, 73
Host: Wolfman Jack (Million Sellers)

Loggins & Messina, "Your Mama Don't Dance"
Billy Preston, "Will It Go Round in Circles"
Stories, "Brother Louie"
Gladys Knight & the Pips, "Midnight Train to Georgia"
Edgar Winter, "Frankenstein"
The Spinners, "Could It Be I'm Falling in Love"
Curtis Mayfield, "Superfly"
From the movie Deliverance, "Dueling Banjos" (outside clip)
Jim Croce, "Bad Bad Leroy Brown"
Dr. Hook & the Medicine Show, "The Cover of Rolling Stone"
Gilbert O'Sullivan, "Get Down"
Al Green, "Call Me (Come Back Home)"
Charlie Rich, "Behind Closed Doors"
The O'Jays, "Love Train"
Dobie Gray, "Drift Away"
Edward Bear, "Last Song"

Episode 50
Host: Dr. Hook & the Medicine Show

Dr. Hook & the Medicine Show, "Please Mrs. Avery (Stoned)," "Tell Her Goodbye"
Jo Jo Gunne, "Run on Out to the Night"
The Spinners, "Life Ain't So Easy"
Canned Heat, "One More River to Cross"
Leo Sayer, "Everything's Gonna Be Alright"
El Chicano, "Tell Her She's Lovely"
Dr. Hook & the Medicine Show, "Roland the Roadie and Gertrude the Groupie"
Jo Jo Gunne, "I Wanna Love You"

Livingstone Taylor, "Somewhere Over the Rainbow"
The Spinners, "How Could I Let You Get Away"
Dr. Hook & the Medicine Show, "The Loneliest People in the World"
Leo Sayer, "I Won't Let the Show Go On"
Dr. Hook & the Medicine Show, "The Soup Stone"
Canned Heat, Fats Domino medley

Episode 51
Host: Smokey Robinson

Smokey Robinson, "Show and Tell"
Eddie Kendricks, "Keep On Truckin'"
Paul Butterfield's Better Days, "Take Your Pleasure Where You Can Find It"
Ann Peebles, "I Can't Stand the Rain"
Edwin Starr, "Ain't It Hell"
Smokey Robinson, "Tracks of My Tears," "Tears of a Clown," "Dum De Dum De La"
Grin, "Come This Beggar's Day"
Johnny Taylor, "It's Cheaper to Keep Her"
Paul Butterfield's Better Days, "Meet Me in the Bar Room"
Smokey Robinson, "Someone"
Eddie Kendricks, "Boogie Down Baby"
Edwin Star, "War"
Grin, "You're the Wait I've Been Waiting For"
Johnnie Taylor, "We're Getting Careless with Our Love Affair"

1974

Episode 52
Host: Steve Miller

Steve Miller Band, "The Joker"
James Gang, "It Must Be Love"
Brownsville Station, "Smokin' in the Boys Room"
James Cotton Band, "Rocket 88"
Tim Buckley, "Do You Ever Think of Me"
Steve Miller Band, "Let's Slip Away"
Genesis, "This Is Your Fate"
James Cotton/Steve Miller, "Big Boss Man"
Steve Miller Band, "Fly Like an Eagle"
Genesis, "This Is My Song"
Tim Buckley, "Honey Man"
Steve Miller Band, "Sugar Baby"

Episode 53
Host: Helen Reddy

Helen Reddy, "Leave Me Alone"
Ike and Tina Turner, "Land of 1000 Dances"
Rare Earth, "Big John Is My Name"
Curtis Mayfield, "If I Were a Child Again"
Kenny Rankin, "Why Do Fools Fall in Love"
Helen Reddy, "Delta Dawn"
The Impressions, "Preacher Man"
Ike and Tina Turner, "It's Gonna Work Out Fine"
Rare Earth, "Born to Wander"
Franklin Ajaye, "Spot"
Helen Reddy, "Don't Mess with a Woman"
Rare Earth, "Don't Fight It"
Kenny Rankin, "Haven't We Met"
Helen Reddy, "Time," "I Am Woman"

Episode 54
Host: Ike and Tina Turner

Ike and Tina Turner, "City Girl Country Boy"
Flash Cadillac & the Continental Kids, "Dancin' on a Saturday Night"
Electric Light Orchestra, "Showdown"

Jose Feliciano, "I Like What You Give"
Mandrill, "Git It All"
Todd Rundgren, "Couldn't I Just Tell You"
Ike and Tina Turner, "With a Little Help from My Friends"
David Essex, "Rock On"
Flash Cadillac & the Continental Kids, "Muleskinner Blues"
Electric Light Orchestra, "Bluebird Is Dead"
Todd Rundgren, "The Dream Goes On Forever"
Ike and Tina Turner, "Proud Mary"
Jose Feliciano, "Blame It On the Sun"
David Essex, "Streetfight"
Ike and Tina Turner's, "I Smell Trouble"

Episode 55
Host: Roy Orbison

Roy Orbison, "Pretty Woman," "Dream Baby," "Running Scared," "Only the Lonely"
The Drifters, "Up on the Roof," "Save the Last Dance For Me"
Del Shannon, "Runaway," "Hats Off to Larry," "Keep Searching"
Jackie Wilson, "(Your Love Keeps Liftin' Me) Higher and Higher," "Lonely Teardrops," "That's Why"
Bobby Vee, "Take Good Care of My Baby," "The Night Has a Thousand Eyes," "Devil or Angel"
Lloyd Price, "Personality," "Stagger Lee"
Duane Eddy, "Rebel Rouser," "Ramrod,"
Tommy Roe, "Sheila," "Everybody," "Jam Up and Jelly Tight"

Episode 56
Host: Gordon Lightfoot

Gordon Lightfoot, "The List"
The James Gang, "Standing in the Rain"
The Guess Who, "Share the Land"
Redbone, "Come and Get Your Love"
Maria Muldaur, "Midnight at the Oasis"
Gordon Lightfoot, "If You Could Read My Mind"
The Guess Who, "Star Baby"
Ravi Shankar, "Raga Jogiya"
Maria Muldaur, "Don't You Feel My Leg"
The James Gang, "The Devil Is Singing Our Song"
Gordon Lightfoot, "Don Quixote," "Affair on Eighth Avenue"
Byron MacGregor, "Americans"
Redbone, "Maggie"
Gordon Lightfoot, "High and Dry," "Sundown"

Episode 57
Host: Dr. Hook & the Medicine Show

Dr. Hook & the Medicine Show, "Ever Come"
The Stylistics, "Rockin' Roll Baby"
Foghat, "Home in My Hands"
Peter Yarrow, "Old Father Time"
Al Wilson, "Show and Tell"
Dr. Hook & the Medicine Show, "The Yodel," "Marie Lavaux"
Foghat, "Honey Hush"
Melissa Manchester, "Never Never Land"
Peter Yarrow, "Jelly Jelly"
Dr. Hook & the Medicine Show, "Cops and Robbers"
Uncle Crusty, "Badly Bent"
Al Wilson, "Touch and Go"
The Stylistics, "You Make Me Feel Brand New"

Episode 58
Host: Gladys Knight & the Pips

Gladys Knight & the Pips, "I've Got to Use My Imagination"
Curtis Mayfield, "Right On for the Darkness"
Spooky Tooth, "I Am the Walrus"
Freshflavor with Richie Havens, "Prometheus Bound"
Jobriath, "I'm a Man"
Gladys Knight & the Pips, "Best Thing That Ever Happened to Me"
Jim Weatherly, "Loving You Is Just an Old Habit"
Les Variations, "Moroccan Roll"
Curtis Mayfield, "To Be Invisible"
Jobriath, "Rock of Ages"
Gladys Knight & the Pips, "On and On"
Les Variations, "I Don't Know Why"
Gladys Knight & the Pips, "Midnight Train to Georgia"
Jim Weatherly, "Same Old Song and Dance"
Freshflavor with Richie Havens, "Loser"

Episode 59
Host: The Pointer Sisters

The Pointer Sisters, "Yes We Can Can"
Focus, "Hocus Pocus"
Billy Paul, "Thanks for Saving My Life"
Dan Hicks, "There Ain't a Guy That Wouldn't Like to Be in My Shoes"
The Crusaders, "Lay It on the Line"
The Strawbs, "Hero and Heroine"
The Pointer Sisters, "Little Pony"
The Butts Band, "Love Your Brother"
Billy Paul, "The Whole Town's Talking"
Focus, "House of the King"
The Strawbs, "Round and Round"
The Butts Band, "Kansas City"
The Pointer Sisters/Wolfman Jack, "Salt Peanuts"
The Pointer Sisters, "Bangin' on the Pipes," "Steam Heat"
Dan Hicks, "Hummin' to Myself"
Bonnie Pointer, "Black Coffee"
The Pointer Sisters, "Wang Dang Doodle"

Episode 60
Host: Bill Withers

Bill Withers, "Ain't No Sunshine"
Rory Gallagher, "Tattoo'd Lady"
Bobby Womack, "Lookin' for a Love"
Melissa Manchester, "Bright Eyes"
Montrose, "Rock the Nation"
Buddy Miles, "You Really Got Me"
Bill Withers, "The Same Love That Made Me Laugh"
Cliff de Young, "My Sweet Lady"
Bobby Womack, "Nobody Wants You When You're Down and Out"
Melissa Manchester, "He Is the One"
Bill Withers, "Lean on Me"
Bill Withers/Cliff de Young, "Sunshine" Film Clip
Cliff de Young, "Sunshine on My Shoulders"
Rory Gallagher, "Cradle Rock"
Bill Withers, "Green Grass"
Montrose, "Good Rockin' Tonight"
Billy Withers/Bobby Womack/Buddy Miles, "Railroad Man"

Episode 61
Host: The Guess Who

The Guess Who, "American Woman"
Wishbone Ash, "Blowin' Free"
Sha Na Na, "Rock Around the Clock," "Teenager in Love"
Slade, "My Friend Stan"
David Essex, "Lamplight"
Judi Pulver, "Statler Hilton"
The Guess Who, "Star Baby"
Wishbone Ash, "Vas Dis"
David Essex, "On and On"
Slade, "Do We Still Do It"
Leo Kottke, "Bean Time"
The Guess Who, "These Eyes," "Clap For Wolfman"
Sha Na Na, "Tell Laura I Love Her"
David Essex, "Rock On"
Slade, "Everyday"
Judi Pulver, "Sing for Your Supper"
The Guess Who, "Hand Me Down World"

Episode 62, 86
Host: The Righteous Brothers

The Righteous Brothers, "Hello Rock 'n' Roll"
New Riders of the Purple Sage, "Panama Red"
Paul Williams, "You and Me Against the World"
The Staple Singers, "If You're Ready (Come Go with Me)"
The Righteous Brothers, medley: "Soul and Inspiration," "Unchained Melody," "You've Lost That Lovin' Feelin'," "Ebb Tide," "You've Lost That Lovin' Feelin'"
The Righteous Brothers, "Roberto and Bill," "Lighten Up"
The Staple Singers, "Touch a Hand Make a Friend"
Paul Williams, "Nice to Be Around"
New Riders of the Purple Sage, "Sunday Susie"
The Righteous Brothers, medley: "Little Latin Lupe Lu," "Koko Jo," "My Babe"
The Righteous Brothers/Paul Williams, "Mr. Sandman"
The Righteous Brothers, medley: "Swing Low Sweet Chariot," "Swing Down Chariot," "Down by the Riverside," "Oh Happy Side"
Bobby Hatfield, "He Ain't Heavy, He's My Brother"
Rosemary, "Wildflower"
The Righteous Brothers, "Rock 'n' Roll Loser"

Episode 63
Host: Roy Clark

Roy Clark, "Rollin' in My Sweet Baby's Arms"
Lynn Anderson, "Listen to a Country Song"
Tom T. Hall, "I Love"
Conway Twitty, "You've Never Been This Far Before"
Diana Trask, "When I Get My Hands On You"
Charlie McCoy, "Orange Blossom Special"
Roy Clark, "Yesterday When I Was Young"
Lynn Anderson, "Smile for Me"
Mel Tillis, "Midnight Me and the Blues"
Roy Clark, "Honeymoon Feelin'"
Roy Clark/Buck Trent, "Dueling Banjos"
Tommy Overstreet, "(Jeannie Marie) You Were a Lady"
Conway Twitty, "It's Only Make Believe"
Tom T. Hall, "The Year That Clayton Delaney Died"
Roy Clark, "Thank God and the Greyhound," "Riders in the Sky"
Mel Tillis, "Sawmill"
Conway Twitty, "There's a Honky Tonk Angel," "I'm Not Through Loving You Yet"
Roy Clark, "Black Mountain Rag"

Episode 64
Host: Curtis Mayfield

Curtis Mayfield, "If There's a Hell Below We're All Gonna Go"
Gladys Knight & the Pips, "Best Thing That Ever Happened to Me"
Status Quo, "Big Fat Mama"
Phil Ochs, "The Power and the Glory"
Sugarloaf, "Green Eyed Lady"
The Impressions, "I'm a Changed Man"
From the movie Claudine (outside clip)
Gladys Knight & the Pips, "On and On"
Curtis Mayfield, "To Be Invisible"
Sugarloaf, "I Got a Song"
Curtis Mayfield, "Give Me Your Love"
The Impressions, "People Get Ready"
Phil Ochs, "Changes"
Curtis Mayfield, "No Thing on Me"
Gladys Knight, "Get Off" drug spot

Episode 65
Host: Charlie Rich

Charlie Rich, "Lonely Weekends," "Life Has Its Little Ups and Downs"
The Staple Singers, "I Ain't Raisin' No Sand"
Anne Murray, "You Won't See Me"
Charie Rich/Anne Murray, "Break My Mind"
Charlie Rich, "How I Became a Country Singer," "Behind Closed Doors"
The Staple Singers, "Touch a Hand Make a Friend"
Charlie Rich, "The Most Beautiful Girl"
Dobie Gray, "Rockin' Chair"
Anne Murray, "A Love Song"
Charlie Rich, "A Very Special Love Song"
Dobie Gray, "I Never Had It So Good"
Charlie Rich, "Big Boss Man"
Dobie Gray, "Drift Away"
The Treasures, "The Right Combination"
Charlie Rich, "Dance of Love"

Episode 66
Host: The Spinners

The Spinners, "One of a Kind Love Affair"
Bobby Womack, "Let It Hang Out"
Bedlam featuring Cozy Powell, "Dance with the Devil"
Bloodstone, "Outside Woman"
Peter Yarrow, "Isn't That So"
Martha Reeves, "Power of Love"
The Spinners, "Mighty Love"
The Lockers, "Outta Space" dance routine
Bobby Womack, "Copper Kettle"
Peter Yarrow, "That's Enough for Me"
The Spinners, "I'm Coming Home"
Bloodstone, "Everybody Needs Love"
Bedlam featuring Cozy Powell, "Set Me Free"
The Spinners, "It's a Shame," "Could It Be I'm Falling in Love"

Episode 67
Host: George Carlin

Leo Sayer, "The Show Must Go On"
George Carlin, comedy spot
Buffy Sainte-Marie, "Sweet Little Vera"
The Dramatics, "Choosing Up on You"
Waylon Jennings, "Good Hearted Woman"
Livingston Taylor, "Hallelujah I Love Her"
George Carlin, comedy spot
Puzzle, "Everybody Wants to Be Somebody"
Buffy Sainte-Marie, "Generation"
Leo Sayer, "Goodnight Old Friend"
Livingston Taylor, "Sit On Back"
Waylon Jennings, "Louisiana Women"
Puzzle, "My Love"
The Dramatics, "And I Panicked"
Livingston Taylor, "Cornbread and Buttermilk"

Episode 68
Host: Frankie Avalon

Sam and Dave, "Hold On I'm Comin'"
Frankie Avalon, "Why"
The Fleetwoods, "Come Softly to Me"
Jimmie Rodgers, "Kisses Sweeter Than Wine"
Frankie Ford, "Sea Cruise"
Fabian, "Rock Around the Clock," "Turn Me Loose," "Tiger"
Frankie Avalon/Fabian, "Scrapbook," "Fireball 500"
Frankie Avalon, "Just Ask Your Heart"
Shirley and Lee, "Let the Good Times Roll"
Sam and Dave, "Soul Man"
Lou Christie, "Lightnin' Strikes"
Jimmie Rodgers, "Honeycomb"
The Royalteens, "Short Shorts," "The Great Midnight Special Rock 'n' Roll Opera"
Frankie Avalon, "De De Dinah," "Gingerbread," "Bobby Sox to Stockings"
Jimmie Rodgers, "Oh Oh I'm Falling in Love Again"
Lou Christie, "The Gypsy Cried"
The Fleetwoods, "Mr. Blue"
Frankie Avalon, "Venus"

Episode 69, 206, 385
Host: Richard Pryor

Bobby "Blue" Bland, "Ain't That Loving You"
Richard Pryor, comedy spot
Olivia Newton-John, "Let Me Be There"
Boz Scaggs, "You Make It So Hard to Say No"
New Riders of the Purple Sage, "Glendale Train"
Marvin Hamlisch, "The Entertainer"
Richard Pryor, comedy spot
Olivia Newton-John, "If You Love Me Let Me Know"
Melvin Van Peebles, "A Birth Certificate Ain't Nothin' But a Death Warrant Anyway"
Marvin Hamlisch, "The Way We Were"
Bobby "Blue" Bland, "Gotta Get to Know You"
Richard Pryor, audience improv
Boz Scaggs, "Slow Dancer"
Olivia Newton-John, "If Not for You"
New Riders of the Purple Sage, "South American Man"
Melvin Van Peebles, "Eyes on the Rabbit"
Gladys Knight, "Get Off" drug spot

Episode 70
Host: Marty Robbins

Marty Robbins, "I Couldn't Believe It Was True"
Anne Murray, "You Won't See Me"
Johnny Rodriguez, "Louisiana Man"
Don Gibson, "Touch the Morning"
Bill Anderson, "If You Can Live with It"
Tammy Wynette, "My Man"
George Jones, "A Picture of Me"
Marty Robbins, "Home on the Range," "Down in the Little Green Valley"
Freddie Hart, "Easy Loving"
Charlie McCoy, "Silver Threads and Golden Needles"
Johnny Rodriguez, "Something"
Diana Trask, "Lean It All on Me"
Marty Robbins, "La Paloma"
Anne Murray, "Children of My Mind"
Marty Robbins, "If I Were Howard Hughes"
Tommy Overstreet, "Gwen (Congratulations)"
Tammy Wynette, "My Man"
Bill Anderson, "My Life"
Marty Robbins, "Don't You Think," "Lord You Gave Me a Mountain"

Episode 71
Host: The Kinks

The Kinks, "You Really Got Me"
Electric Light Orchestra, "Showdown"
Buddy Miles, "Life Is What You Make It"
Alan Price, "In Times Like These"
Suzi Quatro, "All Shook Up"
The Kinks, "Money Talks"
Rory Gallagher, "Hands Off"
Electric Light Orchestra, "Bluebird Is Dead"
Suzi Quatro, "Glycerine Queen"
The Kinks, "Here Comes Yet Another Day,"
    "Celluloid Heroes"
Alan Price, "Between Today and Yesterday"
Rory Gallagher, "Who's That Comin'"
The Kinks, "Skin and Bone"

Episode 72 (see Episode 46)

Episode 73 (see Episode 49)

Episode 74, 156
Host: David Steinberg

Monty Python's Flying Circus, comedy spot
David Steinberg, comedy spot
Kentucky Fried Theater, gashion show
David Steinberg/Wolfman Jack, comedy spot
Freddie Prinze, comedy spot
Ace Trucking Company, comedy spot
Kentucky Fried Theater, "Shaving Blindfolded"
Franklin Ajaye, comedy spot

Episode 75
Host: Anne Murray

Anne Murray, "You Won't See Me"
The Wet Willie Band, "Keep On Smilin'"
Eddie Kendricks, "Son of Sagittarius"
Buffy Sainte-Marie, "Sweet Fast Hooker Blues"
Rufus, "Tell Me Something Good"
Anne Murray, "A Love Song"
Buffy Sainte-Marie, "Hey Baby Howdja Do Me
    This Way"
Golden Earring, "Radar Love"
The Wet Willie Band, "Trust in the Lord"
Country Joe McDonald, "Jesse James"
Eddie Kendricks, "Boogie Down"
Buffy Sainte-Marie, "That's the Way You Fall in
    Love"
Anne Murray, "Robbie's Song For Jesus"
Country Joe McDonald, "All My Love in Vain"
Rufus, "You Got the Love"
Anne Murray, "He Thinks I Still Care," "Ease
    Your Pain"

Episode 76
Host: Bobby Womack

Bobby Womack, "Nobody Wants You When You're
    Down and Out"
Kool & the Gang, "Hollywood Swinging"
David Essex, "Lamplight"
Tim Weisberg, "Dreamspeaker"
Chi Coltrane, "Who Ever Told You"
Bobby Womack, "Lookin' for Love"
Bobby Womack/Wolfman Jack, "Tired of Living
    in the Country"
Kool & the Gang, "Jungle Boogie"
Elliot Murphy, "How's the Family"
Tim Weisberg, "Streak-Out"
David Essex, "Streetfight"
Bobby Womack, "You Send Me"
Chi Coltrane, "Let It Ride"
Bobby Womack, "Fact of Life," "He'll Get There
    When the Sun Goes Down"
Elliott Murphy, "Last of the Rock Stars"
Bobby Womack, "I Take It On Home"

Episode 77
Host: Helen Reddy

Helen Reddy, "Keep On Singing"
Brownsville Station, "I'm the Leader of the Gang"
Paul Williams, "You Know Me"
Janis Ian, "Applause"
Gabe Kaplan, comedy spot
Dave Loggins, "Please Come to Boston"
Helen Reddy, "Pretty Pretty"
Peter Allen, "More Than I Like You"
Brownsville Station, "Kings of the Party"
Paul Williams, "Driftwood"
Helen Reddy, "Love Song for Jeffrey," "You and
    Me Against the World"
Dave Loggins, "Sunset Woman"
Janis Ian, "The Man You Are in Me"

Episode 78
Host: Leon Russell

Leon Russell/Gap Band, "Alcatraz," "Going
    Back," "Smashed," "Streakers Ball"
Gap Band, "Magician's Holiday"
Leon Russell, "Queen of the Roller Derby," "Roll
    Away the Stone"
Gap Band, "Tommy's Groove"
Leon Russell, "Ain't That Peculiar," "Tight Rope"
Gap Band, "You Can Always Count on Me"
Leon Russell, "Delta Lady"

Episode 79
Host: Leon Russell

Leon Russell, "Jambalaya"
Rick Nelson, "Someone to Love," "Garden Party"
Doug Kershaw, "Louisiana Man," "Cajun Joe"
John Hartford, "Turn Your Radio On"
David Carradine, "A Country Mile"
Waylon Jennings, "Pick Up the Tempo," "Willie
    the Wandering Gypsy and Me," "Can You Save Her"
Willie Nelson, "Stay All Night a Little Longer"
Michael Murphy, "The South Canadian River
    Song"
Babby Bare, "Marie Lavaux"
Leon Russell, "Goodnight, Irene"

Episode 80
Host: Sly & the Family Stone

Sly & the Family Stone, "Thank You (Falettinme
    Be Mice Elf Agin)," "Time For Livin'"
Elvin Bishop, "Travelin' Shoes," "Sunshine
    Special"
Roger McGuinn, "Gate of Horn"
Sly & the Family Stone, "Small Talk," "Family
    Affair," "Dance to the Music," "Music Lover,"
    "I Want to Take You Higher"
Henry Gross, "Come On Say It"
Little Feat, "Tripe Face Boogie," "Willin'"
Sly & the Family Stone, "If You Want Me to
    Stay," "Stand"
Elvin Bishop, "Groundhog"
Henry Gross, "Simone"
Roger McGuinn, "Peace on You"
Sly & the Family Stone, "Loose Booty"

Episode 81
Host: Little Richard

Little Richard, "The Midnight Special"
Golden Earring, "Radar Love"
Kool & the Gang, "Funky Stuff"
Aerosmith, "The Train Kept A Rollin'"
Little Richard, "In the Name"
Eddie Kendricks, "Hooked on Your Love," "Keep
    On Truckin'"
David Clayton-Thomas, "Anytime Babe"

Little Richard, "Ooh Poo Pah Doo," "Greenwood,
    Miss"
Aerosmith, "Dream On"
Kool & the Gang, "Who's Gonna Take the
    Weight"
David Clayton-Thomas, "And When I Die"
Little Richard, "Freedom Blues"

Episode 82 (see Episode 42)

Episode 83
Host: B.B King

B.B. King, "Why I Sing the Blues"
Paul Butterfield's Better Days, "Meet Me in the
    Bottom"
Jimmy Witherspoon, "Nothing's Changed"
John Lee Hooker, "Boogie with the Hook"
Big Mama Thornton, "Ball and Chain"
Joe Williams, "Who She Do"
B.B. King, "I Like to Live the Love"
Bobby "Blue" Bland, "Goin' Down Slow"
Papa John Creach, "John's Other"
B.B. King/John Lee Hooker/Papa John Creach,
    "Gettin' It Together"
B.B. King, "The Thrill Is Gone"
Jimmy Witherspoon, "Love Is a Five Letter Word"
Joe Williams, "Tell Me Where to Scratch"
B.B. King, "I Got Some Help I Don't Need," "Why
    I Sing the Blues"

Episode 84, 226
Host: Marvin Gaye

Marvin Gaye, "Trouble Man," "Inner City Blues"
    (Make Me Wanna Holler)," "Come Get to
    This," "Keep Gettin' It On"
Marvin Gaye, medley: "I'll Be Doggone," "Try It
    Baby," "Can I Get a Witness," "You're a
    Wonderful One," "Stubborn Kind of Fellow,"
    "How Sweet It Is," "Distant Lover," "Let's Get
    It On," "Jan," "What's Going On"

Episode 85
Host: The O'Jays

The O'Jays, medley: "Put Your Hands Together,"
    "People Keep Tellin' Me," "Time to Get Down,"
    "This Air I Breathe," "People Keep Tellin' Me"
Mick Jagger, "Happy," "Tumbling Dice" (outside
    clip)
James Brown, "Payback," "Cold Sweat," "I Can't
    Stand to Live," "Papa's Got a Brand New Bag"
Elvin Bishop, "Stealing Watermelons," "Calling
    All Cows"
The O'Jays, "For the Love of Money"
Mick Jagger, "Midnight Rambler" (outside clip)
James Brown, "Hell," "Papa Don't Take No Mess"
The O'Jays, "Sunshine"
Elvin Bishop, "Sunshine Special"
James Brown, "My Thang"
The O'Jays, "Love Train"

Episode 86 (see Episode 62)

Episode 87
Host: Randy Newman

Randy Newman, "Mama Told Me Not to Come,"
    "Simon Smith and the Amazing Dancing
    Bear," "Political Science," "Davy and the Fat
    Boy"
Maria Muldaur, "Sweetheart"
Dr. John, "Let's Make a Better World," "Desitively
    Bonnaroo"
The Turtles, "Happy Together"
Randy Newman, "I Think It's Going to Rain
    Today"
Dr. John and Maria Muldaur, "Three Dollar Bill"
The Turtles, "Feel Older Now," "Let Me Make
    Love to You"

Maria Muldaur, "Lover Man," "Squeeze Me"
Randy Newman, "Rolling"
Dr. John, "Mos'Scocious"
Ry Cooder, "Ditty Wah Ditty"
The Turtles, "You Showed Me"
Randy Newman, "All His Love"
Dr. John, "Mama Don't Allow"
Randy Newman, "Louisiana 1927"

Episode 88
Host: Al Green

Al Green, "Sweet Talk," "Tired of Being Alone,"
    "Sha La La," "Here I Am (Come and Take Me)"
Joe Cocker, "Something," "Delta Lady"
Al Green, medley: "Funny How Time Slips Away,"
    "How Can You Mend a Broken Heart," "For the
    Good Times," "Let's Stay Together"
Al Green, "I'm Still in Love with You," "Love and
    Happiness"

Episode 89
Host: Jose Feliciano

The Main Ingredient, "Just Don't Want to Be
    Lonely"
Jose Feliciano, "My Sweet Lord"
Hot Tuna, "Hamar Promenade"
Buffy Sainte-Marie, "I Can't Take It No More"
Jesse Colin, "Morning Sun"
Hot Tuna, "Day to Day Out the Window Blues," "I
    See the Light"
Jesse Colin, "Light Shine"
Buffy Sainte-Marie, "That's the Way You Fall in
    Love"
Jose Feliciano, "Chico and the Man"
The Main Ingredient, "Everybody Plays the Fool,"
    "Happiness Is Just Around the Bend"
Jose Feliciano, "T.S.O.P.," "Golden Lady," "Love's
    Theme"

Episode 90, 151
Host: Paul Anka

Paul Anka, "You're Having My Baby"
Brownsville Station, "Kings of the Party"
The Tymes, "You Little Trustmaker"
Ohio Players, "Skin Tight"
The Guess Who/Wolfman Jack, "Clap
    for the Wolfman"
Odia Coates/Paul Anka, "One Man Woman"
James Brown, "Papa Don't Take No Mess"
Paul Anka, "Jubilation"
The Guess Who, "American Woman"
Paul Anka, "It Doesn't Matter Anymore,"
    "American Pie"
James Brown, "Good Foot"
Paul Anka, "Let Me Get to Know You,"
    "Jubilation"

Episode 91, 414
Host: David Steinberg

The Committee, comedy spot
Steve Martin, comedy spot
Monty Python's Flying Circus (outside clip)
Freddie Prinze, comedy spot
Burns and Schreiber, comedy spot
Pat McCormick, comedy spot

Episode 92
Host: Fats Domino

Fats Domino, "I'm in Love Again," "Blueberry Hill"
Frankie Valli & the Four Seasons, "Dawn," "Let's Hang On"
The Coasters, "Yakety Yak," "Poison Ivy"
Fats Domino, "Ain't That a Shame"
Frankie Valli & the Four Seasons, "Can't Take My Eyes Off of You," "Sherry," "Walk Like a Man," "Big Girls Don't Cry," "Bye Bye Baby"
Fats Domino, "Josephine," "Walkin' to New Orleans," "I'm Gonna Be a Wheel Someday," "Blue Monday," "I Want to Walk You Home"
Frankie Valli & the Four Seasons, "Stay," "My Eyes Adored You," "Will You Still Love Me Tomorrow," "Rag Doll"
The Coasters, "Charlie Brown"
Fats Domino, "When the Saints Go Marching In"

Episode 93
Host: Redd Foxx

Little Anthony & the Imperials, "What Is Hip?"
Golden Earring, "Big Tree Blue Sea"
Little Anthony & the Imperials, "Goin' out of My Head," "Hurts So Bad"
Orphan, "I've Been Working"
Golden Earring, "Candy's Going Bad"
Little Anthony & the Imperials, "I Don't Have to Worry"
Golden Earring, "She Flies on Strange Wings," "Love Is a Rodeo"
Little Anthony & the Imperials, "The Loneliest House on the Block"

Episode 94
Host: Barry White

Love Unlimited Orchestra, "Love's Theme"
Barry White, "You're the First, the Last, My Everything," "Can't Get Enough of Your Love, Babe," "Never Gonna Give You Up"
The Eric Burdon Band, "It's My Life," "The Real Me"
Love Unlimited Orchestra, "Barry's Theme," "I Belong to You"
The Eric Burdon Band, "When I Was Young"
Barry White, "I'm Gonna Love You Just a Little More Baby"
Love Unlimited Orchestra, "Oh Love We Finally Made It"
Barry White, "I Found Someone"
Love Unlimited Orchestra, "Love Train"

Episode 95
Host: George Carlin

The Kiki Dee Band, "I've Got the Music in Me"
Roy Wood's Wizzard, "Brand New '88"
Roger McGuinn, "Peace on You"
Sparks, "Talent Is an Asset," "This Town Ain't Big Enough for Both of Us"
Roy Wood's Wizzard, "Ball Park Incident"
Roger McGuinn, "Better Change"
Sparks, "Amateur Hour," "Here in Heaven"

Episode 96
Host: Bobby Vinton

Bobby Vinton, "My Melody of Love"
Rufus, featuring Chaka Khan, "You Got the Love"
Neil Sedaka, "Laughter in the Rain"
Al Green, "Sha La La"
Billy Swan, "I Can Help"

Carl Carlton, "Everlasting Love"
Al Green, "I'm Still in Love with You," "Let's Stay Together"
Rufus, featuring Chaka Khan, "Tell Me Something Good"
Bobby Vinton, "Mr. Lonely"
Neil Sedaka, "Standing on the Inside"
Bobby Vinton, "I Honestly Love You," "My Melody of Love"

Episode 97, 123, 168
Host: Tom Jones

Tom Jones, "My Soul Is a Witness," "Greenwood Mississippi," "I Guess You Know Me Girl"
Tom Jones/Paul Anka, "She's a Lady," "My Way"
Tom Jones, "Pledging My Love"
The Kiki Dee Band, "I've Got the Music in Me"
Tom Jones, medley
Chuck Berry, "Johnny B. Goode"
Tom Jones/Chuck Berry, "School Days," "Memphis," "Roll Over Beethoven"
Tom Jones, "It Never Hurts to Be Nice to Somebody," "Danny Boy," "One Night with You," "Right Place, Wrong Time," "Pledging My Love"

Episode 98
Host: Wolfman Jack
(Million Sellers Show, Part I)

Steve Miller, "The Joker"
Rufus, featuring Chaka Khan, "Tell Me Something Good"
Paul Anka, "You're Having My Baby"
The Stylistics, "You Make Me Feel Brand New"
Redbone, "Come and Get Your Love"
Barry White, "Can't Get Enough of Your Love, Babe," "Never Gonna Give You Up"
Olivia Newton-John, "If You Love Me Let Me Know"
James Brown, "The Payback"
Love Unlimited Orchestra, "Love's Theme"
Gordon Lightfoot, "Sundown"
Blue Magic, "Sideshow"
Bobby Womack, "Looking for Love"
Love Unlimited Orchestra, "Love's Theme"
Steve Miller "Get Off" drug spot

Episode 99
Host: Wolfman Jack
(Million Sellers Show, Part II)

Gladys Knight & the Pips, "I've Got to Use My Imagination"
David Essex, "Rock On"
The O'Jays, "For the Love of Money"
Brownsville Station, "Smokin' in the Boys Room"
Kool & the Gang, "Hollywood Swinging"
Olivia Newton-John, "Let Me Be There"
The Main Ingredient, "I Just Don't Want to Be Lonely"
Gladys Knight & the Pips, "Best Thing That Ever Happened to Me"
Marvin Hamlisch, "The Entertainer"
Ohio Players, "Skin Tight"
Kool & the Gang, "Jungle Boogie"
Marvin Hamlisch, "The Way We Were"
Byron McGregor, "The Americans"
Marvin Hamlisch, "The Entertainer"

Episode 100
Host: Charley Pride

Charley Pride, "Is Anybody Goin' to San Antone," "Kiss an Angel Good Morning," "Mississippi Cotton Picking Delta Town"
Doug Kershaw, "Diggy Diggy Lo," "Battle of New Orleans"

Ronnie Milsap, "Rolling in My Sweet Baby's Arms," "Pure Love"
Doug Kershaw, "All I Want to Do Is Make Babies," "Whatcha Gonna Do When You Can't"
Charley Pride, "Cotton Fields"
The Four Guys, "Too Late to Turn Back Now"
Ronnie Milsap, rock medley
Charley Pride, "All I Have to Offer You Is Me," "Kawliga"
Gary Stewart, "Drinking Thing"
Charley Pride, "It's Gonna Take a Little Bit Longer," "Louisiana Man," "Let Me Live," "The Fugitive"

Episode 101
Host: The Guess Who

The Guess Who/Wolfman Jack, "Clap for the Wolfman"
The Guess Who, "Dancin' Fool"
The Spencer Davis Group, "Gimme Some Lovin'," "Workin' on the Railroad"
Montrose, "I Got the Fire"
The Guess Who, "Bus Rider," "Sour Suite"
Charlie Daniels, "Way Down Yonder," "I've Been Down"
The Guess Who, "No Time," "Diggin' Yourself"
Montrose, "Space Station #5"
The Spencer Davis Group, "Don't Throw Your Change on Me"
The Guess Who, "Dirty"
The Guess Who/Wolfman Jack, "Clap for the Wolfman"

Episode 102
Host: The Righteous Brothers

The Righteous Brothers, "Dream On"
The Guess Who, "Dancin' Fool"
Linda Ronstadt, "You're No Good"
George Foreman, "Walk On"
Frankie Valli, "My Eyes Adored You"
Paul Anka, "One Man Woman"
Gloria Gaynor, "Never Can Say Goodbye"
Bobby Hatfield, "You Turn Me Around"
Bill Medley, "Brown Eyed Woman"
Carol Douglas, "Doctor's Orders"
Billy "Crash" Craddock, "Ruby Baby"
The Righteous Brothers, "Rock and Roll Heaven"
Frankie Valli & the Four Seasons, oldies medley
The Righteous Brothers, "Give It to the People"
Carol Douglas, "Baby Don't Let This Good Love Die"

Episode 103
Host: Electric Light Orchestra

Electric Light Orchestra, "In the Hall of the Mountain King," "Great Balls of Fire"
Linda Ronstadt, "When Will I Be Loved," "Willin'," "You're No Good," "Faithless Love"
Electric Light Orchestra, "Can't Get It out of My Head," "Orange Blossom Special"
Rufus, featuring Chaka Khan, "You Got the Love," "I Am Woman," "Packed My Bags"
Electric Light Orchestra, "Laredo Tornado"
The Ohio Players, "Jive Turkey"
Rufus, featuring Chaka Khan, "We Can Work It Out"
Electric Light Orchestra, "Flight of the Bumble Bee," "Roll Over Beethoven"

Episode 104
Host: The Marshall Tucker Band

The Marshall Tucker Band, "This Ol' Cowboy," "24 Hours at a Time," "In My Own Way"
Poco, "Hoedown," "Whatever Happened to Your Smile," "Rocky Mountain Breakdown," "Sagebrush Serenade," "High and Dry"
Olivia Newton-John, "If Not for You"
The Charlie Daniels Band, "The South's Gonna Do It"
Olivia Newton-John, "Let Me Be There"
The Charlie Daniels Band, "Long Haired Country Boy," "Caballo Diablo"

Episode 105, 227, 335
Host: Helen Reddy

The Doobie Brothers, "Listen to the Music," "Jesus Is Just Alright"
Aretha Franklin/Ray Charles, "Takes Two to Tango"
Joan Baez, "Love Song to a Stranger"
Gladys Knight/B.B. King, "The Thrill Is Gone"
Helen Reddy, "Angie Baby," "Emotion," "Raised on Rock," "I'll Be Your Audience," "I Think I'll Write a Song"
David Bowie, "Space Oddity," "Time"
Bachman-Turner Overdrive, "Hold Back the Water"
The Byrds, "Mr. Tambourine Man," "So You Want to Be a Rock 'n' Roll Star"
Bobby Darin, medley

Episode 106
Host: Dave Mason

Dave Mason, "World in Changes," "Bring It On Home to Me," "All along the Watchtower," "Every Woman," "You Can't Take It When You Go"
The Kiki Dee Band, "You Need Help," "Frozen One"
Average White Band, "Got the Love," "Work to Do"
Dave Mason, "Only You Know and I Know"
The Crusaders, "Double Bubble," "Stomp and Buck Dance"
Average White Band, "Nothing You Can Do"
Dave Mason, "Lucille," "Feelin' Alright"

Episode 107
Host: Neil Sedaka

Neil Sedaka, "That's When the Music Takes Me," "The Immigrant," "Laughter in the Rain," "Standing on the Inside," "Don't Let It Mess Your Mind"
The Spinners, "I've Got to Make It on My Own," "Living a Little, Laughing a Little," "Sadie," "Then Came You"
Sister Sledge, "Love Don't You Go Through No Changes on Me"
Todd Rundgren, "Real Man," "Freedom Fighter," "Seven Rays," "Born to Synthesize," "Do Ya"

Episode 108
Host: Steppenwolf

Steppenwolf, "Born to Be Wild," "Gang War Blues," "Smokey Factory Blues"
Linda Ronstadt, "Heat Wave," "Heart Like a Wheel"
Steppenwolf, "Straight Shootin' Woman"
P.F.M., "Celebration"
Herbie Hancock, "Watermelon Man," "Chameleon"
The Headhunters, "God Made Me Funky"
Steppenwolf, "Children of the Night"
P.F.M., "Alta Loma Nine Till Five"
Herbie Hancock, "Spank-A-Lee"
Steppenwolf, "Smokey Factory Blues"

Episode 109
Host: B.T. Express

B.T. Express, "Do It (Til' You're Satisfied)," "This House Is Smokin'," "Express"

Sha Na Na, "Breaking Up Is Hard to Do," "All Shook Up"

Sugarloaf, "Green Eyed Lady," "Don't Call Us, We'll Call You"

Jimmy Witherspoon, "Love Is a Five Letter Word," "Goin' Down Slow"

B.T. Express, "That's What I Want for You Baby"

Sha Na Na, "Sixteen Candles"

Peter Allen, "Just Ask Me I've Been There," "Continental American"

B.T. Express, "Do You Like It," "Do It (Til' You're Satisfied)"

Episode 110, 165, 262
Host: Olivia Newton-John

Olivia Newton-John, "If You Love Me Let Me Know," "Have You Ever Been Mellow," "You Ain't Got the Right," "The Air That I Breathe," "I Never Did Sing You a Love Song"

Ike and Tina Turner, "Sexy Ida," "Bayou Song," "Baby Get It On," "Long Tall Glasses," "Telepath," "In My Life," "The Dancer"

Waylon Jennings, "Honky Tonk Heroes," "You Ask Me To"

Kenny Rankin, "Silver Morning," "Catfish"

Episode 111
Host: Clive Davis

Barry Manilow, "Mandy"

Janis Joplin, "Try" (outside clip)

Blood, Sweat and Tears, "You've Made Me So Very Happy," "I Love You More Than You'll Ever Know"

Melissa Manchester, "Midnight Blue"

Gil Scott-Heron, "The Bottle," "Must Be Something"

Barry Manilow/Martha Reeves, medley

Episode 112
Host: Black Oak Arkansas

Black Oak Arkansas, "Jim Dandy," "Hey Y'all," "Taxman"

Alvin Lee & Company, "Somebody's Calling Me," "Time and Space"

Montrose, "Paper Money," "I Got the Fire"

Black Oak Arkansas, "High and Dry"

Grey Ghost, "Burning Whiskey"

Alvin Lee & Company, "Going Through the Door," "Ride My Train"

Black Oak Arkansas, "Back Door Man"

Grey Ghost, "Old West Outlaws"

Black Oak Arkansas, "Lord Have Mercy," "Hot and Nasty"

Episode 113
Host: Wolfman Jack—International

Golden Earring, "Love Is a Rodeo," "Candy's Going Bad"

The Guess Who, "Diggin' Yourself," "Dirty"

Electric Light Orchestra, "Great Balls of Fire," "Can't Get It out of My Head"

P.F.M., "Celebration"

Rory Gallagher, "Tattoo'd Lady," "Cradle Rock"

Ravi Shankar, "Raja Jogiya"

Brian Cadd, "Think It Over," "Let Go"

Episode 114
Host: Ohio Players

Ohio Players, "Jive Turkey," "Fire" (Part I), "Fire" (Part II), "I Want to Be Free," "Skin Tight" (Part I), "Skin Tight" (Part II), "Pain" (Part I), "Pain" (Part II), "Fire"

Episode 115
Host: Wet Willie/Charlie Daniels

Wet Willie, "Dixie Rock," "Leona," "Keep On Smilin'"

Bonnie Bramlett, "(Your Love Keeps Liftin') Higher and Higher," "Your Love Has Brought Me (A Mighty Long Way)"

The Charlie Daniels Band, "The South's Gonna Do It," "Orange Blossom Special," "Long Haired Country Boy"

John Mayall, "So Much to Do," "Step in the Sun"

B.J. Thomas, "(Hey Won't You Play) Another Somebody Done Somebody Wrong Song," "Hooked on a Feeling"

Wet Willie, "Mama Didn't Raise No Fool"

The Charlie Daniels Band, "Trudy," "Caballo Diablo"

Episode 116
Host: Earth, Wind & Fire

Earth, Wind & Fire, "Shining Star," "Mighty Mighty"

LaBelle, "Lady Marmalade," "What Can I Do for You?"

Leo Sayer, "Long Tall Glasses," "In My Life"

Earth, Wind & Fire, "Devotion"

Melissa Manchester, "Just Too Many People," "Party Music"

LaBelle, "Are You Lonely," "Happy Feelin'"

Melissa Manchester, "Midnight Blue"

Earth, Wind & Fire, "Yearning Learning"

Episode 117
Host: Rod Stewart & the Faces

Rod Stewart, "Bring It On Home to Me," "You Send Me," "Take a Look at the Guy"

Rod Stewart/Keith Richards, "Sweet Little Rock and Roller"

Rod Stewart, "Angel," "I Can Feel the Fire," "You Can Make Me Dance"

Rod Stewart/Keith Richards, "Twisting the Night Away"

Rod Stewart, "You Wear it Well," "Maggie May," "We'll Meet Again"

Episode 118
Host: Billy Preston

Billy Preston, "Nothing from Nothing"

LaBelle, "Space Children," "What Can I Do for You?"

Jeff Beck, "It Don't Really Matter"

Billy Preston, "Found the Love"

Rufus, featuring Chaka Khan, "Pack'd My Bags," "Please Pardon Me"

Billy Preston, "It's My Pleasure," "Let Me Sing My Song"

LaBelle, "You Turn Me On"

Jeff Beck, "Cause We've Ended as Lovers"

Billy Preston, "All My Life"

Tonto, "Bittersweet"

Billy Preston, "Outa-Space"

Episode 119
Host: Wolfman Jack

Ohio Players, "I Want to Be Free"

Roxy Music, "Out of the Blue," "The Thrill of It All," "A Really Good Time"

Graham Central Station, medley Part I, medley Part II

The Strawbs, "Lemon Pie," "The Life Auction"

Larry Gatlin, "Penny Annie," "Help Me"

Graham Central Station, "Feel the Need"

Episode 120
Host: Chubby Checker

Chubby Checker, "The Twist"

Lesley Gore, medley: "It's My Party," "Judy's Turn to Cry," "Maybe I Know," "You Don't Own Me"

Danny & the Juniors, "Rock and Roll Is Here to Stay," "At the Hop"

Bo Diddley, "Bo Diddley"

Chubby Checker, "Pony Time"

The Angels, "My Boyfriend's Back," "Till"

The Drifters, "Up on the Roof," "Save the Last Dance for Me"

Chubby Checker, "Slow Twistin'"

The Tymes, "So Much in Love"

Danny & the Juniors, "Sometimes"

Chubby Checker, "Let's Twist Again"

The Angels, medley of oldies hits

Bo Diddley, "Crackin' Up"

Chubby Checker, "Hound Dog," "I Saw Her Standing There," "Hound Dog," "The Twist"

Episode 121
Host: Don Cornelius

Harold Melvin & the Blue Notes, "Bad Luck"

Disco Tex and the Sex-O-Lettes, "I Wanna Dance Wit' Choo"

Herbie Mann, "Hijack"

Earth, Wind & Fire, "Shining Star," "Mighty Mighty"

Consumer Rapport, "Ease On Down the Road," "Everybody Join Hands"

The Whispers, "A Mother for My Children," "Bingo"

Herbie Mann, "I Can't Turn You Loose"

The Lockers, Dance Routine

Disco Tex and the Sex-O-Lettes, "Get Dancin'"

Harold Melvin & the Blue Notes, "The Love I Lost," "Hope We Can Get Together Soon"

Herbie Mann, "High above the Andes"

Episode 122
Host: Joan Baez

Joan Baez, "Fountain of Sorrow," "Diamonds and Rust"

Kool & the Gang, "Spirit of the Boogie," "Rhyme Tyme People"

Joan Baez, "Jesse," "Children and All That Jazz"

Hoyt Axton, "Will the Circle Be Unbroken," "When the Morning Comes"

Joan Baez/Hoyt Axton, "Lion in the Winter"

Hampton Hawes, "Irene"

Joan Baez, "Simple Twist of Fate," "Never Dreamed You'd Leave in Summer," "Winds of the Old Days"

Hampton Hawes, "Pink Peaches"

Kool & the Gang, "Summer Madness"

Episode 123 (see Episode 97)

Episode 124
Host: Seals & Crofts

Seals & Crofts, "I'll Play For You," "Ugly City"

Ben E. King, "Supernatural Thing," "Happiness Is Where You Find It"

Seals & Crofts, "Blue Bonnet Nation," "Wisdom"

Barry Manilow, "It's a Miracle," "Could It Be Magic," "Avenue C," "Sweet Life," "Ashes in the Snow"

Olivia Newton-John, "(Take Me Home) Country Roads"

Ron Dante, "Midnight Show"

Ben E. King, "Do It in the Name of Love"

Seals & Crofts, "I'll Play for You"

Episode 125
Host: Herb Alpert

Herb Alpert, "Coney Island"

The Captain and Tennille, "Love Will Keep Us Together"

Phoebe Snow, "Poetry Man," "Harpo's Blues"

Supertramp, "Hide in Your Shell"

Herb Alpert, medley: "Lonely Bull," "Spanish Flea," "This Guy's in Love with You," "Taste of Honey," "Zorba the Greek"

Billy Preston, "Song of Joy"

Herb Alpert, "Carmine"

The Captain and Tennille, "Cuddle Up"

Herb Alpert, "Never Never Land"

Supertramp, "Bloody Well Right"

Herb Alpert, "Desert Dance," "Coney Island"

Episode 126
Host: Flip Wilson

The Temptations, "The Midnight Special," "Glass House"

Ace, "How Long"

Jessi Colter, "I'm Not Lisa"

The Temptations, medley of hits

The Temptations, "Memories," "Firefly," "A Song for You"

Leo Sayer, "One Man Band," "Train"

Jessi Colter, "Storms Never Last"

Ace, "Sniffin' About"

The Temptations, "Shakey Ground"

Rose, "Whole New Thing"

The Temptations, "Happy People"

Episode 127
Host: Frankie Valli

Frankie Valli, "Swearin' to God," "My Eyes Adored You"

The Hollies, "Long Cool Woman in a Black Dress," "Another Night"

Freddy Fender, "Before the Next Teardrop Falls"

Frankie Valli & the Four Seasons, "Who Loves You"

Frankie Valli, "Can't Take My Eyes off of You"

The Four Seasons, "Warsaw Concerto"

Orleans, "Let There Be Music," "Dance with Me"

Frankie Valli, "I Got Love for You Ruby"

The Hollies, "Sandy"

Frankie Valli & the Four Seasons, "Silence Is Golden"

Freddy Fender, "Wasted Days and Wasted Nights"

Orleans, "Tongue Tied"

Frankie Valli, "Swearin' to God"

Episode 128
Host: Flip Wilson

Flip Wilson, "Berries in Salinas"

Miss Song, "Deuce"

Jenny Rankin, "Silver Morning"

Carol Wayne, "Rock Rap"

Flip Wilson, tribute to Helen Reddy

Blue Magic, "Never Get Over You"

Kenny Rankin, "Birembau," "Killed a Cat"

Kiss, "Black Diamond"

Blue Magic, "Three Ring Circus," "Berries in Salinas"

Episode 129
Host: Helen Reddy

Helen Reddy, "Bluebird," "I Believe in Music"
Mac Davis, "Burnin' Thing"
Minnie Riperton, "Lovin' You"
Steve Martin, comedy spot
Helen Reddy, tribute to Cat Stevens, "Ain't No Way to Treat a Lady"
Waylon Jennings, "Are You Sure Hank Done It This Way," "Let's All Help the Cowboys (Sing the Blues)"
Minnie Riperton, "Adventures in Paradise"
Helen Reddy, "Free and Easy"
Mac Davis, "Rock and Roll I Gave You the Best of My Life"
Minnie Riperton, "Inside My Love"
Joe Simon, "Get Down Get Down"
Helen Reddy, "Long Time Looking," "I Am Woman"

Episode 130
Host: Helen Reddy

Helen Reddy, "Angie Baby"
Neil Sedaka, "That's When the Music Takes Me"
Helen Reddy, medley: "Leave Me Alone," "I Don't Know How to Love Him," "Delta Dawn"
Tribute to The Bee Gees
Jessi Colter, "I'm Not Lisa"
Helen Reddy/Neil Sedaka, "Don't Let It Mess Your Mind"
Janis Ian, "At Seventeen," "When the Party's Over"
Helen Reddy, "Bluebird"
Kraftwerk, "Autobahn"
Neil Sedaka, "Love Will Keep Us Together"
Jessi Colter, "You Ain't Never Been Loved"
Helen Reddy, "I Am Woman"

Episode 131
Host: Helen Reddy

Glen Campbell, "By the Time I Get to Phoenix"
Helen Reddy, "Peaceful"
Glen Campbell, "Rhinestone Cowboy"
Helen Reddy/Glen Campbell, "By the Time I Get to Phoenix," "Wichita Lineman," "Gentle on My Mind"
Helen Reddy, salute to Aretha Franklin, "Think I'll Write a Song"
Glen Campbell, "My Girl"
Gwen McCrae, "Rockin' Chair"
Uriah Heep, "Devil's Daughter"
Gwen McCrae, "He Don't Ever Lose the Groove"
Uriah Heep, "Return to Fantasy," "Prima Donna"
Helen Reddy, "I Am Woman"

Episode 132
Host: Helen Reddy

Helen Reddy, "L.A. Breakdown"
Charlie Rich, "Midnight Blues"
Melissa Manchester, "Midnight Blue"
Roger Daltrey, "Tommy," "Come and Get Your Love," "Walking the Dog"
The Amazing Rhythm Aces, "Third Rate Romance"
Helen Reddy, "I Got a Name"
Melissa Manchester, "Just Too Many People"
Charlie Rich, "Everytime You Touch Me (I Get High)"
The Amazing Rhythm Aces, "Anything You Want"
Helen Reddy, "I Am Woman"

Episode 133
Host: Helen Reddy

Johnny Rivers, "The Midnight Special"
Helen Reddy, "The Last Blues Song"
Johnny Rivers, "Help Me Rhonda"
Jose Feliciano, "Chico and the Man"
Helen Reddy, salute to Neil Young
Johnny Rivers, medley
George McCrae, "Rock Your Baby"
Helen Reddy, "Crazy Love"
George McCrae, "I Ain't Lyin'"
Jose Feliciano, "Marie," "No Jive"
Waylon Jennings, "I'll Be a Long Time Leaving," "Are You Sure Hank Done It This Way"
Helen Reddy, "I Am Woman"

Episode 134
Host: Helen Reddy

Helen Reddy, "Ain't No Way to Treat a Lady"
Frankie Valli, "Swearin' to God"
Helen Reddy, *Midnight Special* Hit, "Big Yellow Taxi"
KC & the Sunshine Band, "Get Down Tonight"
Helen Reddy, "Lovin' You"
Frankie Valli & the Four Seasons, "Who Loves You"
Hoyt Axton, "Paid in Advance"
Peter Frampton, "(I'll Give You) Money"
KC & the Sunshine Band, "That's the Way (I Like It)"
Peter Frampton, "Nowhere's Too Far," "Baby I Love Your Way"
Helen Reddy, "I Am Woman"

Episode 135
Host: Helen Reddy

The Bee Gees, "Jive Talkin'"
Helen Reddy, "Ain't No Way to Treat a Lady"
Janis Ian, "At Seventeen"
Helen Reddy, "The Midnight Special"
The Eagles, "One of These Nights"
Orleans, "Dance with Me"
Helen Reddy/The Bee Gees, "To Love Somebody"
B.T. Express, "Give It What You Got"
Helen Reddy, "Mama"
The Bee Gees, "Nights on Broadway"
Janis Ian, "When the Party's Over"
B.T. Express, "Peace Pipe"
Orleans, "Let There Be Music," "Tongue Tied"
Helen Reddy, "I Am Woman"
Eagles, "One of These Nights"

Episode 136
Host: Helen Reddy

Helen Reddy, "I'll Be Your Audience"
Animation, "Bad Bad Leroy Brown"
Helen Reddy, salute to David Bowie
The Nitty Gritty Dirt Band, "Dream"
Phoebe Snow, "I Don't Want the Night to End"
Billy Braver, comedy spot
Paul Williams, "Cried Like a Baby"
The Nitty Gritty Dirt Band, "Bayou Jubilee," "Battle of New Orleans"
Helen Reddy, "Time"
The Nitty Gritty Dirt Band, "Mother of Love"
Phoebe Snow, "Poetry Man"
Paul Williams, "Old Souls"
Helen Reddy, "I Am Woman"

Episode 137
Host: Helen Reddy

Helen Reddy, "Body Language"
Barry Manilow, "Could It Be Magic"
Helen Reddy, "Raised on Rock"
Isaac Hayes, "Feel Like Makin' Love"
Helen Reddy, salute to Chuck Berry
The Committee, comedy spot
Helen Reddy, "You and Me Against the World"
Barry Manilow, "I Want to Be Somebody's Baby"
Isaac Hayes, "Come Live with Me," "I Can't Turn Around"
Helen Reddy, "I Am Woman"

Episode 138
Host: Helen Reddy

Helen Reddy/Roger Miller, "In the Summertime"
Helen Reddy, "Mrs. Robinson"
Janis Ian, "In the Winter"
Helen Reddy, "Songs"
The Crusaders, "Creole"
Keith Carradine, "I'm Easy"
Helen Reddy/Keith Carradine, "It Don't Worry Me"
Roger Miller, "All I Love Is You"
Janis Ian, "Bayonne Blues"
Helen Reddy, "Ain't No Way to Treat a Lady"
Larry Beezer, comedy spot
Roger Miller, "The Day I Jumped from Uncle Harvey's Plane"
Keith Carradine, "Honey Won't You Let Me Be Your Friend"
The Crusaders, "Soul Caravan"
Roger Miller, "Fraulein"
Helen Reddy/Keith Carradine, "It Don't Worry Me"

Episode 139
Host: Helen Reddy

Ike and Tina Turner, "Sexy Ida"
Elvis Presley, *Midnight Special* Hit, "Don't Be Cruel"
Helen Reddy, "This Must Be Wrong"
The Bee Gees, "Nights on Broadway"
Wolfman Jack, salute to Joan Baez
The Bee Gees, medley of hits
Billy Joel, "Travelin' Prayer"
Mel Tillis, "Rainy Day Woman," "Mental Revenge"
Ike and Tina Turner, "Baby Get It On"
Helen Reddy, "You're My Home"
Billy Joel, "Ballad of Billy the Kid"
The Bee Gees, "Wind of Change"
Elvis Presley, "Don't Be Cruel" (reprise)

Episode 140 (see Pilot)

Episode 141
Host: Glen Campbell

Glen Campbell, "Rhinestone Cowboy," "Star Talk"
Gwen McCrae, "Love Insurance"
Glen Campbell/Gwen McCrae, "Rockin' Chair"
Glen Campbell, "Country Boy (You Got Your Feet in L.A.)"
Glen Campbell/Mac Davis, "Baby Don't Get Hooked on Me"
Mac Davis, "Naughty Girl"
Glen Campbell, "Star Talk" Part II, "When Will I Be Loved"
Gwen McCrae, "Move Me Baby"
Glen Campbell, "Marie"
Glen Campbell/Ed Davis, "Talk"
Glen Campbell, "Gentle on My Mind"

Episode 142
Host: Gabe Kaplan/Helen Reddy

Helen Reddy, salute to Elton John
Tavares, "It Only Takes a Minute"
Helen Reddy, "Angie Baby"
The J. Geils Band, "Love Itis"
Helen Reddy, "Pretty Pretty"
The Hudson Brothers, "Ma Ma Ma Baby"
The J. Geils Band, "Orange Driver," "Give It to Me"
Tavares, "Free Ride"
The Hudson Brothers, "Stop"
Helen Reddy, "Long Hard Climb," "Talk," "I Am Woman"

Episode 143
Host: Helen Reddy

Helen Reddy, salute to Glen Campbell
Carly Simon, "You're So Vain"
Roger Daltrey, "Come and Get Your Love"
Ohio Players, "Fire"
Helen Reddy, "Travelin' Band"
Helen Reddy/Merle Haggard, "Today I Started Loving You Again"
Merle Haggard, "Working Man Blues"
Ohio Players, "Sweet Sticky Thing"
Helen Reddy, "You Have Lived"
Roger Daltrey, "Near to Surrender"
Merle Haggard, fiddle medley
Helen Reddy, "I Am Woman"

Episode 144
Host: Helen Reddy

Helen Reddy, "Delta Dawn"
Freddie Prinze, comedy spot
Neil Sedaka, "Bad Blood," "Breaking Up Is Hard to Do"
Neil Sedaka/The Captain and Tennille, "Love Will Keep Us Together"
The Captain and Tennille, "Natural Woman"
Helen Reddy/Neil Sedaka, "Sad Eyes"
Neil Sedaka, "Lonely Night (Angel Face)"
Wolfman Jack, "Brown Sugar"
Neil Sedaka, "When You Were Loving Me"
Helen Reddy, "Emotion"
KC & the Sunshine Band, "(That's the Way) I Like It," "Get Down Tonight"
Helen Reddy, "I Am Woman"

Episode 145
Host: Helen Reddy

Helen Reddy, "Angie Baby"
Jimmie Walker, comedy spot
Elton John, *Midnight Special* Hit, "Goodbye Yellow Brick Road"
Brenda Lee, "Bringing It Back"
Wolfman Jack, salute to Jan and Dean
David Essex, "All the Fun of the Fair"
Helen Reddy, "Somewhere in the Night"
Tom Scott/L.A. Express, "Good Evening Mr. and Mrs. America"
David Essex, "Rock On"
Tom Scott and L.A. Express, "Tomcat"
David Essex, "Won't Get Burned Again"
Brenda Lee, "Too Hard to Handle"
Tom Scott/L.A. Express, "Rock Island Rocket"

Episode 146
Host: Helen Reddy

The Four Seasons, "Who Loves You"
John Denver, *Midnight Special* Hit, "Rocky Mountain High"
David Brenner, comedy spot
Helen Reddy, "Birthday Song"
Barry Manilow, "Something's Comin' Up"
Helen Reddy, salute to Harry Nilsson
Frankie Valli, "My Eyes Adored You"
Kiss, "Deuce"
Barry Manilow, "Tryin' to Get That Feelin' Again"
Helen Reddy, "Belle of the Blues"
Barry Manilow, "I Want to Be Somebody's Baby"
Kiss, "She"
Helen Reddy, "I Am Woman"

1976

Episode 184
Host: Jimmie Walker

Johnnie Taylor, "Disco Lady"
Elvin Bishop, "Struttin' My Stuff"
Salute to Neil Sedaka
Henry Gross, "Springtime Mama"
Johnnie Taylor, "Somebody's Gettin' It"
Lynn Anderson, medley: "Rose Garden," "Top of the World," "Cry"
Cate Brothers, "Union Man," "Can't Change My Heart"
1st National Rotagilla Band, "Rotagilla Chorus," "I Feel Like Singing"
Henry Gross, "Southern Band"
Lynn Anderson, "Gone at Last"

Episode 185 (see Episode 170A)

Episode 186
Host: Aretha Franklin

Lou Rawls, "You'll Never Find Another Love Like Mine"
The Marshall Tucker Band, "Long Hard Ride"
The Movies, "Dancin' on Ice"
Aretha Franklin, "Sparkle"
Aretha Franklin/Impressions, "Midnight Train to Georgia," "Easy to Remember," "Ain't No Mountain High Enough"
Salute to Paul Williams
The Marshall Tucker Band, "Fire on the Mountain"
Aretha Franklin, "Mr. D.J."
Lou Rawls, "Groovy People"
The Marshall Tucker Band, "Searchin' for a Rainbow"
Lou Rawls, "This Song Will Last Forever"
Aretha Franklin, "Mr. D.J."

Episode 187
Host: The Spinners

The Spinners, "I've Got to Make It on My Own"
England Dan & John Ford Coley, "I'd Really Love to See You Tonight"
Dr. Hook, "A Little Bit More"
Electric Light Orchestra, "Showdown"
Elton John/Kiki Dee, "Don't Go Breakin' My Heart"
The Spinners, "The Rubberband Man"
Junior Walker, "What Does It Take," "(I'm A) Road Runner," "Shotgun"
Dr. Hook, "Rollin' in My Sweet Baby's Arms"
England Dan & John Ford Coley, "Showboat Gambler"
Junior Walker, "I'm So Glad"
The Spinners, medley: "I Don't Want to Lose You," "One of a Kind Love Affair"
Dr. Hook, "Jungle to the Zoo"
England Dan & John Ford Coley, "Nights Are Forever without You"
The Spinners, "Could It Be I'm Falling in Love"

Episode 188
Host: Lesley Gore

Lesley Gore, "It's My Party," "Judy's Turn to Cry"
Danny & the Juniors, "At the Hop"
Johnny Tillotson, "Poetry in Motion"
The Drifters, "Up on the Roof"
Bobby Vee, "The Night Has a Thousand Eyes"
Lloyd Price, "Personality"
The Shirelles, "Will You Still Love Me Tomorrow"
Del Shannon, "Runaway"
Jimmie Rodgers, "Kisses Sweeter Than Wine," "Honey Comb"

Lesley Gore, medley: "Sunshine, Lollipops and Rainbows," "Maybe I Know," "She's a Fool," "That's the Way the Boys Are," "Sunshine"
Danny & the Juniors, "Rock and Roll Is Here to Stay"
The Drifters, "Save the Last Dance for Me"
Bobby Vee, "Come Back When You Grow Up," "My Girl," "Hey Girl"
The Shirelles, "Soldier Boy"
Lloyd Price, "Stagger Lee"
Johnny Tillotson, medley: "Heartaches by the Number," "Send Me the Pillow You Dream On," "It Keeps Right On A-Hurtin'," "Talk Back Tremblin' Lips"
Del Shannon, "Hats off to Larry," "Keep Searchin'"
Lesley Gore, "I'd Like to Be"
Jimmie Rodgers, "Oh Oh I'm Falling in Love Again"
Lesley Gore, "You Don't Own Me"

Episode 189
Host: George Carlin

George Carlin, monologue
Helen Reddy, "Hold Me in Your Dreams Tonight," "Mama," "Get off Me Baby"
Glen Campbell, "When Will I Be Loved," "Rhinestone Cowboy," "Gentle on My Mind"
Lou Rawls, "You'll Never Find Another Love Like Mine," "Groovy People," "This Song Will Last Forever"
Rick Dees & His Cast of Idiots, "Disco Duck"
Salute to Johhny Mathis
Cliff Richard, "Devil Woman"

Episode 190
Host: James Brown

Black Oak Arkansas, "When the Band"
England Dan & John Ford Coley, "I'd Really Love to See You Tonight"
James Brown, "The Payback"
Walter Murphy, "A Fifth of Beethoven"
The Brothers Johnson, "Get the Funk out Ma Face"
Black Oak Arkansas/Ruby Starr Alan, a tribute to Elvis, "Maybe I'm Amazed"
James Brown, "Cold Sweat," "Papa's Got a Brand New Bag"
Black Oak Arkansas, "Fistful of Love"
England Dan & John Ford Coley, "Nights Are Forever"
The Brothers Johnson, "I'll Be Good to You"
Black Oak Arkansas, "Love Comes Easy," "Lord Have Mercy"
James Brown, "Please Please Please"

Episode 191
Host: Jackie DeShannon/Johnny Rivers

Jackie DeShannon, "Put a Little Love in Your Heart"
Johnny Rivers, medley: "Secret Agent Man," "Seventh Son"
The Byrds, "Mr. Tambourine Man," "So You Want to Be a Rock 'n' Roll Star"
The Turtles, "Happy Together"
Steppenwolf, "Born to Be Wild"
Johnny Rivers, "Poor Side of Town"
Jackie DeShannon, "When You Walk in the Room," "Needles and Pins," "What the World Needs Now"
Gerry and the Pacemakers, "Ferry Cross the Mersey"
Sam and Dave, "Hold On I'm Coming"
Johnny Rivers, "Summer Rain," "Tracks of My Tears"

Gerry and the Pacemakers, "Don't Let the Sun Catch You Crying"
Jackie DeShannon, "The Weight"
Sam and Dave, "Soul Man"
Jackie DeShannon, "What the World Needs Now"

Episode 192
Host: Helen Reddy

The Spinners, "The Rubberband Man"
Wild Cherry, "Play That Funky Music"
Franklin Ajaye, monologue
Martha Reeves, "For the Rest of My Life"
Salute to James Brown
The Spinners, "I Don't Want to Lose You," "One of a Kind Love Affair"
Wild Cherry, "I Feel Sanctified"
Helen Reddy, medley: "Leave Me Alone (Ruby Red Dress)," "Angie Baby," "Delta Dawn"
Wild Cherry, "Hold On"
Martha Reeves, medley: "Jimmy Mack," "Quicksand," "Heat Wave," "Dancing in the Streets"
Helen Reddy, "Long Time Looking," "I Am Woman"

Episode 193
Host: KC & the Sunshine Band

KC & the Sunshine Band, "(Shake Shake Shake) Shake Your Booty"
Bay City Rollers, "I Only Want to Be with You"
Rick Dees & His Cast of Idiots, "Disco Duck"
ABBA, "Fernando"
Salute to Gladys Knight & the Pips
KC & the Sunshine Band, "That's the Way (I Like It)"
Bay City Rollers, "Saturday Night"
ABBA, "Mamma Mia"
Billy Braver, monologue
KC & the Sunshine Band, "Baby I Love You (Yes I Do)"
Bay City Rollers, "Rock 'n' Roller"
ABBA, "S.O.S."
KC & the Sunshine Band, "Get Down Tonight"

Episode 194
Host: Frankie Valli

Frankie Valli, "Boomerang"
The Four Seasons, "December, 1963 (Oh What a Night)"
Loretta Lynn, "Me and Bobby McGee"
Flash Cadillac/Wolfman Jack, "Did You Boogie (With Your Baby)"
Salute to Joe Cocker
Bob Seger: Film
Frankie Valli, "Easily"
Peter Allen, "She Loves to Hear the Music"
The Four Seasons, "Mystic Mr. Sam"
Flash Cadillac, "Your Love Keeps Liftin' me Higher and Higher"
Frankie Valli, "Swearin' to God"
Peter Allen, "This Sideshow's Leaving Town"
Frankie Valli, "Can't Get You Off of My Mind"

Episode 195
Host: Lou Rawls

Lou Rawls, "Groovy People"
Neil Sedaka, "You Gotta Make Your Own Sunshine"
Helen Reddy, *Midnight Special* Hit, "Angie Baby"
England Dan & John Ford Coley, "Nights Are Forever without You"
Salute to Traffic
The Lettermen, medley: "The Way You Look Tonight," "When I Fell in Love," "Summer Place," "Hurt So Bad," "Put Your Head on My Shoulder," "Shangri-La," "Going out of My Head," "Can't Take My Eyes Off of You"

Neil Sedaka, "Steppin' Out"
Lou Rawls/Dorothy Moore, "Mighty High"
Dorothy Moore, "For Old Times' Sake"
Lou Rawls, "Love Is a Hurtin' Thing"
England Dan & John Ford Coley, "I'd Really Love to See You Tonight"
Neil Sedaka, "Good Times, Good Music. . ."
England Dan & John Ford Coley, "Showboat Gambler"
Lou Rawls, "You'll Never Find Another Love Like Mine," "From Now On," "Groovy People"

Episode 196
Host: Helen Reddy

Leo Sayer, "You Make Me Feel Like Dancing"
Elvin Bishop, "Keep It Cool"
Helen Reddy, "Bluebird"
The Ritchie Family, "The Best Disco in Town"
Sasha and Yuri, "My Hope"
David Dundas, "Jeans On"
Salute to War
Leo Sayer, "Reflections"
Elvin Bishop, "Give It Up"
Helen Reddy, "Gladiola"
Sasha and Yuri, "Out of the U.S.S.R."
Elvin Bishop, "Spend Some Time," "Rock My Soul"
Leo Sayer, "Hold On to My Love"
The Ritchie Family, "Brazil"
Helen Reddy, "I Am Woman"

Episode 197, 245
Host: Diana Ross

Diana Ross, "Love Hangover," Motown medley
Jermaine Jackson, "Let's Be Young Tonight," "My Touch of Madness"
Tata Vega, "Full Speed Ahead"
Commodores, "Just Be Close to You"
Franklin Ajaye, comedy spot
Diana Ross, "One Love in My Lifetime"
Commodores, "Come Inside"
Tata Vega, "Been on My Own (Too Long in the Wilderness)"
Jermaine Jackson, "Bass Odyssey"
Tata Vega, "Never Had a Dream Come True"
Commodores, "Fancy Dancer"
Diana Ross/Jermaine Jackson/Tata Vega, "Let's Be Young Tonight"

Episode 198
Host: Wolfman Jack (Million Sellers)

The Captain and Tennille, "Lonely Nights (Angel Face)"
Wild Cherry, "Play That Funky Music"
The Miracles, "Love Machine (Part I)"
Eric Carmen, "All By Myself"
Elvin Bishop, "Fooled Around and Fell in Love"
Dr. Hook, "Only Sixteen"
The Manhattans, "Kiss and Say Goodbye"
Rick Dees & His Cast of Idiots, "Disco Duck (Part I)"
The Captain and Tennille, "Shop Around"
The Bay City Rollers, "Saturday Night"
The Sylvers, "Boogie Fever"
Cliff Richard, "Devil Woman"
Queen, "Bohemian Rhapsody"
Rhythm Heritage, "Theme from S.W.A.T."
Wild Cherry, "Play That Funky Music"

Episode 199
Host: Helen Reddy
Helen Reddy, "Birthday Song"
Judy Collins, "Someday Soon"
Olivia Newton-John, "Every Face Tells a Story"
The Spinners, "The Rubberband Man"
Joe Cocker, "I Broke Down"
El Chicano, "Dancin' Mama"
Salute to Steppenwolf
Joe Cocker, "With a Little Help from My Friends"
Stuff, "How Long Will It Last"
Darvy Traylor, "I Can't Stop Loving You"
Helen Reddy, "Long Hard Climb"
El Chicano, "Para Ti"
Joe Cocker, "Without Love"
Darvy Traylor, "Takin' It to the Streets"
Helen Reddy, "I Am Woman"

Episode 200
Host: Tom Jones
Tom Jones, "Feel the Need"
Glen Campbell/Beach Boys medley
Tom Jones/Sly & the Family Stone, "Everyday People"
Tom Jones/Lynn Anderson, "Don't Go Breakin' My Heart"
Tom Jones, "Delilah," "Third Rate Romance," "Why My Lord," "Get Back," "Feelings," "You Don't Have to Say You Love Me," "Love Machine," "Say You'll Stay until Tomorrow"
Glen Campbell, "Bloodline"
Emerson, Lake & Palmer, "I Believe in Father Christmas"
Sly & the Family Stone, "What I Was Thinkin' in My Head"
Lynn Anderson, "Stand by Your Man"
Tom Jones, "Say You'll Stay until Tomorrow"

Episode 201
Host: None—Million Sellers
Elton John/Kiki Dee, "Don't Go Breakin' My Heart"
KC & the Sunshine Band, "(Shake, Shake, Shake) Shake Your Booty," "Get Down Tonight," "That's the Way (I Like It)"
England Dan & John Ford Coley, "I'd Really Love to See You Tonight"
Hot Chocolate, "You Sexy Thing"
Walter Murphy, "A Fifth of Beethoven"
Gary Wright, "Dream Weaver"
Commodores, "Sweet Love"
Four Seasons, "December, 1963 (Oh What a Night)"
Lou Rawls, "You'll Never Find Another Love Like Mine"
Dorothy Moore, "Misty Blue"
The Staple Singers, "Let's Do It Again"
Henry Gross, "Shannon"

Episode 202 (see Episode 170A)

Episode 203
Host: Judy Collins
Judy Collins, "Send in the Clowns"
Leo Sayer, "You Make Me Feel Like Dancing"
Salute to Rod Stewart
Robert Palmer, "Man Smart Woman Smarter"
Freddy Fender, "Wasted Days and Wasted Nights," "Before the Next Teardrop Falls," "Living It Down"
Judy Collins, "Bread and Roses"
Brick, "Dazz"
Doc Severinsen, "Melody"

Leo Sayer, "When I Need You"
Robert Palmer, "Gotta Get a Grip on You" (Part II)
Freddy Fender, "Fifties medley"
Judy Collins, "Everything Must Change"
Brick, "That's What It's All About"
Judy Collins, "Political Science," "Special Delivery"

Episode 204, 224, 277, 365
Host: Helen Reddy
(Fourth Anniversary Special)
The Bee Gees, "Nights on Broadway"
Linda Ronstadt, "You're No Good"
Kris Kristofferson/Rita Coolidge, "I Never Had It So Good"
Earth, Wind & Fire, "Shining Star"
Monty Python's Flying Circus, comedy spot
Salute to Alice Cooper, Part I
Salute to Alice Cooper, Part II
Neil Sedaka/The Captain and Tennille, "Love Will Keep Us Together"
Aretha Franklin, "Something He Can Feel"
George Carlin, comedy spot
The Bee Gees, "Jive Talkin'"
Linda Ronstadt, "Faithless Love"

Episode 205
Host: Glen Campbell
Glen Campbell, "Southern Nights"
Queen, "Somebody to Love"
Seals & Crofts/Glen Campbell, "Dust on My Saddle"
ABBA, "Fernando"
David Dundas, "Jeans On"
Glen Campbell, "Sunflower"
Salute to the Spinners
ABBA, "Dancing Queen"
Sly & the Family Stone, "Heard Ya Missed Me Well I'm Back"
Seals & Crofts, "Goodbye Old Buddies"
Glen Campbell, "For Cryin' Out Loud," "This Is (Sarah's Song)," "God Only Knows," "Early Morning Song"
Sly & the Family Stone, "What Was I Thinkin' in My Head"
Seals & Crofts, "Cause You Love"
Glen Campbell, "Southern Nights"

Episode 206 (see Episode 69)

Episode 207
Host: Electric Light Orchestra
Electric Light Orchestra, "Livin' Thing"
Mary MacGregor, "Torn Between Two Lovers"
Santana, "Let the Music Set You Free"
Electric Light Orchestra, "Do Ya," "Telephone Line"
George Miller, comedy spot
Don McLean, "Magdalene Lane"
Santana, "Carnaval," "Let the Children Play," "Jugando," "Give Me Love" (outside clip)
Electric Light Orchestra, "Rock Aria" (outside clip)
Don McLean, "Muleskinner Blues," "Cripple Creek"
Mary MacGregor, "I Just Want to Love You"
Electric Light Orchestra, "Livin' Thing"

Episode 208
Host: Loretta Lynn
Loretta Lynn, "Coal Miner's Daughter"
Leo Sayer, "You Make Me Feel Like Dancing"
Mickey Gilley, "Lawdy Miss Clawdy"
Loretta Lynn, "Somebody Somewhere"
Willie Nelson, "Will the Circle Be Unbroken"
Johnny Rodriguez, "Hillbilly Heart"

Leo Sayer, "When I Need Love," "Endless Flight"
Kinky Friedman, "Dear Abby"
Mickey Gilley, "Bring It On Home to Me"
Loretta Lynn/Mickey Gilley, "Release Me," "Honky Tonk," "Crazy Arms"
Mothers Finest, "Rain"
Billy Crystal, comedy spot
Johnny Rodriguez, "Love Put a Song in My Heart"
Kinky Friedman, "Ol' Ben Lucas"
Willie Nelson, "Night Life"
Loretta Lynn, "Your Woman Your Friend"

Episode 209
Host: KC & the Sunshine Band
KC & the Sunshine Band, "(Shake, Shake, Shake) Shake Your Booty"
Heart, "Magic Man"
Gordon Lightfoot, "The Wreck of the Edmund Fitzgerald"
Rocky film clip
ABBA, "Dancing Queen"
Jose Feliciano, "Every Woman"
KC & the Sunshine Band, "Get Down Tonight"
Gordon Lightfoot, "Race among the Ruins"
Andy Kaufman, "I Trusted You"
Jose Feliciano, "The Hungry Years"
Heart, "Dreamboat Annie (Fantasy Child)," "Crazy on You"
KC & the Sunshine Band, "That's the Way (I Like It)"
Heart, "White Lightning and Wine"

Episode 210
Host: Marilyn McCoo/Billy Davis Jr.
Manfred Mann's Earth Band, "Blinded by the Light"
Marilyn McCoo/Billy Davis Jr., "Your Love"
Thelma Houston, "Don't Leave Me This Way"
Manfred Mann's Earth Band, "Spirit in the Night"
Marilyn McCoo/Billy Davis Jr., "I Hope We Get to Love in Time"
Thelma Houston/Marilyn McCoo/Billy Davis Jr., "Proud Mary"
Fleetwood Mac, "Say You Love Me," "Go Your Own Way"
Fleetwood Mac, "So Afraid"
Marilyn McCoo/Billy Davis Jr., "Gone at Last"

Episode 211
Host: Aretha Franklin
Aretha Franklin, "Respect," "Hooked on Your Love"
Glen Campbell, "Southern Nights"
Thin Lizzy, "Jailbreak"
Salute to Neil Sedaka
Queen, "Tie Your Mother Down"
Aretha Franklin, "Sweet Passions"
The Babys, "If You've Got the Time"
Brian Cadd, "White on White Eldorado"
Thin Lizzy, "Don't Believe a Word"
Aretha Franklin, "When I Think About You," "Meadows of Springtime"
Brian Cadd, "Heavenly Night in September"
Aretha Franklin, "When I Think About You"

Episode 212
Host: George Carlin
George Carlin, comedy spot
Natalie Cole, "I've Got Love on My Mind"
Electric Light Orchestra, "Do Ya"
Stephen Bishop, "Save It for a Rainy Day"
Salute to Jose Feliciano
Chick Corea, "Music Magic"
Travis Shook, "The Great Point Song"
Natalie Cole, "Unpredictable You," "Party Nights"
Chick Corea, "So Long Mickey Mouse"
Stephen Bishop, "On and On"

Episode 213
Host: Gabe Kaplan
Gabe Kaplan, comedy spot
Rod Stewart, "Tonight's the Night"
ABBA, "Dancing Queen"
Gary Wright, "Water Sign"
Rod Stewart, "The First Cut Is the Deepest"
Salute to Judy Collins
James Darren/Hattie Winston, "You Take My Heart Away"
The Dirt Band, "Fish Song"
Gary Wright, "I'm Alright"
The Dirt Band, "Disco Swamp"

Episode 214
Host: George Benson
George Benson, "Everything Must Change," "Gonna Love You More"
Van Morrison, "Joyous Sound," "Heavy Connection," "Cold Wind in August"
Carlos Santana/George Benson, "Breezin'," "Valdez in the Country"
Etta James/Dr. John, "I'd Rather Be Blind" (Everyone on the show), "Moondance," "Bring It on Home to Me"

Episode 215, 334
Host: Wolfman Jack (British Rock)
Fleetwood Mac, "Go Your Own Way"
Queen, "Tie Your Mother Down"
Salute to Elton John
Electric Light Orchestra, "Do Ya"
Fleetwood Mac, "You Make Lovin' Fun"
Genesis, "Assault and Battery"
Salute to Rod Stewart
Queen, "Somebody to Love"
Electric Light Orchestra, "Rock Aria," "Telephone Line"
Queen, "Bohemian Rhapsody"

Episode 216
Host: Helen Reddy
Helen Reddy, "You're My World," "The Happy Girls"
Kenny Rogers, "Lucille"
The Kinks, "Sleepwalker"
The Babys, "If You've Got the Time"
James Brown, "Get Up Offa That Thing"
The Sanford/Townsend Band, "Smoke from a Distant Fire"
The Babys, "Looking for Love"
Kenny Rogers, "In and out of Your Heart"
The Kinks, "Juke Box Music"
Helen Reddy, "Midnight Skys," "Aquarius Mirable"
The Babys, "Wild Man"
James Brown, "I Refuse to Lose"

Episode 217
Host: Wolfman Jack
Glen Campbell, "Southern Nights"
Marilyn McCoo/Billy Davis Jr., "Your Love"
Natalie Cole, "I've Got Love on My Mind"
Manfred Mann's Earth Band, "Blinded By the Light"

ABBA, "Dancing Queen"
Heart, "Magic Man"
Mary MacGregor, "Torn Between Two Lovers"
Stephen Bishop, "Save It for a Rainy Day"
Brick, "Dazz"
Manfred Mann's Earth Band, "Spirit in the Night"
ABBA, "Fernando"
Heart, "Crazy on You"
Stephen Bishop, "On and On"

Episode 218
Host: Lou Rawls

Lou Rawls, "Some Folks Never Learn"
Andrew Gold, "Lonely Boy"
Salute to Earth, Wind & Fire
Gino Vannelli, "Summers of My Life"
Leo Sayer, "When I Need You"
Gordon Lightfoot, "Race Among the Ruins"
Lou Rawls/Donna Summer, "Swing Low
    Sweet Chariot"
Lou Rawls, "See You When I Git There"
Melanie, "Cyclone"
Leo Sayer, "Spring Again," "You Make Me Feel
    Like Dancing"
Andrew Gold, "Go Back Home Again"
Lou Rawls, "Some Day You'll Be Old"
Sammy Davis (walk on)

Episode 219
Host: Neil Sedaka

Neil Sedaka, "Oh Carole," "Tin Pan Alley"
The Captain and Tennille, "(You Make Me Feel
    Like A) Natural Woman"
Helen Reddy, "You're My World"
Judy Collins, "Bread and Roses"
Neil Sedaka, "Amarillo"
Janis Ian, "I Want to Make You Love Me"
Salute to Joan Baez
Thelma Houston, "Don't Leave Me This Way"
Kim Carnes, "Sailin'"
Helen Reddy, "The Happy Girls"
Neil Sedaka, "Hollywood Lady," "Sleazy Love"
Janis Ian, "Party Lights"
Thelma Houston, "If It's the Last Thing I Do"
Neil Sedaka, "Breaking Up Is Hard to Do"

Episode 220
Host: Bread

Bread, "Lay Your Money Down"
England Dan & John Ford Coley, "It's Sad
    to Belong"
Andrew Gold, "Lonely Boy"
Johnny Rivers, "Slow Dancin'"
Valentine, "Take You Back"
Salute to Kenny Rogers
Joni Mitchell, "Big Yellow Taxi"
Bread, "The Chosen One"
Eddie Rabbitt, "Rocky Mountain Music"
Andrew Gold, "Go Back Home Again"
England Dan & John Ford Coley, "Soldier
    in the Rain"
Valentine, "I've Got It"
Bread, "She's the Only One," "Lost Without
    Your Love"

Episode 221, 388
Hosts: Emmylou Harris and Little Feat

Emmylou Harris/Little Feat, "Queen of the
    Silver Dollar"
Little Feat, "Dixie Chicken"
Bonnie Raitt, "Runaway"
Jessie Winchester, "Rhumba Man"
Neil Young, "Like a Hurricane" (outside clip)
Paul Barrere, "Old Folks Boogie"

Jessie Winchester, "I Can't Stand Up Alone"
Weather Report, "Birdland"
Bonnie Raitt, "Home"
Jessie Winchester/Emmylou Harris, "Nothing But
    a Breeze"
Little Feat, "Rocket in My Pocket"
Emmylou Harris, "My Songbird"
Bonnie Raitt, "Sugar Mama"
Weather Report, "Teen Town"
Little Feat, "Rock and Roll Doctor"

Episode 222
Host: Neil Sedaka

Neil Sedaka, "Amarillo," "Laughter in the Rain,"
    "A Song," "Bad Blood," "One Night Stand"
Fleetwood Mac, "You Make Lovin' Fun"
Kenny Rogers, "Lucille," "Daytime Friends"
George Benson/Van Morrison, "Misty"
Renaissance, "Carpet of the Sun," "Midas Man"
Salute to Van Morrison
Small Wonder, "Be Part of Me," "Run Run Around"
Carole Bayer Sager, "Sweet Alibis"

Episode 223
Host: Gregg Allman

Gregg Allman, "Let This Be a Lesson to Ya"
Elvin Bishop/Gregg Allman, "Little Brown Bird"
Jennifer Warnes, "Right Time of the Night"
Bad Company, "Run with the Pack" (outside clip)
Jerry Lee Lewis, "Whole Lotta Shakin' Goin' On"
Booker T. and the MG's, "Double Thrust"
Gregg Allman, "Sweet Feelin'," "Midnight Rider"
Elvin Bishop/Booker T. and the MG's, "Don't You
    Lie to Me"
Salute to Little Richard
Jennifer Warnes, "I'm Dreaming"
Jerry Lee Lewis, "The Closest Thing to You"
Elvin Bishop/Booker T. and the MG's, "Dedicated
    to the One I Love"
Gregg Allman, "Don't Keep Me Wondering,"
    "Midnight Rider"

Episode 224 (see Episode 204)

Episode 225 (see Episode 158)

Episode 226 (see Episode 84)

Episode 227 (see Episode 105)

Episode 228
Host: KC & the Sunshine Band

KC & the Sunshine Band, "I'm Your Boogie
    Man"
The Emotions, "Best of My Love"
Peter McCann, "Do You Wanna Make Love"
Cat Stevens, "The Old Schoolyard" (outside clip)
Bay City Rollers, "Saturday Night"
The Emotions, "Don't Ask My Neighbor"
Salute to Willie Nelson
KC & the Sunshine Band, "Keep It Comin' Love"
Peter McCann, "Right Time of the Night"
Flora Purim, "Nothing Will Be As It Was"
The Emotions, "Flowers"
KC & the Sunshine Band, "That's the Way (I Like
    It)"
Flora Purim, "Open Your Eyes You Can Fly,"
    "Sometime Ago"
KC & the Sunshine Band, "(Shake, Shake,
    Shake) Shake Your Booty"

Episode 229
Host: The Spinners

The Spinners, "Could It Be I'm Fallin' in Love,"
    "Rubberband Man"
Andy Gibb, "I Just Want to Be Your Everything"
Rod Stewart, "The Killing of George" (outside clip)
The Spinners, "The Way We Were"
Salute to Blood, Sweat & Tears
Johnny Rivers, "Slow Dancin'"
The Sons of Champlin, "Saved by the Grace of
    Your Love"
Andy Gibb, "Love Is Thicker Than Water"
The Spinners, "Games People Play"
The Sons of Champlin, "Hold On"
The Spinners, "You're Throwing a Good Love
    Away," "Mighty Love"

Episode 230
Host: The Bay City Rollers

The Bay City Rollers, "You Made Me Believe in
    Magic"
KC & the Sunshine Band, "Keep It Comin' Love"
Roger Daltrey, "One of the Boys" (outside clip)
Electric Light Orchestra, "Telephone Line"
England Dan & John Ford Coley, "It's Sad to
    Belong"
The Bay City Rollers, "Yesterday's Hero"
Jimmy Webb, medley
Salute to Hoyt Axton
Billy Braver, comedy spot
Jimmy Webb, "Mixed-Up Guy"
The Bay City Rollers, "It's a Game"
England Dan & John Ford Coley, "Soldier in the
    Rain"
Jimmy Webb, "The Highway Man"
The Bay City Rollers, "Love Fever"

Episode 231 (see Episode 42)

Episode 232 (see Episode 157)

Episode 233
Host: The Captain and Tennille

The Captain and Tennille, "Can't Stop Dancin'"
Chaka Khan/The Captain and Tennille, "Let the
    Good Times Roll"
Lou Rawls, "See You When I Get There"
David Bowie, "Fame" (outside clip)
The Captain and Tennille, "Come In from
    the Rain"
Little River Band, "Help Is on Its Way"
Salute to Janis Ian
Rufus, featuring Chaka Khan, "Everlasting Love"
Neil Young, "Like a Hurricane" (outside clip)
Lou Rawls, "Spring Again"
The Captain and Tennille, "54 Boogie Blues"
Little River Band, "It's a Long Way There"
The Captain and Tennille, "Circles"

Episode 234
Host: David Brenner

Joan Baez, "Diamonds and Rust"
The Brothers Johnson, "Strawberry Letter 23"
Average White Band/Ben E. King, "Keeping It to
    Myself"
REO Speedwagon, "Keep Pushin'"
Joan Baez, "Time Rag"
Salute to Yes
Average White Band, "Star in the Ghetto"
Joan Baez, "Honest Lullaby"
REO Speedwagon, "Ridin' the Storm Out"
Joan Baez, "A Heartfelt Line or Two"

Episode 235
Host: George Benson

Roy Ayers/Herbie Hancock/Harvey Mason/Jean-Luc
    Ponty/John Klemmer/George Benson, "Fever"
George Benson, "The Greatest Love of All"
Bonnie Raitt, "Three Time Loser"
Roger Daltrey, "Say It Ain't So, Joe" (outside clip)
George Benson/Minnie Riperton, "Misty"
Salute to Lou Rawls
George Benson, "Nature Boy"
Minnie Riperton, "Young Willin' and Able"
Bonnie Raitt, "My Opening Farewell"
George Benson/Roy Ayers, "What's Going On"
Minnie Riperton, "Could It Be I'm in Love"
Roy Ayers/Herbie Hancock/Harvey Mason/Jean-
    Luc Ponty/John Klemmer/George Benson,
    "Chameleon"

Episode 236 (see Episode 164)

Episode 237, 366
Host: Kenny Rogers

Kenny Rogers, "Just Dropped In (To See What
    Condition My Condition Was In)"
B.J. Thomas, "Don't Worry Baby"
Debby Boone, "You Light Up My Life"
Supertramp, "Give a Little Bit"
Bob Marley & the Wailers, "Jammin'"
Kenny Rogers/Debby Boone, "Desperado"
Kenny Rogers, "Daytime Friends"
Andy Gibb, "Love Is Thicker Than Water"
Debby Boone, "Baby I'm Yours"
B.J. Thomas, "Play Something Sweet (Brickyard
    Blues)"
Kenny Rogers, "Sweet Music Man"
Bob Marley & the Wailers, "Get Up, Stand Up,"
    "Exodus"
Kenny Rogers, "Oh Lady Luck"

Episode 238
Host: Marilyn McCoo/Billy Davis Jr.

Marilyn McCoo/Billy Davis Jr., "My Very Special
    Darling"
Rod Stewart, "I Was Only Joking"
Eric Carmen, "Marathon Man"
Johnny Rivers, "Slow Dancin'"
Marilyn McCoo/Billy Davis Jr., "Wonderful"
Salute to Randy Newman
Eric Carmen, "She Did It"
Rod Stewart, "Hot Legs"
Marilyn McCoo/Billy Davis Jr./Michael Masser,
    medley
Eric Carmen, "Boats Against the Current"
Marilyn McCoo/Billy Davis Jr., "My Reason to Be
    Is You," "Look What You've Done to My Heart"

Episode 239
Host: Elvin Bishop

Elvin Bishop, "Struttin' My Stuff"
Electric Light Orchestra, "Telephone Line"
Crystal Gayle, "Don't It Make My Brown Eyes
    Blue"
Ronnie McDowell, "The King Is Gone"
Van Morrison, "Domino"
Salute to KC & the Sunshine Band
Thin Lizzy, "Dancin' in the Moonlight"
Elvin Bishop, "Fooled Around and Fell in Love,"
    "Birthday Cake"
Elvin Bishop/Crystal Gayle, "Green Door"
Electric Light Orchestra, "Rock Aria"
Elvin Bishop, "Another Mule"
Crystal Gayle, "Ready for Times to Get Better"
Elvin Bishop/Van Morrison, "Help Me"
Thin Lizzy, "Emerald"
Elvin Bishop, "Rock My Soul"

Episode 240
Host: David Soul

David Soul, "Silver Lady"
Debby Boone, "You Light Up My Life"
David Soul/Debby Boone, "Oregon"
Little River Band, "Help Is on Its Way"
David Soul, "Playing to an Audience of One"
Styx, "Come Sail Away"
Salute to Electric Light Orchestra
Paul Nicholas, "Heaven on the Seventh Floor"
David Soul, "Nobody but a Fool or a Preacher"
Debby Boone, "My Dangerous Heart"
Styx, "Fooling Yourself"
David Soul/Lynne Marta, "Tennessee Blues"
David Soul, "Flute Thing," "Hooray for Hollywood"

Episode 241
Host: Lou Rawls

Lou Rawls, "Lady Love"
KC & the Sunshine Band, "Keep It Comin' Love"
Rod Stewart, "You're in My Heart"
Player, "Baby Come Back"
Lou Rawls, "Tradewinds"
Salute to Harry Nilsson
Lou Rawls/Candi Staton, "You Bet Your Sweet Sweet Love"
Kip Addotta, comedy spot
Alan Parsons Project, "I Wouldn't Want to Be Like You"
Rod Stewart, "Insane"
Player, "Come On Out"
Lou Rawls, "You'll Never Find Another Love Like Mine"
Candi Staton, "Young Hearts Run Free"
Lou Rawls, "There Will Be Love"

Episode 242
Host: Glen Campbell

Glen Campbell, Beach Boys medley
Brick, "Dusic"
Jeff Kutash and His Dancing Machine, *Star Wars* Theme
Dorothy Moore/Glen Campbell, "How Sweet It Is"
Dorothy Moore, "Let the Music Play"
Glen Campbell, "William Tell Overture"
Dianne Steinberg, "Amazing"
Salute to Anne Murray
Dorothy Moore, "I Believe You"
Glen Campbell, "MacArthur Park"
Brick, "Ain't Gonna Hurt Nobody"
Dianne Steinberg, "The Wish"
Glen Campbell, "Amazing Grace"

Episode 243
Host: The Spinners

The Spinners, "I'll Be Around"
Crystal Gayle, "Don't It Make My Brown Eyes Blue"
The Spinners/Ronee Blakely, "Then Came You"
Alan Price, "I Want to Dance"
Salute to Average White Band
The Spinners, "Heaven on Earth"
Ronee Blakely, "Need a New Sun Rising"
Gato Barbieri, "Ruby"
Heatwave, "Boogie Nights"
J.J. Barrie, "Bing's Gone"
Alan Price, "I've Been Hurt"
Gato Barbieri, "I Want You"
The Spinners, "Baby I Need Your Love," "Easy Come, Easy Go"

Episode 244
Host: Frankie Valli

Frankie Valli, "Swearin' to God"
Thudpucker (outside clip)
Salute to Olivia Newton-John
Robin Trower, "Farther Up the Road"
Frankie Valli, "I Need You"
Robert Gordon/Linky Wray, "Red Hot"
Pat Boone, "Ain't Going Down in the Ground Before My Time"
Chris Hillman, "Playing the Fool"
Robin Trower, "Somebody's Calling"
Frankie Valli, "With You"
Chris Hillman, "Heartbreaker"
Robert Gordon/Linky Wray, "The Way I Walk"
Robin Trower, "Bridge of Sighs"
Frankie Valli, "Native New Yorker"

Episode 245 (see Episode 197)

Episode 246
Host: Wolfman Jack

Paul McCartney & Wings, "Mull of Kintyre"
David Bowie, "Heroes"
England Dan & John Ford Coley, "Gone Too Far"
The Jacksons, "Going Places"
Libby Titus, "Fool That I Am"
Air Supply, "Feel the Breeze"
Ricci Martin, "Moonbeams"
Salute to Brenda Lee
Bill Withers, "Lovely Day"
Libby Titus, "Love Has No Pride"
England Dan & John Ford Coley, "Dowdy Ferry Road"
Air Supply, "Do It Again"
Fusion, "You Gotta Find Jesus"

Episode 247
Host: Lou Rawls

Lou Rawls, "See You When I Get There"
Paul Nicholas, "Heaven on the Seventh Floor"
Rod Stewart, "You're in My Heart"
Lou Rawls/Dorothy Moore, "Let It Be Me"
Salute to Electric Light Orchestra, Part II
Dorothy Moore, "With Pen in Hand"
Rod Stewart, "Hot Legs"
Thin Lizzy, "Bad Reputation"
Dorothy Moore, "Let the Music Play"
Lou Rawls, "Pure Imagination"
Rod Stewart, "I Was Only Joking"
Paul Nicholas, "Earthquake, Landslide, Hurricane"
Lou Rawls, "Lady Love," "Tradewinds"

Episode 248
Host: Pat Boone (Christmas Show)

Pat Boone and Family, "Joy to the World"
Debby Boone, "You Light Up My Life"
David Gates, "Goodbye Girl"
Pat Boone, medley of hits
Pat Boone/Debby Boone/David Gates, "Nothing Ever Changes," "If"
Phoebe Snow, "Never Letting Go"
Pat Boone, "Ain't Going Down in the Ground Before My Time"
Pat Boone and the Boone Girls, Christmas medley
Salute to Emerson, Lake & Palmer
Phoebe Snow, "Love Makes a Woman"
Debby Boone, "Until Your Love Broke Through"
Phoebe Snow, "Electra"
Pat Boone, "Break My Mind," "We Wish You a Merry Christmas"

Episode 249
Hosts: Marilyn McCoo and Billy Davis Jr.

Marilyn McCoo/Billy Davis Jr., "You Don't Have to Be a Star to Be in My Show"
Boz Scaggs, "Lowdown," "Lido Shuffle," "Balloons"
Dave Mason, "We Just Disagree"
Gladys Knight, "I've Got to Use My Imagination"
Marilyn McCoo/Billy Davis Jr., disco dance segment
Heart, "Check It Out," "Keep Your Love Alive"
Marilyn McCoo/Billy Davis Jr., "Sad Eyes," "You Got Me Running"
Heart, "Little Queen," "Barracuda"
Dave Mason, "Let It Go, Let It Flow"
Marilyn McCoo/Billy Davis Jr., "Just the Two of Us"

Episode 250
Host: The Bay City Rollers

The Bay City Rollers, "Money Honey"
Randy Newman, "Short People"
Queen, "We Are the Champions"
Black Oak Arkansas, "Race with the Devil"
Kenny Rogers, "Sweet Music Man"
The Bay City Rollers, "The Way I Feel Tonight"
Black Oak Arkansas, "Not Fade Away"
New Riders of the Purple Sage, "Jasper"
The Bay City Rollers, "Pie"
Greg Lake, "C'est La Vie"
The Bay City Rollers, "Don't Let the Music Die"
Kenny Rogers, "Morgana Jones"
New Riders of the Purple Sage, "Take a Red"
Kenny Rogers, "Something's Burnin'"
The Bay City Rollers, "Wouldn't You Like It?"

Episode 251
Host: The O'Jays

The O'Jays, "For the Love of Money"
England Dan & John Ford Coley, "Gone Too Far"
Billy Preston, "Nothin' From Nothin'"
David Bowie, "Heroes"
Sammy Hagar, "Red"
The O'Jays, "Message in Our Music"
Salute to the Animals
The O'Jays, medley: "Backstabbers," "Wildflowers," "Sunshine," "Love Train," "Put Your Hands Together"
Dee Dee Sharp Gamble, "I'd Really Love to See You Tonight"
Emerson, Lake & Palmer, "Tiger in the Spotlight"
Billy Preston, "I'm Really Gonna Miss You"
Sammy Hagar, "You Make Me Crazy"
Billy Preston, "Wide Stride"
The O'Jays, "Stand Up"

Episode 252 (see Episode 181)

Episode 253
Host: Aretha Franklin

Aretha Franklin, "Touch Me Up"
Dan Hill, "Sometimes When We Touch"
Aretha Franklin, "Keep On Loving You"
Barry White, "It's Ecstasy When You Lay Down Next to Me"
Salute to Black Oak Arkansas
Four Tops, "Ain't No Woman (Like the One I've Got)"

Dan Hill, "Hold On"
Aretha Franklin, "Almighty Fire"
Aretha Franklin/Four Tops, "Isn't She Lovely"
Fred Travalena, comedy spot
Four Tops, "The Show Must Go On"
Aretha Franklin, "Joy Baby," "Keep On Loving You"

Episode 254
Host: Shaun Cassidy

Shaun Cassidy, "Hey Deanie"
Paul McCartney & Wings, "Mull of Kintyre"
Peter Allen, "I Go to Rio"
Bob Welch, "Sentimental Lady"
George Duke, "Reach For It"
Salute to ABBA
Shaun Cassidy, "That's Rock and Roll," "Teen Dream"
Tom Dressen, comedy spot
George Duke, "Searchin' My Mind"
Bob Welch, "Ebony Eyes"
Peter Allen, "She Loves to Hear the Music"
George Duke, "We Give Our Love"
Shaun Cassidy, "That's Rock and Roll"

Episode 255
Host: Natalie Cole

Natalie Cole, "This Will Be"
KC & the Sunshine Band, "Boogie Shoes"
Rick Danko, "Java Blues"
The Bee Gees, interview
Yvonne Elliman, "If I Can't Have You"
Ronnie Laws, "Friends and Strangers"
Natalie Cole, "Lucy in the Sky with Diamonds"
Rick Danko, "Brainwash"
Natalie Cole, "Our Love"
Yvonne Elliman, "Sally Go Round the Roses"
Ronnie Laws, "Always There"
Natalie Cole, "Be Thankful," "Just Can't Stay Away"

Episode 256, 281, 349
Host: Wolfman Jack

Elton John/Kiki Dee, "Don't Go Breakin' My Heart"
Electric Light Orchestra, "Telephone Line"
Andy Gibb, "I Just Want to Be Your Everything"
Queen, "We Are the Champions"
Rod Stewart, "Hot Legs"
Debby Boone, "You Light Up My Life"
Cat Stevens, "(Remember the Days of The) Old Schoolyard"
Olivia Newton-John, "Sam"
Manfred Mann's Earth Band, "Blinded by the Light"
Leo Sayer, "When I Need You"
The Emotions, "Best of My Love"
Johnny Rivers, "Slow Dancin'"
Crystal Gayle, "Don't It Make My Brown Eyes Blue"
Player, "Baby Come Back"

Episode 257
Host: Donna Summer

Donna Summer, "I Feel Love"
Kenny Rogers, "Daytime Friends"
Kenny Rogers/Dottie West, "Every Time Two Fools Collide"
Salute to Elvin Bishop
The Captain and Tennille, "Sad Eyes"
Journey, "Lights" (outside clip)
Donna Summer, "Last Dance"
Brooklyn Dreams, "Music, Harmony and Rhythm"

Kenny Rogers/Dottie West, "Anyone Who Isn't Me Tonight"
Kenny Rogers, "Love or Something Like It"
Donna Summer, "I Love You"
Journey, "Feeling That Way"
Brooklyn Dreams, "Don't Fight the Feeling"
Donna Summer "A Man Like You," "I Feel Love"

Episode 258
Host: Rick Nelson

Rick Nelson, "I Wanna Move with You"
Paul Davis, "I Go Crazy"
10cc, "The Things We Do for Love" (outside clip)
Rick Nelson, "Gimme a Little Sign"
Salute to The Captain and Tennille
Sweet Inspirations, "Dance"
Rick Nelson, "Something You Can't Buy," "Garden Party"
George Benson, "Here Comes the Sun"
Rick Nelson, "Mystery Train"
Paul Davis, "Bad Dream"
Sweet Inspirations, "Sweet Inspiration"
Paul Davis, "I Never Heard the Song At All"
10cc, "Five o'Clock in the Morning" (outside clip)
Rick Nelson, "I Wanna Move with You"

Episode 259
Host: Ronnie Milsap

Ronnie Milsap, "Let My Love Be Your Pillow"
Ronnie Milsap/Larry Gatlin, "Lovesick Blues"
Crystal Gayle, "Ready for the Times to Get Better"
Larry Gatlin, "Love Is Just a Game"
Salute to Jerry Lee Lewis
Ronnie Milsap, musical impressions: Elvis/Fats Domino/The Platters/Jerry Lee Lewis/Eddy Arnold
Ronnie Milsap, medley: "I'm a Stand By Your Woman Man," "What Goes On When the Sun Goes Down," "Daydreams," "About Night Things"
Conway Twitty, "It's Only Make Believe"
Ronnie Milsap, "What a Difference You've Made in My Life"
Larry Gatlin, "I Just Wish You Were Someone I Love"
Crystal Gayle, "Let's Do It Right"
Conway Twitty, "Maybellene"
Larry Gatlin, "Broken Lady"
Ronnie Milsap, "Country Cookin'," "It Was Almost Like a Song," "Let My Love"

Episode 260
Host: Player

Player, "Baby Come Back"
Jay Ferguson, "Thunder Island"
Starland Vocal Band, "Afternoon Delight"
Salute to Queen
ABBA, "Name of the Game"
Player, "Cancellation"
The Rutles, "Hard Days Rut," "Ouch"
Player, "This Time I'm in It for Love"
Jay Ferguson, "Losing Control"
New Birth, "It's Been a Long Time"
Player, "Come On Out"
Starland Vocal Band, "Late Night Radio"
New Birth, "Coming from All Ends"
Player, "Baby Come Back"

Episode 261
Host: Tom Jones

Tom Jones, "Goin' Places"
Dan Hill, "Sometimes When We Touch"
Tom Jones, "I Just Want to Be Your Everything," "You Light Up My Life"
Salute to Electric Light Orchestra, Part II
The Emotions, "I Don't Want to Lose Your Love"
Tom Jones, "Delilah," "Back in Love Again," "No One Gave Me Love," "I Can See Clearly Now"
Dan Hill, "Hold On"
Tom Jones, medley: "Are You Lonesome Tonight," "Can't Help Falling in Love with You"
The Emotions, "How'd I Know That Love Would Slip Away"
Tom Jones, "Have You Ever Been Lonely"

Episode 262 (see Episode 110)

Episode 263, 276
Host: Roger Miller

Roger Miller, "King of the Road"
KC & the Sunshine Band, "Boogie Shoes"
The Dirt Band/Roger Miller, "Promised Land"
Gene Cotton, "Before My Heart Finds Out"
Salute to Herb Alpert
The Dirt Band, "In for the Night"
Raydio, "Jack and Jill"
Roger Miller, "Orange Blossom Special"
Andy Kaufman, comedy spot
The Dirt Band, "For a Little While"
Gene Cotton, "Save the Dancer"
Roger Miller, "There's Nobody Like You," "Baby Me Baby"
The Dirt Band, "Escaping Reality"
Roger Miller, "King of the Road"

Episode 264
Host: England Dan & John Ford Coley

England Dan & John Ford Coley, "We'll Never Have to Say Goodbye Again"
Wet Willie, "Street Corner Serenade"
Kansas, "Dust in the Wind"
Salute to the Commodores
England Dan & John Ford Coley, "You Can't Dance"
Barbara Carroll, "Isn't She Lovely"
Meatloaf, "Bat out of Hell"
England Dan & John Ford Coley, "Nights Are Forever without You"
Kansas, "Point of No Return"
Wet Willie, "One Track Mind"
Barbara Carroll, "At Seventeen"
Wet Willie, "Make You Feel Loved Again"
England Dan & John Ford Coley, "Some Things Don't Come Easy," "Maybe Tonight"

Episode 265
Host: Jay Ferguson

Jay Ferguson, "Thunder Island"
Bob Welch, "Ebony Eyes"
Yvonne Elliman, "If I Can't Have You"
David Bowie, interview
Jay Ferguson, "Losing Control"
Hoyt Axton, "Joy to the World"
Le Blanc-Carr Band, "Falling"
Kelly Warren, "I Got the Music in Me"
Chris Bliss, juggling, "Day in the Life"
Jay Ferguson, medley: "Run Run Run," "Mr. Skin," "I Got a Line on You"
Le Blanc-Carr Band, "Something About You"
Jay Ferguson, "Paying Time"
Hoyt Axton, "Flash of Fire"
Jay Ferguson, "Thunder Island"

Episode 266
Host: Journey

Journey, "Wheel in the Sky"
Eddie Money, "Baby Hold On"
Rita Coolidge, "The Way You Do the Things You Do"
Al Jarreau, "So Long Girl"
Eddie Money, "Don't Worry"
Chris Bliss, juggling, "Carry On"
Journey, "Feeling That Way," "Anytime"
Lou Reed interview with Flo & Eddie
Eddie Money, "Two Tickets to Paradise"
Journey, "Patiently"
Rita Coolidge, "Words"
Al Jarreau, "Better Than Anything"
Journey, "La Do Da," "Wheel in the Sky"

Episode 267
Host: Yvonne Elliman

Yvonne Elliman, "If I Can't Have You"
Rubicon, "I'm Gonna Take Care of Everything"
Salute to Tavares
Be-Bop Deluxe, "Panic in the World"
Bonnie Tyler, "It's a Heartache"
Robin Trower, "Bluebird"
Yvonne Elliman, "Sally Go Round the Roses"
Walter Egan, "Magnet and Steel"
Chris Bliss, juggling, "Stairway to Heaven"
Rubicon, "Cheatin'"
Be-Bop Deluxe, "New Precision"
Walter Egan, "Blonde in the Blue T-Bird"
Yvonne Elliman, "Up to the Man in You," "If I Can't Have You"

Episode 268
Host: Dicky Betts

Dicky Betts/Elvin Bishop/Charlie Daniels/Bonnie Bramlet, "Southbound"
Frank Marino/Mahogany Rush, "Johnny B. Goode"
Genesis, "Follow You, Follow Me"
George Benson, "Lady Blue"
Oak Ridge Boys, "Heavenbound"
Dicky Betts/Elvin Bishop/Charlie Daniels/Bonnie Bramlett, "Midnight Creeper"
George Benson, "On Broadway"
Frank Marino/Mahogany Rush, "I'm a King Bee"
Dicky Betts, "Good Time Feelin'"
Oak Ridge Boys, "You're the One"
Kelly Warren, "Rocky Top"
Dicky Betts, "Good Time Feelin'"

Episode 269
Host: Helen Reddy

Helen Reddy, "Ready or Not"
Player, "Cancellation"
Elton John, "Ego"
Salute to Billy Preston
Samantha Sang, "Emotion"
Player, "This Time I'm in It for Love"
Helen Reddy, "Lady of the Night"
Andy Kaufman, comedy spot, "Oklahoma," "My Way"
Helen Reddy, "We'll Sing in the Sunshine"
Samantha Sang, "You Keep Me Dancing"
Joe Brooks interview with Flo & Eddie
Helen Reddy, "Poor Little Fool," "We'll Sing in the Sunshine"

Episode 270, 291
Hosts: Donna Summer and Wolfman Jack

Linda Clifford, "Runaway Love"
Tuxedo Junction, "Chattanooga Choo Choo"
Donna Summer, "Once Upon a Time"
Love and Kisses, "Thank God It's Friday"
Paul Jabara, "Queen of the Disco"
Linda Clifford, "If My Friends Could See Me Now"
Salute to KC & the Sunshine Band
The Village People, "San Francisco"
Hot Song, "No Love in the Morning"
Wolfman Jack dance lesson with Jeff Kutash
Brooklyn Dreams, "Street Dance"
The Village People, "Macho Man"
Donna Summer, "Last Dance"

Episode 271, 360
Host: Crystal Gayle

Crystal Gayle, "Don't It Make My Brown Eyes Blue"
Tom Petty & the Heartbreakers, "American Girl"
Eddie Rabbitt, "Crossin' the Mississippi"
Outside clip from The Last Waltz
Chuck Mangione, "Feels So Good"
Andy Kaufman, comedy spot: "Confidence," "The Cow Goes Moo," "Mighty Mouse"
Crystal Gayle, "Why Have You Left the One You Left Me for"
Tom Petty & the Heartbreakers, "I Need to Know"
Eddie Rabbitt, "You Don't Love Me Anymore"
Chuck Mangione, "Hide and Seek (Ready or Not Here I Come)"
Crystal Gayle, "Cry Me a River"
Tom Petty & the Heartbreakers, "Listen to Her Heart"
Crystal Gayle, "Someday Soon"
Peace and Quiet, "And Here She Is"
Crystal Gayle, "Don't It Make My Brown Eyes Blue"

Episode 272
Host: Elvin Bishop

Elvin Bishop, "Raisin' Hell"
Cory Wells, "When You Touch Me This Way"
Paul McCartney & Wings, "With a Little Luck"
Salute to Leo Sayer
Nick Lowe, "So It Goes"
Alessi, "All for a Reason"
Elvin Bishop, "Travelin' Mood"
Cory Wells, "Midnight Lady"
Elvin Bishop, "Stealing Watermelons"
Andy Gibb, "Shadow Dancing"
Nick Lowe, "Heart of the City"
Alessi, "I Don't Want to Lose You"
Elvin Bishop, "Fishing," "Raisin' Hell"

Episode 273
Host: Mac Davis

Mac Davis, "You Put Music in My Life"
Andrew Gold, "Thank You for Being a Friend"
Johnny Paycheck/Mac Davis, "Take This Job and Shove It"
Rod Stewart, "I Was Only Joking"
Todd Rundgren, "Can We Still Be Friends"
Salute to George Benson
Mac Davis, "Shee Moe Foe"
Andrew Gold, "The Gambler"
Johnny Paycheck, "Me and the I.R.S."
Todd Rundgren/Mime Piece, "Bread"
Mac Davis, "Rock 'n' Roll, I Gave You All the Best Years of My Life"
Andrew Gold, "Never Let Her Slip Away"
Johnny Paycheck, "Rollin' in My Sweet Baby's Arms"
Mac Davis, "You Are," "You Put Music in My Life"

Episode 274
HOST: BURTON CUMMINGS
Burton Cummings, "Roll with the Punches"
Randy Bachman, "Takin' Care of Business"
Teddy Pendergrass, "Only You"
Patti Smith interview with Lisa Robinson
Ronnie Montrose, "Town without Pity"
Burton Cummings, "Break It to Them Gently"
Burton Cummings/Randy Bachman, "American Woman"
Randy Bachman, "Is the Night Too Cold for Dancing"
Ronnie Montrose, "My Little Mystery"
Burton Cummings, "Guns, Guns, Guns"
Teddy Pendergrass, "Close the Door"
Randy Bachman, "Survivor"
Burton Cummings, "Dream of a Child," "Roll with the Punches"

Episode 275
HOST: MARTIN MULL
Burt Reynolds (walk on)
Martin Mull, "I'm Everyone I've Ever Loved"
Martin Mull, comedy spot, "Yellow Face"
Robert Palmer, "Every Kinda People"
Jethro Tull, "Heavy Horses"
Martin Mull, "The Humming Song"
Mink De Ville, "Guardian Angel"
Flo & Eddie, "Natural Man"
Martin Mull/Flo & Eddie, "Get Up, Get Down"
Martin Mull, comedy spot, "Record Album Promo"
Robert Palmer, "You're Gonna Get What's Coming"
Martin Mull/Flo & Eddie, "Puff the Magic Dragon"
Martin Mull, "I'll Do the Samba"
Mink De Ville, "Just Your Friends"
Martin Mull, "Goodnight"

Episode 276 (SEE EPISODE 263)

Episode 277 (SEE EPISODE 204)

Episode 278
HOST: EDDIE MONEY
Eddie Money, "Two Tickets to Paradise"
Todd Rundgren, "Can We Still Be Friends"
Gerry Rafferty, "Baker Street"
Eddie Money, "So You Want to Be a Rock 'n' Roll Star," "Baby Hold On"
Stanley Clarke, "Rock and Roll Jelly"
Jay Ferguson, "Losing Control"
Peter Noone, English rock & roll segment
Todd Rundgren/Mime Piece, "Bread"
ABBA, "Take a Chance on Me"
Stanley Clarke, "More Hot Fun"
Eddie Money, "So Good to Be in Love Again," "Call On Me," "Two Tickets to Paradise"

Episode 279
HOST: LEO SAYER
Leo Sayer, "How Much Love"
Raydio, "Jack and Jill"
Chuck Mangione, "Feels So Good"
Wolfman Jack/Gary Busey, "The Buddy Holly Story"
Bonnie Tyler, "It's a Heartache"
Leo Sayer, "Dancing the Night Away"
Randy Newman, "Baltimore"
Raydio, "Is This a Love Thing"
Demis Roussos, "I Just Live"
Chuck Mangione, "Hide and Seek"
Leo Sayer, "Rainin' in My Heart"
Demis Roussos, "That Once in a Lifetime"
Leo Sayer, "Something Fine," "The Show Must Go On"

Episode 280 (SEE Pilot)

Episode 281 (SEE Episode 256)

Epsidoe 282, 298
HOST: FRANKIE VALLI
Frankie Valli, "Grease," "Save Me, Save Me," "Needing You," "Sometimes Love Makes Me Cry"
Walter Egan, "Magnet and Steel," "Hot Summer Nights," "Finally Found a Girlfriend"
Nick Gilder, "Hot Child in the City," "Got to Get Out"
A Taste of Honey, "Boogie Oogie Oogie," "Distant"
Atlanta Rhythm Section, "I'm Not Going to Let It Bother Me Tonight," "Imaginary Lover"

Episode 283
HOST: TODD RUNDGREN & UTOPIA
Todd Rundgren, "Real Man"
Warren Zevon, "Werewolves of London"
Tom Petty & the Heartbreakers, "I Need to Know"
Todd Rundgren, "You Cried Wolf"
Exile, "Kiss You All Over"
Carlene Carter, "I Once Knew Love"
Warren Zevon, "Nighttime in the Switching Yard"
Meatloaf, "Paradise By the Dashboard Light"
Todd Rundgren, "Love in Action," "Sometimes I Don't Know What to Feel"
Exile, "Never Gonna Stop"
Tom Petty & the Heartbreakers, "American Girl"
Carlene Carter, "Never Together but Close Sometimes"
Tom Petty & the Heartbreakers, "Listen to Her Heart"
Todd Rundgren, "Just One Victory"

Episode 284 (SEE Episode 152)

Episode 285
HOST: KC & the Sunshine Band
KC & the Sunshine Band, "Do You Feel Alright?"
Donna Summer, "Last Dance"
Jimmy "Bo" Horne, "Dance around the Floor"
Paul McCartney, "I've Had Enough"
KC & the Sunshine Band, medley: "Get Down Tonight," "That's the Way (I Like It)," "(Shake, Shake, Shake) Shake Your Booty," "I'm Your Boogie Man," "Keep It Comin' Love," "It's the Same Old Song"
Teddy Pendergrass, "Close the Door"
Cheryl Ladd, "Think It Over"
Salute to Otis Redding
Cheryl Ladd, "Lady Gray"
KC & the Sunshine Band, "Who Do You Love?"
Jimmy "Bo" Horne, "Let Me (Let Me Be Your Lover)"
Donna Summer, "I Love You"
Teddy Pendergrass, "Only You"
KC & the Sunshine Band, "Come to My Island," "Do You Feel Alright?"

Episode 286
HOST: LARRY GATLIN
Larry Gatlin, "Colorado"
Tony Orlando, "Don't Let Go," "That's Rock 'n' Roll"
Tavares, "More Than a Woman"
Larry Gatlin, "Do It Again Tonight"
Evelyn "Champagne" King, "Shame"
The Cars, "Just What I Needed"
Tony Orlando, "Save the Last Dance for Me"
Tavares, "Heaven Must Be Missing An Angel"
Jeff Kutash Dancers, "Copacabana"
Larry Gatlin, "Done Enough Dying Today"
Devo, "Come Back Johnny"

The Cars, "My Best Friend's Girl,"
Larry Gatlin, "Penny Annie"
Jeff Kutash Dancers, "Saturday Night Fever"
Larry Gatlin, "Do It Again Tonight"

Episode 287
HOST: REO SPEEDWAGON
REO Speedwagon, "Keep Pushin'"
Little River Band, "Reminiscing"
A Taste of Honey, "Boogie Oogie Oogie"
Climax Blues Band, "Couldn't Get It Right"
Ozark Mountain Daredevils, "If You Wanna Get to Heaven"
REO Speedwagon, "Time for Me to Fly"
Little River Band, "Help Is on Its Way"
Atlanta Rhythm Section, "I'm Not Going to Let It Bother Me Tonight"
REO Speedwagon, "Roll with the Changes," "Say You Love Me or Say Goodnight"
Climax Blues Band, "Mistress Moonshine"
Atlanta Rhythm Section, "Champagne Jam"
Little River Band, "Shut Down, Turnoff"
Ozark Mountain Daredevils, "Tough Luck," "Roll with the Changes"

Episode 288, 300, 354, 376
HOST: DOLLY PARTON
Dolly Parton, "Two Doors Down"
Paul McCartney & Wings, "With a Little Luck"
Dolly Parton, "Here You Come Again"
Frankie Valli, "Grease"
Dolly Parton, "Heartbreaker"
Rita Coolidge, "You"
Crystal Gayle, "Cry Me a River"
Yvonne Elliman, "If I Can't Have You"
Dolly Parton, "Baby I'm Burnin'"
Alice Cooper, "How You Gonna See Me Now"
Salute to Queen
Chuck Mangione, "Feels So Good"
Dolly Parton, "Jolene"
Paul McCartney & Wings, "I've Had Enough"
Dolly Parton, "I Will Always Love You," "Heartbreaker"

Episode 289 (SEE Episode 158)

Episode 290, 301
HOST: THE DIRT BAND
The Dirt Band, "Whoa Babe"
McEuen/Steve Martin, banjo duet, "Pitkin Country Turnaround"
Steve Martin, "King Tut"
The Dirt Band, "In for the Night"
The Who, "Who Are You"
Michael Johnson, "Bluer Than Blue"
The Dirt Band/Steve Martin, "Ramblin' Man"
Fish, comedy spot
Steve Martin, "Maxwell's Silver Hammer"
McEuen and LeRoux, "Tokin' Funk"
LeRoux, "New Orleans Ladies"
Steve Martin/LeRoux/The Dirt Band, "Will the Circle Be Unbroken"
The Dirt Band/Steve Martin, "White Russia"
McEuen Song, "Opus '36"
Michael Johnson, "Almost Like Being in Love"
LeRoux, "Slow Burn"
The Dirt Band, "For a Little While"

Episode 291 (SEE Episode 270)

Episode 292
HOST: WOLFMAN JACK
Evelyn "Champagne" King, "Shame"
Anne Murray, "You Needed Me"
The Trammps, "Disco Inferno"
Exile, "Kiss You All Over"
Little River Band, "Reminiscing"
Cheryl Ladd, "Think It Over"
Linda Clifford, "If My Friends Could See Me Now"
Anne Murray, "You Won't See Me"
Stonebolt, "I Will Still Love You"
Little River Band, "Help Is on Its Way"
The Trammps, "Season for Girls"
Paul McCartney & Wings, "London Town"
Stonebolt, "The Shadow"
The Trammps, "Disco Inferno"

Episode 293 (SEE Episode 13)

Episode 294
HOST: Hall & Oates
Hall & Oates, medley: "She's Gone," "Sara Smile," "Rich Girl"
Hall & Oates, "I Don't Want to Lose You," "It's a Laugh," "Melody for a Memory," "Don't Blame It on Love"
Daryl Hall, "August Day"
Nick Gilder, "Hot Child in the City"
Alice Cooper, "How You Gonna See Me Now"
Heart, "Cook with Fire," "Crazy on You," "High Time," "Straight On"

Episode 295
HOST: THE ATLANTA RHYTHM SECTION
Atlanta Rhythm Section, "Champagne Jam," "Imaginary Lover," "I'm Not Going to Let It Bother Me Tonight," "I'm So Into You"
Atlanta Rhythm Section/Sea Level, "Long Tall Sally"
The Cars, "My Best Friend's Girl"
Salute to the Beach Boys
Paul Davis, "Sweet Life"
Paul Davis/Crystal Gayle, "I Don't Want to Be Just Another Love"
Sea Level, "That's Your Secret"
Van Morrison, "Wave Length"
Ambrosia, "How Much I Feel"

Episode 296
HOST: TED NUGENT
Ted Nugent, "Cat Scratch Fever," "Free for All," "Need You Bad," "Stranglehold"
Cheap Trick, "Surrender," "California Man"
AC/DC, "Sin City"
REO Speedwagon, "Say You Love Me or Say Goodnight"
Thin Lizzy, "Cowboy Song"
Golden Earring, "Grab It for a Season"
Aerosmith, "Come Together"

Episode 297
HOST: WOLFMAN JACK (DISCO SHOW)
Chic, "Everybody Dance," "Dance, Dance, Dance," "Le Freak"
Sylvester, "You Make Me Feel (Mighty Real)," "Grateful"
Rick James/The Stone City Band, "You and I," "Mary Jane"
Pattie Brooks, "The House Where Love Died," "After Dark"
Disco Hit, "MacArthur Park" (Vocal: Donna Summer)
Jeff Kutash Dancers, "Get Off," "Sweet Lucy"
Jeff Kutash Dancers/Sylvester, "Dance (Disco Heat)"
Laura Taylor, "Dancin' in My Feet"
Gallagher comedy spots throughout show

Episode 318, 326, 336
HOST: THE BEACH BOYS

The Beach Boys, "Good Vibrations," "Here Comes the Night," "Surfin' U.S.A.," "Angel Come Home," "Lady Lynda"
Blondie, "Heart of Glass," "One Way or Another," "Hanging on the Telephone"
Tavares, "Straight from Your Heart," "More Than a Woman," "Never Had a Love Like This Before"
Bad Company, "Rock 'n' Roll Fantasy," "Can't Get Enough of Your Love"
McGuinn, Clark and Hillman, "Don't You Write Her Off," "Surrender to Me, "Backstage Pass"
Beach Boys/Roger McGuinn/Wolfman Jack, "Rock 'n' Roll Music"

Episode 319
HOST: AMII STEWART

Amii Stewart, "Knock on Wood," "Light My Fire," "Bring It on Back to Me," "Get Your Love Back," "Closest Thing to Heaven"
G.Q., "Disco Nights (Rock Freak)," "This Happy Feeling"
Peaches & Herb, "Reunited"
Elvis Costello, "(What's So Funny) 'Bout Peace Love and Understanding," "Oliver's Army"
Tasha Thomas, "Shoot Me with Your Love," "Midnight Rendezvous"
Badfinger, "Look Out California," "Love Is Gonna Come at Last," "The Winner"

Episodode 320, 333
HOST: PEACHES & HERB

Peaches & Herb, "Shake Your Groove Thing"
Raydio, "Rock On"
Melba Moore, "Pick Me Up, I'll Dance"
Peaches & Herb, "We've Got Love"
Charlie Lucas, "Dance with You"
Rickie Lee Jones, "Young Blood"
Peaches & Herb, "Reunited"
Raydio, "You Can't Change That"
Little River Band, "Reminiscing"
Peaches & Herb, "Love It Up Tonight"
Melba Moore, "Where Did You Ever Go?"
Rickie Lee Jones, "Chuck E's in Love"
Carrie Lucas, "Danceland"
Melba Moore, "You Stepped into My Life"
Peaches & Herb, "Reunited"

Episode 321
HOST: JOURNEY

Journey, "Loving You Is Easy," "Just the Same Way," "Lovin' Touchin' Squeezin'," "City of the Angels," "Too Late"
Journey/Herbie Hancock, "I'm a Roadrunner Baby"
Herbie Hancock, "Ready or Not," "Tell Everybody"
The Jacksons, "Shake Your Body (Down to the Ground)," "Destiny," "Things I Do for You"
Levi and the Rockats, "All Through the Night," "Rockabilly Idol"
Anita Ward, "Ring My Bell," "Make Believe Lovers"

Episode 322 (SEE EPISODE 316)

Episode 323 (SEE EPISODE 307)

Episode 324
HOST: GLORIA GAYNOR

Gloria Gaynor, "I Will Survive," "I Said Yes," "Anybody Wanna Party?," "Never Say Goodbye," "You're All I Need to Get By"
Jay Ferguson, "Thunder Island," "Shake Down Cruise," "Turn Yourself In," "No Secrets"
The Gap Band, "Shake," "Baby Baba Boogie," "Open Up Your Mind (Wide)"
Rod Stewart, "Ain't Love a Bitch," "D'Ya Think I'm Sexy"
Ron Wood, "Buried Alive"

Episode 325, 332
HOST: BOB WELCH

Bob Welch, "Precious Love," "Ebony Eyes," "Three Hearts," "Danchiva," "Church"
Thelma Houston, "Saturday Night, Sunday Morning," "Don't Leave Me This Way," "I Wanna Be Back in Love Again"
Paul McCartney & Wings, "Goodnight Tonight"
Foxy, "Hot Number," "Get Off"
Olivia Newton-John, "Deeper Than the Night"
Fast Fontaine, "Hard Working Girl," "Real Life"

Episode 326 (SEE EPISODE 318)

Episode 327
HOST: RAYDIO

Raydio, "Rock On," "You Can't Change That," "Jack and Jill," "Hot Stuff," "More Than One Way to Love a Woman"
England Dan & John Ford Coley, "Hollywood Heckle and Jive," "Love Is the Answer," "Rolling Fever"
Dolly Parton, "You're the Only One," "Great Balls of Fire," "Star of the Show"
Anita Ward, "Ring My Bell," "Make Believe Lovers"
McFadden and Whitehead, "Mr. Music," "Ain't No Stoppin' Us Now"

Episode 328 (SEE EPISODE 10)

Episode 329
HOST: WOLFMAN JACK

Steve Martin/John McEuen, "Pitkin Country Turnaround"
Steve Martin, "King Tut"
Donna Summer, "I Feel Love"
The Who, "Who Are You"
A Taste of Honey, "Boogie Oogie Oogie"
Kenny Rogers, "Love or Something Like It"
Yvonne Elliman, "If I Can't Have You"
Atlanta Rhythm Section, "Imaginary Lover," "I'm Not Going to Let It Bother Me Tonight"
Nick Gilder, "Hot Child in the City"
Teddy Pendergrass, "Close the Door," "Only You"
The Dirt Band/Steve Martin, "White Russia"
Kenny Rogers/Dottie West, "Every Time Two Fools Collide"

Episode 330
HOST: SUZI QUATRO

Suzi Quatro, "Stumblin' In," "Evie," "If You Can't Give Me Love," "Breakdown," "Non-Citizen," "Passing Lane"
Queen, "Love of My Life"
David Naughton, "Makin' It"
Roger Voudouris, "Get Used to It," "Can't Stay Like This Forever," "Just What It Takes"
Carly Simon, "Vengeance," "We're So Close"
David Bowie, "Boys Keep Swingin'," "D.J."
Paul Warren/Explorer, "The Others," "Faded Glory"

Episode 331
HOST: MAC DAVIS

Mac Davis, "Somethin's Burnin'," medley: "Best Disco in Town," "I Love the Nightlife," "Le Freak," "Love to Love You Baby," "'D'Ya Think I'm Sexy," "Don't Leave Me This Way," "Dancin' Fool," "Soul Man," "I Love Music," "Y.M.C.A.," "Dance (Disco Heat)," "Instant Replay"
McFadden and Whitehead, "Ain't No Stoppin' Us Now," "Mr. Music"
Bonnie Pointer, "Heaven Must Have Sent You," "Free Me from My Freedom," "Aw Shoot"
ABBA, "Does Your Mother Know?"
Lisa Hartman, "Hold On I'm Comin'," "Oh Me Oh My"
Gerry Rafferty, "Days Gone Down"

Episode 332 (SEE EPISODE 325)

Episode 333 (SEE EPISODE 320)

Episode 334 (SEE EPISODE 215)

Episode 335 (SEE EPISODE 105)

Episode 336 (SEE EPISODE 318)

Episode 337
HOST: LITTLE RIVER BAND

Little River Band, "Lonesome Loser"
Kiss, "I Was Made for Loving You"
Maxine Nightingale, "Lead Me On"
Moon Martin, "Rolene"
The Who, "Baba O'Reilly"
Little River Band, "It's Not a Wonder"
Maxine Nightingale, "Bringing Out the Girl in Me"
Moon Martin, "Bad Case of Loving You"
Beckmeier Brothers, "Rock 'n' Roll Dancing"
Kiss, "Sure Know Something"
Little River Band, "Mistress of Mine"
Moon Martin, "I've Got a Reason"
Little River Band, "Man on the Run"
Beckmeier Brothers, "Snakes in the Grass"

Episode 338
HOST: BOB WELCH

Bob Welch, "Outskirts"
Paul Butterfield/Rick Danko, "Mystery Train"
Elvin Bishop, "Honest I Do"
Electric Light Orchestra, "Don't Bring Me Down"
Bob Welch, "Big Towne 2061"
John Mayall, "Falling"
The Jam, "Rock Me Baby"
Van Halen, "Dance the Night Away"
Bob Welch, "Rebel Rouser"
The Whizz Kids, "Cheesecake Baby"
Bob Welch, "Hot Love Cold War"
Bob Welch "Ghost of Flight 401" (outside clip)
The Whizz Kids, "Get Your Hooks Off Me"
Van Halen, "Bottoms Up"

Episode 339
HOST: THE CHARLIE DANIELS BAND

The Charlie Daniels Band, "The Devil Went Down to Georgia," "Jitterbug," "Johnny B. Goode," "Blind Man," "Passing Lane"
Paul McCartney & Wings, "Arrow through Me"
Journey, "Lovin' Touchin' Squeezin'," "Too Late," "City of the Angels"
Gerry Rafferty, "Right Next Time," "Days Gone Down"
Robert John, "Sad Eyes," "Lonely Eyes"
Timothy Leary

Episode 340
HOST: THE CARS

The Cars, "Let's Go," "Moving in Stereo," "Candy-O," "Dangerous Type," "Got a Lot on My Head," "Nightspots"
The Records, "Starry Eyes," "Teenarama," "Affection Rejected," "All Messed Up and Ready to Go"
M, "Pop Muzik"
Iggy Pop, "Five Foot One," "I'm Bored"
Lene Lovich, "Lucky Number," "Say When"
Suicide, "Dream Baby," "Ghost Rider"

Episode 341
HOST: BLONDIE

Blondie, "Dreaming," "Slow Motion," "Heart of Glass," "The Hardest Part," "Accidents Never Happen"
Robert Palmer, "Bad Case of Loving You," "Jealous," "Can We Still Be Friends"
Bram Tchaikovsky, "Girl of My Dreams," "Lady from the U.S.A."
Supertramp, "Goodbye Stranger," "The Logical Song," "Breakfast in America"
Rick James, "Love Gun," "Fool on the Street"
Robert Fripp, "God Save the Queen"

Episode 342 (SEE EPISODE 306)

Episode 343
HOST: THE CAPTAIN AND TENNILLE

The Captain and Tennille, "You Never Done It Like That," "How Can You Be So Cold," "No Love in the Morning," "Do That to Me One More Time," "Love on a Shoestring"
Yvonne Elliman, "Love Pains," "Savannah"
Dr. John, "Renegade"
Yvonne Elliman/Dr. John, "Hit the Road Jack," "Sticks and Stones"
Salute to Willie Nelson
Cher, "Hell on Wheels"
Chicago, "Runaway," "Street Player"

Episode 344
HOST: PEACHES & HERB

Peaches & Herb, "Roller Skate Mate," "Gypsy Lady," "Howzabout Some Love," "I Pledge My Love"
France Joli, "Come to Me," "Let Go," "Don't Stop Dancing"
Salute to Elton John
Maureen McGovern, "Different Worlds," "Save Me Save Me"
Salute to Olivia Newton-John

Episode 345
HOST: KC & THE SUNSHINE BAND

KC & the Sunshine Band, "Please Don't Go," "Do You Wanna Go Party?," "Ooh I Like It," "I Betcha Didn't Know That," "I've Got the Feeling"
Deniece Williams, "I Found Love," "I've Got the Next Dance"
Kool & the Gang, "Ladies Night," "Too Hot"
The Dirt Band, "Happy Feet," "An American Dream"
Michael Jackson, "Don't Stop Till You Get Enough"
The Who, "Won't Be Fooled Again"
M, "Pop Muzik"

Episode 346, 353, 387, 406
HOST: THE COMMODORES

The Commodores, "Brickhouse," "Sail On"
Frankie Valli, "Passion for Paris"
Frankie Valli/The Commodores, "Grease"
The Captain and Tennille, "Do That to Me One More Time"
The Commodores, "Three Times a Lady"
The Commodores/Wolfman Jack, "Midnight Magic" (a capella)
Destination, "Move On Up"
The Commodores, "Still"
The Captain and Tennille, "You Never Done It Like That"
Salute to ABBA
Destination, "Dance Dance Party Party"
The Commodores, "Midnight Magic"

Episode 347
HOST: ROGER MILLER

Roger Miller, medley: "Dang Me," "Kansas City Star," "Chug a Lug," "England Swings," "King of the Road," "Lady America," "The Fiddle Song," "This Here Town," "The Hat"
Tina Turner, "Love Explosion," "Sunset on Sunset"
Blondie, "Dreaming," "The Hardest Part"
Brenda Russell, "So Good So Right," "Way Back When"
Ian Hunter, "Ships," "Just Another Night"
Salute to the Beach Boys

Episode 348
HOST: THE POINTER SISTERS

The Pointer Sisters, "Fire," "Who Do You Love," "Dreaming As One," "(She's Got) the Fever," "Don't Let a Thief Steal into Your Heart"
Linda Clifford, "I Just Wanna Wanna," "Bailing Out," "Here Is My Love"
Carlene Carter, "Two Sides to Every Woman," "Do It in a Heartbeat," "Lies"
Jackie DeShannon, "I Don't Need You Anymore"
Pointer Sisters/Linda Clifford/Jackie DeShannon/Carlene Carter, "What the World Needs Now Is Love"
Salute to Rod Stewart

Episode 349 (SEE EPISODE 256)

Episode 350
HOST: DOC SEVERINSEN/FRANCE JOLI

Doc Severinsen/France Joli, "Come to Me"
Doc Severinsen, "Luv Ya," "Peg," "Dance of Animals," "Song of Our Friends"
France Joli, "Don't Stop Dancing," "Let Go"
Chic, "Good Times," "My Feet Keep Dancing," "My Forbidden Lover"
Comedy segment, hosted by David Steinberg
Kermit the Frog, "Rainbow Connection"

Episode 351
HOST: THE VILLAGE PEOPLE

The Village People, "Ready for the '80s," "Y.M.C.A.," "Save Me," "Rock and Roll Is Back Again"
Rupert Holmes, "Escape," "Him"
The Spinners, medley of hits: "Games People Play," "I'll Be Around," "Could It Be I'm Falling in Love"
The Spinners, "Working My Way Back to You"
The Little River Band, "Cool Change," "Lonesome Loser"
Comedy segment, hosted by David Steinberg

Episode 352
HOSTS: LOU RAWLS AND RITA COOLIDGE

Lou Rawls/Rita Coolidge, "Fever"
Lou Rawls, "Sit Down and Talk to Me," "You'll Never Find Another Love Like Mine," "Time Will Take Care"
Rita Coolidge, "I'd Rather Leave While I'm in Love," "(Your Love Keeps Liftin') Higher and Higher," "The Way You Do the Things You Do"
Jan and Dean, "Little Old Lady from Pasadena," "Barbara Ann"
"Outrage" comedy segment: Bruce Vilanch, Pat McCormick, Rufus Shaw Jr., Emily Prager, Gary Mule Deer, David Rupprecht

Episode 353 (SEE EPISODE 346)

Episode 354 (SEE EPISODE 288)

1980

Episode 355
HOST: DR. HOOK

Dr. Hook, "When You're in Love with a Beautiful Woman," "Better Love Next Time," "What Do You Want," "Clyde," "Ooh Pooh Pah Doo"
Rupert Holmes, "Escape," "Him"
Cliff Richard, "We Don't Talk Anymore," "Carrie"
Prince, "I Wanna Be Your Lover," "Why Do You Wanna Treat Me So Bad"
"Outrage" comedy segment: Bruce Vilanch, Pat McCormick, Rufus Shaw Jr., Sandra Bernhard, Ron Stevens, Joy Grdnic

Episode 356
HOST: ISAAC HAYES

Isaac Hayes, "Don't Let Go," "A Few More Kisses to Go," "What Does It Take"
The Emotions, "Best of My Love," "What's the Name of Your Love"
Isaac Hayes/The Emotions, "Money"
KC & the Sunshine Band, "Please Don't Go"
Kool & the Gang, "Ladies Night"
"Outrage" comedy segment: Bruce Vilanch, Rufus Shaw Jr., Joyce Burditt, Paul Mooney, Harry Reems, Dee Dee Fay

Episode 357, 370
HOST: THE CAPTAIN AND TENNILLE
(7TH ANNIVERSARY SPECIAL)

The Jacksons, "Shake Your Body (Down to the Ground)"
The Captain and Tennille, "Love Will Keep Us Together"
Rod Stewart, "Da Ya Think I'm Sexy?"
Jim Croce, "Operator," "Bad Bad Leroy Brown"
Barry Manilow, "Mandy," "It's a Miracle"
Donna Summer, "Heaven Knows"
Elton John, "Your Song"
Linda Ronstadt, "Long Long Time"
Talk segment: Bruce Vilanch, Rufus Shaw Jr., Joyce Burditt, Eugenie Ross-Leming, Ronnie Graham, Steve Dahl

Episode 358, 371
HOST: THE CAPTAIN AND TENNILLE

The Captain and Tennille, "Do That to Me One More Time"
Crystal Gayle, "Don't It Make My Brown Eyes Blue"
The Commodores, "Still"
Dolly Parton, "Here You Come Again"

Outrage comedy segments: "The Allies," "The Draft," "Fat People"
The Village People, "Macho Man"
Olivia Newton-John, "Have You Never Been Mellow"
Willie Nelson, "Blue Eyes Crying in the Rain"
The Commodores, "Sail On"
Dolly Parton, "Two Doors Down"
Andy Kaufman, "Stayin' Alive"

Episode 359
HOST: TOM JONES

Tom Jones, "Star," "We Don't Talk Anymore," "Do That to Me One More Time," "I'll Never Love This Way Again," "Ladies Night," "She Believes in Me," "Don't Let Go"
Queen, "Crazy Little Thing Called Love"
Teri De Sario/KC, "Yes I'm Ready," "Dancin' in the Streets"
Insert segment: Bruce Vilanch, Rufus Shaw Jr., Eugenie Ross-Leming, Jaye P. Morgan, David Steinberg

Episode 360 (SEE EPISODE 271)

Episode 361
HOST: BONNIE POINTER

Bonnie Pointer, "I Can't Help Myself," "Heaven Must Have Sent You," "Nowhere to Run," "Deep Inside My Soul"
Electric Light Orchestra, "Last Train to London" (outside clip)
The Spinners, "Working My Way Back to You," "Let's Boogie, Let's Dance"
Nicolette Larson, "Let Me Go Love," "Back in My Arms Again"
Comedy segment: Bruce Vilanch, Rufus Shaw Jr., Eugenie Ross-Leming, Lonnie Shorr, Carol Wayne

Episode 362 (SEE EPISODE 164)

Episode 363
HOST: MAC DAVIS

Mac Davis, "Tequila Sheila," "Why Don't We Sleep on It," "It's Hard to Be Humble," "I Wanna Wake Up with You"
Thelma Houston, "Suspicious Minds," "What Was That Song"
ABBA, "Gimme Gimme Gimme" (outside clip)
Andy Gibb, "Desire"
Comedy segment: Jay Wolpert (host), Bruce Vilanch, Rufus Shaw Jr., Eugenie Ross-Leming, Lonnie Shorr, Carol Wayne

Episode 364
HOST: ANDY GIBB

Andy Gibb, "Desire"
Tom Petty & the Heartbreakers, "Refugee"
The Whispers, "And the Beat Goes On"
Paul Warren & Explorer, "One of the Kids"
Saccharin, comedy spot
Queen, "Crazy Little Thing Called Love"
Andy Gibb, "After Dark"
Tom Petty & the Heartbreakers, "There Goes My Girl"
Paul Warren & Explorer, "For the Love of a Girl"
The Whispers, "Lady"
Andy Gibb, "Falling in Love with You"
Paul Warren & Explorer, "Taking My Girl Back"

Episode 365 (SEE EPISODE 204)

Episode 366 (SEE EPISODE 237)

Episode 367
HOSTS: JANIS IAN AND THE BABYS

The Babys, "Back on My Feet Again"
Janis Ian, "Fly Too High"
Rupert Holmes, "Him"
Heart, "Even It Up"
Comedy segment (#1)
The Babys, "Midnight Rendevous"
Janis Ian, "The Other Side of the Sun"
Rupert Holmes, "Partners in Crime"
Heart, "Break"
Comedy segment (#2)
The Babys, "True Love Confesssions"
Janis Ian, "Memories"
Comedy segment (#3)
Janis Ian/The Babys, "When a Man Loves a Woman"

Episode 368
HOST: THE SPINNERS

The Spinners, "Working My Way Back to You"
Dancers, "Special Lady," "Second Time Around," "Ride Like the Wind," "Too Hot"
Sister Sledge, "I Got to Love Somebody"
Dancers, "Him," "Call Me"
The Byrds, "Mr. Tambourine Man," "So You Want To Be a Rock 'n' Roll Star"
Dancers, "Crazy Little Thing Called Love," "Desire"
Andy Gibb, "Desire"
Herman's Hermits, "Mrs. Brown You've Got a Lovely Daughter"
Dancers, "Working My Way Back to You"
Pink Floyd, "Another Brick in the Wall"
The Spinners, "Body Language"
Dancers, "The Wall," "Cherry Pink and Apple Blossom White"
The Spinners, "Let's Boogie, Let's Dance"
Dancers, "Funkytown"
Gary Numan, "Cars"
Sister Sledge, "Reach Your Peak"
The Spinners, "Not That You're Mine Again"

Episode 369, 400
HOST: SISSY SPACEK AND LEVON HELM

Cast from the movie *Coal Miner's Daughter*: Sissy Spacek, Levon Helm, Beverly D'Angelo, Phyllis Boyens
Outside Clips: "There He Goes," "Back in Baby's Arms," "Honky Tonkin'," "Coal Miner's Daughter," "America's Farm," "Walking After Midnight," "Smooth Talkin' Daddy," "Rivers of Babylon," "Grandma Belle," "Sweet Dreams," "Watermelon Time in Georgia," "China Girl," "Crazy," "Girl Cowboy," "Working Girl Blues," "Watermelon Time in Georgia"
Queen, "Crazy Little Thing Called Love" (#10)
Rupert Holmes, "Him" (#4)
The Spinners, "Working My Way Back to You" (#1)
Top Ten Countdown, Steve Merritt Dancers
"Desire" (#9)
"Special Lady" (#8)
"Another Brick in the Wall" (#7)
"Off the Wall" (#6)
"I Can't Tell You Why" (#5)
"Too Hot" (#3)
"Call Me" (#2)
#1 Country, "It's Like We Never Said Goodbye"
#1 Disco, "Love and Passion"
#1 Album, Bob Seger, *Fire Lake*
30 Year Oldie, "Mona Lisa"
Pick Hit of the Week, "I Pledge My Love"
Golden Moment, Anne Murray, "Snowbird"

Episode 384

Hosts: Glen Campbell and Tanya Tucker

Glen Campbell/Tanya Tucker, "Dream Lover," "Texas When I Die," "Something 'Bout You Baby I Like"

Glen Campbell, "Milk Cow Blues," "Rollin' in My Sweet Baby's Arms," "Southern Nights" (Golden Moment)

Tanya Tucker, "Somebody Must've Loved You Right Last Night," "Not Fade Away"

Ambrosia, "You're the Only Woman," "Living on My Own," "No Big Deal"

Olivia Newton-John, "Magic" (#1)

Top Ten Countdown, Steve Merritt Dancers
"In America" (#10)
"Gimme Some Lovin'" (#9)
"More Love" (#8)
"Love the World Away" (#7)
"Shining Star" (#6)
"Let Me Love You Tonight" (#5)
"One Fine Day" (#4)
"I'm Alive" (#3)
"It's Still Rock 'n' Roll to Me" (#2)
#1 Album, *The Empire Strikes Back*
#1 Country, "You Win Again"
#1 Disco, "Hang Together"
Pick Hit of the Week, "Take Your Time (Do It Right)"

Episode 385 (see Episode 69)

Episode 386 (see Episode 157)

Episode 387 (see Episode 346)

Episode 388 (see Episode 221)

Episode 389

Host: Ted Nugent

Ted Nugent, "Wango Tango," "Hard As Nails," "Violent Love," "Scream Dream" (outside clip)

Pete Townshend, "Let My Love Open the Door" (#10), "Rough Boys"

AC/DC, "You Shook Me All Night Long," "What Do You Do for Money Honey," "Hell's Bells" (outside clip)

Roger Daltrey, "Free Me" (outside clip)

Robbie Dupree, "Hot Rod Hearts" (Pick Hit of the Week)

Olivia Newton-John, "Magic" (#1)

Jackson Browne, "Running on Empty" (Golden Moment), "No Nukes" promo (outside clip)

Top Ten Countdown, Steve Merritt Dancers
"Late in the Evening" (#9)
"Give Me the Night" (#8)
"All Out of Love" (#7)
"Fame" (#6)
"Take Your Time (Do It Right)" (#5)
"Upside Down" (#4)
"Emotional Rescue" (#3)
"Sailing" (#2)
#1 Country, "Lookin' for Love"
#1 Disco, "Upside Down"
#1 Album, Jackson Browne, *Boulevard*
25 Year Oldie, "Naughty Lady of Shady Lane"

Episode 390

Host: Christopher Cross

Christopher Cross, "Ride Like the Wind," "Sailing" (#1), "Never Be the Same"

Christopher Cross/Nicolette Larson, "Say You'll Be Mine"

Johnny Lee, "Lookin' for Love" (#10)

The S.O.S. Band, "Take Your Time Do It Right" (#6), "S.O.S."

Irene Cara, "Fame" (#4), "Out Here on My Own"

Genesis, "Misunderstanding" (outside clip), "Turn It on Again"

Queen, "Bohemian Rhapsody" (Golden Moment)

Amy Holland, "How Do I Survive"

Top Ten Countdown, Steve Merritt Dancers
"Into the Night" (#9)
"Magic" (#8)
"Give Me the Night" (#7)
"Late in the Evening" (#5)
"Upside Down" (#3)
"Emotional Rescue" (#2)
#1 Album, Rolling Stones, *Emotional Rescue*, "She's So Cold"
Pick Hit of the Week, "All Over the World"
#1 Country, "Misery Loves Company"
#1 Disco, "Hot Lunch Jam"
20 Year Oldie, "The Twist"

Episode 391, 420

Host: Cher and Black Rose

Black Rose, "Never Should Have Started," "Julie," "You Know It," "Ain't Got No Money"

Eddie Rabbitt, "Drivin' My Life Away" (#10), "Gone Too Far," "Suspicions"

The Rolling Stones, "She's So Cold," "Emotional Rescue" (#1) (outside clip)

The Everly Brothers, "All I Have to Do Is Dream" (Golden Moment)

Paul Simon, "One Trick Pony," "Ace in the Hole" (outside clip)

David Bowie, "Ashes to Ashes" (outside clip)

Top Ten Countdown, Steve Merritt Dancers
"Into the Night" (#9)
"All Out of Love" (#8)
"Lookin' for Love" (#7)
"Give Me the Night" (#6)
"Fame" (#5)
"Sailing" (#4)
"Upside Down" (#3)
"Late in the Evening" (#2)
25 Year Oldie, "Only You"
Pick Hit of the Week, "You're the Only Woman"
#1 Country, "Making Plans"
#1 Disco, "Upside Down"
#1 Album, Rolling Stones, *Emotional Rescue*, "Let Me Go"

Episode 392

Host: Chevy Chase

Chevy Chase, "Short People," "I Shot the Sheriff," "16 Tons"

The Rolling Stones, "Emotional Rescue" (#2) (outside clip/repeat), "She's So Cold"

Benny Mardones, "Into the Night" (#9), "Hometown Girls"

Irene Cara, "Fame" (#8)

Johnny Lee, "Lookin' for Love" (#4)

Richard Tee, "Now," "A Train"

Johnny Nash, "I Can See Clearly Now" (Golden Moment)

Richard Belzer, comedy spot

Top Ten Countdown, Steve Merritt Dancers
"Driving My Life Away" (#10)
"Give Me the Night" (#7)
"All Out of Love" (#6)
"Sailing" (#5)
"Late in the Evening" (#3)
"Upside Down" (#1)
Pick Hit of the Week, "One in a Million You"
#1 Disco, "Love Don't Make It Right"
#1 Album, *Urban Cowboy*
#1 Country, "Misery and Gin"

Episode 393

Host: America

America, "Sister Golden Hair," "Survival," "Valentine," "You Could've Been the One," "A Horse with No Name" (Golden Moment, outside clip)

Pure Prairie League, "Let Me Love You Tonight," "I'm Almost Ready" (outside clip)

Larry Graham, "One in a Million You" (#10), "When We Get Married"

The Cars, "Touch 'n' Go," "Panorama" (outside clip)

Air Supply, "All Out of Love" (#1, outside clip)

Keith Carradine, "I'm Easy" (Golden Moment)

Top Ten Countdown, Steve Merritt Dancers
"I'm Alright" (#9)
"Give Me the Night" (#8)
"Drivin' My Life Away" (#7)
"Fame" (#6)
"Upside Down" (#5)
"Another One Bites the Dust" (#4)
"Late in the Evening" (#3)
"Lookin' for Love" (#2)
Pick Hit of the Week, "Real Love"
#1 Disco, "Love Sensation"
#1 Country, "Old Flames Can't Hold a Candle to You"
#1 Album, *The Game*
20 Year Oldie, "Teen Angel"

Episode 394

Host: The Spinners

The Spinners, "I Just Want to Fall in Love," "Now That You're Mine Again," "Cupid," "Working My Way Back to You"

Ambrosia, "You're the Only Woman," "No Big Deal"

The Pointer Sisters, #10 "He's So Shy" (#10), "Could I Be Dreamin'" (outside clip)

Jose Feliciano, "Light My Fire" (Golden Moment)

Joan Armatrading, "All the Way from America," "Me Myself I"

Robbie Dupree, "Hot Rod Hearts" (outside clip)

Top Ten Countdown, Steve Merritt Dancers
"Xanadu" (#8)
"One in a Million You" (#7)
"I'm Alright" (#6)
"Woman in Love" (#5)
"Another One Bites the Dust" (#4)
"Give Me the Night" (#3)
"All Out of Love" (#2)
"Upside Down" (#1)
Pick Hit of the Week, "The Wanderer"
#1 Disco, "Can't Fake the Feeling"
#1 Country, "Old Flames Can't Hold a Candle to You"
#1 Album, *The Game*
20 Year Oldie, "It's Now or Never"

Episode 395, 405

Host: Mac Davis

Mac Davis, "Me and Fat Boy Pruitt," "Rock 'n' Roll I Gave You All the Best Years of My Life" (Golden Moment), "Texas in My Rear View Mirror," "Secrets," "Rodeo Clown"

Olivia Newton-John/Cliff Richard, "Suddenly"

Cliff Richard, "Dreaming" (#10), "Everyman"

Cher and Black Rose, "Never Should've Started," "You Know It," "Ain't Got No Money"

Peaches & Herb, "Funtime"

From the movie *Cheaper to Keep Her* (outside clip)

Top Ten Countdown, Steve Merritt Dancers
"Midnight Rocks" (#9)
"Upside Down" (#8)
"All Out of Love" (#7)
"I'm Alright" (#6)
"The Wanderer" (#5)
"Xanadu" (#4)
"Give Me the Night" (#3)
"Real Love" (#2)
"Woman in Love" (#1)
20 Year Oldie, "Running Bear"
#1 Album, *The Game*, "Dragon Attack"
#1 Country, "Lovin' Up a Storm"
#1 Disco, "Can't Fake the Feeling"
Pick Hit of the Week, "How Do I Survive"

Episode 396

Host: The Oak Ridge Boys

The Oak Ridge Boys, "Trying to Love Two Women"

Queen, "Another One Bites the Dust"

Debby Boone, "Are You on the Road to Loving Me Again"

Pat Benatar, "You Better Run"

The Oak Ridge Boys, "Leaving Louisiana in Broad Daylight"

Ray, Goodman & Brown, "Special Lady"

Amy Holland, "How Do I Survive"

The Oak Ridge Boys, "Beautiful You"

Robert Palmer, "Looking for Clues"

Debby Boone, "Take It Like a Woman"

Pat Benatar, "I'm Gonna Follow You"

Ray, Goodman & Brown, "My Prayer"

The Oak Ridge Boys, "Dream On"

Robert Palmer, "Johnny and Mary"

Ray, Goodman & Brown, "You"

Episode 397 (see Episode 383)

Episode 398

Host: Stephanie Mills

Stephanie Mills, "Never Knew Love Like This Before"

The Pointer Sisters, "He's So Shy"

Leo Sayer, "More Than I Can Say"

Pete Townshend, "Rough Boys"

Stephanie Mills, "Sweet Sensation"

Leo Sayer, "When I Need You"

707, "I Could Be for You"

John Cougar, "This Time"

Stephanie Mills, "Try My Love"

The Pointer Sisters, "Could I Be Dreaming"

Leo Sayer, "Time Ran Out on You"

Pete Townshend, "A Little Is Enough"

707, "Tonight's Your Night"

Stephanie Mills, "I Just Wanna Say"

John Cougar, "Ain't Even Done with the Night"

Episode 399

Host: Billy Crystal

Billy Crystal, three monologues

Susan Anton, "Dreaming My Dreams," "Love Won't Always Pass Me By"

Susan Anton/Fred Knoblock, "Killing Time"

David Bowie, "Ashes to Ashes" (outside clip)

The Bus Boys, "Did You See Me," "There Goes the Neighborhood," "Johnny's Soul'd Out"

Yes, "Into the Lens" (outside clip)

Korgis, "Everybody's Gotta Learn Sometime" (outside clip)

The Vapors, "Turning Japanese" (outside clip)

Don McLean, "Vincent," "Dreidel"

Episode 400 (see Episode 369)

Episode 401
Host: The Captain and Tennille
The Captain and Tennille, "Until You Come Back to Me," "This Is Not the First Time," "Do That to Me One More Time," "Keeping Our Love Warm," "But I Think It's a Dream"
Bette Midler, "My Mother's Eyes" (outside clip)
Leo Sayer, "More Than I Can Say," "Time Ran Out on You," "Where Did We Go Wrong"
The Ramones, "Rock 'n' Roll High School," "Do You Remember Rock 'n' Roll Radio" (outside clip)
David Bowie, "Fashion" (outside clip)
Neilsen/Pearson, "Two Lonely Nights," "If You Should Sail"
LaToya Jackson, "If You Feel the Funk," "Night Time Lover"

Episode 402
Host: REO Speedwagon
REO Speedwagon, "Time for Me to Fly," "Keep On Loving You," "Don't Let Him Go," "In Your Letter," "Roll with the Changes"
Rod Stewart, "Oh God," "Passion" (outside clip)
Randy Meisner, "Hearts on Fire," "Got to Get Away," "Trouble Ahead"
Randy Meisner/Kim Carnes, "Deep Inside My Heart"
The Babys, "Sweet 17," "Turn and Walk Away," "She's My Girl"
Thin Lizzy, "Chinatown," "Killer on the Loose"

Episode 403
Host: Robert Klein
Robert Klein, comedy monologues
Kool & the Gang, "Celebration," "Ladies Night," "Jones vs. Jones"
Cliff Richard, "Dreaming," "Everyman"
ABBA, "The Winner Takes It All" (outside clip)
Dire Straits, "Skateaway" (outside clip)
The Rolling Stones, "She's So Cold" (outside clip)
The Tremblers, "Green Shirt," "You Can't Do That"
Susan Anton/Fred Knoblock, "Killing Time"

Episode 404
Host: The Pointer Sisters
The Pointer Sisters, "He's So Shy," "Fire," "Could I Be Dreaming," "Where Did the Time Go," "Here Is Where Your Love Belongs"
Blondie, "The Tide Is High" (outside clip)
The Temptations, "Struck By Lightning Twice," "Power," "Take Me Away"
Supertramp, "Dreamer" (outside clip)
Harry Chapin, "Sequel"
Korgis, "Everybody's Gotta Learn Something" (outside clip)
Spyro Gyra, "Cafe Amore," "Percolator"

Episode 405 (see Episode 395)

Episode 406 (see Episode 346)

Episode 407
Host: Harry Chapin
Harry Chapin, "Sequel," "Remember When the Music," "Taxi," "Story of a Life"
ABBA, "The Way Old Friends Do," "The Winner Takes It All," "Super Trouper" (outside clip)
Leo Sayer, "More Than I Can Say," "Time Ran Out on You"
The Pointer Sisters, "Could I Be Dreaming," "He's So Shy"
Moom Martin, "Signal for Help," "Five Days of Fever"
Prince, "Uptown" (outside clip)

Episode 408, 419
Host: Larry Hagman
Larry Hagman, "Ballad of the Good Luck Charm," "My Favorite Sins"
George Burns, "Using Things and Loving People"
Marie Osmond, "It's the Falling in Love"
Tanya Tucker, "Can I See You Tonight," "Pecos Promenade," "Love Knows We Tried"
Rod Stewart, "She Won't Dance with Me," "Passion," "Oh God"
Olivia Newton-John, "Don't Cry for Me Argentina," "Suspended in Time"
Olivia Newton-John/Cliff Richard, "Suddenly"
Heart, "Tell It Like It Is" (outside clip)
Bette Midler, "My Mother's Eyes" (outside clip)

Episode 409, 421
Host: Andy Kaufman
Andy Kaufman, profile segments: "Andy's Other Job," "Andy Wrestling," "Andy the Entertainer," "Parents' Reaction"
Comedy segments: Foreign Man (impressions), Puppets
Songs, "I Beg of You" (Elvis), "It's a Small World" (Joe Clayton Group), "Too Much" (Elvis)
Tony Clifton, "Carolina in the Morning," "If You're Happy . . .," comedy routine
Slim Whitman, "I Remember You," "That Silver Haired Daddy of Mine," "When"
Freddy Cannon, "Tallahassee Lassie," "Palisades Park"
Queen, "Flash Gordon" (outside clip)

Episode 410
Host: Lily Tomlin
Lily Tomlin, "Suzi Sorority," "Crystal"
From the movie *The Incredible Shrinking Woman* (outside clip)
From television special, "Born Free" (outside clip)
Fred Willard, "Beware of the Letter," "Ride 'Em High," from the movie *First Family* (outside clip)
Hall & Oates, "You've Lost That Lovin' Feelin'," "Kiss on My List," "How Does It Feel to Be Back"
Police, "De Do Do Do De Da Da Da" (outside clip)
Kool & the Gang, "Celebration"
The Motels, "Envy," "Danger"
Robert Hilburn interview with Martha Davis of The Motels

Episode 411
Host: Lynda Carter
Lynda Carter, "Last Song"
Charles Grodin Profile, Part 1
Lynda Carter Feature, Part 1
Gail Davies, "I'll Be There"
Charles Grodin Profile, Part 2
Devo, "Whip It"
Robert Hilburn interview with Devo
Lynda Carter Feature, Part 2
Lynda Carter, "Tumble Down Love"
Charles Grodin Profile, Part 3
T.G. Sheppard, "Do You Want to Go to Heaven"
Gail Davies, "It's a Lovely, Lovely World"
Lynda Carter, "Fantasy Man"
T.G. Sheppard, "I Feel Like Loving You Again"
Lynda Carter Profile, Part 3
Lynda Carter, "Tumble Down Love"

Episode 412
Host: Bob Uecker
Bob Uecker, comedy spot
Neil Diamond interview, Part 1
Bellamy Brothers, "Do You Love As Good As You Look"
Neil Diamond interview, Part 2
Blondie, "Rapture"
Bellamy Brothers, "Let Your Love Flow"
Neil Diamond interview, Part 3
Rick Nelson, "It Hasn't Happened Yet"
Neil Diamond interview, Part 4
Bob Uecker, comedy spot
Bellamy Brothers, "If I Said You Have a Beautiful Body"
Neil Diamond interview, Part 5
Rick Nelson, "Believe What You Say," "Almost Saturday Night"
Bellamy Brothers, "Let Your Love Flow"

Episode 413
Host: Marilu Henner
Marilu Henner, three-part feature with Judd Hirsch, Jeff Conaway, Tony Danza, Danny DeVito, Christopher Lloyd, Michael Lembeck, Jim Jacobs
Michael O'Donoghue, four-part "Mr. Mike" feature with Paul Klein, Lorne Michaels, Tim White
Peter Ustinov, interview
Sir Douglas Quintet, "She's About a Mover," "Who'll Be the Next in Line," "Mendocino"
Firefall, "Staying with It," "Strange Way," "I Don't Want to Hear It"

Episode 414 (see Episode 91)

Episode 415
Host: Laraine Newman
Laraine Newman/Van Dyke Parks, "Cheek to Cheek"
Juice Newton, "Angel of the Morning," "Queen of Hearts," "Ride 'Em Cowboy"
Cliff Richard, "A Little in Love," "Give a Little Bit More"
David Bowie, "Fashion" (outside clip)
Peter Gabriel, "Games Without Frontiers" (outside clip)
Etta James, "Take It to the Limit," "Miss You"
Michael O'Donoghue, "Mr. Mike" feature
Catch a Rising Star, feature with Rick Newman, Richard Belzer, David Sayh, Adrianne Tolsch, Pat Benatar

Episode: 416
Host: John Schneider
John Schneider, "It's Now or Never," "34 in Atlanta," "Those Good Old Boys Are Bad"
John Schneider, three-part feature with Denver Pyle, Catherine Bach, Sorrel Booke, Tom Wopat, James Best
Donna Summer, interview with Robert Hilburn
Dottie West, "Are You Happy Baby," "Sorry Seems to Be the Hardest Word," "Lesson in Leaving"
Sheena Easton, "Morning Train (Nine to Five)," "Modern Girl"

Episode 417
Host: Patricia Davis
Patricia Davis, "Dark Side of the Night," "Crying Over You"
Rich Little/Patricia Davis, comedy segment with Little Playing Ronald Reagan
Albert Brooks, four-part feature with Carl Reiner, Kathryn Harrold
From the movie *Modern Romance* (outside clip)
The Police, "Don't Stand So Close to Me" (outside clip)
Emmylou Harris, "Mr. Sandman," "I Don't Have to Crawl" (outside clip), interview with Robert Hilburn, Part 1, "White Girl," "Once Over Twice," Interview with Robert Hilburn, Part 2

Episode 418
Host: Skip Stephenson and Byron Allen
Skip Stephenson, comedy monologue
Byron Allen, comedy monologue
Robert Urich, feature with Heather Menzies, Bart Braverman, Phyllis Davis, Howard Cosell
Cathy Moriarty, feature
Waylon Jennings, Interview with Robert Hilburn
Creedence Clearwater Revival, "Proud Mary," "Green River," "Midnight Special"
Yarbrough and Peoples, "Don't Stop the Music," "Easy Tonight"

Episode 419 (see Episode 408)

Episode 420 (see Episode 391)

Episode 421 (see Episode 409)

Episode 422 (see Episode 10)

Episode 423 (see Pilot)

PHOTOGRAPHY CREDITS

p. 14, top right: Jeffrey Mayer/Star File;
bottom right: Leif Ericksen/Globe Photos;
bottom center: Herm Lewis/Globe Photos

p. 15, top center: Walter Iooss/Globe Photos;
center right: NBC/Globe Photos

p. 16, bottom left: NBC/Globe Photos;
bottom right: Don Bradburn/Globe Photos

p. 18, bottom center: Richard E. Aaron/Star File

p. 19, second from top at left: Brian D. McLaughlin/
Globe Photos

p. 20, top right: Globe Photos

p. 22, top right: Hans Ruedelstein/Globe Photos

p. 24, bottom right: Herm Lewis/Globe Photos

p. 25, left: Gary Merrin/Globe Photos

p. 26, bottom left: M. J. Pokempner/Globe Photos;
second from top at right: Gary Merrin/
Globe Photos

p. 27, top right: Bob Gruen/Star File

p. 29, top center: Bob Gruen/Star File

p. 30, top right: NBC/Globe Photos

p. 31, second from top at left: Jeffrey Mayer/
Star File; top right: Mick Rock/Star File

p. 37, bottom center three images:
NBC/Globe Photos

p. 38, top left: Globe Photos;
top right: Bob Alford/Star File

p. 39, large center image: Lynn McAfee/Globe
Photos; top right: Mitchell Tapper/Globe Photos

p. 40, second from top at left:
Richard A. Adshead/Globe Photos

p. 43, background image:
Walter Iooss/Globe Photos

p. 44, top right: Bob Gruen/Star File

p. 45, second from top on left:
Brian D. McLaughlin/Globe Photos

p. 47, left center: Barry J. Morgan/Globe Photos

p. 49, left center: Ashiki Taylor/Globe Photos

p. 52, top right: Richard E. Aaron/Star File;
bottom center: Jeffrey Mayer/Star File

p. 53, top center: Brian D. McLaughlin/Globe
Photos; bottom center: Jeffrey Mayer/Star File

P. 58, top center: Jeffrey Mayer/Star File

p. 64, bottom center: John Cameola/Globe Photos;
bottom left: Waring Abbott/Globe Photos;
all other images: Bob Gruen/Star File

p. 65, left center: Andy Sackheim/Globe Photos;
right center: NBC/Globe Photos;
all other images: Bob Gruen/Star File

p. 67, second from top at left: Adam Scull/Globe
Photos; left center: NBC/Globe Photos

p. 68, second and third from top at left:
Michael A. Norcia/Globe Photos; top right:
Bob Gruen/Star File

p. 69, bottom left: Herb Steinberg/Globe Photos

p. 70, second and third from top at left:
Jeffrey Mayer/Star File

p. 72, bottom left: Lynn McAfee/Globe Photos

p. 73, center: Lynn McAfee/Globe Photos

p. 77, bottom center: Jeffrey Mayer/Star File

p. 78, bottom left: Brian Wolff/Globe Photos

p. 79, bottom right: Steve Joester/Star File

p. 80, top and bottom right: Herb Ball/NBC/Globe
Photos; all other images: NBC/Globe Photos

p. 81, all images: NBC/Globe Photos

p. 83, left center, Gary Merrin/Globe Photos

p. 84, second from top at left: Richard Corkery/
Globe Photos; top right: G. Thompson/Globe
Photos; bottom right: Gary Merrin/Globe Photos

p. 85, clockwise from top left: Mick Rock/Star File;
Bob Gruen/Star File; Bob Gruen/Star File;
Bob Gruen/Star File; Mick Rock/Star File;
Jeffrey Mayer/Star File

p. 89, right: Jeffrey Mayer/Star File

p. 93, second from top at left: Ian Dickson/
Globe Photos

p. 94, bottom left: Globe Photos; bottom right:
Dennis Barna/Globe Photos

p. 95, bottom left and right: Ken Kaminsky/
Globe Photos

p. 100, bottom right: Lydia Criss/Star File

p. 101, second from bottom at left: Virginia Lohle/
Star File

p. 103, center: Lynn McAfee/Globe Photos;
top right: Jeffrey Mayer/Star File

p. 105, second from bottom at left: Lynn McAfee/
Globe Photos; bottom left: John Blau/
Globe Photos

p. 108, center and left center: Jeffrey Mayer/
Star File

p. 117, right center: Brad Markel/Globe Photos

p. 118, top left: Bob Gruen/Star File; top center:
Bob Gruen/Star File; top right: Larry Kaplan/
Star File; center: Larry Kaplan/Star File

p. 121, clockwise from top left: Mick Rock/Star File;
Pictorial Press/Star File; Chuck Pulin/Star File;
Chuck Pulin/Star File; Chuck Pulin/Star File;
Bob Gruen/Star File

p. 127, center: Bob Alford/Star File

WHO'S WHO ON THE COVER

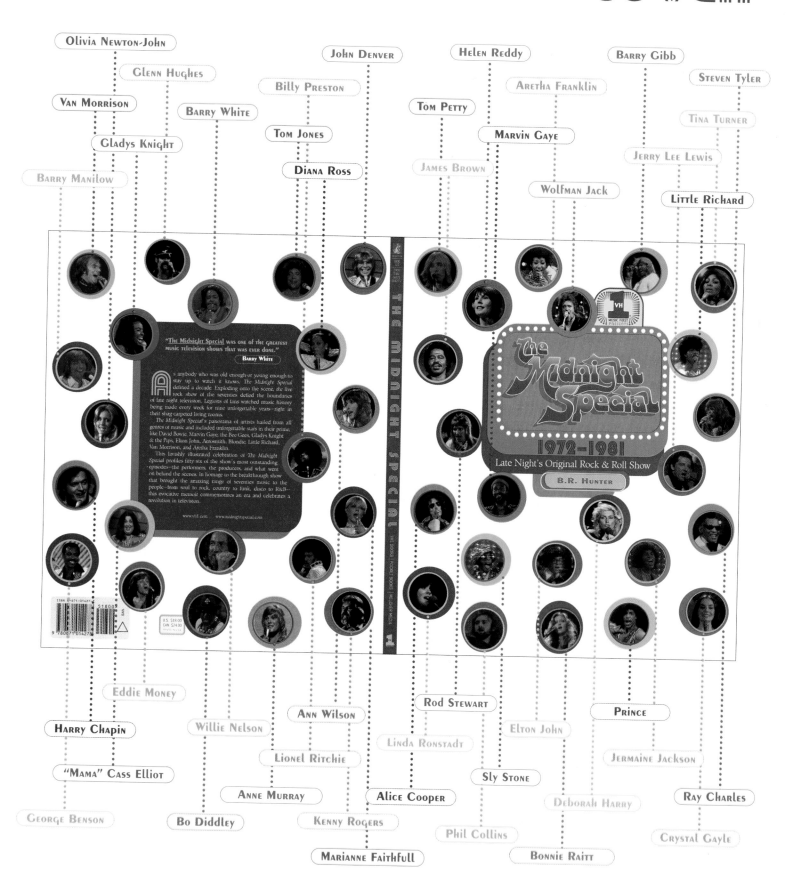

Olivia Newton-John
Glenn Hughes
Van Morrison
Barry White
Gladys Knight
Barry Manilow
Billy Preston
Tom Jones
Diana Ross
John Denver
Tom Petty
James Brown
Helen Reddy
Aretha Franklin
Marvin Gaye
Wolfman Jack
Barry Gibb
Steven Tyler
Tina Turner
Jerry Lee Lewis
Little Richard

"The Midnight Special was one of the greatest music television shows that was ever done."
Barry White

As anybody who was old enough or young enough to stay up to watch it knows, *The Midnight Special* defined a decade. Exploding onto the scene, the live rock show of the seventies defied the boundaries of late night television. Legions of fans watched music history being made every week for nine unforgettable years—right in their shag carpeted living rooms.

The Midnight Special's panorama of artists hailed from all genres of music and included unforgettable stars in their prime, like David Bowie, Marvin Gaye, the Bee Gees, Gladys Knight & the Pips, Elton John, Aerosmith, Blondie, Little Richard, Van Morrison, and Aretha Franklin.

This lavishly illustrated celebration of *The Midnight Special* profiles fifty-six of the show's most outstanding episodes—the performers, the producers, and what went on behind the scenes. In homage to the breakthrough show that brought the amazing range of seventies music to the people—from soul to rock, country to funk, disco to R&B—this evocative memoir commemorates an era and celebrates a revolution in television.

www.vh1.com   www.midnightspecial.com

THE MIDNIGHT SPECIAL

The **Midnight Special**
1972-1981
Late Night's Original Rock & Roll Show

B.R. Hunter

U.S. $18.00
CAN $24.00

Eddie Money
Harry Chapin
"Mama" Cass Elliot
George Benson
Willie Nelson
Bo Diddley
Ann Wilson
Lionel Ritchie
Anne Murray
Kenny Rogers
Marianne Faithfull
Linda Ronstadt
Alice Cooper
Rod Stewart
Sly Stone
Phil Collins
Elton John
Deborah Harry
Bonnie Raitt
Prince
Jermaine Jackson
Ray Charles
Crystal Gayle